YOU KNOW I

*love you*

DUET

WALL STREET JOURNAL & USA TODAY BESTSELLING AUTHOR

# WILLOW WINTERS

YOU KNOW I

# love you

WILLOW WINTERS

I married the bad boy from Brooklyn.

The one with the tattoos and a look in his eyes that told me
he was bad news.
The kind of look that comes with all sorts of warnings.

I knew what I was doing.
I knew by the way he first held me that he would be my
downfall; how he owned me with his forceful touch.

I couldn't say no to him, not that I wanted to. That was
then, and it seems like forever ago.

Years later, I've grown up and moved on. But he's still the
man I married. Dangerous in ways I don't like to think
about and tried to ignore for so long.
I did this to myself. I knew better than to fall for him.

I only wish love were enough to fix this …

*You Know I Love You* is book 1 of a duet. It is the second
duet in the You Are Mine series, but it can be read first.

YOU KNOW I

love you

# prologue

## Kat

It only took one night; one moment, and my fate was sealed. He knew I would never tell him no.

I wonder what would have happened if I'd never met Evan. The thought makes my stomach sink and twist, and a cold chill flows in waves over my body.

It *pains* me to consider such a thing. To have never been with the man I love.

Dragging in a lungful of cold air, I steady myself with deep breaths.

It physically hurts to imagine not having him in my life for the last six years.

I didn't know I was setting myself up for heartbreak all those years ago. Yet here I am, and that reality is what keeps me up at night. My eyes burn from both exhaustion and the tears begging to be shed.

That chance encounter set everything into motion, and only months ago I would have said it was a blessing, bestowed upon me by fate, or maybe kismet. But now I know better.

I wish I'd never stopped that night.

I wish I'd never met Evan at that gas station.

Whoever said it's better to have loved and lost than never to have loved at all was a liar and a fool.

This pain isn't worth it.

If only I could go back, because I don't know how we'll get through this.

# CHAPTER
## one

*Kat*

*Tell me a lie and make it sweet,*
*Like the vows you made on our wedding day.*
*Tell me a lie, don't make it hurt,*
*The pain in my chest won't go away.*
*Don't tell me the truth, I can't face what's to come.*
*I'll yell and I'll kick, I'll fight it, I'll run.*
*Don't tell me the truth, I don't want to hear.*
*Tell me pretty lies with whispers sincere.*

THE CHILL ON MY SKIN LINGERS AND FLOWS DOWN my shoulders. It's an odd sensation that travels across my arms and I'd like to blame it on the alcohol, but I've felt it all day. From the very start of this morning, before the drinks came easier and easier. For days, really, I've been feeling this strange sensation of not quite being in my own body. As if I'm not really here. This isn't really happening to me.

It's been going on for more than a few days if I'm honest … maybe even weeks, but I've been ignoring the signs and whispers, pretending like they weren't real.

Now that this sickness won't leave me, I can't deny it.

Ever since I let the words slip through my lips.

*I hate you.*

*You're a fucking liar.*

*I want a divorce.*

An ache in my chest prompts me to take a sip of wine. Letting it slide down my throat, I pretend that it soothes me. It's numbing, that's what it is. That's what I need. Tears prick at my eyes, but I don't let them fall. Instead a shuddering breath leaves me and I lift up my glass, downing the remaining wine. It's too sweet for being so dark.

Startled by a sound from the floor above me, the glass nearly tips over as I set it down quickly to wipe under my eyes. I don't want him to see me cry; I won't let him. But the creak I heard was a false alarm. I don't hear the heavy footsteps of him coming down the stairs to our townhouse. I'm still alone in the dining room, waiting for him to leave.

Left only with bittersweet memories and the constant question: *How did this happen?*

The thick, dark drapes behind me are pulled shut but even they can't completely drown out the night sounds of busy New York City. There's always a bit that travels through. It used to bother me when I initially moved here, but now it's soothing. It calms me as my gaze drifts toward the empty stairwell, where it lingers.

I shouldn't be drunk, not when I'm supposed to be preparing to meet with a potential client tomorrow. As one of the top literary agents in New York City, I'm damn good at what I do but tonight, I don't care.

I shouldn't have closed my laptop and logged off all social media when I have promotions and advertisements running around the clock for these launches.

I shouldn't be doing a lot of things.

But here I am, sitting at the head of the dining room table, and I refuse to do anything but watch the stairs and wait for him to leave. The very thought of staring at his back as the front door closes forces me to reach for the bottle.

I listen carefully as I pour the last of the wine into my glass. He's packing at the last minute, like he always does, but this time it's so much different. He's traveling for work, but when he leaves from his rendezvous in London, he's not coming back here. That sudden realization brings a fresh flood of unshed tears to burn my eyes, but I remain very still. As if maybe playing dead will hold back these emotions.

"He better not," I mutter beneath my breath, holding on to my resolve.

I lift the glass to my lips, the dark cabernet tasting sweeter and sweeter with each sip, lulling me into a lethargy where the memory of yesterday fades.

Where the article doesn't exist. Where the denial of an affair can fall on deaf ears. The picture itself was innocent. But Evan doesn't have a single explanation for me. He can't make clear to me why he's lying, why he's stumbling over his words to come up with a justification.

What hurts the most is the look in his eyes when he lies to me. The paparazzi photo is of him with his boss's wife Samantha, who just so happens to be in the middle of a vicious divorce. He was with her at 3:00 in the morning in her hotel lobby. Three fucking a.m. *Nothing good happens past 2:00 a.m.* He used to make that joke all the time when we first met. I used to laugh with him when he said it.

There's only one explanation for that photograph and both of us know it. Even though he can't come up with a plausible excuse, he still denies it. It's a slap in my face. I'm done pretending like I can forgive him for this. If he can't give me his truth, I'm left with my own, which is that my husband is not the man I fell in love with. Or at the very least, his decisions aren't ones I can live with.

I suck in a long, deep breath, pushing my phone away as it beeps again with a message from a friend and I lean back in my chair. I don't want to read it. With the palms of my hands, I cover my eyes, suddenly feeling hot. Too hot.

They keep asking me the same things, but with different words.

Maddie: *Are you all right?*

Julia: *Is it true? It can't be true.*

Suzette: *So you went through with it? Is there anything I can do?*

Messages from my friends have been hitting my phone one by one, each of them making it vibrate on the table throughout the day.

It takes everything in me to face them, as if they were

really here in person asking me all these questions. I don't have answers to give them, none that I want to say out loud anyway. I'm not pushing away my husband because I want to. I'm doing it because I have to and I don't have the resolve to speak that confession.

Even I'm disappointed in myself.

My friends want what's best for me. They only want to help me and I know that's the truth, but it doesn't keep me from being angry at the phone as it goes off again.

Heaving in a deep breath, I wish I wasn't in the big city. I wish I wasn't well known. I wish I could hide under the guise of anonymity and just be no one. More importantly, I wish no one knew. I'd crawl back to him if that were the case. I'd beg him to hold me every time I cried, even if he's the one who brought out this side of me.

I'd beg him to love me. He would, I know it. And then I'd hate myself.

*You deserve better than this.* Another message from Suzette comes through next and I can only run the pad of my thumb down the screen over her words. It's an attempt to make myself believe it.

Just leave me alone. Everyone get out of my life, my marriage. It wasn't for them to see. It's not for them to judge like every fucking gossip column in New York City. It's not the first time our marriage has been mentioned in the papers, but I pray it'll be the last.

My knuckles turn white as I grip the phone with the intent of throwing it, letting it smack against the wall to silence it, but I don't. It's the sound of Evan's boots rhythmically hitting each step as he walks down the stairs that forces me to compose myself. At the very least I pretend to; he's always seen through it, though. He knows how much this kills me.

I hit the button to turn off my phone and ignore the texts and calls, squaring my shoulders as I attempt to pull myself together.

I haven't answered a single message or email since this morning when Page Six came out with an article about our separation. It's funny how I only uttered the words two nights ago, yet it was already circulating gossip columns before the weekend hit, blasted all over social media. I wonder if he wanted this. If that was Evan's way of finally pushing his work-aholic wife to the brink of divorce.

My gaze morphs into a glare as he comes into view, but it doesn't stay long. My skin is suddenly feeling hotter, but in a way that's joined with desire. I can't help but to imagine how his rough stubble would feel against my palm as I caressed his cheek, how his lips would taste as he leaned down to kiss me. A very large part of me wants to savor it. Our last goodbye kiss. It's funny how the goodbye kisses are the ones I value most, but I won't let him kiss me before he leaves this time. Not when the last things that came from his lips were lies.

My deep inhales are silent, although the heavy rise and fall of my chest betrays me. If he notices, he doesn't let on as he places his luggage by the front door. My own hands turn numb watching his.

Even if he is only wearing a pair of faded jeans and a plain white T-shirt, he's still devilishly handsome. It's his muscu-lar physique and tanned, tattooed skin that let you know he's a classic bad boy regardless of what he's wearing. My heart beats slower as the seconds pass between us; it's calming just to look at him. That's how he got me in the beginning. The desire and attraction are undeniable despite what he's done.

He's the first to break our gaze as he runs his fingers through his dark brown hair and lets out an uneasy sigh. In response my lips curl into a sarcastic smile, mocking both me and my thoughts. I'm not the only one to fall for his charm and allure, but I should have learned my lesson by now. My fingers slip down the thin stem of the wineglass as I smile weakly and force back the sting in my eyes, pretending I'm not going to cry, pretending that I've made my decision final. Like I don't already regret it.

"I have to go," Evan states after a moment of uncomfortable silence, apart from the constant background hum of traffic.

My blood rushes and I try to swallow the lump in my throat. I focus on the wine, the dark red liquid pooling in the base of the glass. I try to swirl it, but it doesn't move; there's so little left.

"Is she going to be there?" I ask him, staring straight ahead at a black and white photo of the two of us taken years ago on vacation in Mexico.

Why? Why even bother? Why did I let it slip out? I'd planned to just say goodbye. Just end this suffering already.

As he answers, I continue to stare at the genuine smile on my face and then to where his arm is wrapped possessively around my waist in the photograph.

I hate that I asked. It's my insecurity, my hate. My envy even.

"No, she's not. And I already told you it doesn't matter."

9

Any trace of a smile or even of disinterest leaves me. I can't hide what it does to me, what his lie has done to me.

*It doesn't matter. Let it go.* They're all non-answers. They're words to hide the truth and we both know it.

My elbow is planted on the table as I rest my chin in my hand and try to cover up how much it hurts. To keep it from him just like he's keeping the truth from me, even if I sniff a little too loud. I speak low as I stare straight ahead at nothing in particular. "You told me it's not true, but you didn't deny it to the press," I tell him and finally look him in the eye. "You didn't deny it to anyone but me, and I know you're lying." My words crack at the end and I have to tear my gaze away. "It's been different since you came home." My last statement is drawn out and practically a whisper. It's been difficult between us over the past year, but the last two weeks … The tension between us changed the second he came home. I knew something bad had happened. I knew it.

Everyone told me to be careful and warned me about Evan six years ago when I first started seeing him. I knew what I was doing when I first said yes to a date with him, when I gave myself to him and let myself fall for someone like him. I'm a fool.

"I told you, Kat, it's not what it looks like," he says and his voice is soft, like he's afraid to say the words louder.

"Then why not tell them?" I ask, staring into his pleading expression. "Why let the world believe you've cheated on me? What could you possibly gain?" Each question gets louder as the words rush out of my mouth. I'm ashamed of how much passion there is in my voice. How much of my pain is on display.

In stark contrast is how little pain he shows and I don't miss how he hasn't budged. He hasn't made a single move to come to me. So I stay planted in my seat as well.

I know why he doesn't deny it, and it's because it's true. Years of just the two of us have shown me who he is and I know he's not a liar, but he's lying to me now. I've never been more sure of anything in my life. "It's been weeks, hasn't it?" I say, forcing out the words from between clenched teeth. This morning I couldn't talk without screaming. Without slamming my fists onto the table, making it shake and causing a glass of water to fall and shatter on the hardwood floor.

I reached my breaking point when he looked me in the eye and told me there was nothing to that picture. I refuse to listen when he lies; not when he does such a horrible job of it.

"Stop it, Kat," Evan commands firmly and his voice is harsh and unforgiving, like I'm the one in the wrong.

"Oh, I see," I respond, raising a brow and feeling a sick smile tug at my lips. "You can cheat, you can lie, but I should be quiet and give you a kiss on the way out to go do whatever you want to do?"

"Don't do this," he says with a rawness that makes my heart clench.

"Then tell me what happened. I know something did." He's been distant, even cold toward me ever since he came home.

A moment passes and I lose my composure again, bared to him in every way as I wait for an answer. But I don't get the one thing I need. The truth. *Or a believable lie.*

"I have to go," is all he says as he gathers his luggage.

Slinging a black duffle bag over one shoulder, gripping a suitcase with his other hand, he adds, "I love you."

He says the words without looking at me.

*I love you.*

It hurts so damn much because he knows I love him. He knows it and he throws the words back at me like it doesn't matter that he's risking it all.

"If you won't tell me the truth," I say lowly as I stare at the table, pushing out the words and feeling each one slice open the cut in my heart that much deeper, "then don't bother coming back." My throat tightens and my lungs refuse to fill as silence is all that answers me.

There's only a slight hesitation, a small creaking sound as he adjusts his grip on the luggage. That's all I get. That's it. The creak of the floorboards that's barely heard over my racing heart.

He leaves without attempting to kiss me or approaching me in the least. His strides don't break in cadence until the heavy walnut front door opens and closes, leaving me with nothing but the tortured sob that's desperate to come up and the faint sounds of the city life filling the empty space once again.

My hands tremble as I close my eyes and try to calm down.

If he really loved me, he wouldn't have let it come to this.

If he loved me, he'd tell me the truth.

Secrets break up marriages.

I keep telling myself that he's to blame, but as a cry rips up my throat and I bring my knees into my chest, my heels resting on the seat of the chair, I replay the last few years and I know I'm at fault too. Deep down, I know. I bury my face in my knees and rock slightly, feeling pathetic as I break down yet again.

If I were him, I'd have cheated on me too.

He says he didn't. He swears it's a lie.

But he doesn't explain it. He can't even look me in the eye.

I did this to myself. I should've known better.

# CHAPTER
## two

### *Evan*

**W**HEN DID I TURN INTO THE PIECE OF SHIT I am right now?

*Pathetic.* That's how I feel as the plane rumbles beneath my feet and I shake my head slightly, waving off the flight attendant and whatever small bag of snacks she was offering.

I crack my neck to the left and right as a ding indicates the seatbelt sign is off and everyone can move about the cabin. I have no intention of getting up or doing a damn thing other than sit here and try to figure out exactly where it all went wrong.

The Wi-Fi is available and I take my time setting it up, prolonging the moment when I'll have to face the fact that she most likely hasn't messaged me. She can yell at me, hit me, take it all out on me, but her silence is what kills me. Her shutting me out is like a knife to the heart.

There's no way to make it right, but I'm not letting her go.

Kat's mine. My wife. *My love*. She's everything to me, even if she hates me to the point where I'm nothing to her.

We used to be … Something special. Something other assholes dream about and pray for. And now? I couldn't even kiss her before leaving. The very thought of doing it felt too much like goodbye. Like the kind of goodbye that would kill me.

She's kidding herself if she thinks I'm not coming home to her. I don't care that we're going through this, I don't care how bad our fighting is or that I fucked up beyond repair. She doesn't know what happened and I hope she never will, but that doesn't change the fact that she's mine. Above all else, I love her and she loves me. She can't deny that.

My seat groans as I readjust in first class. I clear my throat and clench my teeth as the plane rumbles again, reminding me that she's miles and miles away. Reminding me that I left her again.

I can't bring myself to feel like I deserve her forgiveness. Or that I deserve her at all. That's always been the case between us. She's always been too good for me. The guilt is all-consuming and now I'm trapped in a corner, desperately looking for a way out of the mess I've gotten myself into.

My computer pings as the plane continues to fly across the ocean taking me farther away from her, and I lean forward to check it. I'm far too quick to do it too, praying it's Kat.

Praying's never helped me before and sure enough, it

didn't this time either. It's only a message from James, my boss and Samantha's now ex.

My teeth grind against one another, making my jaw even more tense as I read the message. It's the schedule for the rest of the day and my room number for the hotel.

It feels like a slap in the face. I can't keep up this façade and live each day as if nothing's happened. Pretending like nothing's changed.

The back of my head pushes into the seat as I take a calming breath.

Stuck between a rock and a hard place is an inadequate saying.

*I'm fucked.* Just waiting for them to pick, pick, pick away at me while I have my hands tied behind my back.

Only years ago, I loved my life. It was a high most would be envious of. This is what I wanted more than anything. On the outside, it's glamorous. I stay at five-star resorts, party with celebrities and have every sinful pleasure at my finger-tips. That's what a life of helping the rich and famous avoid prison has afforded me.

I protect the clients from any bad press, keep charges from sticking, and avoid any altercations that could lead to something … unwanted. In return, I'm paid generously and live the high life.

I didn't sign up for *this*, but I sure as fuck cashed every check along the way. My email beeps and it's another message from James, as if confirming that exact thought: this is exactly what I signed up for. It's what I asked for.

*Let me know when you land.* That's all the email says.

I clear my throat as my hand clenches into a fist and I run

16

the rough pad of my thumb over my knuckles slowly. My reflection in the screen stares back at me and I note the scowl, the dark circles under my eyes. *The anger.*

When I was younger, this was all I wanted. I get paid to party and live in a perpetual state of drunkenness. I lived for the thrill.

Kat used to love it too. Years ago, when we first met and things were different. I glance at the empty seat to my left and picture her sitting beside me. She used to play with the buckle on every flight. Unbuckle, buckle, unbuckle, buckle. At first I thought it was a nervous habit that had to do with a fear of flying, but it was just due to the excitement.

She loved coming with me to events. It was what we did together. Back when everything was the way it was supposed to be.

Back when life was less complicated.

Back when we were kids and I didn't realize that life was going to catch up to me and her career was going to take off, placing us on two very different paths in life.

A huff of a sigh leaves me as I shift in my seat and look back to my computer.

I click over to the flight tab and see there are four hours remaining until we land in London. Four hours to sit in silence and dwell on each and every moment where I fucked up. Every step I took that led me to this very hour.

I turned thirty-two just four months ago, but I'm living the same life I had when we were in our twenties.

She's the one who changed.

She grew up and I'm the one who screwed up.

17

I run a hand down my face, trying to get the images out of my head.

She can never know, but I was a fool to think I'd hidden it from her.

There's no way out of this.

*How can she love me when she knows I'm lying to her?*

*How can she forgive me for a sin she has no idea I've committed?*

*How can I keep her when I don't deserve her?*

# CHAPTER
## three

### *Kat*

"SO THIS IS ALL BULLSHIT?" Sue asks with a tone that says she believes otherwise as she motions to the newspaper. Her voice is soft, but my nerves make it seem louder than it is here in this small coffee shop. I almost shush her before realizing she's not speaking loudly at all.

"It doesn't look like it's …" I can't finish my thought, my eyes drawn to the same picture I stared at for hours last night, plus the night before.

"Well, she's all over him. There's no denying that."

"Women are always all over him." My answer comes out flat. I'm nothing if not blunt and transparent. It's one of the reasons my clients trust me.

"I used to like it … when they'd try to be all over him," I

admit to her but bite my tongue at the urge to voice the additional confession: *I loved it.* "How they'd fawn over him, desperate for Evan's attention. But he only had eyes for me."

"Why is this one any different then?" The paper hits the slick surface of the coffee table as she tosses it down and immediately digs into her large Chanel hobo bag. I know she believes exactly what Evan denied. It's written all over her perfectly red, pursed lips. This is only an attempt to appease me.

It's not the first, the second, or even the third time Evan's had his name in the tabloids for less than angelic reasons. Suzette has her opinions, but she's always refrained from voicing them when it comes to Evan.

His reputation and his livelihood depend on the fact that he's gotten away with things that would send most people to jail for the night.

That was the case before I met him, anyway. Now he gets paid to make sure his clients meet the same fate.

Sue talks as she pulls out a tube of deep red lipstick and a compact mirror. "Do you think he really did it this time?" she asks as if the weight of our marriage doesn't rest on my answer.

The reason this time is different is because I know there's truth to it.

It's because of how he reacts.

It's how he looks at me as if he's guilty.

"He says it's not what it looks like," I answer and roll my eyes as I do, trying to downplay the pain that coils in my chest. My throat goes tight, but I'm saved by the return of Maddie.

For so many years, since I first moved here really, there's been one constant. It's these women. Jules, my first client and the New York socialite who brought us all together, isn't here.

I owe her so much for helping my career take off as quickly as it did, but Jules has everything and all she really wants is companionship. She's getting settled into married life, but she'd be here if I asked. Maddie and Sue were both available and to be honest, I'd prefer them right now. They're not helplessly in love and therefore blind as a bat.

"Pumpkin spice," Maddie says as she sets a hot cup of coffee down in front of me. She doesn't look me in the eyes, like she's afraid doing even that will make me cry.

The strong scent of cinnamon smacks me in the face, but I wrap my hand around the cup, giving her a grateful smile as she takes her seat to my right. I don't like flavored coffee—I don't even like pumpkin, but I'll drink it. I desperately need the caffeine.

My gaze travels to Sue, sitting straight across from me as she returns to the conversation and says, "He says it's not what it looks like?" Her brow quirks as she adds, "… And what does that mean?" It's not a question, it's an accusation and the two of us know it.

"What does what mean?" Maddie asks innocently, the legs of her chair scraping along the floor.

"It means he's lying," Sue answers matter-of-factly and folds the newspaper over, reading the article again. It's only a paragraph, maybe two. It doesn't say much other than the fact that Samantha Lapour and her husband James are now separated, due to an affair she had with my husband, Evan Thompson. Which is a blatant lie. Their marriage has been on the rocks for months and they were separated long before this happened.

Inwardly I cringe at defending my husband at all. An

affair is an affair. In an effort to ease the guilt that weighs down my chest, I rub the small spot just below my collarbone.

Maddie's expression turns hard with a look of warning that would normally make me laugh considering how petite and naïve she is. "We're talking about Evan," she says under her breath. Her eyes stay on Sue, who slowly purses her lips and acknowledges Maddie with only a short nod.

The newly divorced Suzette doesn't give men a chance to explain. For good reason, seeing as how she's been through hell and back.

"I'm sorry," Maddie whispers and then clings to her own coffee. French vanilla if I had to guess.

"It's fine," I say lowly, shaking off the emotions rocking through my body and easing the tension at the table. "There's no reason for us to get into this." I don't look at either of them, blowing on the hot coffee and reluctantly drinking it. I don't taste it on the way down, though.

"Well, what do you think?" Maddie asks me and then she puts down her own cup. The coffee shop on Madison Avenue is fairly empty, probably due to the rain and chill of the late fall in the air.

As the shop door opens with a small chime and the busy sounds of the street flood into the small space for a moment, I think of how to answer her.

I don't know what to say.

I think he cheated on me.

I think he's sorry and he regrets it.

I think he loves me. No, I know he loves me.

And I feel like a fool for still loving him and wanting him.

That's what's in my head as I look around the small coffee

shop, taking in every detail of the bright white chair rail and cream walls. The framed macro photographs of coffee pots and coffee beans keep my attention a little longer. I've never really noticed them before. This place is so familiar, yet I couldn't have described any of these details if someone had asked me. I've been coming here for years and yet I'd never cared enough to look at what was right here in front of me.

"Why would he lie to you?" Maddie asks, pulling my attention back to her. She huffs, sitting back and causing the chair to grind against the floor as she does. "I just can't imagine Evan doing this." My shoulders rise with a deep intake of breath as I pick at a small square napkin on the table.

I roll the tiny piece I've ripped off between my forefinger and thumb, watching as it crumples into a small ball.

"I don't know why," I answer softly. I can feel all the overwhelming sadness and betrayal rise up and make my throat tighten as I try to come up with a response. "Maybe I'm stupid, but I can't remember him ever lying to me before." I swallow thickly and flick the tiny ball onto the table. "Not like this." Defeat drips from my words.

"Sorry," I tell them and wipe under my tired eyes, hating that I could possibly feel the telltale prick of tears behind them given how much I've already cried. "I tried not to let it …" I can't finish. I watch as the rain batters the large glass window in the front of the shop and I slip my internal armor back on.

"Don't you dare be sorry," Sue says with a strength that pulls my attention back to her. Her jet-black hair cut into a blunt bob sways as she leans forward, moving closer to me while she speaks with an undeniable authority. "If you want to cry, cry. If you want to scream, do it. Whatever you need to do, just let it out."

Maddie nods her head in my periphery, but I can't do the same. Looking at the two of them, the stark contrast between Maddie and Suzette is more than obvious. Maddie's a young brunette with large doe eyes, equally in love with love itself and the big city. Sue's a recent divorcée with a bitter sense of humor she's earned. Even their fashion choices are at odds. Maddie's wearing a maxi dress and has a teal raincoat and clear umbrella hanging off the back of her chair, while Sue's in a black and white tweed dress with a matching jacket, plus a broad-brimmed, black Breton hat she wears to keep people away.

Somewhere in the middle is where I fall.

*What if I want to deal with it by falling into his arms and letting him lie to me?* I bite my tongue, letting the silence be eaten up by the ticking of the clock. I know it's not okay, yet that's all I want. I want him to fight for me. I want him to love me. I want to forgive him, even if he won't admit what he's done.

And that makes me a coward and a pathetic excuse for a modern-day woman, doesn't it?

The snide thought makes me turn my attention back to the dreary state of affairs outside. The clouds have set in and the sky quickly turns dark.

"This is crap weather for a first meeting," I say out loud, not really meaning to.

"Way to change the topic," Sue half jokes as she picks up her coffee cup and takes a sip, the smirk ever present on her lips. Her light blue eyes stare back at me from over the rim and it almost makes me laugh. Almost.

"So you're meeting your client here?" Maddie asks, gracefully accepting my invitation to talk about anything else. I've never loved her more than in this very moment.

I nod, still not trusting myself to speak and take another gulp of my coffee. I forgot it was pumpkin spice and I nearly spit it out, startled by the flavor, but then I swallow it down. It's not so bad.

Maddie pulls her dark brown, curly hair over her shoulder and scrunches her nose as she takes in my expression. "You don't like pumpkin?" she asks, raising a brow in disbelief.

"It's okay," I say, answering her with a straight face and Sue erupts with a laugh that catches the attention of an elderly couple behind us. Her good humor is infectious and I find myself smiling. This is what I need. To talk and think about something else. Anything else.

"I'll get you something else," Maddie says as Sue starts to speak. "Just regular? Cream and sugar?"

"Thanks, but don't worry about it, Maddie. It's good." I wave off her concern and take another sip. "I just needed some caffeine."

"Well, you look professional," Sue says with a nod. "The rain didn't ruin your hair."

I shake out my hair playfully in response to Sue's attempt at a distraction but Maddie doesn't pick up on the hint, and when I yawn, she goes right back to the conversation I hoped we were done with.

"Trouble sleeping?" Maddie asks and I nod my head once then turn back to the cup, hating that we're back on this again.

"I just wish I had …" I can't finish the sentence and I struggle to come up with something to say as I push the hair from my face while trying to remember what I want. I haven't got a clue. "I wish I had my life together," I practically whisper, but they hear and I know they do.

"You do have your life together. You're an established publisher. An entrepreneur and a hard worker."

I have work. Yes. Maddie happily agrees with Sue, reminding me of how many people in this very city would kill for my job.

But I don't have a damn thing else. Not enough to hold on to a life I somehow strayed from.

The thought makes me miserable and I focus on the coffee again, knocking it back as if it'll save me. When I set it down, I notice how empty it is as I tap the bottom of it against the table and hear a hollow sound. I'm going to need a refill. I'll get it myself, though. I push away from the table slightly. "I'm going to grab another. At this rate it'll be empty before Jacob gets here."

"Oh, Jacob." Sue says his name with a hint of something I can't describe in her voice. A devilish smile grows on her face and it makes me roll my eyes. Of all the girls, Sue's the one who gets over one man by getting under another. And she's given the advice freely to our tight group of friends. I can practically feel her elbow in my ribs.

"Yes, *Jacob*," I echo, mocking the way she said it, feeling irritable and juvenile, but it only makes Sue smile.

"Well I hope he's a good distraction for you," Sue says then winks and slides her bag off her lap, onto her shoulder.

"Work is always a good distraction." My tone destroys the bit of lightness. "I'm good at burying myself in it." The girls are quiet as my words sit stale in the air. It's part of the reason my marriage is tainted. I don't have to say it out loud and they don't have to tell me. Everyone already knows it.

*She worked herself to death* will be written on my tombstone. It's all I think while I stand at the counter and order another coffee. Regular this time, with a splash of cream and plenty of sugar.

"I read his book you gave me," Maddie says when I retake my seat a moment later, changing the subject back to Jacob Scott. "I looked him up online too," she adds as a smile spreads across her lips and her cheeks brighten with a blush. She scoots to the back of her seat and holds her cup in both hands, gladly taking the attention off of me. "He's cute," she says and smiles in a way I don't see often from her. My left brow raises as I watch her pink cheeks turn brighter. *Little Miss Innocent.*

"Is he now?" Sue comments and the two share a look as Maddie nods.

"Want me to put in a good word for you?" I question—it's meant for either of them really—and reach into my Kate Spade satchel for my laptop and notebook, setting them up on the table as Sue stands and puts on her jacket. There's no way Maddie would actually make a move. She's so sheltered and inexperienced. There's also no way I'd let someone like Jacob near her.

"You can always stay and wait for him to get here?" I say jokingly. "Or maybe leave something behind and have to come back for it?"

She doesn't answer, merely shakes her head and slides off her seat to join Sue in leaving me to my fresh coffee and waiting laptop.

"I wouldn't want to impose," Maddie finally says and then walks over to give me a hug. Even in her heels, I still sit a little higher at the bar-height table as she embraces me.

I half expect her to say something in my ear, to tell me it'll be all right or that Evan's made a mistake. But she doesn't say a word until she lets me go. "I'm just a call away," she says with a chipper tone that wouldn't clue in anyone around us that I'd need to call her because my life is falling apart. Both of her hands grip my shoulders just a second too long.

My heart goes pitter-patter.

"Same here, darling," Sue adds, placing her own hand on Maddie's shoulder as a cue, and then the two walk off. The sound of Sue's heels starts to fade as she opens the door. But the chime sounds just the same as when we first walked in here.

"Later, loves." I force a smile on my face as they leave me here alone.

But my expression doesn't reflect anything I truly feel.

And nothing's changed.

# CHAPTER
## four

*Evan*

BERKELEY SQUARE IN LONDON FEELS THE SAME AS it has for years. The crisp air and old trees that tower over the park always feel timeless when I'm here. The black iron and white stone that speak to the history of this place never fail to impress. The dark, narrow alleys and the nightlife tucked away in the shadows of this city are what make my blood heat and my foot tap anxiously on the floorboard of the car.

It's always given me a rush to come here. There are a number of cities I'm fond of, cities that are playgrounds for the wealthy and where the best parties are had. Los Angeles, San Francisco, and New York City, of course. But London is one of the best. There's something to be said about being away from your normal life and getting to you don't have any obligations to stay in, yet welcomes you as if it's always been home.

The cabby clears his throat and his accent greets me as he tries to make small talk. I give him a curt nod and as many one-word answers as it takes to make it clear he doesn't need to fill the time with needless conversation. I'm not interested.

Rubbing sleep from my eyes, I lean back in the leather seat, feeling more and more exhausted as we pass the park, the dark green landscape fading from sight and rows of homes taking the place of the public areas.

I've felt comfortable here for years. It's a constant go-to for the PR company and I've been sent here to look after clients multiple times. But as the sky turns gray and the rain starts to beat against the tin roof, the welcoming feeling leaves me, and I'm left empty. Brought back to the present and brooding on how much the past has fucked me over.

The cab takes a left onto Hay Hill and I pass an old townhome where I used to crash. I've had so many close calls here. I was too much of a hothead, always looking for a thrill and pushing my luck further and further.

The cabby comes to a stop before I'm ready. The memories play on a loop in the back of my head of all the years I spent wasted. I can still feel the crunch of bone from the last fight I got into not three blocks from here.

"Here we are," the cabby states, turning in his seat, but before he can say anything else, I jam some cash into his hand and grab my bags on my own.

"Have a good day, sir," I hear him call out as I shut the door, the patter of rain already soaking through my collar at the back of my neck.

I have to walk with my head down to keep the rain from hitting me in the face. The door opens easily and I drag my luggage in, tossing it to the right side where the coatrack and desk are meant to greet clients. This condo's been converted into an office space. It's blocks from the nightlife and blends in with the community. A perfect location for client drop-off.

The high ceilings and intricate crown molding make the already expensive building feel that much wealthier. It's all been done in shades of white and cream, without an actual color in sight. It makes the bright neon sticky note atop a stack of papers sitting on the edge of the welcome desk stand out even more.

Sterile, but rich.

"You were supposed to tell me when you landed." I hear James's voice before I see him, his heavy steps echoing in the expansive room.

"I did," I tell him flatly, not bothering to take out my phone and check. I'm positive I did, as I always do, and he ignored it. That seems to have been his preference for the last two weeks. The air about him has changed; ever since that night, things have been tense between us. As if we're in a silent war, each waiting for the other to show weakness.

I'm not interested in this shit. The only thing I give a damn about is my Kat, keeping her safe from the crossfire. So I'll play nice. I'll do what he says. But I'm not his bitch and I don't play games.

"I didn't get it," he says, stopping in front of me in the foyer. He has to tilt his head back slightly to look me in the eyes since he's a few inches shorter.

I shrug as if it doesn't matter, not bothering to confirm

or deny whether a text was sent. "Well, I'm here now," I tell him as I slide off my jacket, soaked from the usual London rain, and hang it on the coatrack.

"You look like shit," he comments and an asymmetric grin tilts up my lips.

"Thanks." Running a hand over my damp hair and wiping it off on my jeans, I respond, "I'd say I feel better than I look, but that'd be a lie."

I've known James a long time, nearly a decade and I expect him to ask why, even though he already knows. I anticipate him starting the conversation, but instead he says nothing. Avoiding the obvious and walking down the hallway of the townhouse.

That's right, how could I forget? We're at war.

My feet move on their own, following him even though adrenaline courses faster in my blood. It makes me feel sick to not talk about it. To not clear the air.

"Whiskey?" he asks me as he pours himself a glass in the converted dining room. It's more of a bar now with a long plank of cedar serving as a makeshift counter in the back of the room. The recessed lighting shines softly on the bottles of clear and amber liquids and creates an intimate feel in the room. The humidor full of Cuban cigars and pair of dark leather wingback chairs on either side of it must have been added after I was here last.

"Kane Buchan," he says, speaking the name and then hands me a manila folder. I'm sure it's filled with the same shit that was emailed to me. I've got Kane's profile memorized already. He was the lead singer in a rock band from the Bronx. They had one smash hit and then he split from the rest of them. He decided to go his own way thinking he was too good for the band. Most said it was his ego, but it turns out he was right. Three number one hits on the top record charts and now he's a client.

They all want the same. To flaunt their wealth, get drunk or high. Fuck whomever they want. Kane Buchan is no different.

"He said something about going to Annabel's tonight," James tells me and I nod my head. I've been there more than a time or two. It's exclusive and ridiculously overpriced, so of course an up-and-coming star wants to be seen there.

I already know exactly how the night's going to play out. I just have to keep it clean enough so there are no problems. Kane's had enough of them from the fallout with his previous drummer.

"Did you even hear what I said?" James asks in a raised voice laced with irritation.

"Annabel's," I answer as I look him in the eyes and hope he was still going on about the club.

"No, I said he's married now so make sure there are no pictures if he does something stupid."

"I know." That's a given.

"He's staying a few days, maybe less depending on what his agent wants. Just keep an eye on him, show him a good time—" He's pissing me off. Treating me like a new hire and nothing more.

"I know what to do," I say, cutting off James deliberately with my retort. "I've been here before."

I've had days to think of how to approach this, but I still hesitate to get everything off my chest.

He huffs a response, sounding something like disbelief and then grabs the tumbler of whiskey from the table. The ice clinks as he takes a sip and holds it in front of him.

"Buchan's agent doesn't need any more press other than what they've arranged."

"I want you to know," I start to say as I stare him in the eyes, forcing him to listen to what I'm telling him. "I think it was a setup." Maybe I'm paranoid, but I don't give a fuck. I have to tell someone. And I'm sure as shit not going to Samantha. "It was an accident, but it just doesn't seem right. Something's off."

He shrugs and says, "It was handled." He takes a sip of his whiskey before adding, "So I don't give a shit if it was."

"I do." My words come out hard and bitter, but James is already walking away from me. I know if I move an inch, if I even breathe, I'll beat the piss out of him for leaving this all on me. And risk losing everything.

# CHAPTER
## five

*Kat*

M Y BLOODSHOT EYES HATE ME. THEY BURN FROM the onslaught of cool air as I finally sit back down in my office. I'm always here. I never leave this room unless I have to.

When I do decide to perch on the sofa or go to bed, I always bring my laptop with me.

*Workaholic* is a word for it. I'm not sure even that does it justice. I gave up everything for this. For sitting in this damn office, making deal after deal.

It's why I came to New York.

It's why I spent years in the publishing industry, collecting contacts and building a brand that's recognizable. I do it on my own and it's always been rewarding. Up until recently, this was my dream.

While Evan stayed the same and carried on with a life that was a fun distraction, I buried myself in work. Growing farther and farther apart from my husband. Knowingly creating distance between us. I thought it was worth it and that they'd all understand.

Ignored friends ... at least I didn't have family to ignore. Other than Evan.

I rub my eyes again and try to soothe them, but the darkness is all I can see. It begs me to sleep.

I desperately need it. I can't even read an email right, partly from how tired my eyes are and partly from my inability to focus on anything at all. I've reread this pending message about a dozen times and I couldn't tell a soul what the content is to save my life. My meeting with Jacob is *next* week. I spent an entire hour on my own sitting mindlessly in the coffee shop before I bothered to check the time and date.

The errors are piling up and so is my anxiousness.

At least the coffee in the shop was comforting and the little biscuits were delicious. But the rain was coming down in sheets, and any sense of ease was gone by the time I dragged my ass back home to an empty townhouse with soaking wet jeans slick around my ankles.

My shoulders rise and fall as I take another glance at the screen. The contrast of the black and white is too harsh and I almost shut the laptop down and give in to sleep, but my phone goes off, scaring the shit out of me.

*Evan.*

It's my first thought and I hate how disappointed I am when I see it's not him. It's his father. My heart sinks and I pretend it doesn't hurt.

In my contact list, it still says "Evan's parents' house." It's tied to the number for the landline at the house where he grew up. He said he had the number memorized when he was only six years old.

Marie gave the number to me the night I first saw her, so she could call me about next Sunday's dinner, all those years ago. Every time I see the words *Evan's parents' house*, I'm reminded that only Henry remains.

It brings a number of memories I don't welcome. Just the same as the reminder of my own parents' sudden death in a car crash. Tragedy brought us together. It wasn't love. It was a need for love and that's something else entirely.

That's something Evan and I had in common, both of us losing our loved ones so quickly. He still has his father at least, but I've had no one for most of my life.

The phone rings and rings as I attempt to gather my composure. We'd only been seeing each other for a few months when I got the first call from this number. I was expecting it to be Marie, but it wasn't his mother making the call, it was Evan because his cell phone had died.

He told me he couldn't make it to our date and the first thought I had was that he was breaking up with me, simply because of the tone of his voice. It wasn't until he apologized that I realized it was something else.

He couldn't hold it together on the phone. His voice shook and his sentences were short. I'll never forget that feeling in my chest, like I knew something horrible had happened and there was nothing I could do about it.

There was something in his voice that I recognized. It's

how I sound when I'm trying to convince someone else I'm okay, but I'm not. I knew it well.

After my parents died, I got tired of having to convince people there was more to me than tragedy. People who didn't bother to get to know me, because I was just the sad girl at the end of the block. The *poor child* everyone talked about.

It was why I moved to New York. Living in the small town where my family died wasn't a healthy place for someone who just wanted to feel like there's something else in this world other than the past.

For Evan it wasn't a sudden car crash, it was the phrase "two weeks to live" that brought him to his weakest moment.

I insisted on seeing him and meeting him at his parents' place and even though I thought he'd object, he didn't. He'd never been so passive toward anything like he was that night.

Evan's only cried twice since I've known him.

That night after his mother had finally gone to bed and we went back to his childhood bedroom. And nineteen days later, when she was put in the ground.

My hand itches to hold his right now. Instead I hold a ringing cell phone in an empty home.

"Henry," I say, answering the phone as if nothing's wrong although I'm very aware my voice sounds nearly breathless. Clearing my throat, I repeat his name. My voice is peppy and full of life, even though it's nearly 10:00 p.m. and I feel nothing but dead inside.

I squint at the clock on the computer and wonder why he's calling so late. "Is everything all right?" I ask, rushing out the words, my heart beating slower and a deep fear of loss settling in.

"My favorite daughter-in-law," Henry says and his greeting makes a soft smile lift up my lips. I even feel the warmth from it.

"Your *only* daughter-in-law," I correct him, picking at a bit of fuzz on the sleeve of my shirt.

"Still my favorite," he replies and I give him the laugh that he's after, even if it is a little short and quiet.

"What are you calling for?" I ask him and rest my elbow on the desk, chin in my hand. I absently minimize the document on my screen and clear out all my tabs, checking my email yet again as Henry talks.

"I just wanted to check on you, make sure everything's going well."

Again, I get the sense that something's off. "That's sweet of you," I tell him but before I can say everything's fine, he gets right to the real reason he called.

"You two all right?"

"Yeah," I say and instantly feel like shit. The single word is a vicious lie on my lips. I question what I should tell him: I don't know if my marriage to his son will last? That I'm falling apart and I have no idea how to make this better? That his son is a liar and I hate him for the pain he's putting me through?

"I spoke to Evan and he said he's not sure about the holidays coming up," Henry tells me and his tone reflects that he's baiting me. Henry's kind, polite, keeps to himself and doesn't want to be a bother, but he has a way of getting the truth out of people. Evan certainly inherited his charm from his father.

The screen of my laptop dims, ridding the room of any light so I hit the space bar and bring it back to life.

"It's a bit away, but," I say then pause and swallow, not

39

knowing how to articulate the onslaught of thoughts. They all crowd themselves into a jam at the back of my throat, refusing to come out. I don't have family, so it's not as if I can use them as an excuse. "Work may be a little much." I finally say the words and breathe out slowly, giving him a lie I'm sure he knows is exactly that.

"He said you're going through something." There's no bullshit in his voice as he adds, "That you two aren't doing the best."

A pricking numbness dances across my hands as I ask weakly, "Did he?" Staring blankly ahead, the rhetorical question is like a knife in my back. It's a betrayal. That's how I feel hearing that Evan's told his father what we're going through. It makes the crack in my heart that much wider.

*We aren't doing the best.* I hear it over and over and each time the knife stabs deeper.

It's not fair that he invites so much attention. I don't need the judgment, because I don't want their opinions. I don't want them to know we're flawed. I just want us whole again. I wish no one knew so I could silently be the weak wife I am. The one willing to turn a blind eye for the unfaithful man she loves more than herself.

"I don't want to talk about it, Henry," I say bluntly as my eyes close at the confession. I can tell the computer has gone into sleep mode again and this time I don't hit the keys to bring it back to life. The darkness is too comforting.

"I just want you to know I'm here for you," Henry says clearly into the phone. "You're my daughter," he adds and it breaks my composure.

I push away from the desk, the chair legs catching on

the rug and nearly tipping over. With a heavy inhale, I walk slowly to the door and then to my bedroom, the phone still pressed to my ear. I'm just going through the motions and trying to be numb to it all.

"Thank you," I finally say as I lean against the bedroom door, closing it. I almost tell him he's like a father to me.

Almost, but when we do get a divorce, Henry won't be there for me. It doesn't matter what he says. It doesn't matter that I'll be alone, because that's how I've been most of my life anyway.

"I love you and I'm sorry you two are going through this." I let Henry's words echo in my head.

He's not the only one who's sorry.

# CHAPTER

## six

### *Evan*

THE MUSIC POUNDS AWAY, THE BASS CRANKED UP so high it vibrates my chest. The interior of the nightclub alternates between dark shadows and bright, colorful lights that flash in time with the beat. Vibrant reds and greens scatter across the slim bodies that come and go from sight with the sudden darkness in between the beats.

"Another!" Kane's friend Mikey yells on my left, a little too loud, a little too close to my ear for comfort. I give him a smile in return and pretend to take another swig of my beer. I'm used to guys like him.

Another time in my life, I'd actually be drinking. The feel that I get on the right side of a heavy buzz is comforting. That light-headedness where you still have control, but

YOU KNOW I love you

a damn thing matters. That's the place I craved to be for so long, but not anymore.

Not when so much is slipping through my fingers.

It's been a few hours since we got to Annabel's and so far the job's been easy. Kane and his friends are trashed and most importantly, the rock star is having the time of his life. His crew is saddled up to the bar with a few women pressing their bodies against the men who welcome it, letting their hands stray every so often. One in particular for Kane, which has me on edge and keeping an eye out for the telltale glow of a cell phone in the air, ready to capture a snapshot.

She's the woman closest to Kane, Christi is what she said her name was, and the loudest by far. The more she drinks, the louder she gets, and the closer to Kane. Not that Kane seems to notice any of that.

According to his file, the tall, loudmouthed blonde is his type and it wouldn't be the first time he's strayed from his wife. Fame and fortune tend to do it. I've seen it too many times to keep track.

*Kat thinks this is the type of shit I do.* The thought makes me sick to my stomach, a scowl marring my face. I can't change what my clients do; I learned that all too fast. You can't change people. You accept it and work with what you're given. A prick's a prick. He's never going to be anything but that. So I raise the beer to my lips and take a long swig, nearly draining the bottle.

With the change of music bringing the group a little closer as the lights fade, I watch them each carefully, but all I can think about is Kat. What she'd think of this mess.

She's never questioned me before, but last night she let

out shit I had no idea about. Insecurities and accusations that made me feel like less of a man.

I can't blame her, can I? Not when I have secrets. Not when I can't look her in the eyes and tell her I haven't fucked up.

A strong grip on my arm rouses me from my thoughts.

"Can you get me something?" Kane asks, sidling up next to me. The smell of whiskey is heavy on his breath. It takes great effort not to put immediate distance between us.

Just like Mikey, he's a little too close as he slurs his request to the point where I can't tell what he's saying.

"What are you looking for?" I ask him to clarify and stare at the half-empty bottles of liquor lining the top shelf of the bar.

"Something a little stronger," he says as he tilts his head and tries to be subtle, but fails miserably, putting his hand to his nose and sniffing loudly. Cocaine.

I hesitate and waver on my answer. Luckily, I don't have to respond. Instead a loud, high-pitched voice on my right screams out, "We've got absinthe!" Apparently Christi was eavesdropping. *Surprise, surprise.* Her bright red talons are digging tight into Kane and I know she's going to stay within hearing range until we're out of here, just like she's been doing since she recognized him from across the room. She's leaning over a barstool, her breasts on full display and when I look back at Kane, the only thing he's looking at is her chest.

"Never had it," Kane says too low and the blonde screams, practically in my ear, "What?"

Giving them distance and getting out from between the two of them, I wait for him to agree. I know he will. She's got him wrapped around her little finger. I'll do it with a smile on my face and babysit this fucker. I used to think of this differently. This all used to be fun. But it wasn't like *this*, was it?

It doesn't take more than one feminine mewl and a *please* from her to convince Kane that absinthe is good enough and that we should all head to her place.

It's two blocks down and up a set of iron rails to get to the apartment. The sidewalk's still wet and this late at night, there's no one else on the streets. Just a bunch of drunk assholes stumbling on their way home. We fit in perfectly. I keep my eyes ahead, but occasionally look back and in all directions casually. I know the street and the apartment complex well. There aren't any cameras or storefronts for onlookers. Still, I watch and wait for any type of paparazzi.

I follow them as Kane and his friend cling to the group of women. There are three of them, two blond chicks and a dark brunette with curls, each barely covered in skimpy clubwear as they grip the railing to the apartment stairs and laugh as they stumble their way up in heels. It's difficult to tell with the other blonde if it's an act and she's playing up the drunkenness, or if she's really that plastered.

Kane's hands are all over Christi, moving from her hips to her ass as he walks behind her. Mikey's into the other blond chick and the brunette's checked out, only interested in smoking weed and getting trashed.

I tolerated the attention and flirting in the beginning of the night, but after a few minutes of ignoring the women, they lost interest and moved on. I'm certain this brunette is well aware there's nothing happening between us. The number one rule of my job is to not bring down the vibe. So I offer her a smile when she peeks at me, but then go back to scanning the surroundings and blocking the view from the street. One thought gnaws at me as the group travels along: I just want to get back to Kat and make her take it all back. Make her forget what happened and remind her why we're meant to be together. Remind her why she's mine.

I don't want this life anymore. Not when it makes Kat doubt me and what we have. Rightfully so.

I can't take this shit. I'll give it up for her. She'd take that, wouldn't she?

As the girls laugh nearly in unison to something that Mikey yelled out and the door opens, I take my phone out of my pocket, glancing up to make sure none of the girls have theirs out.

The number two rule of my job: no pictures.

That's my second concern. The first is getting Kane and peacing out of here. He's had a good time; he'll remember enough of it at least. I'm not interested in being here any longer than I have to be.

I'm distracted for only a moment. Half a second, but the moment I stop watching these girls, one of them breaks rule number two.

The second Christi's blond friend pulls out her iPhone, flicking her long hair behind her as if she's only taking a selfie, turning and posing with Kane in the background, I snatch it from her. She gasps and tries to grab it back like this is a game and I'm making a move on her. Her smile widens and she lets out a small laugh, again trying to snatch it from me.

Keeping the smile in place, I'm firm. It takes her a minute

to realize no matter how much she pulls on my arm and makes that girlish cry, I have no intention of giving it back.

"No pictures," I tell her simply, my voice low and admonishing. I don't have time for this shit or her antics. She knows what she's doing and it's not cute or funny.

The smile drops from her face, her disappointment evident. I force myself to stare into her drunken hazel gaze until she looks down and then holds out her hand. The flirtation is completely gone. "I get it," she snaps.

I place the phone in her palm after I shut it off and she huffs like I'm an asshole, but she'll listen. They always do. It's obvious she's biting her tongue over wanting to tell me off and I can't really blame her. She wouldn't be the first. I've been slapped more times than I know. Mostly by women. Years of doing this have led to plenty of fights and unfortunate events.

I've beaten the shit out of assholes.

Called doctors and paid them in cash to come to hotel rooms.

I've paid off cops, bouncers, bookies. At this point I've seen it all, done it all. And I'm tired of this shit.

This little blonde, though? She'll pout and listen, even if she tries to make a move on me and probably attempt even more pictures throughout the night.

The bright green of the absinthe bottle catches my eye as the blonde I just pissed off brings it to the coffee table. I watch as she sets it in the center and lines up three shot glasses before going back to the small kitchen only ten feet away to grab more.

Kane's in the middle of the sofa with both arms draped across the back as Christi and the brunette cuddle up next to him. The sounds of them laughing and Kane saying something in a low voice as they huddle closer to him are barely on my mind as I turn my focus back to my phone.

I text the driver and let him know I'm going to need the car in about thirty minutes then send him the address.

It takes fifteen minutes for the alcohol to hit their systems. Heavy pours and three shots each will have them all out on their asses. Normally I'd feel bad cutting their party short, but I don't give a shit. All I can think about is Kat.

I need to get back to her.

With an asymmetric grin forced onto my face, I roll up my sleeves, letting the tats show. "Let me get it, doll," I tell the blonde as I make my way to the kitchen. "You sit back and relax," I add, taking the bottle from her hands. I'll pour the second round while they're throwing back the first. She gives me a flirtatious smirk. "I knew you weren't *all* asshole," she teases with a playful peek up at me and then sits on her knees next to the coffee table. Too close, too presumptuous.

"You had it right the first time," I murmur under my breath as I fill all six glasses and pass them out.

"Let's do a couple rounds and get this party started."

# CHAPTER
## seven

*Kat*

*"I'm stronger than this. I deserve so much more."*
*They're the words I breathe, then collapse on the floor.*
*My eyes close tight; tears trapped, lungs still.*
*I can't speak the truth; I can't fight the chill.*
*"I'm stronger than this." I whisper the words, my face hot.*
*But I know I'm a liar, and I know that I'm not.*

EVAN ALMOST NEVER TEXTS ME WHEN HE'S working but he did tonight, and I can't take my eyes away from my phone because of that little fact. In all the years we've been together, I can count on one hand when he's messaged me while out on a job. I've never minded it; he's working. I've never needed a message that said he missed me, I always knew he did and that he'd be home soon. I had work to occupy me while he was away. Come morning, there was always a message to greet me, but while he was out, he was simply unavailable.

My body's still and my focus is nonexistent when it comes to work now, though. There's not a damn thing keeping me company but the memories of us and the constant worry of what'll happen when—and if—he comes home.

Staring down at my cell, I swallow thickly. *He messaged me. He reached out to me.* I can't explain why it makes my bruised heart hurt even more. Maybe I wish he'd just be cruel and not try or not care. It hurts so much more to think that he's trying. Hope is an odd little thing. I want to cling to it, but if I do, the inevitable fall will be that much more deadly.

He always messaged in the morning, though, after the late night of whatever the hell he'd been up to. I've always thought it was cute how he'd text me to tell me good morning, even if he was only just then getting into bed.

But it's 2:00 a.m. in London, his prime time, and my phone's lit up on the desk with a message from him.

I was finally getting some work done, the keys clacking and the to-do list shrinking somewhat although for every item crossed off, I feel as if I've added two. Focusing and managing to write up some feedback along with creating a marketing tactic for a client has been a highlight of my night ... Until that message came through.

Half of me doesn't want to answer him. Cue the grinding halt to any progress I'd made. I don't want to read whatever he's sent and go back into the black hole of self-pity. But I can't resist. He is a drug and I am an addict. We could go days without speaking before, but in this moment, every second that I stare at my phone knowing there's an unread message from him feels like an eternity in hell.

My hand inches toward it, the need to see what he has to say overriding the anger and the sadness. The need to be wanted by him and to feel loved winning out over my dignity.

So I click on the damn thing and my heart does a little pitter-patter of acknowledgment. When I swallow, it's as if I'm shoving my heart back down where it belongs.

*I hate it when you're mad at me.*

I stare at his message, feeling the vise in my chest tighten. My fingers hesitate over the keys as I read it again and again. Before I can respond, another message comes through.

*Forgive me.*

That's the crux of the situation. The dams break loose.

*Forgive you for what exactly?* I message him back without even thinking. Whatever he's hiding is bad, I know it is. I can feel it deep down in my core. Just like I knew that night when his mother was diagnosed. Whatever he's done is enough to ruin us.

But we were already ruined, weren't we? It's been a slow burn of destruction. My intuition is hardly ever wrong. We've grown apart. We're different people now. *We don't belong together.* We never did, not really. Admitting that is what hurts the most.

With my body trembling, I force myself to get up and move, even if it's just to walk through the house. I'm only wearing a baggy shirt and a pair of socks. I wore the shirt to bed last night and I should really shower and get dressed. It's a rule I've had since I started working from home.

Every day, I dress as if I'm going into the office. Right now I just don't have the energy.

Evan sends two texts, one right after the other as I walk to the kitchen.

*We can work through this.*

*I love you.*

I only glance at them before putting the phone down on the counter and heading straight to the fridge for some wine. Taking in a staggered breath, I focus on ignoring the pain. *Think logically*, I command myself. *Don't fall back into his arms without having a grasp on the problem. Because otherwise it will happen again. That's what happens when you accept a behavior without acknowledgment and a plan to change.*

There's only half a glass left in the dark red bottle, but it'll have to do.

I glance at the clock as I sip it. It's after 9:00 p.m. I've barely slept, barely worked and hours passed before I realized I hadn't brushed my teeth today. At least I'm drinking from a clean glass.

It only takes one sip before I tell him what's on my mind. Communication is key. All the years of therapy taught me that. There is no relationship worth keeping if you don't trust what someone says.

*I don't understand why you won't tell me what you did.*

*Won't tell you what?* he texts back and it pisses me off.

"Does he think I'm stupid?" I mutter beneath my breath as my blood boils. The anger is only an ounce stronger than the pain. In the back of my mind I note that only crazy people talk to themselves, but even if that's the case, I accept it. This man makes me crazy. I can admit that much.

*Don't treat me like this*, I answer him, feeling weak. I'm practically begging him in my head but when I reread the text it sounds strong. *I deserve better.*

I down the remaining wine after sending the last line, the cool red soothing a tiny bit of an ache. I don't know exactly what it is I deserve but I have a rough idea. Him telling me the truth. Him confiding in me. Or a better husband altogether.

As I grab the last bottle of red wine on the rack and bring it back to the kitchen, I realize this is how women feel when they stay in these marriages.

They'd rather be told a sweet little lie and believe it than face the truth. Those are my choices: demand the truth and accept the lie he gives me or … I don't know.

Right now, it's exactly what I want. Just lie to me. Tell me there's nothing that happened. That it's blown out of proportion. *That it was just a kiss.* Yes, that one. That last one. I could forgive it, but better yet, I could believe it. I could allow myself to believe it, even if deep down inside I know it was more.

Lie to me and love me. He knows I'll still love him. It would make everything better.

The barstool legs scratch on the floor as I sit down to uncork the new bottle.

I just want him to come home. Tell me everything is fine and make up something that's easy to forgive. It was only a kiss.

With a bottle of wine and a full glass in front of me, I go back to the beginning. Back to when I was stronger and I actually had self-respect.

Back to when I knew better.

The memory and the wine are the only things to keep me

company for the rest of the night, because Evan doesn't text me back with the truth or a lie. He gives me silence.

*Six years ago*

*The wind blows in my face, alleviating some of the stifling summer heat as I pull into the gas station parking lot in Brooklyn. It's late and the hustle and bustle of New York has waned, but the nightlife on this side of the city is only getting started.*

*Some would say it's the bad part of town, but others say it's the fun part. I guess it depends on what circles you run in. New to New York and struggling to find where I belong, I suppose I'm keeping an open mind. The bright lights and sophistication are what I came here for, but making it here isn't so easily achieved.*

*I'm slow to step on the brakes and pull into the last spot that lines the front of the small convenience store. I've only been here a few times, either needing to stop for gas or a quick bite to eat on my way to or from work on the west side of the city. It's a clerical job for a newspaper, but beggars can't be choosers and the bills need to be paid while I learn the ropes, snag clients and rub elbows, so to speak.*

*Several cars are parked in front of the store and a few men head inside as I pull up. They vary from obviously expensive to looking like they're falling apart. The vehicles, that is.*

*I notice the men, and they notice me. Averting my eyes to avoid making small talk, I turn down my radio and put my car in park.*

*I mind my business and everyone around me seems to do the same. In the city that never sleeps, there's always something happening. And I'm not interested in a damn one of those some-things. Distractions get a bad rap for a reason.*

*Grabbing my purse and keys in the same hand, I make haste, opening the car door to step out in a rush, but my eyes glance back to the cars and straight into a man's gaze.*

*Not just any man, a man exuding power and confidence, along with defiance. Although he's wearing a simple shirt and faded dark jeans, the way he wears them makes me think they were made to be fitted to his muscular body. He's hot as hell, and given the way he looks at me, he could be a temptation the devil made just for me.*

*My driver's side door shuts with a loud bang as I stand there caught in the heat in his gaze. He leans against the hood of a car, I'm assuming is his, a shiny black Mercedes that reflects the light from the store in its slick exterior. The windows are rolled up and tinted so dark it's hard to see the inside. As my eyes move back to the man, my movements are slowed and I grip my keys tighter.*

*He doesn't stop looking, taking me in and letting his eyes follow along the curves of my body. Arrogance and sinful thrill dance in his cocky grin. He obviously wants me to know that he's watching me. Something about that small fact forces a blush to rise to my cheeks.*

*My breathing picks up and I subconsciously pull the hem of my dress down just slightly, smoothing out the cherry red pleats and wishing I hadn't been wearing it all day. I take one step and the click of my heels keeps time with my racing pulse as I walk forward, knowing I have to pass him on my way in.*

*I can't help that my eyes flicker over to his as I grip my purse strap and settle it in place. His shirt is pulled taut and over his muscular frame and his tanned skin is decorated with ink. Tattoos* travel down his chest and arms, peeking out below his collarbone from the crisp white cotton shirt and leaving a trail of intricate designs all the way down to his wrists. I'm too far away to see what they say or what they are. I know if he were in a suit, the tattoos would be hidden, but something tells me he's proud to have them on full display.

"What are you up to?" he asks me and catches me off guard.

"I don't think that's any of your business," I answer him easily, although I don't know how, swaying a little from side to side in a flirtatious way I didn't intend. My body can't help but be attracted to his. Some part of me is eager to know how his tattooed skin would feel against my fingertips.

There's a scar over his left eyebrow and it's subtle, but even from this distance I notice it. As his deep rough chuckle fills the night air and drowns out the other sounds of the city, I find myself wondering how he got it.

"A man can wonder, though," he says, causing a hot blush to creep slowly into my cheeks. I bite down on my lower lip, but that doesn't stop the shy smile from showing. I have to stop and give him the attention he's looking for as he leans forward, holding me captive to whatever's on his mind.

"You're pretty, you know that?" he says and I roll my eyes. Even if I know this flirtation isn't just for me, that he's simply playing with me, I still enjoy it. I crave it even. I'm sure he's already used these lines tonight.

"Sure, and you're not too bad looking either." I enjoy the flirting, the attention. At least coming from him. He makes me feel things I haven't before.

He splays a hand over his heart and cocks his head as he says, "Well thank you, beautiful, I aim for 'not bad.'" This time

I'm the one laughing, a short, soft snicker as I kick the bottom of my heels against the ground and stare at them for a moment, readying myself to say goodbye and end his bout of teasing. I don't trust myself not to say anything and instead I just wave and carry on, expecting him to do the same.

"You didn't answer me," he calls out after I take a few steps. "What are you doing out here so late?" he asks. It's forward of him and I usually despise that, but instead I savor the challenge in his voice. Something about it tells me he thinks I'm already his. And that ownership makes my blood that much hotter.

I know I shouldn't give him any information at all, but I find myself telling him the truth before I can stop myself. "I'm hungry and overworked. So I stopped to grab a bite to eat."

"You're getting your dinner from here?" he asks, gesturing to the store and I nod. "A woman like you should be taken out, not eating dinner from the gas station."

A woman like you plays over and over in my head. He doesn't know what type of woman I am. "You don't even know my name," I say, the half smile and challenge firm on my expression.

He nods and grins, flashing me a cocky smile as he replies, "Don't make me guess."

I chew on my lip for a moment, rocking from side to side. He's bad news and I'm flirting with fire … but I love the thrill. I can't deny it. "It's Kat," I tell him and a smile is slow to form on his face. One of complete satisfaction, as if hearing my name is the best thing that's happened to him all night.

"I'm Evan," he says and I taste his name on the tip of my tongue, nearly whispering it. "Let me take you to dinner, Kat," he suggests with an easiness I don't like. I wonder how many times that's worked for him before.

"I'm not your type," I respond, intentionally looking past him at the bars that wrap around the glass door to the convenience store. I just need a late-night snack to hold me over till morning. That's all this little errand was supposed to turn into.

"I don't think you should tell me what is and isn't my type." Although it comes out playful, there's a hint of admonishment, and my naïve little heart doesn't like that. "You might be surprised," he adds.

I clear my throat and try to breathe evenly, wanting this flirting session to end so I can get back to work. I have to admit the attention is very much appreciated, though. And the desire in his eyes looks genuine.

"Sorry, Charlie, didn't mean to upset you," I tell him with a playful pout as I walk past him.

"It's Evan," he says, repeating his name and that makes a wicked grin play at my lips, "and you're wrong." The last part is spoken with a seriousness I wasn't expecting. His tone is hard and when I turn around to face him fully, finally taking a step onto the curb, he's no longer leaning on the hood of the Mercedes. He takes a few strides across the asphalt parking lot and stops in front of me as I ask, "Wrong about what?"

Up close he's taller than I first thought, more intimidating too and his shoulders seem broader, stronger. Even his subtle moves as he brushes his jaw with his rough fingers and licks his lower lip again, are dominating. He glances to the left and right before opening his mouth again and letting that deep, rough voice practically ignite the air between us.

"You're wrong that you aren't my type and that I'm not your type."

The compliment makes my body feel hotter than it already

*is in the hot summer night. Someone behind me exits the store, the telltale jingle of the bells and the whoosh of air-conditioning reminding me that I'm supposed to be in and out of this store. Reminding me that Evan isn't a part of my to-do list tonight.*

*"I never said you weren't my type," I say and my voice comes out sultry, laced with the desire I feel coursing in my blood. I try to hold his gaze, but the fire and intensity swirling in his dark eyes make me back down.*

*I can try to be tough all I want, but he's a bad boy through and through and I should know better.*

*"Good to know," he says with a cocky undertone that makes my eyes whip up to his. I half expect him to blow me off now that his ego's been fed. He licks his lower lip and my eyes are drawn to the motion, imagining how it'd feel to have his lips on every inch of my skin. "Come out with me tonight," he says. As if I don't have anything better to do. As if he can just command me to do what he wants.*

*"Sorry … Evan. I can't tonight," I tell him and turn back around, hiking my purse up higher on my shoulder, ready to go about my business.*

*"Tomorrow night then," he says, raising his voice so I can hear him as I wrap my hand around the handle and pull the door open. Again the chill of the store greets me, but this time it's unwanted.*

*I'm all too aware of what this man could do to me. He's the type to pin you down as he takes you how he wants you and doesn't stop until you're screaming. And I can't lie, just that thought alone makes me desperate to say yes.*

*He takes another step closer as I stand with the door wide* open and hesitate to answer. Shoving his hands into his pockets, he manages a shrug as if it's a casual question.

"Just one date," he adds as he looks at me with a raised brow and his version of puppy dog eyes. It's enough to force a smile on my face.

"And what am I supposed to do? Meet you here at ten?" I ask him.

"How about at Jean-Georges in Central Park?" he asks and I'm taken aback. It's an expensive place and my eyes glance back to his car, to his ripped body and tattooed skin. There's something about the air that follows him that screams he's no good. The danger in the way he looks at me is so tempting, though.

"I just want to feed you," he adds as the time ticks by slowly and a short, older man with salt-and-pepper hair walks out of the exit, stealing our attention and making my hand slip slightly on the handle.

I chew on the inside of my cheek. The answer is an easy one. No. Simple as that. He's a bad boy who only wants one thing, but I can't deny that I want it too.

I said yes.

To the date, and then again a year later to marrying him.

That initial yes, pushed through my lips by an undeniable attraction, was my first mistake on a list of too fucking many.

All because I can't tell him no.

# CHAPTER
## eight

*Evan*

I TRY TO SHUT THE FRONT DOOR SOFTLY, AS QUIETLY as I can so I don't wake up Kat if she's passed out.

I know she told me not to come back. She says a lot of things and then apologizes and changes her mind. Silence isn't better, though. It still hurts, just in a different way. Our loft is small and the walls are thin so you can hear everything in here. I stop in the foyer, setting down my duffle bag and luggage then toss the bunched-up chenille blanket that's in a puddle on the floor onto the sofa in the living room.

The room is mostly gray, just like the city. There's a paned glass mirror above the long sofa and black and white accents everywhere. I hated that mirror from the moment we got it, but Kat loved it, so I never said a word. It belongs in some farmhouse up north, not in the heart of New York, the devil's playground. But it made her smile. I'll be damned if that isn't reason enough to keep that cheap-ass mirror.

My eyes scan the room in the faint light from the city that's shining through the gap in the curtains.

Five years of marriage, six of creating this place together.

Each piece of furniture is a memory. The wine rack that we purchased was the first thing we bought together. The gray sofa with removable pillows was a fight I lost. I didn't want the cushions to be removable, because they always end up sagging, but Kat insisted the brand was quality.

The plush cushions still look like they did in the store, and I wonder if she was right or if it's just because we don't even sit on the damn thing. Maybe both but I lean toward the latter.

I'm never here and she's always working. What's the point of it?

The bitter thought makes me kick the duffle bag out of my way and head past the living room and dining room, straight to the stairs so I can get to bed and lie down with Kat. It's been almost a week since I've slept in the same room as her and I refuse to let that go on for another night. I pause to look at the photos on the wall, the light streaming in leaving a sunbeam down the glass.

Almost all are in black and white, the way Kat likes her décor. All but one, the largest in the very center. It's also the only one that's not staged.

She's leaning toward me, and her lips look so red as she's mid-laugh, holding a crystal champagne flute and wrapping her fingers around my forearm. Her eyes are on whoever was giving a speech. I don't remember who it was or what they said, but I can still hear her laugh. It's the most beautiful sound.

She was so happy on our wedding day. I thought she'd be stressed and worried, but it was like a weight was lifted and the sweetest version of her was given to me that day. There's nothing but love in the photo. No work, no bullshit, just the two of us telling the world we loved each other enough to stay together forever.

My eyes are on her in that picture, with a smile on my face and pride in my reflection.

I tear my gaze away and keep walking, feeling the weight of everything press down on my shoulders. I'm exhausted and like the childish fool I am, I wish I could just go to sleep and this would all be a dream. A huff of sarcasm accompanies my gentle footsteps up the stairs.

I want to go back to when we first got married. Before we both got caught up in work and started to live separate lives. Before I fucked up.

If only we could start over and go back to that day.

As I pass the open office door, I hear the clacking of the computer keyboard. So many nights I've come home to this, so many mornings I've woken up to it. She's always in her office, which is a shame. There's hardly any light, or anything at all in the room. File cabinets, papers, a shredder and a desk. There's not a hint of the woman Kat is in this room.

I guess it's the same as the living room, but at least a classic elegance is present there. It's nothing but cold in here. If a to-do list could be made into décor, that's what this cramped room resembles.

"Hey, babe," I say softly and Kat ignores me. I clear my

throat and speak louder. "I'm home," I tell her and again, I get nothing from Kat, just the steady clicks. There's an empty wineglass and two bottles on the floor by her feet.

Maybe she's a little drunk, maybe she has her earplugs in too, but still, she'd hear me. Was it a long shot that she'd kindly accept me coming home? *Yes.* It's not too much to ask for an acknowledgment, though. Even if she tells me to fuck off. I'd take it.

My teeth grind together as I grip the handle of the door harder. She deserves better. I know she does. This is exactly what I deserve, but I don't want it. I won't go down without fighting for what I want.

The standing floor lamp in the corner of her office is on, but it's not enough to brighten the room. Even the glow of the computer screen is visible.

"Do you want to talk?" I ask her and her only response is that her fingers stop moving across the keys.

She doesn't turn to face me or give any sign that I've spoken to her. She heard it, though, and her gaze drops to the keyboard for a second too long not to give that away.

"I don't want to fight, Kat," I tell her and force every bit of emotion I'm feeling into my words. "I don't want this between us."

She turns slowly in her seat, a baggy T-shirt covering her slim body and ending at her upper thighs. Her exposed skin is pale and the dark room makes her look that much paler. Her viridian eyes give her away the most, though. Nothing but sadness stares back at me.

My body is pulled to her, and I can't help it. I can't stand that look in her eyes. Before I can tell her I love her and I'm sorry, before I can come up with some lame excuse, she cuts me off.

"I wanted to last night," she says and then crosses her arms. She looks uncomfortable and unnatural. Like she's doing what she thinks she should be doing, not what she wants. "When you texted me and then I texted you back. I was ready to talk then."

"I'm here now," I offer and walk closer to her, the floorboards creaking gently. There's a set of chairs in the corner of the room from our first apartment and I almost drag one over, but I'm too afraid to break eye contact with her. It's progress. I'll be damned if I stop progress for a place to sit.

At least she's looking at me, talking to me, receptive to what I have to say.

"Ask me whatever you want." My voice is calm but deep down I'm screaming. Because I know I'll answer her. I'll tell her everything just to take that pain away, even if it's only temporary, even if it fucks her too.

Her doe eyes widen slightly and she cowers back, swallowing before answering me. "Aren't you tired?" she says softly and her eyes flicker to the door and then to the floor.

She doesn't want to know the truth.

"Yeah, I'm exhausted. But I'm not going to bed until you do." I lick my lips and clear my throat, hoping she'll give in to me. For nearly the past year when I'm home, I've tried to stay up with her or brush off the fact that I'd pass out while she was still working and vice versa. Not tonight, not from this point forward. The advice my father gave me on our wedding night was to go to bed together. I should have listened. I'll make it better, I can at least fix that.

65

"I can stay up for you," I say, offering her the suggestion. It's not what she wants, but it's something.

"Well, this has to get done, and it's going to take hours."

"I can wait," I tell her but the second the words slip out she turns back to the computer and says, "Don't."

With her back to me and her fingers already flying across the keys again, I've never felt more alone and crestfallen.

"I'll go unpack and relax on the bed then," I say as I grip the doorframe to stay upright and keep myself from ripping her out of that chair and bringing her to bed.

"Here?" Shock coats the single word.

It takes me a moment to realize why the hell she's asking me that and when I do, it's like a bullet to the chest.

A mix of emotions swell in my gut and heat my blood. Anger is there, but the dejectedness is what cuts me the most.

"Is that all right?" I ask sarcastically.

She nods, conceding to let me stay in my own damn house, but the look in her eyes doesn't fade. She really wants me out. She wants me to just leave? Did she think I wouldn't fight for her? That I'd let this destroy us? It may ruin me, but I'd rather chew on broken glass than let it ruin *us*.

"I said I don't want a divorce." My words come out hard. I'm sick of this. "I want you," I tell her with conviction and walk closer to her, not leaving any space between us.

"I don't know what I want," Kat responds in a murmur, gripping the armrests of the desk chair as her lips form a painful frown and her eyes gloss over. Like she's on the verge of breaking. The last thread that was holding her together has snapped, leaving her falling. I'm not there to catch her, because I'm the one that pushed her over the edge. I hate myself for it.

It's my fault, and this is all on me, but I'll make it right.

"You don't have to, Kat," I say, softening my voice and moving just a little closer. I need a chance. She's vulnerable; I can feel it coming off of her in waves. *Give in to me, baby.*

I cup her cheek in my hand to lean down and kiss her, but she pushes back, quickly standing and making the chair slam against the desk.

My pride, my ego, whatever it is that makes me a man, is destroyed in this moment. My limbs freeze and the tension makes me feel like I'm breaking. Literally cracking in my very center.

I lick my lips, finally letting out a breath as Kat whispers, "I'm sorry, I'm just …" She doesn't finish, and I have to look up at her before I can stand upright again.

"You just what?"

"I don't know, Evan," she answers with desperation in her voice.

"Don't think," I tell her, grasping for anything to keep her from running. "Just let me make it better," I offer and she stands there, in nothing but that T-shirt, and looks at me as if I'm both her savior and her enemy.

I walk slowly, each step making the floor groan in quiet protest. I don't quicken my pace until I'm close enough to her to feel her heat. And she lets me, standing still and giving me the chance I need.

My lips crash against hers, my body molding to her small frame and forcing her back. For each step she takes, I take one with her.

"Stop," she tells me and pushes me away. My breathing is ragged as my hands clench to keep from holding on to her as she leaves me. I can still taste her, my body ringing with desire to make it up to her.

To ease her pain and remind her how good I make her feel. It's what she needs. It's been weeks and I can't deny I need her even more. I need to bury myself inside her warmth.

My hands grasp her hips and I push her back against the wall. Her arms wrap around my neck as she comes in for the kiss this time. Taking the passion from me, letting me give her what she needs. Comfort and an escape from reality. A welcome distraction to the fact that our marriage is at risk.

Right now there's nothing but what we feel for each other. Nothing else. No logic or reason. Just the devotion and intense desire.

I'm grateful it still exists. I only wish this moment would last forever. Where we're both weak for each other, desperate and drunk with lust.

"You're mine, Kat," I whisper against the shell of her ear. My breath is hot and it's making the air between us that much hotter.

Her back arches against the wall and she pushes her soft curves into mine. A quiet moan spills from her sweet lips. I stare at her face, the expression of utter rapture with her eyes closed and her lips parted just slightly.

I rock my palm over her again and again, putting pressure on her swollen nub and feeling her cunt get hotter and wetter.

"This is mine," I whisper louder, not holding back the possession in my voice.

A strangled moan fills the air. At first I don't know if it's from me or her, but the sweet cadence of her voice prolongs the sound of pleasure as her body writhes against mine. She's so close.

I tear the thin lace fabric of her panties off in one tug after ripping it with my thumb and watch her face as her eyes pop open. The gorgeous greens stare back at me with a mix of emotions, the overwhelming two being desire and vulnerability.

I don't give her the chance to second-guess this. This is how we're meant to be. Together, raw and bared.

I only release my grip on her to unzip my pants. The sound mixes with Kat's heavy breathing.

"Evan," she says, whispering my name as if it's a question.

She wants me, although she knows we shouldn't do this. Fuck, I know she's going to question this. Maybe even regret it. But she just needs to feel me again; she needs this as much as I do.

I press the head of my dick against her opening and slide myself through her slick folds, teasing her and watching as her eyes close tight. She squirms when I just barely touch her clit.

So close.

"Evan," she whispers again and this time it's a plea. One I can satisfy.

In one swift stroke I slam into her all the way to the hilt, making her scream out.

Her blunt nails dig into my shoulders as her body is forced against the wall and her head falls back.

I kiss her throat ravenously, desperate to taste her, but not willing to mute the sounds of pleasure she's making.

My thrusts are primal, ruthless. I take from her over

and over. Each time her back hits the wall, her whimpers get louder and louder.

Her grip tightens as my balls draw up. My spine tingles with the need to release, but I need her to find hers with me. I'm desperate to feel her walls tighten around my cock. Desperate to feel her pulsing and lost in pleasure.

The moment I think I can't take any more, she gives me what I need. Screaming out my name as her orgasm rips through her body.

"Fuck," I groan into the crook of her neck. My dick pulses and I come hard, buried deep inside of her. My heart hammers hard and fast and refuses to stop as she clings to me for dear life. A cold sweat lines my skin. Her eyes are closed and her teeth are digging into her bottom lip when I finally look at her.

"I love you, Kat," I whisper as I pull away from her, finally breathing and starting to come down from the highest high.

"I love …" Kat starts to reply, but she doesn't finish. She doesn't look me in the eyes.

She's so ashamed to love me, she can't even say it back.

# CHAPTER
## nine

*Kat*

I DON'T KNOW WHAT I'M MORE ASHAMED ABOUT AS I carelessly toss the throw blanket over one arm of the sofa and force myself get up, still feeling the ache between my thighs.

The fact that I fucked my husband.

Or the fact that I then refused to go to bed with him.

Not that I told him so much. I hid behind work and then snuck out here to the living room. I didn't sleep on the sofa for more than a few hours. Maybe that's all I'm entitled to for being so weak and falling right into his arms the moment he pulled me in.

It's like our union is a spiraling dark hole and I'm falling deeper and deeper, to the point where what I want and what I'm feeling don't make sense and nothing adds up. Not that I could hold on to anything anyway; I've lost all control.

I couldn't possibly feel more pathetic at this point.

Because I love him and hate myself for it.

I glance at my phone on the dining room table as I make my way to the kitchen, the charging cord is in a tangled heap on the floor.

I already know what Sue would say. She'd feel sorry for me for going back to the man who cheated on me. Her lips would purse in that way where it's obvious she's holding back some snarky remark.

Pity and sorrow for the pathetic girl, clinging to an unfaithful man. Even the bitter thought echoes what I already know she'd say.

The thing about love though is that it's not a light switch. You can't just turn it off. No matter how much you may want to, you can't erase the memories and move on. Sue knows that much, she just chooses to forget that it's not so easy.

My head throbs and I'm not sure if it's from the lack of sleep or the absence of caffeine. Even the faint sounds of city life from stories down are enough to make my temples pulse. I've felt more put together with a hangover than I do now. This is not the unfortunate side effect of too much cabernet last night. I wish it was only that.

I groan as I rest against the wall of the living room and try to calm the headache. I close my eyes and feel the weight of all the stress from the last two weeks.

I need aspirin or coffee. Or both. My heart sputters as I slowly walk up the stairs, knowing Evan's lying in bed alone and that it was my choice.

As I pass the office, I remember last night and my thighs clench; I can still feel him inside of me. His warm lips on my neck, his rough hands on my body ... it's more than a memory, the act still lingers on my skin. He took from me. Relentlessly, possessively. Each step brings my body temperature higher and higher, yet my heart hurts more and more.

Why won't the pain just go away? Why can't my head just shut the fuck up so I can pretend I'm okay for a single moment? Jules told me once I overthink everything. She was referring to some edits I gave her but still, the woman had a point.

The bedroom door is open and as I walk through the door, I can't take my eyes off the perfectly made bed. The cream and white comforter printed with black dahlias is pulled tight, looking pristine. A crease forms in the center of my forehead as I walk to the bathroom, listening to my heart beat with each step, but finding the bathroom empty. *Evan wasn't downstairs*, I think as I open the medicine cabinet and silently grab a bottle of aspirin. He wasn't downstairs, and he's not up here.

I swallow the pills without water, staring into the mirror as my heart clenches, the dark bags under my eyes looking significantly worse than yesterday morning. Did he even stay last night? Did he find me asleep on the sofa and decide to leave? *It's what I wanted, wasn't it?*

The cabinet door slams shut; I give the push more force than I meant to, but I ignore it, striding quickly down to the kitchen, the baggy T-shirt flowing around my thighs as one sleeve slips down my shoulder.

I just need coffee. Coffee will wake me, rid me of this headache and give me the energy I need to deal with this mess.

It is such a chaotic mess; I'm not sure how it possibly got worse than it was. A mix of emotions and desires that thrashes me side to side like an unforgiving earthquake. The only thing certain is that I can't stand on my own two feet. At least not without a cup of coffee.

A sarcastic huff of a humorless laugh leaves me as I round the bottom of the stairs and head to the kitchen, a pitiful smile adorning my lips. Ask and you shall receive; I'm a spiteful self-fulfilling prophecy.

All the plans I had are threatening to blow away like the stubborn seeds of a dandelion. Marriage, traveling, success and recognition. Then what? A small bump at my stomach cradled by his hand on top of mine.

Using the wineglass from last night I left next to the sink, I fill it with water and pour it into the back of the coffee maker, remembering the days when having a child was on my mind. Back when my career was only a long shot of a dream, when my time was monopolized by Evan and we owned the world together. We could be and do anything we wanted.

I slip a fresh coffee pod into the machine and turn it on as I remember how he'd hold my belly and plant a kiss there, just below my belly button, telling me what a wonderful mother I would be one day to his son.

With my throat tight I admit one thing: *we were fools*. I knew this would never last. I knew it back then. Just like I know it now.

I bite the inside of my cheek and take in a heavy breath,

slipping the ceramic mug with *Rise and Shine* scrolled on the side under the spigot to the coffee machine.

My bare feet pad on the tiled kitchen floor as I open the fridge and search for the creamer, ignoring the old dreams and memories being dredged up. I stare longer than I should at the empty spot on the shelf. *I can't even remember to get creamer.* My teeth grind back and forth and the throbbing comes back with a vengeance to my temples.

I slam the fridge door shut as the coffee maker sputters to life. It's quite something when you've fallen so hard that a mundane task like going to the grocery store is enough to push you over the edge. Maybe I've truly gone crazy.

The creak of the front door opening is the last thing I need right now. The door closes softly, as if Evan didn't want to wake me. I wipe under my eyes and push my hair out of my face as I lean against the wall with my arms crossed, waiting for him to make his way in here.

I can't explain why I feel guilty. It's all I feel, like everything I've done is wrong and I'm the one to blame. Is this normal? I feel like this is what I deserve. Like somehow I've orchestrated all of this just so I could feel lonely and miserable. Maybe I had it too good and I decided I needed to go right back to the mental space where I used to feel like I was drowning.

"Morning." I hear Evan's voice and the sound of a plastic bag crinkling before I see him.

My lips part to tell him good morning, but then I catch sight of him.

He looks tired, his scruff a little too grown out, his dark hair a little too long and a bit of darkness under his eyes. For the first time I've laid eyes on him, he looks older, more mature but still as handsome as ever.

It all brings me to an abrupt halt. His jaw tenses as he rests the bag on the counter and then looks over his shoulder at me. "Did you sleep well?" he asks, barely looking at me before turning his attention to the corner cabinet and grabbing a mug for himself.

"No," I say, forcing out the word. "Evan …" I try to keep talking but my heart slams at the same time that Evan shuts the cabinet and turns around to face me. He leaves the stark white mug on the granite countertop where it clinks in protest, and I stare at it, rather than at him.

I have to spend time away from him. That's what I need. To get used to being alone again and stopping this back and forth.

"I need you to leave," I tell Evan evenly and then peek up at him. It hurts to say the words after last night. I should have said them before, but I was so tired and felt so alone. It was selfish to need him then. I used him in a way, but I won't do it again. I won't keep pretending.

He shakes his head, not once or twice but continuously as if he's in disbelief. Like I didn't actually tell him that. He had to know it was going to come to this.

"Last night—"

"Was a mistake," I say, cutting him off forcefully and my voice cracks. My chest feels tight and it's harder to breathe, but I stand my ground.

"We're different people, Evan." I try to say more but my words are stuck in my throat, threatening to choke me.

"We've always been different, Kat. Always," Evan says and

76

his words come out hard. I can already hear him convincing me. I can already see myself falling right back into his arms because that's where I feel so safe and so loved. But he can't hold me forever.

"I can't do this, Evan," I tell him honestly, feeling my heart break as I voice the words. It's a slow break, one meant to be torturous.

"Do what?" he asks me cautiously and it pisses me off. The plastic bag rustles as he reaches behind him, brushing against it and bracing himself against the counter.

"This. I can't." I look him in the eyes even as mine water. I let the tears fall as my blood turns to ice, yet my skin heats.

Evan takes a step toward me, my name falling from his lips as his arms open and spread wide.

"If you won't tell me the truth about what happened, you need to get out."

With his eyes still widening, he shakes his head, an apology from his subconscious before he has the chance to say the words himself.

"Get out!" I yell at him, feeling the weakness threatening to consume me. Threatening to bring me right back to him. "I don't want this. I don't want you here."

"It's going to be all right," he says, attempting to calm me, that placating tone in his voice making me even angrier.

"Well, it's not now, and you need to get the fuck out," I say and seethe. I fold my arms across my chest as I look him in the eyes and tell him again. "I need space, and that means you're leaving." This townhouse is in both our names, I'm more than aware of that and he could easily bring that up. He has a right to be here and part of me wishes he would fight me on that, but he doesn't. He stares at the ground for a moment, his broad shoulders rising slowly with each heavy breath. My body shakes as he snatches his keys off the counter and leaves, slamming the door behind him.

I try to convince myself as I move to the counter, bracing my hot palms on the cold granite and focusing on breathing. This is the worst it's ever been between us. I know it's the end of us. I can feel it deep down in my bones. Shattering my core.

Out of the need to move, to do something and just go through the motions, I reach for the bag on the counter.

It's a mistake. Inside is a bottle of coffee creamer.

It's so stupid that something like this could shred me. That it can make me fall to the floor. That it can make me feel like I've made the worst decision of my life.

That it makes me feel like I'm alone. And that it's my fault for pushing Evan away.

# CHAPTER
## ten

*Evan*

*It happened so slowly,*
*So slowly I couldn't see.*
*She ruined me, damned me,*
*And brought me to my knees.*
*I can't deny there was only one,*
*Only her for me.*
*One true love is a lie,*
*But with her, it has to be.*

I
T'S ODD HOW LOVE WAS THERE RIGHT FROM THE
start and I didn't even know it. Hindsight is twenty-
twenty; I've made enough mistakes to know that. It
doesn't explain how I couldn't see how obvious it was, right

from the first night. Everything I did and said was different, everything I wanted changed.

My old bedroom in my father's house reminds me of all the times I spent here, but more than anything it reminds me of the last time I was in here. When I was crying like a bitch on my bed, burying my head into the pillow and refusing to accept that my mother was dying.

The red plaid flannel sheets are tucked in tight. It feels like this room's been frozen in time since I was here last. Kat fixed the sheets the same way when she made the bed the next morning. She held me all night. She let me cry and didn't tell me to stop or tell me to do anything at all. She just loved me. Freely and for no good reason.

I think she loved me from the very beginning, though. Looking back on it all, I know I had to have loved her right from the moment she stepped out of that car. The door shut with a click and my heart was finally in motion.

I remember that first date we had a few days after we met. I could still feel the beat of the heavy music in the club pumping through my veins as I opened the door to my apartment on the edge of Brooklyn. I glanced over my shoulder to take a peek at her, knowing the alcohol was wearing off and what I wanted was more than obvious. Part of me expected her to back out of coming upstairs.

I could tell she was surprised by how nice my place was. Maybe I can credit her curiosity for why she gathered up the nerve to follow my lead. There was a lot of remodeling going on in the city and I spent my money wisely, always have. Investing in properties is what my father did when he had the chance. I learned from him, but did it on a much larger scale.

The second the door closed, my hands were all over her just like they had been in the taxi and in the club. We were drawn toward each other.

That's why I think it was love. Lust is one thing. It comes and goes. The moment you're filled and satisfied, disinterest takes its place. But that's never been the case for us. There was always more. Even as we grew apart, it only made what could be that much more tempting.

I turn the lights off in my bedroom as a distant siren drowns out the silence of the room and headlights from a passing car leave stripes of light moving through the small space.

Again, I remember what we used to have. Who we used to be. The first night we spent together is all I can think about. The day she ruined me forever. And I didn't even know it was happening.

She wrapped those sweet lips of hers around my dick before I could stop her. We'd only just gotten inside and I was planning on moving a little slower. I would've skipped the foreplay and gone straight for what I wanted if I didn't think she'd appreciate taking my time. When she dropped to her knees in front of me, taking me by surprise, I wasn't going to tell her no.

I was paralyzed as she dug her fingers into my thighs and sucked her way down my length. Her cheeks hollowed as she moaned and I swear I almost came just from the sight of her.

My balls tightened as she pulled back, letting my dick pop out of her mouth and then licking the tip. Her tongue slid up my slit as she worked my shaft and then did it again. The sight of her on her knees and practically worshipping my cock is something I can never forget. It was the shock mostly, I think. A woman who was already too good for me. A woman who was probably slumming it, was on her knees devouring me and loving every second of it.

My fingers speared through her hair as I closed my eyes and let myself enjoy it. Only for a moment, though. I wanted more of her and I was sure I only had the night.

Time moved so slowly as I savored each second of her, wanting more and knowing I could have it, but not ready for it to end.

She stared up at me, licking her lips and shaking her head when I tugged on her to come up and stop. Her lips were already swollen as she panted and then leaned forward. Ignoring me and taking what she wanted.

I watched as she closed her eyes and pushed me all the way to the back of her throat, forcing me to groan from deep in my chest. My dick twitches remembering how her mouth felt like heaven. I fisted my hand in her hair and pulled her off of me; it was fucking torture, wanting what she was giving me, but knowing I'd need more.

"Strip down," I groaned out, my head leaned back and my eyes closed. As if I had any control at all over her.

She shook her head again and I couldn't believe the plea that slipped from her lips.

"I want you to come in my mouth." She said it so simply, although breathlessly with her chest rising and falling, but full of truth. Her voice was laced with desire, but it was the way her shoulders rose and fell with her heavy breathing and the way she scooted closer to me, eager and begging for more that convinced me.

I could never say no to Kat. She doesn't ask for a damn thing. Never has, and I've wished she would. I'd give her the world if I could. But that night there was no fucking way I was going to deny her that.

I'm a selfish man, after all.

I slipped my hand around the back of her head as my toes curled. I was almost embarrassed by how quickly she got me off.

She didn't stop swallowing until I was spent and even then, she bobbed lightly on my dick and sucked like she wanted more. My greedy little sex kitten.

After she was done with me, when I'd pulled my pants up and stared down at her, the atmosphere changed.

"I don't have sex on the first date," she stated shyly, wiping her lips. A blush rose to her cheeks as she slowly stood up, trying to keep her balance by gripping onto my arm. She was hesitant, embarrassed maybe. I think it was vulnerability. I think she was afraid I'd be done. *She was afraid it was only lust.*

"Oh yeah?" I responded, still trying to catch my breath and get a sense of who this girl was. "So what's this then?"

When I looked in her eyes, I knew what the real reason was. She thought I'd be done with her if I got her in bed.

More importantly, it meant she wanted to keep me.

The cockiness at that realization has never felt so good.

She wanted more and all the same, she was terrified to have me. Maybe scared she couldn't keep me, or scared to keep me. I still can't tell which was the motivating factor.

The thought made my still-hard dick even harder. And I stroked myself once and then again until she noticed. A smirk lifted up my lips as I saw her eyes widen.

"What if I want you? What if I want to take care of you now?" I asked her, taking a step forward and forcing her back. Her knees hit the bed and she nearly collapsed, the heat growing between us and nearly suffocating me.

I kissed my way down her neck, letting the heat between us climb higher and higher.

"Not just yet," I said as I stroked my dick again, feeling it turn hard as steel again already. "Let me taste you," I whispered.

Her gorgeous eyes peeked up at me through her thick lashes.

"Take it easy on me, will you?" Her words were playful, again feigning a strength that wasn't quite there. She was exposed and weak for me. Both of us knew it, only she was pretending she wasn't.

It's something that made me crave her more.

"Sure," I whispered in her ear as I pushed her onto the bed. But I never had any intention of holding back when it came to her.

I fucked her as hard as I could into that mattress. I buried myself inside her and held off as long as possible, taking her higher and higher each time until she was holding on to me for her life. Her nails scratched and dug into my skin as she screamed out my name.

I destroyed her the best way I could. And I've never been more satisfied of anything else in my life.

Kat's an emotional woman. I didn't see it at first, but that night, our first night, I got my first taste of it. I could practically hear her tell me she loved me. If nothing else, I know she loved what I did to her.

I wanted to hear her tell me those words so badly. More

than anything else, I wanted *this* woman to admit it. She fell in love with me that first night.

I was desperate for it.

I didn't realize that night that the look in her eyes was exactly what I felt too. Desperate to keep her, but knowing it was never supposed to happen.

I turn on my heels, facing the door as the sound of someone coming up the stairs brings me back to today. Six years later, that night is just a distant memory.

The door to my bedroom opens wide, creaking as it does and revealing my father. I haven't seen him like this in a long damn time.

His hair's been gray for a while, but it's just a bit too long and thinner. With the deep wrinkles around his eyes and only wearing a T-shirt and flannel pants, he looks older and frailer than I remember. Beaten down. Just a few years can change everything. Has it been that long since I really looked at him?

"You getting comfortable in here?" Pops asks me as he walks in and takes a look at the dresser. He runs a hand along it and then makes a face as he turns his hand over and sees the dust there. As he wipes his hand on the flannel pajamas he adds, "It's about time you came back to clean your room."

A rough chuckle barely makes its way up my chest.

"When are you moving out of this place?" I ask him jokingly.

"When I'm dead and gone," my father answers me the same way he has for years now. Ever since Ma passed, I've wanted him to move. He won't, though, and I can't blame him.

"Good thing I'm not in a nursing home. Don't think you'd like to crash there, would you?"

I give him a tight smile, feeling nothing but shame. I run my hand through my hair searching for some sort of an explanation, but I can't lie to my father and I don't want to tell him the truth. So I don't say anything and stare past him instead.

The silence is thick between us until he speaks, glancing around the room rather than looking at me.

"I messed up before with your mother, you know. She kicked me out. I thought it was over." My father flicks on the light and stalks slowly toward the bed, ignoring the fact that I just wanted to pass out and try to sleep. As if I'd be able to in this room.

"I was younger than you, though. By the time I was your age, we'd had you. I'd settled down and stopped being stupid."

"What'd you do?" I ask my father out of genuine curiosity. I'd never seen anything but love from my parents. They never fought in front of me and the one time I came home early, catching them in the heat of a fight, they stopped immediately.

Later that night, when I was sitting in front of the TV, cross-legged and way too close, all I could hear was him apologizing in the kitchen. It'd been quiet all afternoon and night.

"I don't want you to go to bed mad at me," I heard him tell her.

It was the only fight I'd ever witnessed and I remember being scared that he'd done something that Ma wasn't going to forgive.

But she did. I never asked back then, and I'm sure if I did he wouldn't remember. This fight he's talking about obviously isn't that.

"What do you think I did?" he answers me. "We were young and stupid and had a bad fight over money or something. I got drunk, kissed a girl at a bar ... went back to her place. I felt like shit about it and she smacked me right across the face too." He smirks at the memory. "She beat the hell out of me. Kicked me out." The smile falls and he shakes his head as he adds, "I deserved it."

"I can't imagine you ever doing that."

"I loved your mother. I was angry at her over something stupid, I can't even remember what."

The silence stretches between us again as he struggles to come up with what to say next. "I proposed to her a few months after we got back together." A huff of a laugh leaves him and he adds, "God rest her soul," as he twists the wedding band around his ring finger. He's never taken it off. For the same reason he'll never leave this house.

He still needs her. Even if it's just the memory of her.

"The point is, we all make mistakes," he says and then squares his shoulders at me, raising both of his hands and shaking them, "when we're young and allowed to be stupid."

"I'm not that old," I tell him half-heartedly, trying to play it all off. I know what he's getting at, but I don't need to be lectured. I'm well aware of how stupid I've been. He's the one who has no idea how badly I've fucked up. "I'll fix it, Pops."

The silence drags on again and all I can think about is every position I've put myself in where not being faithful to my wife would have been the easy thing to do. I focus on that truth and not the night that still haunts me.

"What are you doing, Evan?" my father asks as I dump my bag on the bed. "You've fucked up more than you should have. You're too old to be carrying on like this."

My initial reaction is to bite back that he's wrong. That he has no idea what's going on. But it wouldn't matter.

I nod my head and let the strap from the bag fall off my shoulder. "Yeah, I know."

"You need to make this right," he tells me, holding my gaze and pointing a finger at me.

I swallow thickly, knowing he's right. But I haven't got a clue how to make this better. I can't take back what's been done.

I'm fucked.

"Yeah, I know."

# CHAPTER
## eleven

*Kat*

*Just get it over with,*
*Tell me that we're done.*
*Leave me to this madness,*
*I accept that you have won.*

*You've broken me to pieces,*
*Left me numb and blind.*
*Made me only yours—*
*I've completely lost my mind.*

I NEED A DISTRACTION, THAT'S WHAT I NEED." I speak the words on my mind without realizing it. It gets the attention of both Maddie and Jules and that's when I realize I've said anything at all. Cue swallowing down another sip of wine.

We've been here in Jules's house helping her unpack for at least two hours now, and everyone's been kind enough to not only *not* ask about what's going on between Evan and me, but to not treat me like I'm some wounded animal either.

That's what friends are for, although the girls do seem to be walking on eggshells around me. I'm grateful, but I need to talk and have someone sift through this mess and give me a straight answer as to what I should do.

I roll my eyes at the thought. I'm a grown woman. I should know what to do and make the decision with certainty. But I've never felt so uncertain in my life.

"A distraction?" Jules questions, a little more pep in her tone than she's had all night.

"That makes sense," Maddie says and nods her head as she takes out a picture frame, wrapped in thick brown packing paper. She's careful with it as she removes the wrapping and exposes the pristine silver frame. "Distractions are a good thing," she adds with a small nod. "Sometimes."

I don't know what photo is already nestled inside of the frame, but whatever it is, it makes her smile. I can only imagine it's a wedding photo … I lift the glass to my lips again.

"I can't go home to the townhouse with all his things and our things and every reminder of everything …" Pausing to take in a lungful of air, I try to steady myself then add, "Let alone go to sleep in the same bed we've had together for forever."

I stare at the artwork centered over Julia's fireplace as I talk.

The crinkling of the packaging paper is all the response I get from the other side of the expansive room. It's so loud that

I'm not sure anyone but Maddie even heard me. We've been working in relative silence save for the soft sound of music flowing from the kitchen behind us.

"We should go on a girls' trip," I offer up and look over my shoulder at Maddie. I shift in my seat and wait for her to meet my gaze.

"Hell yeah," she answers without hesitation. "What does the newlywed think?" Maddie asks and instantly Jules brightens.

She shrugs as if the word *newlywed* didn't make her day and puts the attention back on me as she says, "I'm happy to do whatever you want, Kat." I hate that Jules is holding back. Every response from her tonight seems muted. She's happy and she knows I'm not. She's a newlywed and my marriage is falling apart.

I get it, but she should be happy. She doesn't have to hold back her joy because I'm falling apart.

"You're glowing," I tell her and wait for a response to the compliment, feeling guilty that I haven't said it sooner. My chest feels tight and I shift into a cross-legged position on the plush carpet as I grab a plastic bottle of water, drinking it down slowly even though it's room temperature now. The sweeping room of this new build is ridiculous. The entire house still smells of fresh paint. I can imagine they spent several million on it and the movers did most of the work carrying in all the heavy furniture. Jules didn't trust them with these boxes, though.

Maddie quirks an eyebrow. "You already make a baby?" she asks Jules, her tone devious. I can't help that my brow raises comically.

"Oh my God, Jules, are you pregnant?" I pile on and Maddie snickers as Jules pulls her tawny hair back and rolls her eyes.

"Shut up," Jules says playfully and then goes to the granite counter behind us and makes a show of drinking from her glass of wine. Her simple yet chic rose dress flutters as she waves her glass in the air. She's the epitome of an upper-class socialite.

We exchange amused looks, waiting for her to reply with a straight yes or no.

"Not yet," Jules finally answers.

"Yet!" Maddie practically shrieks. "First comes love, then comes marriage—"

"Then comes a new home and a fresh start," Jules says, cutting her off and Sue laughs from her spot in the corner of the living room where she's been silent all night. Something's definitely gotten to Sue too.

Although maybe it's me, maybe I'm why everyone seems off.

"House first, then the baby," Jules states and then switches the song playing to something more upbeat and less sad. I agree with that decision wholeheartedly.

"Love your house," Sue comments, not bothering to bring up the idea of a child. "Or is it technically a mansion?" she half jokes.

It's grand and spacious and much more like Jules's style than her new husband Mason's previous home. She got a deal on this property and the amount of space is making me regret buying a place so close to the park. It reminds me how tiny our townhouse is. At least compared to this. Location is everything and we paid handsomely for our little place.

This is also a family home, and I live in a townhouse that's not meant for anything more than two people … potentially one child, but it would be cramped. I force my lips to stay in place and swallow down the frown and all the feelings threatening to come up.

Full circle I go, all day long. My thoughts always come back to Evan and what we had and everything we could still have.

With a bitter sigh I hope no one heard, I finish my water and get up to grab another drink, shimmying past the three opened boxes and paper sitting on the floor. I made this decision. I need to own up to it and deal with the consequences.

"I'm not sure I can do this girls' trip," Sue says seemingly out of nowhere. I'd nearly forgotten about the mention of a trip. I guess that's how much it means to me.

"It's just that work …" she adds and then pauses to chew the inside of her cheek. She braces herself on a polished wingback chair before rising and picking up her wineglass. "I've got a new boss and he's a dick with a capital D. There's no way he's going to give me time off."

"It's not really his position to give it to you," Maddie says skeptically. "Like, you *earn* your days. And we haven't even set a date yet." The aggressiveness in Maddie's voice catches me off guard.

Sue stands, an empty glass in hand, meeting me at the small sink filled with ice and bottles of rosé and cabernet. With a glass of wine in her right hand and a ball of packaging paper in her left, she strides past a very young and not at all familiar with the corporate world Maddie, and responds with certainty, "He'll give me shit."

"So fuck him," Maddie says, a little anger coming out. She doesn't usually get worked up, so I'm taken aback. Everyone is off today ... there must be something in the air.

"It's fine, it was just a thought," I say and try to smooth the tension flowing between the two of them. "You okay?" I direct my question at Maddie, who doesn't seem to notice it's for her, picking up her wineglass and throwing it back.

"I don't want to set a bad precedent," Sue states staring directly at Maddie, who refuses to look back at Suzette.

My gaze moves between the two of them and I'm only distracted by the loud clap behind me from Jules. "Who wants some charcuterie?" Jules says and we all turn slowly to see her lifting a tray of cut meats and cheese as if it's the peace treaty between us.

Sue has the decency to laugh and the small moment of tension is immediately diffused.

I feel odd sitting in this room all of a sudden. Looking around the room, I'm surrounded by friends, but I feel alone. I take another sip of water. It's all in my head, I'm more than aware of that, but it doesn't change how I feel.

"Have you slept with him?" Jules regards me as she grabs a contraption from one of her drawers that she uses to un-cork the wine bottles. The kitchen is all white. White cabinets and a sleek white countertop. The only color is in the ebony floorboards. It's luxurious and would be fitting for an editorial photoshoot. Which I promptly told her the moment I stepped foot in this place. I am her agent after all.

"Who with who?" Maddie asks for clarification with a sly

smile on her face. "Is Sue sleeping with her boss?" Her question makes Suzette tense and stare back at Maddie with daggers. But Maddie's oblivious. The two of them should have their own show. If it was up to me, they would and the ratings would be through the roof. Maddie would probably go for it, Sue would never.

"Kat," Jules answers and her tone is casual, not sympathetic or pushy, no motive apparent. "Have you slept with Evan since it all happened?" she asks again, but more directly and pops the cork from the bottle.

It fizzes as my face heats, knowing the other two women are looking at me, but I wait for Jules. The second she raises her eyes to mine, although it was only meant to be a glance, I nod my head.

I anticipate the scoff of disdain from Sue, the tilted head with a sympathetic look from Maddie, but I don't know what to expect from Jules.

She shrugs her shoulders, the soft pink fabric slipping down and making her look that much thinner, that much more beautiful. "Was it any good?" she asks and lifts the glass to her lips. It's dark red wine, the same color she wears on her lips. It's one thing I like about Jules; she's nothing if not consistent.

Rolling my eyes, I wipe my face with my hand. It's always good with Evan. "It was a mistake," I tell her instead. My dismal tone immediately changes the mood and frustration flows through me.

"People make mistakes," Jules says low, so low I almost didn't hear her. And then she looks at me and adds, "It happens." She sounds so sad and I can't help but to wonder what's going on with her. For just a moment, a short glimpse, there's something there other than the perfect façade she always carries. But the moment she registers that I can see it, the crack in her demeanor, she straightens her shoulders and takes in a heavy breath.

Silence passes and the only thing that can be heard is the rustling of paper as Maddie unwraps something. Staring down into the newly poured glass of wine I realize I've never felt so alone and unwelcomed. It's not them, it's me and my head, I know it is. "I just don't know what to do," I say, speaking to all of them or none of them, it doesn't matter, I just needed to say it. "We slept together and I think it was a mistake … Because I kicked him out the next morning." A groan leaves me, nearly comical, as I take a small sip but it's not satisfying. Not nearly large enough either.

"You don't need to decide right now," Jules says easily. "There's a lot to consider and talk about." She nods her head as she talks, almost like she's talking to herself.

"The thing is … I don't know what I want, but I know he'll convince me to stay with him."

"Men have a way with words," Sue chimes in, agreeing with me, and tips her glass in an air-cheers with me. "It's called lying."

I huff in agreement, opting for my water instead of more wine, as I watch Sue saunter over to the tray of cheese.

"I mean … not that he lied … he's just …" Sue says softly and then clears her throat to add with a touch of sympathy, "I keep letting my shitty experience color my opinion. Sorry," she says, looking me in the eyes. The sincerity there kills me.

"It's fine. It's called experience."

"So you're indecisive, and that makes sense. You're married. You love him. But you're hurt." Maddie cuts through all the silence and unease like it's so simple and easy to comprehend. But it's not. There's a raging war of emotions inside of me. I don't know that I can trust my husband, and that alone is enough to end it and what pushed me to kick him out this morning.

Rather than confess about my lack of trust, I offer a partial truth. "I slept with him last night and then kicked him out this morning." I shake my head realizing how awful that sounds, how crazy it seems.

"Sounds like a divorce to me," Sue says and then fills her glass again. "I did it for years, Kat. Years of back and forth. Forgiving but not forgetting." Her slender fingers play on the stem of the glass. "Wish I had those years back."

The need to defend Evan overrides my common sense. "I don't know what I did that pushed him away." Even as I say the words, I know that's not true. I let distance grow between us. I ignored him in favor of my career.

"Nothing, it's not you. It's not your fault." Sue's words are hard, with no negotiation allowed. So I don't correct her.

Maddie adds in, ever comforting, "It's not your fault in the least. Don't let him make you feel that way."

They don't understand. They just don't get it.

"What if—"

Sue cuts me off to say, "If you want to sleep with him, do it. Want to kick him out, do it. Want to hurl something at his head … maybe don't because that's assault." Her joke forces a bark of a laugh from me and a snicker from Jules. Her glass setting down on the counter offers a clink and she adds, "Yes please, for the love of all things holy don't make us come bail you out."

"You would, though," I say and cock a brow, knowing any of the three of these women would bail me out in a heartbeat.

"It's whatever you want," Maddie continues and Jules and Sue both nod. "You can be friends with benefits if that's what you want, fuck buddies, you can use him for revenge sex. I don't think any of us have any answers other than we're here for you." She side-eyes Sue and adds, "Although Sue is cock-blocking our girls' trip."

"Oh my Lord, someone ... get her," Sue groans and Jules and I laugh while Maddie purses her lips and tosses a balled-up bit of paper at Sue's back. It doesn't reach, but the comic relief helps to calm all the nerves I've been feeling. Most of them, anyway. There's still a little flutter in the pit of my stomach.

"We'll plan a girls' trip," Jules states as if it's a fact. "It just might be a bit difficult, but we will make this happen and it'll be great for you to get out."

"I think it will be fun, and I'll figure out how to make it work," Sue says all the while staring at Maddie who finally smiles.

"Yes. Girls' trip and fuck or dump whomever we want ... Except Jules. Because she might be pregnant."

I nearly choke on my wine at that thought.

# CHAPTER
## twelve

*Evan*

I TRIED IT. I SWEAR I TRIED TO GIVE HER SPACE.

Kat says that's what she needs, but I know it's not. This plan of hers isn't what she needs and it's sure as hell not what I want.

She needs me. Period. She needs me to be there and that's where I've failed. Not just in the last few weeks. For years, I chose a lifestyle that forced us apart.

I can fix this, but not by running to Pops and leaving her all alone with nothing but this city whispering in her ear.

My arm stiffens as I slide the key into the lock to our townhouse. My heart doesn't beat until it turns, proving she didn't change the locks. I let out a breath I didn't know I was still holding and push it open. I'm prepared with what

I need to say. Prepared to hold my ground and not take no for an answer.

But it only takes one step inside of our living room for all of it to slip away from me.

Kat looks so tired, so worn out propped up in the corner of the sofa with her laptop sitting to the left of her, but the screen's black. She has a cup of coffee in her hands as well as bags under her eyes. She turns to me slowly, wiping the sleep from her eyes and adjusting herself slightly. With the gentle protest of the sofa, I shut the door behind me.

"What are you doing here?" she asks me, still seated with her legs tucked underneath her on the sofa. I'm stunned for a moment because she's so fucking beautiful, even in this state. My body's drawn to her. If it were another time, I'd go to the sofa, push the laptop off and lie down, making her take a break. I'd kiss her until her body writhed against mine.

*And she'd let me.* She'd let me make her relax. At least she would have a year ago.

"This is my house." I try not to say the words too firmly. "Our house," I correct myself and swallow before continuing and taking a single step closer to her. "I worked my ass off—"

"Then I'll move out," Kat quickly states matter-of-factly, but the pain is barely disguised. She seems to snap out of whatever daze had her captive before I came in here.

"I don't want you to move out. We don't need this." I emphasize my words.

"I asked for time and space because I don't know what to do, Evan. You aren't giving me any options without telling me what happened."

"You want to know?" I look her in the eyes, feeling my blood pulse harder in my veins.

"Are you going to tell me the truth?" she asks me in a cracked whisper. "All of it?"

*All of it?* I have to break her gaze. I can't. I can't confess everything. I'd lose her forever.

The second I break eye contact, she scoffs. "You're so full of shit. Why are you doing this to me?" she asks me, although it's rhetorical. There's a loathing in her tone but more than that it's pain.

*Why am I doing this to her?* If it was only so easy as *doing* something. There's nothing I can do.

"I didn't come home to fight."

"Neither did I … but here we are," she retorts, taking in a shuddering breath. "I asked for time, Evan."

Tossing my keys on the coffee table, I make my way into the living room and sit across from her in the armchair. I'm not foolish enough to think she'd let me sit close enough to touch her. Even as I sit here, feet away, she bends her legs in closer and pushes the laptop to the side. Like she's ready to run at a moment's notice.

Time slips by as I lean back, letting a long exhale take up some of it. "I just want to be home with you while this blows over."

"Blows over?" I don't know how she can make a whisper seem hysterical. I'm not good with words. I never have been, but I wish I had the wisdom to say the right thing right now.

"Maybe this is the moment," she states with a sad smile on her beautiful face.

"The moment?"

"The moment that changes everything for the rest of my life. I've been wondering exactly what moment it was, but thought maybe it hasn't happened yet."

Her words settle deep in my very core and a tingling runs through my fingers up my arms. Slow, yet all-consuming. Her face changes from the sarcastic disappointment that she had when she said the words. As if only just now realizing the magnitude of them herself.

"We can go back. I promise," I tell her softly, raising my hands just slightly, but the fear of losing her keeps my blood cold and my motions subtle.

"It's called separating for a reason," she says, whispering her response. As if what we had the other night meant nothing. As if there's no reason for us to be together. Maybe she really doesn't love me anymore. The fissure in my chest deepens, feeling like it's cracked wide open.

"We're not separated."

"Yes we are."

"We didn't decide to do that," I answer her. "You were angry."

"Rightfully so," she spits back.

"I told you it's not true," I plead with her as I stare deep into her eyes. I watch as they gloss over and her lower lip trembles. "Just …" I swallow thickly, the lump growing in the back of my throat suffocating any plea I have for her. *Just love me. Just forgive me.*

I turn away from her for a moment, not able to voice what I'm feeling. I lean forward in the chair, and it creaks as I rest my weight in it. Kat starts to get up in response.

"I don't want to fight," I remind her.

"I don't want this, Evan. I didn't ask for this," she says, raising her voice for the second part, the anger coming back. She stops moving, though, and I can tell she's losing the will to fight. It's by the way her lips are parted just so, and her breathing is quicker and she has that little crease in the center of her forehead.

"I don't know what to do or say, or what to think. I feel crazy." She stares at me wide eyed, her voice sounding hoarse. "Do you understand what that's like? To be so stupid? To know I'm being stupid and setting myself up for you to hurt me again."

"I won't hurt you—" The truth rushes out of me in a single breath, but she doesn't let me finish.

"But you did," she says, cutting me off and rocking forward just slightly as she points out the obvious. "And you won't even tell me why." Her shoulders shudder, but she doesn't cry, she holds her ground.

"I don't want to lose you, Kat," I manage to speak and peek up to look at her. I'm such a piece of shit. "I just want you. It's the honest to God truth. I just want you."

"I want you to quit," she tells me and rocks on her feet to stand. She nods her head and visibly swallows. "You need to quit." She stares at me, her emerald eyes pleading. Her body's still, like she's not breathing. Just waiting.

"It's not that easy," I say and God I wish she knew. I want to tell her everything, but I can't risk it. I can't leave right now. I just need time.

"It is that easy; you quit or leave." I stare into her eyes that swirl with nothing but raw vulnerability, and hesitate.

"You're giving me an ultimatum?" Even as I ask her, I know that's what she's doing.

She has no idea.

"I just need time." I need her to just give me time. As soon as I'm out of this, I can do whatever she wants.

But not right now.

I can feel her slipping away. Every second that passes where I don't tell her, she's turning colder toward me. But she can't know. No one can.

My lips part and I can feel my lungs still. The words are right there. Begging me, and desperate for her to hear. I need her more than anything.

"Kat." I say her name but it's so much more. It's me begging for her to love me blindly, to trust that I love her and that I'd never do anything to hurt her.

I can't. I can't risk losing her, and I won't do it.

My mouth closes and I turn away from her, running my hand over my face.

"Get out," Kat states and her voice hitches at the end. I turn to see her cover her face.

The next bit happens so fast. It's a blur as I close the distance between us. It only takes three steps, but by the time my arms wrap around her, she's pushing me away. Her hands slam into my chest. She tries to knock me back, but only manages to throw herself off-balance instead.

I grip her hips to steady her, but she slaps me. Hard across the face and the sting catches me by surprise.

I flex my jaw as she screams at me to get out. Her body's shaking. The sinful mix of hatred and betrayal ring in the air between us.

*How the hell did I let this happen?*

"Do you really want me out?" I ask her, genuinely not knowing anymore. I don't know at what point I lost her completely. There's only so many times I can ask her to give me everything while I hold back.

I guess I should be more surprised it hasn't happened sooner.

Rubbing my jaw as I take a step back, I give her the only bit of space I'm willing to offer. "I know you still love me," I tell her and watch as she rips her eyes from me. Her face is blotchy and red and her breathing is frantic.

But she calms as she stands there not able to answer me. That's all I needed. Just a little bit. *Please, Kat. Just hold on a little while longer.*

"Just tell me the truth," she begs me and I wish I could. I feel my throat tighten and my body tense. My hands clench as I swallow.

"I didn't sleep with her." I answer without wasting a second and even I don't believe my words. But it's not what she thinks. I wish I could tell her, but the moment she finds out, everything will be at risk.

"Why don't I believe you?" she says and I don't have the decency to answer.

"I swear, Kat."

"So you've never slept with her?" she asks me and I know it's over. Her expression changes and her eyes darken when the silence stretches too long. So many secrets have built up. Too many to hide. She was never supposed to know. "Since we've been married," I start to say, knowing I'm toeing the line of truth, "I've never slept with anyone. Never kissed anyone

105

but you." I look her in the eyes so she can see it's the truth. "The day I put that ring on your finger, it was only you."

"Then why put me through this?" she asks me with tears in her eyes. "And what were you doing?" I struggle to keep my breathing calm as the questions start piling up. "What were you doing with her in that hotel if you weren't sleeping with her."

I lick my dry lips and take a step forward. "Things got out of hand."

"Why were you with her?" Kat presses and I know she wants an answer right now.

"Because it's what I had to do," I say, telling her the truth with my eyes closed.

"What you had to do? You had to go to her hotel at three in the morning?" I can't look at her as I nod my head. "And you couldn't tell me this before?" I nod my head again.

"You tell me everything right now, or you leave."

"Another ultimatum?" The words drip with disdain.

"Don't talk to me like that," she says. Her tone is dismissive and I can hear her resolve harden.

"It's better if you didn't know everything," I answer gently yet firmly just the same.

"Are you serious right now? You're throwing away our marriage over her? Over your job?"

"Kat, just—" I start to say, but she cuts me off.

"Fuck you," she sneers then yells, "I said get out."

"I'm not leaving," I tell her firmly, staring back at her, even as she turns her back to me.

"It doesn't matter, the weekend's coming," she says beneath her breath as she leaves me.

I keep my feet planted as she stomps up the stairs and I wait for more. I wait for her to push me out, to yell at me, to demand more from me. I'm ready to fight, ready for war with her to keep her. But that's not what I get.

She gives me back exactly what I gave her. *Nothing.*

# CHAPTER
## thirteen

*Kat*

FOUR MANUSCRIPTS TO GO THROUGH THIS weekend.

Four authors waiting to hear back from me.

I doubt I'll be able to focus enough to comprehend a full page. I've been reading the same paragraph over and over and not a damn sentence is staying with me.

It doesn't matter, though. None of this really does.

All that matters is that I stay in this office for as long as Evan's here. He's like a ghost in this house. A ghost of his former self.

So I do what I've always done, I bury myself in work. That was the plan anyway, but now I can't focus on anything but the sounds of him moving through the house.

He walks by the door every few hours, making the floor

groan, and I know he wants to open it, wants me to talk to him. All I can hear is him saying it'd be better if I didn't know. To hell with that.

I'm not going to give him all of me when he can't be bothered to do the same. There is nothing more important than us. Not a single thing that should come between us; yet it feels like he's got plenty in the space between my heart and his.

So we're at a standstill, him refusing to leave and me refusing to blindly forgive.

His voice plays in my head over and over again, telling me it's only ever been me. I want to believe it. It's everything I've been praying for him to say.

*But then what is he hiding?*

My eyes flicker to the screen as my nails tap on the pale blue ceramic mug next to my laptop. *Tick, tick, tick.* I read the line over and over: *Love is a stubborn heart.*

Magdalene, the editor, highlighted the line. She thinks it's beautiful and she wants repetition of the metaphor throughout the book.

*Love is a stubborn heart.*

Is it, though? My forehead scrunches as I think back to the story in the manuscript. The tale about a modern-day Romeo and Juliet. Two families who hated each other and their children who wanted nothing more than to run away together. It's not a tragedy but it doesn't have a happily ever after either. It's too realistic.

If love really was that stubborn, wouldn't they have been together in the end?

Maybe it wasn't really love.

Or maybe love just wasn't enough.

I don't know that I agree that love is stubborn. I suppose it is, but more than that, it's stealthy and lethal. I nod my head at the thought.

Love is deadly.

Rolling my eyes. I push the laptop away. My comments don't belong on this manuscript right now.

I don't know the very moment I fell in love with Evan. It felt like I was counting the days until it would be over, and then one day, I simply decided on forever. Just like that, a snap of my fingers. Slow, so slow and resistant, and then in an instant, I was his and he was mine. And that's how it was going to be forever.

I smile at the thought and try to focus on the lines staring back at me from the computer. I try to read the words, but I keep glancing at the wall behind me. At a photo of the first night he took me to meet his parents. It was after I'd decided on forever.

I'd never felt that kind of fear before. The fear of rejection. Not like I did that night and I know why: it's because I'd never put my heart out there for anyone to take.

I was very much aware that Evan had every piece of me. Unless he didn't want me. In which case, I'd be broken and I didn't know how I'd recover.

The thought consumed me the night he brought me to his family home. I was sure his family wouldn't like me. It'd been so long since I'd been with a family for dinner. I used to go to my friend Marissa's when I was in high school. But that's not the same. Not at all. It was also a rarity that I accepted Marissa's parents' offer for dinner.

When you lose your parents at fifteen, people tend to

look at you as though they've never seen anything sadder. I'd rather be alone than deal with that.

So I was, until Evan. And he didn't come on his own, he had a family that "had to meet me."

My back rests against the desk chair as my gaze lingers on the photograph. I had it printed in black and white. It's the four of us on the sofa in his family home's living room. It's funny how I can see the colors of the sofa so clearly, the faded plaid, even though there isn't any color in the picture that hangs on my wall.

All four of us are smiling. His mother insisted on taking the photo. Just as she'd insisted he bring me that night.

It's only now that I can remember how Evan's father looked at her. I didn't think anything of it at the time, but that's because they hadn't told us that she was sick.

I guess in some ways it was the last photograph. If that isn't accepting someone into your family, I don't know what is.

I have to hold back the prick of tears as I think of her. I only met Marie a handful of times. The dinner was the second. The third was after she'd told Evan; she didn't have a choice, seeing as how she had to be hospitalized. The last time I saw her was at the funeral.

I may not know when I fell in love with him, but I think I know the moment he fell in love with me. The moment a part of his heart died and he needed something, or someone, to fill it. Maybe I got lucky that it was me. Or maybe it was a curse.

I roll my eyes, hating that I'm stuck in the past because I can't move ahead with the future.

Maybe we weren't really meant to be. Maybe it was never the type of love that's meant to keep people together. Just the type of love when you feel compelled to give someone compassion.

*Are there types of love?* I find myself leaving the question as a comment on the book and then deleting it.

If there are, then maybe Evan's love is the stubborn kind. He's not so stubborn that he'll stay this weekend, though. Come Friday he'll be gone again. Maybe it's a different kind of love then …

It's only when I hear the bedroom door shut that I finally look back at the manuscript and email the editor back. I need more time before I can give feedback on any of these to the author and I'm ready to fall asleep in the corner chair, or any place I can where Evan will leave me alone.

I need more time for so much more. I need time and a clear head to move forward with my own life. I need someone to tell me I'm not walking away from the only man who will ever love me, but there's no email I can write for that unfortunate request.

# CHAPTER
## fourteen

*Evan*

*If I could focus on the hate and leave her all alone,*
*I'd be able to move forward, if only I had known.*
*I can't speak the truth, I don't want to make it real,*
*I can't stand what I've done or what it makes me feel.*
*Regret will settle in my chest and suffocate the day.*
*If only I could make it right, if only there was a way.*

"IT'S GOOD TO SEE NEW YORK AGAIN," JAMES SAYS as I walk into his office on Greene Street in lower Manhattan.

Even as he speaks, he stares out the office window. It's an impressive eight-by-eight-foot picture window, making the view seem like it's not quite real.

I don't return his sentiment. I'm fucking miserable

regardless of the scenery or location. I want to drop to my knees and confess everything to Kat. The weight of it all is burying me. I think she'd forgive me. I can see it in her eyes that she wants to accept anything I'm willing to divulge. I could tell her almost everything and I think she'd let me stay.

I'm too scared to do it, though, and bring her into this mess. If they find out she knows ... she just can't know. Not until I end things here at least. It's step one to getting my Kat back.

"It's crazy how you miss it, isn't it?" he continues as he turns to me. He's more relaxed than he was in London, although his suit is crisp and fresh from the dry cleaner. I close the door as he takes a seat at the desk, unbuttoning his dark gray jacket.

"Sorry you had to wait a minute, I was just getting this paperwork wrapped up." He leans back in his chair, loosening his slim navy tie and unfastening the top button of his crisp white dress shirt.

"Are we going to talk about it?" I ask, needing to get this shit off my chest. I kept quiet in London, but I can't anymore. It's been weeks. That must be enough time.

*Is that how long it takes to get away with murder?*

"Talk about what?" he questions and his voice is gravelly and low.

"Talk about the fact that the charges against Bruce are dropped?" I say then hold his cold gaze with one I hope informs him I have no time for bullshit and I'm out of patience.

He may have been relaxed before I sat down, but now he's still. And silent. I let my eyes fall to the stack of papers on his desk, then drift to a small picture frame. It's a cube and matte black on all sides, and I have no idea who the woman in the picture is.

I absently pick it up, ignoring how his eyes bore into me, how his icy gaze heats as I let the question hang in the air, forcing him to answer.

The block is lighter than I thought it'd be and I don't recognize the broad with a closer look either. It's not his ex-wife, or his current girlfriend. Not that I thought Luna or whatever her name was, the fling of the month, would have a place in his office.

"My sister," James says, answering the unasked question. "A Christmas gift."

I nod my head once, putting the block back down and waiting for him to answer me.

"Bruce didn't *do* anything, so of course the charges didn't stick," James states in an eerily calm voice. "We knew he was innocent." James pulls out a drawer and shuffles something inside of it, but I can't see what. He doesn't elaborate or give any room to further the conversation that we should have.

"What's done is done, and there's nothing more to say."

"That's not what Sam told me. She told me she's scared." It's the only reason I let her get so close. She's terrified that the truth is going to come out. She helped me, so she'd go down with me.

"Whose fault is that?" James sneers.

"She's your wife," I say, pushing out the words through my clenched teeth.

"I don't have a wife," he answers me with a sly smile, as if he's clean of this mess. As if it's all on me. Deep down in my gut, I know it is.

"Ex then," I concede and add, "I didn't know the divorce had been finalized." He picks up a pen and taps it against the desk but doesn't take his eyes off me. It hasn't gone through yet, according to Samantha. All the money needs to be split one way or the other, and neither him nor Samantha, his ex-partner in this business and future ex-wife, wants to take less than the other.

"Either way, what's done is done and the two of you need to let it die."

"An innocent man—"

"Got off!" He looks me in the eyes as he leans forward and adds, "And a guilty man got away."

"We should have come forward."

"Should have, but you listened to a shady bitch. That's your problem, not mine."

My gaze falls to the desk as my fingers itch to form a fist. I called *him*. The number I dialed that night was to *his* office. I had no idea she'd be the one who answered.

"I panicked—" I start to say, but he cuts me off.

"Because you fucked up. And now I have to clean up your mess and make sure you stay out of trouble."

"Is that what this is? You doing me a favor?" I ask sarcastically, letting the memory of that night fade. I can't quit while there's still an investigation. I can't bring more attention to myself or to the company. One of my clients dies and I get fired or quit shortly after? Yeah, that'll get the police's attention.

I wish I could tell Kat everything, but then she'd know she was married to a murderer. Even if it was just an accident. I'm a coward and I'll never be a man she deserves. But every day that goes by, I want to be more of the man I was the day before it all changed.

"I need time off," I state, fed up with the conversation. I imagine this isn't the first time something like this has happened and I sift through the memories of all the shit that's gone on behind the scenes for years. I never questioned anything, I never suspected a thing. Not until James brought me into the inner circle.

"No," James answers immediately with no negotiation in his voice.

"Then I quit," I tell him as my fingers dig into the chair. The only thing I can think about is Kat. She'll get over the fact I kept this from her. I know she will. It's not the first time I've kept a secret from her. We'll be okay as long as I'm through with this shit.

His thin lips twist into a half smile as he says, "Well, that can't happen." He looks at me with a calculated glint in his eyes. Like he's been waiting for this and he's ready for my rebuttal, eager for it even.

"Why not?" I question as my muscles coil. Even though I'm aware it could cause suspicion, I can do whatever the fuck I want. "I'm not going to work for this company anymore."

"That's not—"

"It's called quitting," I spit back at him. I don't need this job; I've got plenty of money in the bank and my investments, and Kat's career is finally stable. She bled money for years, but it's leveling out. We'll be all right financially and this is what she wants and what I need.

"You can't just quit."

"I can, and I am."

James's smile fades and he tilts his head to the side, an expression of the utmost sympathy on his weathered face. His deep brown eyes look darker as he picks up a folder on the left side of his desk. It wasn't hidden, but it's not labeled and it looks like all the rest.

My eyes follow his movement and my brow furrows until he opens it.

"The hotel had cameras. They're gone now, of course, but a few snapshots were taken. Some I think you'd find particularly interesting. Maybe enough so to stay."

I can imagine what they are before he flips the folder open. The eight-by-ten glossy photo paper shows the one thing that proves I lied. I'm walking into the hotel lobby I claimed I didn't enter. And I'm not alone. Standing right next to me is Tony. Only hours before he was found dead in the rec room of the hotel. The one reserved for our company and the division Bruce is the head of. The photograph of Tony and his bloodshot eyes takes me back to that night. To the moment I found him dead on the floor.

My limbs freeze in waves. Like the betrayal that moves through me.

"It's a security net on my end," James says and then closes the folder, pulling it off the desk and into his lap.

"So if I quit," I start to say, but instead I stop and stare ahead out of the window. I want to kill him. There's never been a time in my life when I've desired someone dead. But right now, it's all I want.

"Then I assume it's for less than moral reasons," James says, spelling it out for me. "I need to protect myself."

"That's bullshit," I tell him and my words are hard. My

hands turn to fists as they tremble with the need to get this anger out.

"I know, trust me I know," James says. "And I don't like this any more than you do."

A sarcastic huff of a laugh leaves me. "Fuck off," I sneer at him.

I stand up from the office chair so quickly it nearly falls over. I grip it so tight I think I'll break it. Fuck, I want to break it. I can picture beating the piss out of him with the broken wood.

My body is hot, my mind in a daze of regret and sickness.

"I'm leaving," I barely speak as I turn my back to him and start to walk off.

"The fuck you are," he says.

My body whips around, tense and ready to let it all out. Every day it's been building and building, the tension winding tighter and the need to destroy something climbing higher and higher. I only took a few steps away, and with his words I'm right back across the desk, ready to do something stupid.

My body heats as my fist moves from the chair to the desk and I lean closer. He may not want to show it, but I see the fear in his eyes.

He should be scared. He's fucking with me. Threatening me. No one is going to take my wife from me. I won't allow it.

"I need to get away from this. From you."

I never should have listened to him and tried to cover it up. He set me up. He used that night to his advantage and I played right into his hand.

It takes everything in me not to reach across the desk and

haul him up by his collar. To fist the fine cloth in my grip and spit in his face.

Pure rage and adrenaline pump through my blood.

"Careful now, Evan." James smiles as he says it, but I notice how he leans back. Both of us know he's scared. If I throw this punch, if I push, he could bring it all to light.

*And then I'll lose her forever.*

"I'm going home, and I'll let you know when I'm available again." *Never.* The word is whispered in the back of my head. I'm never returning to this office. I'm never doing another thing for this prick.

"You can't leave me. I'll ruin you," he practically whispers with nothing but hate. He says the words I already know.

"Ruin me then," I respond easily, looking into his dark eyes as I turn the doorknob and leave him behind me. On the surface I'm calm, but brewing just beneath my skin is nothing but chaos. Everything I've feared has finally come.

Proof I was there.

Proof I lied to the police.

I leave the office with the threat echoing in my head. I did this to myself, digging the hole deeper and deeper.

There's no way Kat will stay when it all goes down.

# CHAPTER
## fifteen

### *Kat*

*Never trapped, never alone,*
*This city never sleeps.*
*Even in the daylight,*
*The sins are left to creep.*
*They tempt me and pull me,*
*And make me feel alive.*
*My mouth is dry, my body hot.*
*In temptation regrets will thrive.*

M Y IPHONE LIGHTS UP AS I PUSH THE TOP button to check the time again, and then again to look at the date. I'm anxious for this meeting; unusually so. Then again, I'm anxious all the time now.

Evan hasn't come home; he isn't talking to me. It's been

four days and each day I feel like I need to cave more and more. I didn't know how much I wanted him there until he was gone. I just need him back.

A huff leaves me and I shake my head at the thought. Breakups are always hard and that's what this is, so there's only one way to move on and that's to get it over with.

I don't want to be in our townhouse, but I have nowhere else to go.

An easy breath leaves me as I stand behind the only woman in line at Brew Madison and tilt my head to read the sign on the back wall. All the beverages they have to offer are written on a large chalkboard, and large bakery cases house all the treats they have available. From small pastries to toasted breakfast sandwiches, all lined up as if they're plastic replicas, even though I know they're freshly made and just simply that good.

I haven't had much of an appetite, but every sip of my coffee this morning made me nauseated, so a blueberry muffin top it is.

The brunette curls of the woman in front of me swing from side to side as she gives her order. I can't see her face, but I know she's young. From her bright red high heels and black leather jacket paired with white shorts a bit too short for fall, she's definitely a downtown girl.

I smile at the thought as she waits for her coffee: pumpkin spice.

I used to be like her. Stylish and in charge of my destiny. New to the city and ready to tame it.

I thought I had.

A career and reputation in this publishing industry that

I reached within only a few years. I'm an agent worth my weight now and everyone knows it. My name and brand have a meaning to them. The clients are coming in and I'm able to hire more reps and editors. It's the business I've always wanted. More than that, I'm married to a man who still drips of sex appeal and has an edge to him that is irresistible. We own our townhouse near Madison Square Garden. Even if it is small, it's the closest we could get. And it's New York, so location is *everything*.

And my closet ... the girl in front of me would kill for my closet. Not that she would know it based on how I'm dressed at the moment.

My name has a purpose and strength to it that made me proud. Evan and I were a powerhouse in the social scene. The couple everyone wanted to be. But envy comes with threats and in its nature, ruins. Rumors and gossip created a wedge between the two of us.

In the last few years, the highs of this world have crashed as my marriage slowly dissolved.

I let it. I spent my life not living it, wanting more and more from my work. Running as fast as I could, just to stay still while I ignored every other change in the world around me. How could I not have seen it deteriorating?

As the woman turns and I get a look at her cat eye makeup that's subtle enough to still be businesslike and red lips that match her heels, I remember that feeling that used to flow through me. The one that said I could conquer anything.

Yeah, I used to be like her. I still have the heels and even the stylish clothes, although I lean toward professional these days with my wardrobe and those shorts sure as heck don't lean that way.

"What can I get you?" the young man asks me from behind the counter. He's got to be in his early twenties at most. I catch a glimpse of his sleeve tattoo and it reminds me of Evan's tattoos for only a moment.

More thoughts of Evan. Everything reminds me of him.

"A chai and a blueberry muffin top," I answer him with a tight voice and clear my throat as I reach for my card in my wallet. It's a Kate Spade and the soft pink and white match the purse, but I'm only just now realizing that it looks a bit dingy. Not so much so that it's noticeably dirty. Just enough where it doesn't look so new anymore.

As I wait for my chai, I get a look at my reflection in the glass. I guess the same can be said about me. My fingers tease my hair at the roots, putting a little more volume there and I apply a coat of stain on my lips while I wait.

I wrap the belt around my shirt a little tighter, showing off my waist and lean to my right in the reflection.

I'm not done yet. There's still life in me. There's still that girl who wants more buried deep down inside. But what exactly she wants more of remains a question.

Evan, the silent answer, is obvious.

But instead the voice in my head whispers *love*.

Even if he can't give me everything, I know what I'm desperate for: to love and be loved.

The bells to the door chime as I accept my chai and muffin top. I silently pray that it's not Jacob so I can have a moment to try to shovel this down.

No such luck.

I smile broadly when I see him, hiding everything I was just thinking and focusing on my potential client and his career. I mentally tally up how much work we both need to do to get his branding both going in the right direction and noticed by the right market.

"Jacob," I greet him and his deep green, hazel eyes focus on me.

"Katerina, it's wonderful to finally have a one-on-one," he says as he steps over the welcome mat and slips off his thin, black wool jacket. He has a downtown style that would pair well with the woman who was just here. From his gray shirt that hangs low but is fitted tight across his chest, to the boyish grin and messy dark hair. He's sex on a stick for sure.

"It is wonderful to see you in person, thank you so much for meeting me here," I say as I make my way to the front of the shop, making sure not to spill the hot drink in my hand.

"Finally meeting my maybe new agent," he says with both an asymmetric smile and pride.

"I'm so happy you're thinking of signing with us," I answer sweetly.

"The rain this fall is ridiculous," Jacob states as he runs his hand over his hair and then wipes it off on his worn jeans.

His white Chuck Taylor sneakers squeak on the floor as he takes a step closer to me. His expression is comical. With both hands full, one of chai and the other with the muffin top, I gesture to the table where I already have my laptop set up. "Right over here," I tell him and put both the chai and the pastry to the left side of my computer before turning around to face him.

I have to crane my neck. "You're so much taller in person,"

I tell him and hold out a hand for a handshake. His right hand engulfs mine and his shake is firm.

The grin on his face grows to a wide smile and his perfect teeth flash back at me.

He's damn good looking and the fact that his face isn't anywhere on his profiles or brand is a mistake. I watch him as I take my seat, keeping the smile where it belongs on my expression.

"You are too good looking for every one of your readers not to see your face. I know this is a meeting to see if you're interested in coming on board and if our goals align, but the way I like to approach things is to treat you like a client from the start so you know what you're getting. There's so much we have to offer at the agency and I'm sure you'll appreciate not wasting time."

"I like to know what I'm getting; let's dive in. What do you want from me, Katerina?" Jacob asks me and for a split second, a thought enters my mind.

It's only a fraction of a second. A glimpse of his mouth on mine, his hands on my body. Pushing me against the wall like Evan did only a few nights ago.

Thankfully, it vanishes before I can show any admission of what I was thinking.

With a deep inhale, I shake off the unwanted thought and I focus on the plan I have laid out for him as I rotate the computer around on the table.

"We're going to start with your strengths. Obviously, your writing is one of them. Let's also work our way into other aspects of marketing and social media that I think you're ignoring. We can come up with a solid plan that you're comfortable with, but more importantly, one that will work to give you momentum before this upcoming release."

The words come out of my mouth smoothly even though my mind's racing.

It's been a while since I've looked at a man and thought the things running through my head. I tell myself it's because I'm looking for comfort. Searching for someone to desire me like Evan does.

So I don't feel trapped and alone.

"Lead the way, Miss Thompson."

I shake my head, ready to correct him, ready to tell him it's *Mrs.* Thompson. Instead I bite my tongue. In fact, I find myself hiding my left hand behind the computer.

It's only because the attention is nice.

A *distraction*, a sweet voice whispers in the back of my head as I smile at Jacob and hit the right arrow on the keyboard to move to the first point I want to make.

I leave my hand where it's hidden and when he tells me goodbye, again referring to me as "Miss," I still don't correct him.

# CHAPTER
## sixteen

*Evan*

*She makes my blood heat,*
*My breathing tense and ragged.*
*Love's not a straight line,*
*It's reckless and it's jagged.*
*Beyond the lust, beyond desire,*
*There's something in its wake.*
*It's jealousy that makes me weak,*
*It's hate that makes me break.*

BREW MADISON IS MY WIFE'S FAVORITE PLACE IN this whole damn city. My shoes smack on the wet pavement and rain spits from the sky as I close the door a block down and stride down the sidewalk to the coffee shop.

For years she's come here. She and Jules used to write together in the corner. Jules was her first client here in New York. It's how she met her now close friend. I huff and my breath turns to steam as I peek in through the glass window.

It used to be a habit of mine to stop here before going home when I landed. Nine times out of ten, she'd be in the same back corner, immersed in a book or a contract. Half the time she was in a meeting.

But then things changed. She stopped going out with too much work piling up as her business grew, and I stopped searching for her when I left the airport. I knew she'd be home, stuck in her office and working no matter what time of day it was.

Work will take as much time as you give it. And Kat gives it all her time and then some.

Today is a different day, though. Given I just told my boss to fuck off knowing he has evidence that could get me locked up, I need to find Kat. I have to see her.

Just before I get to the glass door, I spot my wife. But more importantly, I see who she's with.

Some asshole is with her. I'm sure he's only a client, but as they walk toward the exit, Kat's eyes on her purse as she rummages through it, looking for her keys I'd think, his eyes are all over her body.

The bastard licks his lower lip, and his gaze flickers to Kat's breasts and then to her eyes as she peeks up at him.

She smiles so naively and tucks her hair behind her ear, but what lights up the anger and the possessiveness running through me, is the blush that rises to her cheeks. My body goes cold and my feet turn to cement standing outside of the shop, watching the two of them unknowingly walk toward me.

She knows he's looking. She knows he likes what he sees. And she's letting him.

The chill that runs through my body fuels something deep inside of me. Something primal and raw. The rain that crashes down on me as the clouds roll in and the sky turns darker by the second does nothing to calm the rage growing inside of me.

I open the door just as the two of them are leaving. My grip on the handle is tight and unforgiving as I wait for them to look up at me.

Kat doesn't stop talking, her sweet voice rattling off something about a signing and who needs to be called to schedule some event.

The dick with a hard-on for my wife sees me first, his eyes widening slightly as he takes in my expression. His first instinct is to angle his body, putting himself between me and Kat. It pisses me off even more and I force my body to stay still, keeping myself from shoving him away from her.

My teeth grind against one another as I stare at his hand, still on her lower back as if he has any right to touch her.

"Evan." Kat looks up at me surprised at first, without a hint of anything other than shock, but instantly her expression changes. "What are you doing? You're getting soaked!" she admonishes me in front of the fucker still standing far too close.

Pride flows through me as she pulls me into the coffee shop, even if she's doing it out of frustration.

She looks from my wet shoulders and the rain dripping down my hair to my forehead and back and then glances outside the shop. She hasn't even acknowledged the man she's with. The demon inside me is at least appeased by that small fact. Her small hands focus on wiping off as much water as she can as she positions me over the large welcome mat at the front of the store.

"Nice to meet you," I say to the man eyeing the two of us. "I'm Kat's husband."

Kat looks up at me and it's obvious she bites her tongue from how her expression scrunches.

"Didn't know she was married," the fucker says and I read him loud and clear. I knew there was a crack in my marriage. But this shit isn't something I'm going to let ruin us. It takes everything in me not to be aggressive toward this shithead.

Kat turns a bright shade of red, but instead of defending us and our relationship, instead of taking my side, she says the worst thing she could to me right now.

"I don't know what we are right now," she states more to me than to him as she looks me in the eyes, daring me to say another word. When I'm quiet, she turns to him.

"I'm sorry for the interruption, Jacob."

"Jake, you can call me Jake," he answers and doesn't even bother to look at me. The awkward tension heats. The thumping of blood rushing in my ears is accompanied with an uncomfortable heat. It was between us. Our problem was only between us. And she made it known to him?

"I'll touch base with you after I get the schedule drawn up, and make sure you get me those summaries as soon as you're able to."

Jake nods his head at Kat and then looks at me to say, "Nice to meet you." He takes his time leaving, glancing over his shoulder more than once, with the rain now coming down in sheets.

"You don't know what we are?" I ask her, feeling the rage wane as the door closes and the sound of the rain is muffled again.

"When you make an ass out of yourself in front of a client, what do you expect me to do?" she hisses.

The rain gets harder and louder as we stand off to the side of the entrance. I take a look around and there are only two other people in the entire place. Both of them women who look like they're on a lunch break, dressed for office jobs. One on each side of the room, both of them on their phones and one with headphones in her ears.

"We can wait out the rain. Get a cup of coffee?" I ask her.

At first Kat looks up at me like I'm crazy. Maybe I am.

"And do what?" she asks. "Play let's-keep-a-secret and hide-away-for-days?"

I ignore her brutal tone and take a chance, wrapping my arm around her waist.

She jumps back for a second, but only because I'm soaking wet.

I chuckle at her response, deep and rough and it makes her smile. She's quick to hide it, but it's there.

"I know you're mad at me," I tell her softly. "I don't want to make you angry, Kat. I love you, and I'm trying."

The trace of all humor fades and she peeks up at me and whispers, "I wish you wouldn't."

I brush the hair from her face and smile down at her as I tell her, "I'll never stop fighting for you."

At my words, she pushes away from me and says, "Then

let's talk until the rain lets up." She looks over her shoulder and out of the window, as if checking to see if our time is already up.

We head to the back corner of the shop, to her spot and her safe place. I can't count the number of times I've sat here with her while she rambled on and told me about her day. Although that was before. It's been too long.

The rest of the seating in the place is all high-top tables and bar-height seats, but in the corner is an L-shaped booth. The same shiny white tabletop, but the seating is for customers who want to spend a while in here and that's what I need with her right now, more time.

She doesn't look at me as she tosses her purse into the booth and then fishes out her wallet.

"You like him?" I question, feeling small pieces of my heart crumble off. Kat's eyes narrow as she huffs out a breath of frustration.

"Knock it off," she answers and I feel torn. I saw the look in her eyes. She's a natural flirt and so am I, but I know she liked the attention more than she should. She felt comfortable with it.

"I don't like him."

"Good to know," she answers me immediately, crossing her arms as she walks toward the counter to order something.

I follow her like a lost fucking puppy. It's quiet between us and the tension is thick as she orders a coffee or whatever the hell it is. The blood is pounding so hard in my ears, I can't hear a damn thing.

"I mean it. He wants you, Kat," I tell her and then nearly

flinch from the look in her eyes. "I don't want anyone else's hands on you."

"It was innocent."

"The hell it was," I bite back instantly, keeping my voice low. I don't give her a chance to speak.

"You can't look me in the eyes and tell me you didn't like it." The air between us turns hot instantly.

"He's a client," she says beneath her breath. My eyes dart from her to the man behind the counter. As soon as I look at him, he averts his eyes, pretending like he didn't just hear the venom in Kat's voice.

"Client or not," I say, standing my ground but all it does is wind Kat up more.

"I'm not the one keeping secrets and lying, I'm not the one who's breaking up this marriage," she says much lower, so much so that it sounds like it was hard for her to even get the words out.

"Stop it," I tell her and grip her hip as she tries to walk past me, back to the booth and undoubtedly to get her stuff and leave.

"I'm sorry," I whisper in her ear and hold her closer to me. I splay my hand on her lower back, feeling the tension in her body slowly leave her. Her body is hot next to mine.

I could fight this, but it's not worth it to upset her. I wait, giving her a moment to calm down and forget about that asshole. For now.

I sit back in the seat, watching the steam rise from her cup as she slips the lid off and grabs a packet of sugar from the center of the table.

The packet makes a flapping sound as she shakes it back

and forth between her forefinger and thumb to get the sugar down. The motion is forceful and she stares at it as she does it, before finally ripping it open and dumping the sugar into the cup.

"I don't tell you everything." The words slip out as the need to win her back takes over everything else.

She's still for a moment, waiting for more, but not looking me in the eyes.

"It's not like I do anything that's … that I want to hide from you. You know what it's like when I go to work."

"I know," Kat says with zero trace of a fight in her voice. "I remember."

"I loved it when you came out with me. You know that, right?"

She finally looks up at me, but only for a moment before she nods her head then slips on the cap to her coffee cup. Her voice is full of remorse as she tells me, "I don't have time for that anymore."

I love that her mind immediately went to the thought of me asking her to come with me. At the beginning of this year, that's all I wanted from her. So we could spend more time together and I could show her off. But the answer was always "no, I can't take time off" so I stopped asking. My heart thumps hard in my chest, remembering how we got into a fight over her not wanting to come with me to Rome a few months back.

"I gave my notice," I tell her and her eyes fly to mine, looking accusing more than anything. "Because you wanted me to." I say the words as if they're the truth and for a moment it feels like they are. But then I remember that's not the

135

reason. I remember what happened. I remember everything in a flood and I have to turn away to breathe in deep and focus on keeping Kat. That's the only thing I care about while everything else collapses around me.

"And because I want to quit too."

"When's your last day?" There's a small bit of hope in her voice, and I watch it shatter as I hesitate to answer.

"I don't know. He ... umm. James." I run my hand down the back of my head and I hate how Kat sees through it all. Her head shakes with disappointment. "It's not finalized."

I nearly forget everything I planned on telling her, but somehow I hold on to it and continue, "I regret a lot of the things I've done this year and maybe for a while now—"

"For a while?" Kat repeats and her eyes reflect the pain that's in her voice.

"I didn't cheat on you, Kat. It's not what you think," I tell her and feel like a liar. "I told you, you're the only one for me."

Before I can say anything else, she shakes her head and that false smile mars her face. "I don't know what you did. But I don't want to know anymore," she says quietly, staring at the cup in her hands before looking back up at me. "We're different people and I think it was only a matter of time before something like this ..." her voice cracks, but she doesn't cry. She simply looks away.

My heartbeat slows. So slow that it's painful.

"Where are you sleeping tonight?" Kat asks me and I have to swallow the spiked lump deep down in my throat before I can answer.

"You still don't want me to come home?"

"It would be easier if you didn't."

"Easier for what?"

"Easier for the breakup, Evan." Her lips part and then she adds, "It's not about love anymore or about what we had. It's about trust and what we've become. I need a fresh start and a life I'm proud of. And I don't think it includes you in it."

"It does," I answer her instantly. "And I want the same."

She stares back at me with an expression that shows how vulnerable she is. How much she wants to believe what I'm telling her.

I take her hand in mine and tell her, "I'll do whatever you want, so long as when it's all said and done I get to keep you."

I stare in her eyes knowing I've never said anything more truthful, but something deep down inside tells me that's not how this story will end.

"It's too little, too late, Evan. I'm sorry."

# CHAPTER
## seventeen

*Kat*

THE BED GROANS AND DIPS AS I TURN BACK ONTO my right shoulder, pushing the pillow between my knees and trying to force myself to sleep. My mind won't stop playing back every minute of the coffee shop. Every little moment. Even sleeping pills aren't working.

I've been alone all my life. Until Evan. When he first started sleeping over, it was hard to fall asleep. Unless he fucked me to the point of exhaustion, which was often.

You'd think it'd be easy going back to being alone. I was a pro at it for years and worse yet, I was proud of it. The train goes by and the sound cuts through the white noise of the city. The windows are closed, but I still hear it. I can even feel the rumble and vibrations as I try to lie still on the bed. And that's when I get a hint of Evan's scent. When I'm alone, missing him, I sleep on his side of the bed. It's easiest the first night he's gone. It smells just like him. Each day it gets a little harder and working late nights gets more appealing. But even the masculine scent that drifts toward me as I inch my head closer to his pillow isn't enough to comfort me. Why would it? I'm losing him and everything we had.

I toss the heavy comforter off my body and sit up, wiping the sleep from my eyes and dangling my feet over the side of the bed. It's nearly 1:00 a.m. and pitch black in the room. I should be sleeping, considering the fatigue plaguing my body and all too conscious it should come easy.

My fingers run through my long hair, separating it and braiding it loosely before I take a sip of water from the glass on the nightstand. If I get up and start working, I know I won't sleep at all tonight. The very thought makes my heart thump harder. Work is killing me, lack of sleep is destroying me. But both are because I'm completely and utterly alone.

*Just breathe.* I let my head fall back and slowly creep back under the covers. All I need to do is breathe.

But that hope is short lived as I hear Evan climb the stairs. I had one condition to him coming home, and that was leaving me the bedroom. Even if it hurts me, I'd rather feel pain in his absence than a fraction of that pain in his presence.

I close my eyes as I hear the door open. For a moment I think I should pretend to be asleep, but I don't want any more lies in our relationship. Whatever our relationship even is now.

"I thought you were going to sleep on the sofa?" I ask him and then hold my breath. I should want him to leave. That's what a sane woman who's getting a divorce should want. But there isn't an ounce of me that wants to see him walk out that door.

"I was going to," Evan answers and then slips his shirt off over his head. He keeps his eyes on me, daring me to say something, but my eyes focus on his broad chest.

In six years his body has changed, as has mine. But he's still lean and muscular. My body heats and my thighs clench, but I play it off, turning my back to him to lie on my left shoulder.

"Is this all right?" he asks me, his voice carrying through the dark night and cutting me down to my deepest insecurity. It's not all right and nothing about this situation is, but those aren't the words that come out of my mouth.

My eyes squeeze shut tight and I give in to what I want, slowly moving my body toward his. Wouldn't it be a lie to deny it?

"I'm afraid I'll like it too much if you stay," I finally answer with my eyes closed as the bed dips. I stay perfectly still as I lay out the bare truth. "I'm afraid I'll forgive you and I'll forget why we shouldn't be together." All the words pour out from deep down in my soul, leaving my lips in a rush.

A rough sound comes from deep in his throat as the comforter pulls just slightly. "You don't know what you want, Kat," Evan tells me although the confidence is missing. "You want me to leave because you're afraid. You won't fight for me to stay because you know I will regardless of what you say, isn't that right?"

My brow furrows as I take in his assessment. He scoots closer to me, making the bed shift beneath my still body. When I turn to meet him, still under the covers, his dark gaze stares at me as if I'm his prey and that's just how I feel. "No. I want you to leave because we're leading different lives." I have to second-guess my words.

"Then let's get back on track. Let's start over," he whispers and then leans closer to me. As if testing my boundaries, he rests his hand on the pillow above my head. I don't push him away, but I don't move toward him either.

I'm fucked no matter what I do.

I'm empty and hollow. All the sadness and regret has been shed from me, leaving nothing behind but faint memories of what we had and the hint of all the hopes and dreams I had so long ago to make my heart flutter. As I close my eyes and swallow the lump in my throat, Evan lies next to me, gently resting his hand on my hip. He's silent but I can hear his steady breath and smell a hint of his scent. I inhale deeper. God, what that scent does to me. My head dips further into the pillow as I readjust under the covers and when I do, Evan lifts his hand slightly. Waiting to see which way I'll turn.

And I turn toward him.

"You make me a foolish woman," I tell him as my eyes slowly open. His hazel eyes are so clear at this angle. Maybe it's the moon creeping in from the slit between the curtains.

He smirks at me, although there's a sadness in his smile as he brushes my hair from my face.

"Tell me you'll stay with me."

"Tell me why I should," I reply instantly and the soft look of longing in his eyes fades away as the soothing motion of his thumb rubbing along my temple falters. My eyes drop to his chest and my heart plummets to the pit of my stomach.

"You said you didn't cheat," I tell him, but mostly I make a promise to myself. "So I believe you."

"Thank you," he says so softly beneath his breath I hardly hear him. His shoulders sag slightly and it makes the bed creak with relief.

I want to say more. I want to make some sort of demand or ultimatum … or ask why he was there in that hotel lobby in the middle of the night. Why he lied to the world. Why he's lying to me. But instead I curl into him.

"Don't leave me," he says, giving me the request and wraps his arms around me, pulling me closer to him. Closer to his scent, his warmth, to the man I've been desperate to be with for so damn long. His heat wraps around me in the most comforting of ways.

"I won't promise you that," I answer with honesty with my eyes open, staring at a small scar on his left shoulder. I lift my hand up and let my fingers play along the silvery indent of it. "You're right that I don't know what I want. So we'll just have to find out."

He's quiet for a long time. And part of my heart, a very large part of it, aches. It's a horrible feeling and it makes my eyes sting. But I won't mourn what I'm not even sure I've lost. It's just the threat of ending something I've valued so dearly and for so long that hurts.

My shoulders shake slightly as I take in a shuddering breath, and that's when he cups my chin and forces me to look at him.

"You know I love you," he says with a ragged breath. "More than anything, anything in the world."

I sniffle and try to ignore how the pain grows. "I do," I

tell him and then try to hide my face, but his grip on my chin is too strong and I can only close my eyes, feeling the smallest bit of tears threaten to spill over and soak into my lashes.

"Don't cry, Kat," Evan whispers as he rests his forehead against mine. "I love you, and that's all that matters." For some reason it seems so obvious to me in this moment that those words were more for him than they were for me. My eyes open to find his still closed. To see the pain there. To see how desperate he is.

That's what I can blame it on. And it's my undoing.

It always has been. He needs me, and I crave it.

"Kiss me—" Before the command leaves my lips, his are on mine. Devouring me and taking every little piece I'm willing to give. I crumble underneath him. My hands fly to his hair as he deepens the kiss. The air turns hotter as my skin heats and our breathing quickens.

"Kat." He barely breaks away from me to whisper my name and then presses his lips harder against mine as he grabs my hips and pulls me toward him.

My gasp is muted as his tongue dives into my mouth. My back arches and my breasts push against his hard chest as he climbs on top of me.

Every second I'm acutely aware that I'm falling backward. It pains my heart as I pull away from him, digging my head into the pillow to feel the cool air. But I can't stop this. I never could. He nips along my neck and my body clenches with need as my legs wrap around his waist.

My heels dig into his ass while I close my eyes tight and let my body do what it wants. It's only ever wanted him and I won't deny my own needs.

Not when he worships me like this, kissing his way down my body as he strips the clothes from me. The only sound is our breathing as I cautiously open my eyes to watch.

His fingertips brush against my skin as he takes off the last piece and stares at my glistening sex.

"You're wet for me." He says the words out loud, although I don't think he meant for me to hear. Another time, I'd blush. But there's no shame or embarrassment right now. It's desperation.

He parts from his clothes faster than I can steady my breath. The moonlight casts shadows on his chiseled chest and every sensitive bit of me is on fire and singing with need. My eyes are drawn to his hands as he strokes his length. When he does it again, I can't help how my lips part with desire and my legs spread wider. My body's ready, willing and aching for him to take me.

"I'm the only one who can satisfy you like this, Kat." My gaze shifts to Evan and he captures it with an intensity that pins me down. "Don't ever forget that."

I can't respond, I don't have time. In one swift motion he's buried to the hilt inside of me. Stretching my walls and sending a spike of heat, desire and a bit of pain through me. Every nerve ending screams to life as a strangled moan tears through me.

It's nothing but pleasure as he stills deep inside of me. Waiting for me to adjust to his girth. He takes his time kissing his way up my collarbone to my lips.

The touches are softer now. Small pecks and nips until I open my eyes and he brings them to a halt.

"I love you," he whispers. My legs wrap around his waist

and my fingers dig into his strong shoulders as he moves slowly at first. Burying his head into my neck before I can tell him the same.

He rocks his hips, his rough pubic hair rubbing against my clit with each small movement and bringing me higher and higher. My release feels so close but so far away just the same.

I can only make small whimpers as he speeds up, knowing he's going to send me crashing in the end. All the while he rides through my orgasm, fueled by my cries of pleasure. I cling to him for dear life as my body seems paralyzed and he continues to take from me. Pounding into me, harder and harder. Pistoning his hips until the headboard slams against the wall rhythmically in time with his relentless thrusts. He has his way with me, and then he holds me. I would do it all again just for this moment in time. Just to be held by him, as if he'll never let me go.

# CHAPTER
## eighteen

*Evan*

I T'S BEEN A LONG DAMN TIME SINCE I'VE MADE breakfast for Kat. It's probably been a year or more since we've woken up together, that's how fucked our schedules have become.

Her bare feet pad down the stairs as I set the last plate on the table. It's brimming with fresh diced pineapple and strawberries. Bacon's still the prominent scent, though. Bacon and eggs for breakfast. Plus a platter of hotcakes with fruit in the center and of course, her coffee.

I grab her mug from her spot on the table. It's still burning hot but I make sure to put it handle out as I turn around to face her. Maybe I'm pussywhipped. Maybe I'm sucking up. Either way, I don't give a fuck.

The sight of her messy halo of hair and wide eyes with

bit of mascara still lingering from yesterday makes my heart pump hard in my chest. She's gorgeous even when she's a mess. She's got nothing on but a baggy Henley of mine and it makes her seem even more petite than she already is. My Kat's never been an early riser. Only when she has to, or apparently when the smell of breakfast is in the air.

"You have good timing," I tell her as she hesitantly grabs the coffee. I can see her shoulders sag just a bit and her eyes close as she takes in the smell, though. It gives me a sense of pride. Even if it's just for the moment.

"Good morning," she says with a soft smile, but it's barely hiding her true feelings. I force a smile back and pull out her chair.

"I don't know the last time I had an actual breakfast," she says as she takes the seat and then looks up at me. "Thank you." It's genuine, but with her shoulders hunched and that sad look in her eyes, I don't give her a response.

I wish I could hold on to last night forever. But the sun had to rise, and I need to come clean to her. She deserves that much.

The chair legs scratch on the wooden floor as I pull out my seat. I grimace slightly and then clear my throat as I sit down, noticing how Kat doesn't seem to care. She's not nearly awake enough; sleep still dominates her expression.

With both hands cradling her mug, she leans back in her seat and gives me a small smile but doesn't reach for any food. She doesn't say anything either. All she does is wait. I wish I had something better to offer her than what's going to come out of my mouth.

"I want a fresh start ... and the marriage we were

supposed to have," I say as I push a fork through the pancake on my plate, but I don't eat it. I'm already sick to my stomach.

A heavy breath leaves me and I rub my forehead to get out some of the tension. I can't tell her everything, but I can give her something that has killed me for years; a truth I wish didn't exist.

My skin's hot and my throat's dry. It's been years, and I never intended on telling Kat. I didn't want her to know and it was before things changed for me. Before my mother told me she was dying. Before Kat came to me and showed me she was the person I needed in my life forever. It happened before I realized she was mine and I was never going to let her go.

"You okay?" Kat asks and there's genuine pain in her voice. Sadness and concern I wish weren't there. She's too good for me. I've made so many mistakes and this is going to crush her and hurt her more than it should. It meant nothing to me back then, but it'll mean everything to her right now. And I hate it.

"There's something I have to tell you." As I say the words I look Kat in the eyes, and her expression changes. The corners of her lips turn down and a deep crease settles between her brows. She has this way of hiding her emotions, but it doesn't last long. She offers me a hard stare with her lips pressed into a thin line. She gives it to me all the time, but I know the second I give her silence, Kat's mouth will open and every emotion she's feeling will show. She can't hide it from me.

"When you asked me about Samantha, if I'd slept with her ..." I have to break off from my thought and pause to take in another breath.

The clink of Kat's fork hitting the plate makes my chest

feel tight. She lets out a small sound, almost like a sigh but weighted down with a bitter hopelessness.

"I told you the truth, that I haven't been with anyone since we got married," I say and watch her eyes, her expression, everything about her, but she doesn't look back at me. Her shoulders rise like she's holding her breath and waiting for a bomb to go off.

"It was years ago, Kat. Before I knew how much you meant to me." The words come up my throat as if they're scratching and clawing to stay buried down deep inside of me.

Her expression crumples the second I hint at the affair. If you can even call it that. "I felt like I was lying to you. Every. Single. Time." I bang my fist on the table and the plates rattle with each word and make Kat jump, but I can't help it. "I felt like a bastard when I looked you in the eyes and said nothing happened, because you should have already known."

"When?" Kat asks me.

"I swear that night in the papers was about something else. Something that has nothing to do with that woman or sleeping with her. It was—"

"When?" She screams out the question as her eyes gloss over. She doesn't stop staring at me, but the emotion I expect to see isn't there. It's only anger, a furious rage that stares back at me. "When did you sleep with her?"

"The night I got the call from my mother." I swallow thickly and add, "I was with her."

"The night she told you?" she asks me with a morbid tone and I nod, feeling that acidic churning in my stomach as my clammy hands clench. "You were at the company party?" she

149

asks instantly, although it's more of her recalling that night than an actual question.

"You were supposed to take me out that night afterward," Kat says and each word sounds sadder and sadder as she looks away from me. "You were fucking her while at work."

"It was a one-time thing. A mistake. I didn't know who she was and things were getting serious with us, Kat. You don't understand. It wasn't how it seems." I stumble over my words. Leaning closer to her and reaching for her, she abruptly pushes away from the table, slamming her palms against it and scooting the chair back.

My hands fly into the air, keeping them up. As if I'm not a threat. Trying to keep her here with me to give me a chance to explain.

"Look, we were getting serious and I needed ... I don't know how to explain it."

"You didn't want to be with me anymore so you went and slept with the first girl to bat her eyelashes at you?" she asks although it's less of a question and more an accusation, a bitter one at that.

I can't explain how pathetic I feel as she looks at me like I'm the devil. It was a game back then. I wish I could change it. If I'd known what Kat would mean to me, I'd have put a ring on her finger the moment I laid eyes on her. I never would have done anything to risk what we had. *Lies. So many lies*, a voice in the back of my mind whispers. If that was the truth, I wouldn't have needed to call Samantha with my eyes on a lifeless body in the corporate hotel room. If she knew every-thing, she'd hate me.

"I messed up and I made a lot of mistakes," I say and lean toward her, but she's not having it.

"How many women have you fucked since I've been with you?" Her voice is hard and full of nothing but bitterness.

"Just her, just Samantha and just that once. Please, Kat." My voice begs her for mercy as I lean forward but she's quick to stand up, nearly toppling the chair over just so she can get away from me.

Regret consumes me. I wish I hadn't told her. Fuck. I don't know what to wish for anymore.

I swallow thickly and try to remember everything else I was going to say and the point of bringing up the past. "It's why I feel so guilty about these allegations and why I didn't say anything to the press. I needed them to think it'd happened and it kind of did, just years ago."

"Why were you in the hotel lobby with her at three in the morning?" she asks me—for the dozenth time—as she crosses her arms over her chest, bunching the shirt and finally letting her gaze trap mine.

I have to swallow the hard lump in my dry throat before I can answer her. "I needed an alibi."

"Are you fucking serious, Evan?" she says, spitting out her words as she looks at me with more disgust than I've ever seen on her face.

"I'm sorry. It was an accident."

"It's always an accident. Always a mistake. Why do you do this? Why do you put yourself in these situations?" She screams at me with a rage I know she's had pent up inside of her for a while now. I'm too old to be this stupid. I never should have continued working for James once her career took off. But the money and the lifestyle were so addictive. It was a high I couldn't refuse.

"I told you, I quit. I'm not going to put myself in—" As I shake my head, trying to get out the words, I can't remember a damn thing I'd planned on saying.

"It's too little, too late, Evan," Kat says, cutting me off before leaving me alone in the room, whipping around and not bothering to say another word. I stare at her back as she storms up the stairs.

I've never felt this way before in my life. Like I've hurt the one person in the world who would never hurt me. Like I betrayed her. Like I'm not worth a damn thing.

And there's no way to make that right.

I don't know how to make any of this right.

# CHAPTER
## nineteen

*Kat*

*I knew the truth,*
*I didn't want to believe.*
*But deep in my gut,*
*The agony did seethe.*
*Call me a fool,*
*Say what you will.*
*But I can't help it,*
*I love him still.*

I CAN'T STOP THINKING ABOUT HOW EVAN FUCKED her. Samantha is ... the opposite of me. Everything about her is exactly the opposite. Disgust doesn't begin to cover it. All I can imagine is how that night would have played out had his mother not called him. If tragedy hadn't stepped in to intervene. He fucked her, and then what? Was he going to bail on our date or was he still planning on seeing me?

I should be focused on the fact that he told me he needed an alibi. The fact that only weeks ago he was doing shit he knows is wrong and could send him to jail. But that's the man he's always been. I knew better than to turn a blind eye, but that's exactly what I've been doing, isn't it?

It's an odd feeling, like waking up from a long and deep sleep or having a blindfold taken off after wearing it for days. Has it always been this way?

I knew what kind of life he was leading and the risks that came with it. I didn't do a damn thing about it. I should be ashamed, mortified.

And yet all I can think about is him fucking her.

Not to mention how many times I've seen that woman at events and socialized with her. Not once did she make it seem like anything had happened between them. She comes off sweet and innocent. She's slim like me, but taller and she prefers soft, muted colors. Samantha always has perfectly manicured, pale pink nails. She pretties herself up like a little doll, prim and proper. I never would have expected it. I remember how genuinely happy for me she seemed when she gushed over my engagement ring.

*That fucking bitch.*

The door to my office opens behind me, the telltale creak forcing my eyes to shoot open. They narrow as I see his reflection on the black computer screen. I don't even know if the damn thing is on anymore or how long I've been sitting here. All I've done is stare at a worn spot on my desk and think about how he fucked her, even knowing he was going to see me only hours later.

What would have happened if his mother hadn't chosen that moment to tell him to come home and that she wasn't well? Maybe that would have been the night he chose to break it off with me. After all, every day with him was like ticking off a checkbox. I knew it wasn't going to last. I was waiting for it to end.

Marie screwed me over by telling him.

"Kat." Evan calls my name from behind me. Hearing his voice causes a shudder to run down my spine. It's a slow one that sends a chill over my body.

"I'm going to do everything I can to prove to you how much I love you."

"Do I even know you?" Even as I whip around and sneer at him a sick voice in the back of my head answers me. *Yes. Yes, you knew what you were doing. You knew the man you married.*

"You're the only one who does," he answers, looking me in the eyes as his broad shoulders fill the doorframe to my office. "You know I love you."

I scoff at him, choosing to ignore the truth and how much I blame myself.

Right now, it's all on him. I didn't cheat on him. I didn't continue to live a lifestyle that was obviously going to tear us apart.

He did. And fuck him for that.

"I hate you right now." The words slip out in a breath and he visibly flinches.

"You're angry, and you have every right to be."

"Angry doesn't cut it!" I scream, my throat feeling raw as

the salty tears burn my eyes. "I loved you. I would have done anything for you!" I grit out the words through my clenched teeth and try to grip the chair as I stand on shaky legs.

"I loved you so much. And this is how you treat our marriage. With lies and secrets and all this shit I don't even know about."

"I'm sorry I kept that from you, but that was it." He says *that was it* as if it's easily accepted. As if he's never told a lie or done anything else that would ruin us.

"Liar! How many laws have you broken at work?" I let the words tumble from my mouth, all the rage coursing through my blood. "But you kept at it. You were never going to stop until something made you. You didn't care about me or what it did to us!

"What kind of marriage is that!" As the words tear from my throat and Evan stares back at me a guilty man, the reality hits me like a bullet to the chest.

I was blinded by my lust for him. Maybe even my love. Either way, I've been denying the reality.

"I want more than this. I deserve better."

"I love you," he says like that's the answer to all of this. Like it will save us.

"You keep saying that, but I don't think you know what it means." *Or maybe love just simply isn't enough anymore.*

"What really gets me," I start to say then take in a long, ragged breath, finally taking a step toward him but immediately stop when he does the same.

Standing across from him in the small office I look him in the eyes and get what I've been thinking about out of me. "You saw her all the time. You were with her at every function."

My voice lowers as I add, "Even *I* was with her so many times. And you didn't bother to tell me."

"What happened was a mistake for her too."

"Don't talk to me like she didn't know what she was doing. She was married and she knew we were together. How could you? How could you stand to be around her?"

"I was working. If you'll recall, you were broke and we needed money. What was I supposed to do? Quit?"

"Does your boss know?" His expression turns to stone, although he looks more pissed off than anything else. "Does James know?" I ask him again.

"I don't know."

It's silent as I breathe out a huff of disgust.

"I'm sorry. I fucked up but it was years ago."

"It wasn't just years ago. Every day you went back was a mistake. Every day you kept it from me was a mistake!"

"What part of it being my job don't you get?" he asks me in a low voice full of anger as he takes another step forward.

"You could have gotten another job." All I can see is red. The words come out automatically, but my mind is racing. My breathing is heavy.

"Who would hire me?" he asks with sincerity. "You were just starting out and needed every penny I could earn."

"Don't act like you did this for me!" I spit at him with anger. My fist pounds against my chest. "Don't you dare blame this on me!"

Tears prick my eyes as he stares at me without saying a word.

Shame and guilt heat my body. Both of us are raging with emotion. Both of us want to tear the other person apart. That realization is all I can take. Tears spill over and I have to turn away from him. With my back to him, he tries to touch me and I rip my arm away from him. I shake my head and firm my resolve.

"Please leave me alone. I'm begging you, Evan. If you love me, please get away from me."

# CHAPTER
## twenty

*Evan*

*The truth I cannot change,*
*I'm a sinner and I confess.*
*But I refuse to let her go,*
*She's my love and nothing less.*

I LOVE YOU, KAT, AND I'M SORRY.

I text her again, the cellphone screen lighting up the dark bedroom in Pops's house, my old bedroom. The glossy posters reflect the light that scatters into the room in stripes from the blinds on the window. The sound of the traffic is louder here and everything about it reminds me of the life I used to lead. The one before Kat. The one I'm so damn ashamed of now.

I'll never forget the look of disappointment on his face

when I showed up a few hours ago with a duffle bag. It's like even he lost hope in me making it right with Kat.

It's crushing to leave her. But it's different this time. I get exactly why she needs space. This is why I never told her. She needed something to hold on to, though, she needed a solid reason to be pissed at me, so we could get through it and move on.

Still, I didn't expect it to go down like it did. I'm worthless and it's never been more apparent to me that my life is meaningless without Kat in it.

I swallow thickly as I lean back on the bed and fall against the pillow. I've never felt so alone. I wish I could take it all back.

My eyes close as I feel my heart slow and my blood turn cold. Being here like this makes me remember one of the last conversations I had with my mother.

She'd seen me with Kat while we were out one night. Just a coincidence, but she acted like it was more than it was.

Kat was a fling and a good time. She was someone I wanted more and more of and I made damn sure to monopolize her time until I had my fill, but of course that time would never come. I just didn't know it back then or I liked to pretend I didn't anyway.

"She seems sweet," my mother told me when I came home for Sunday dinner. Looking back at that night now, I realize how much slower she was to set the table. How everything was a little off, but to me, Sunday dinner was just an obligation I had to my mother before I would be leaving to go out and have a good time.

"You didn't really talk to her," I said and laughed at my

mom, shaking my head and taking a drink from whatever was in my cup. I leaned back and looked at my father, waiting for him to agree with me. When he didn't, I added, "Plus she's the only girl you've seen me with."

"That's true," Ma replied and shrugged. "I like the way you two look together," she stated matter-of-factly and then looked me in the eyes as she smiled. "Is it too much to ask that you pretend to value your mother's opinion?"

I let out a small laugh and shook my head. "I'm glad you approve," I told her. More just to make her happy than anything else, but it only opened the door for Ma to invite her over for the next family dinner. I had already started coming up with reasons to end it that night.

It was too much. I was young and in my prime and working a job that would keep my appetite well-fed.

I was ready to end it too the next night; it was too serious, too soon. But her smile and the way she laughed at me when I pulled up wearing an old rugby shirt caught me off guard in a way I found completely endearing. She thought it was the oddest thing and I'll never forget the way her soft voice hummed with laughter and it carried into the night. Who was I to take that away? I knew she'd end it with me anyway. I didn't know it would be after marriage and six years later.

If I could go back to that night, I would change it all and I'd make sure I told Ma she was right.

"I'm heading to bed." My father's voice catches me by surprise and my body jolts from the memory. I pretend to rub the sleep from my burning eyes and clear my throat to tell my father good night. It's tight with emotion and it takes me a second to sit up in bed.

"You look like hell," Pops says.

Nodding in agreement, I take a moment to set my feet on the floor. My head is still hung low and my shoulders are sagging as I rest my elbows on my knees.

"How did you keep Ma out of it? All the stupid shit you did?" I ask him. I know he led a wild life. He's got the stories and the scars to prove it. I came by my lifestyle honestly.

I lift my head and look him in the eyes, forcing a small smile to my face. "I need to know what to do. I need advice."

"You can't. It's gotta stop." He shrugs his shoulders, the faint light from the hallway casting a long shadow of him into the room, ending at my feet. "That's the advice I can give you. Don't keep a thing from her. You should already know that."

I swallow, or try to, as a ball of spikes grows in my throat. "What if you can't stop? What if I can't quit this job and this life?" The image of Tony dead on the floor remains firm in my sight. Even as I blink it away and look up at my father, I can still see him. Dead from an overdose and staring back at me with glassy, lifeless eyes as if it was my fault.

I brought him to that room. The one reserved for partying in our company.

I gave him the coke, but I didn't know it was laced. And then I left him there to get whiskey and cigarettes.

I brought him to his death.

I can never tell her that. I can barely admit it to myself.

"Did you ever mess up so bad, you thought you could never make it right?" I ask even though his answer doesn't matter. I guess I just don't want to feel so alone.

"We all do; you just find a way. I'm sorry, but it's the best I've got."

"Find a way …" I say the words softly, barely moving my lips as I look at the edge of the comforter, wishing it were that easy.

"I don't know what to tell you, Evan. I did everything for your mom, and I'd do it all again. Maybe that's where you went wrong?"

"What's that?" I'm quick to ask him, my gaze focused on Pops and whatever it is he has to say. I'm desperate for an answer to all this shit. I need to take it all back.

"You weren't thinking about her."

His words sink in slow, but deep.

I shake my head and agree, "No, I wasn't."

"The best thing you ever did was marry that girl." I nod my head, feeling a jagged pain move through my body. "Worse thing you ever did was leave her side."

He doesn't know how true his words are.

# CHAPTER
# twenty-one

## Kat

*You left a space beside me,*
*You left me all alone.*
*You left a space beside me,*
*I thought my heart would turn to stone.*
*You left a space beside me,*
*Desire creeps in the night.*
*You left a space beside me,*
*Lust fills the emptiness up just right.*

THE EVENING SKYLINE IS GORGEOUS. THE COLORS of autumn dance along the buildings and the beautiful hues of orange and soft reds travel up to the bright full moon.

It's early for the moon to be out, but as I walk away from

the townhouse, down the stone steps as the heavy walnut door shuts behind me, I can't help but admire it. There's beauty in nature and having the small bit of it above the city is something I've taken for granted for so long.

With each step, my boots click on the concrete, until my body stumbles forward and I nearly fall down the last two stairs.

"Shoot!" I cry out as I frantically reach for the iron rail and just barely get a grip tight enough to keep me upright. My purse is flung down to the crook of my arm, spilling odds and ends, including my phone, onto the busy street.

I curse beneath my breath as my cheeks heat with embarrassment and I keep my head down. Most people walk around me, and I'm fine with that. Better than fine. I'm happy that they're just ignoring me and my clumsiness.

I crouch down low to grab the fallen items, ignoring the bystanders as they steer clear of me but as I stand up, I realize someone didn't miss my fall and their eyes haven't left me.

"You okay?" Jacob asks as he comes toward me, nearly out of breath. His cheeks are slightly red, the chill of the air getting to him. His hand is cold on my shoulder as he helps me stand upright. His thick black wool jacket brushes against mine and the heavy scent of pine, a masculine fragrance I love, fills my lungs.

"I saw you from across the street," he tells me as I blink away my surprise. Not only from his presence, but from my reaction.

I brush the hair from my face and give him a grateful smile as the crowd continues to walk around us. This city doesn't stop for anything or anyone. Jacob walks with me to move out of the way and stand on the stairs to my townhome.

"Just a clumsy moment," I say in a breathy voice and reluctantly laugh at myself as I steady the bag back onto my shoulder. This is so embarrassing.

Jacob shrugs and slips his hands into his pockets as he says, "I expected worse." As he speaks, his perfect teeth show, and I can't help but eye his lush lips. "Honestly, that was a nice save."

A warmth flows through me.

"Well thanks," I say, shifting my weight and shaking my head. "What are you doing here?"

"I'm checking out a townhouse down the street. Moving to the city was definitely the right move for me."

"And have you thought of the contract at all?" I ask him and then bite the inside of my cheek. "I don't mean to be forward. I'm just excited to work together."

I don't miss how his eyes stray slightly to my breasts when I breathe in deep. He turns away, toward the street to try to play it off and licks his lower lip. Maybe it was a subconscious thing on my part. I almost feel the need to apologize.

"I'm thinking I should get to signing it. I just was hoping maybe we could meet up to go over a few minor details?" he asks as he brings his attention back to me.

I smile and nod my head, my hair falling back in front of my shoulders. "I'd be happy to," I answer a little too eagerly. His eyes flash with something they shouldn't, but I ignore it.

"Well, I should get going," I say and the words rush out of my mouth.

"Me too," Jacob says and looks back across the street. "My realtor is over there somewhere waiting on the steps to let me in to 'my dream home,'" he says, mimicking what must be his realtor's nasally voice, and then he gives me another view of his gorgeous smile.

"If you ever need anything, I'm always home or a call away," I offer and then bite the inside of my cheek. *What the hell was that?*

"Sounds good. Be safe," he says comically and then takes a few steps forward. "I'll text you," he says over his shoulder and I simply nod. Not able to speak, just standing there, gripping my purse strap with both hands and wondering why he gets to me so much.

I won't deny that he does.

That's not the part that bothers me.

It's why. Is it him? The timing?

What is it about Jacob that makes me want him, when I haven't lusted for a man other than my husband in years?

# CHAPTER
## twenty-two

*Evan*

"HAVE YOU TRIED ROSES?"

My gaze moves from the cell phone in my hand to my father. With his arm braced against the wall, he taps his knuckles against the cream wall.

"I'm not sure roses are going to help," I reply and give him a weak smile.

"You'd be surprised. Flowers are a girl's best friend."

A small but genuine smile graces my lips as I toss the phone onto the end table. "It's diamonds, Pops. The saying is diamonds are a girl's best friend."

"Then get her diamonds," he replies with a stern look before making his way to the worn, caramel-colored leather recliner in the corner of the living room. There's a the TV. I'm not sure who's playing since the volume is so low I can barely hear it.

"She still hasn't messaged you back?" he asks.

"Nothing yet," I answer lowly, not bothering to hide my disappointment, and then look back at the phone, wishing it would go off.

"You going back home to talk? Or what's the plan?"

"I don't know," I tell him. "I know she wants space; I just don't know if it's what's best."

From my periphery, I watch him nod and then he says, "It's hard to know. Especially when she's not talking to you."

"I wouldn't talk to me either," I say, mostly out of the need to defend her. "I'd have kicked me out too."

"It was a long time ago," my father says, but there's hardly any conviction in his voice.

It's quiet for longer than I'd like. Both of us not knowing where to go in the conversation.

"I remember when you moved in with her," Pops finally says and breaks the silence.

"It feels like forever ago. I hardly even remember what it was like before her."

"Feels like it just happened to me. All the boxes and her wanting to paint first and then wanting everything in a specific order. She sure has a certain way of going about things."

I lean my head back, staring at the ceiling fan as I say, "Yeah she does" with a hint of a smile on my lips. "She's particular."

"That's one word for it," Pops says back with a small laugh, the kind where I can feel his smile in the laugh, not missing a beat.

"You love her, though. Particular and all," I remind him.

He nods his head. "I love her for it too." He clears his throat and says, "I never told you this, but I felt like I'd lost your mother and then lost you."

"Pops, no—" I try to stop that shit, but he's already moved on before I can get a thought out.

"It was a short-lived feeling. Kat came over more than you did after the move, if you remember."

"She's the one who wanted the family dinners. I remember her pushing for that. Probably wouldn't have happened if it wasn't for her. I think she was just trying to make things right."

"I know she was. She's a lot like your mother in that regard. You did good picking her."

I can't respond to my father. He's never talked to me about Kat really. Now of all times, it's just making the pain that much worse.

"You remember that heavy-ass dresser?" Pops asks me and it makes me huff a laugh as I nod. More than anything I'm thankful for the change in topic.

"She had to have it," I say absently. "It was her mother's."

"Oh, I know. I remember her telling me a dozen times."

"She kept talking about the movers." I shake my head. "We didn't need any movers."

"Sure, sure. I remember that squabble."

"Squabble," I repeat and run my hand over my hair. "She knew I could handle it."

Pops laughs at the thought. A deep laugh, and then he leans back in his chair.

"You guys can handle that, then you guys can handle anything."

"It feels different, Pops." I swallow and fight back the swell of emotion. "This isn't just a fight."

"How would you know? You haven't even really had a fight, have you?"

I stare at him blankly, knowing me and Kat haven't ever gone at it before, not really. A little bickering here or there, but this isn't some argument over dishes. This is worse than he can imagine, and I'm ashamed to speak that truth.

"Just get her something shiny. Spoil the woman," he says, throwing his hand up.

I let a trace of a smile linger on my lips as I picture handing Kat a bouquet of roses. I'd pick the dark red ones, but make sure there's some baby's breath in the package too. One of the large bouquets. The ones that make you lean in and smell them. Too good to resist. That's the kind I'd get her.

I can see her soft smile as she peeks up at me, holding it in both her hands.

A warmth settles through me. I wish it were that easy. I'd buy every flower I could if that were the case.

"Whatever you do," Pops says, distracting me from the vision of Kat forgiving me, "just don't give up."

"I won't," I tell him and I damn well mean it.

# CHAPTER
## twenty-three

*Kat*

MY FINGERS RELENTLESSLY TAP ON MY PHONE and my gaze drifts to the door. He's coming. Soon. Evan needs to get his things and get out. Mistake after mistake after mistake. That's what this relationship has been. There's undeniable love between us. I won't argue with that. But some people aren't meant to be together and at this point in my life, I should be concerned with having children and not the possibility of having to bail my husband out of jail.

There's a bit of anger that's carried me through the last two days. It's what I focus on. It's what gives me the strength to tell him I don't want to be with him anymore. To tell him it doesn't matter when he says he loves me.

I know it matters, and I'd be a liar if I didn't admit that

I'll always want him and have love for him. I'll always want to feel loved like I did when we first got together.

But there's only one way for the story of the two of us to end and that's with him packing his things and getting out. Loving each other simply isn't enough when we're so far apart in other ways.

As if he heard my thought, the front doorknob jiggles and the sound of keys clinking creeps into the room.

Fate hates me. No, that's not strong enough of a word. It must *loathe* me because the sight of my husband standing in our doorway shatters my heart.

I attempt to keep my expression cold, but my body goes numb and the same coldness that swept over my body only weeks ago when I felt my marriage falling apart drifts over my skin now. His eyes are bloodshot. He can't force a look of anything but agony as he turns his gaze from me and walks slowly into the room, closing the door behind him. The shock to my system is crippling and I can't look him in the eyes. He doesn't try to hide the desperation. His disheveled hair and all-around rough appearance make my body itch to touch him. To comfort him. To make the obvious pain go away.

I think that's why I'll never be able to deny that I love him. The image of him in pain destroys me to my core. My soul hurts for his, and I want nothing more than to take his misery away.

I need to love myself more than I could ever love him. I'm trying to. My God, am I trying.

He nods his head as he tosses his keys down on the coffee table and stands awkwardly in front of me.

I have to swallow the tightness in my throat and ignore

the heat flowing through my body begging me to give in. "Hi."
I'm the first to say anything at all and break the uneasy tension in the living room.

"How are you?" he asks and it feels so odd. Like we're just old friends or acquaintances.

"Not the best," I answer him. I try to find that anger, I remember everything as my eyes shift to the entrance to the dining room, but there's not an ounce of anger that will come to my rescue.

"I miss you," he says as the last word spills from my lips.

"I miss you too," I admit, my voice cracking and I lick my lips.

"Things have gotten rough, but I never stopped loving you. You're the only thing that matters."

"What you say is everything I want to hear, Evan. But it's what you've done that makes it impossible for me to stay with you."

His boots smack on the hardwood floor as he makes his way to me. And I don't move. I don't object. I even lean into him slightly when he sits down next to me. At first he's angled away from me, his elbows on his knees but then he looks at me with a hurt in his eyes that makes me inch closer to him, and he does the same.

I may be angry about what he's done. What I've done as well. But no amount of anger can outweigh the pain we both feel in this moment.

The pain from knowing we're damaged beyond repair.

"Will you ever forgive me?" he questions and then takes a chance, moving his large hand to my thigh and gently rubbing his thumb back and forth.

"I already have," I tell him and feel slightly less strong. Weak for being okay with what's happened. Or at least for accepting it.

"Do you just not love me anymore then?" he asks me, his eyes piercing into mine and holding me captive. His words are raw, coming from a damaged man.

My lungs still and the words hang on the tip of my tongue. They're too afraid to leave me. I'm so weak for him, so bendable and disposable. If I admit such a flaw, he may never give me a fighting chance for something more.

What's worse, I may be content with that.

"Please just tell me you love me," Evan whispers. "I know I fuck up, more than I should. But please don't stop loving me."

"I've never felt so alone." It's one thing to be left alone. It's quite another to choose it. In this moment, I don't want it. I don't want to be alone another day, but I know I have to.

"I don't want to be alone. I don't want to be mad at you," I tell him, wiping from under my eyes and leaning my body into his. He kisses my forehead before enveloping me in his arms. And I let him. My biggest flaw.

"Then don't," he whispers and then pulls away to look down at me, waiting for my eyes to meet his. "Forgive me, please," he says and when I look to him, his dark hazel eyes beg me. His voice is raw and full of nothing but pain and remorse. "For everything. For being so stupid. For putting you through all this shit."

The question is right there, right on the tip of my tongue. I should ask, I should know what he's hiding. But the look in his eyes is so familiar.

"I meant what I said," I tell him. "I need you to leave."

"But you still love me?" he asks me even though it comes out as a statement.

My body heats, my breath stutters and the words get caught in my throat, refusing to come out. I'm on the edge of leaving him, of ruining this man I love so much.

"Yes, I still love you. So much," I admit and the confession is like a weight off my chest, but one that only leaves a gaping, painful hole in its absence.

"I can fix this."

"I need you to leave, Evan," I plead with him weakly.

"Just give me time."

"We're separated, Evan. That's what that means."

"I don't want this. Please, Kat." Evan closes his eyes and buries his face in the crook of my neck. I've never seen him so weak. So desperate for mercy.

I've never wanted to forgive so badly in my life, but it's not forgiveness that I need. It's a different life that I need moving forward and I won't get that with Evan.

"I'm sorry." My lips move but the words aren't audible, and I have to say it again.

His fingers dig into me, holding me closer and tighter, as if the moment he loosens them, I'll leave his grasp forever.

"I'm sorry, but it's what I want," I tell him and I've never heard such a horrible lie in my life. But he nods his head, pulling away slightly although still refusing to let go.

"It's what I deserve," he says beneath his breath. His eyes are glossy and his breathing slower as he looks away from me, still holding on but trying to gather the strength to say something. I don't trust myself to speak. So I just wait, praying for this moment to be over. Praying for something better to come once this has all left me. But how? I have no idea. I've never felt so dead inside.

"One last time. Please, just once more. I love you, Kat. I swear I've never loved anyone like I love you. And maybe it's not enough to keep you, but for tonight?"

Again I don't trust myself to speak. I'm not sure what words would pass through my lips. But I know what I want and I lean forward to take it, spearing my fingers through his hair and pressing my lips to his. It's only when I feel the wetness against our lips that I realize I was crying.

I let him hold me, and I try my best to remember every detail.

The way he smells, masculine like fresh pine and dew.

The way his heart beats just a bit faster than mine as I rest my palm against his hard chest.

I try to remember everything. I pray that I will, because even though he said he can make it right, I know he can't. I know that time will aid in the growing distance between us. I know we're leading two different lives.

I know I need more, and that I deserve someone who won't hide things from me and make me feel like I've lost myself.

So I need to remember this, because I want it to be the last time.

Not for him, not for us, but for me.

# CHAPTER
# twenty-four

## *Evan*

*Don't throw me away, don't tell me you're through.*
*Don't stop loving me, I can't live without you.*
*That ring on your finger, that makes you my wife.*
*You're my everything, my love and my life.*

I DIDN'T MEAN IT WHEN I SAID ONE LAST TIME. It's the same way an addict is desperate for more and will say anything to get it. All I have to do is be next to her when she needs a single thing. Anything. Just one small crack in her armor. At least that's what I keep hoping for.

It's what's keeping me from dissolving into the nothingness I feel in my hollow chest.

I wonder if she'll get over me before that time comes. If the few years we had together was enough to make her love me even when she doesn't want to. That's all I keep thinking about as I stare at her sleeping form. There's only a thin sheet over her gorgeous body, hiding it from me. Her back is toward me as she lies on her side, her hair fanned out along the pillow. I've been awake for hours; I'm not even sure I slept at all.

It feels like it's over, but that can't be true. I can't let her go this easily and walk away. But somehow it doesn't feel like letting her go. It feels like I don't have her anymore. Like I don't even have the option to keep her anymore.

A sudden buzz from my phone vibrating on the nightstand strips my thoughts from me and causes Kat to stir next to me.

I keep my eyes on her as I reach for it. She slowly turns to look over her shoulder and then looks away, pulling the sheet tighter around her. Closing herself off from me.

There's a heaviness on my chest as I let it sink in that she doesn't belong to me anymore. The bed dips as Kat pulls the sheet with her and walks quietly to the bathroom.

I would think my life couldn't get any lower than this, but the text from James mocks that thought.

My hands rake over my face as the phone drops and I inhale deeply, grateful Kat left when she did. There's still so much shit that I need to fix and make right. So much damage I've caused that's leaving cracks under each and every footstep I take.

*Come to the office.*

I stare at the text as Kat flicks on the light switch in the bathroom, the warm yellow hue filtering from under the closed door. She turns on the water as I toss the phone down.

James can go fuck himself.

It's like he knew I'd think that, because the second the phone drops to the nightstand, it goes off again.

*It's not about work. You know what it's about.*

*I was given new information today.*

The texts come one after the other in rapid speed and it makes adrenaline slowly pour into my veins, breathing life into me.

The creak of the bathroom door opening and the light switching off forces me to look up at Kat. She slipped on a robe in the bathroom. It's some sort of black and pink kimono from a bachelorette party I think. I've never seen her wear it but it's been hung up by the towels for years. I guess it's all she could find in there to hide herself from me.

She doesn't return my gaze and I can already see that she regrets last night.

*Our last night.*

I refuse to let it be true. I refuse to give up. But I'll give her time since that's what she thinks she needs.

"You can come whenever you need to," she says and then pulls a shirt over her head as she lets the robe fall into a puddle around her feet. The sight would make my dick hard as steel if it weren't for the words that hit me at full force. "To get whatever you need. I know you can't take everything all at once."

"You really want me to go?" I question even though I know I need to leave regardless of what she tells me. I need time to sort out my shit and get my life to be one that belongs beside hers.

I wish she'd lie to me. I can see it in her eyes, her posture; I can hear it in her voice that she needs me to go. *Tell me a pretty lie, Kat. Make me believe you still want me.*

"I think it's for the best," she answers as her eyes flicker from me to the door and she pushes her hair out of her face. The dark circles under her eyes are evidence of how worn out she is. She's tired of my bullshit.

"I want to be happy and I feel like we're so used to being something else that it's not going to work."

The argument stirs in my chest, but she's right in a way and I know I can prove to her that we're going to be fine. I just need time. "I'll go now, but I'm coming back when I fix things."

"That's what you do, isn't it? You fix things?" A sarcastic, sad laugh accompanies her comment.

Fixer. That's what they call this job, but really I'm supposed to prevent anything from breaking. There's another small huff of a laugh that leaves her, but it's not the joyous sound I've grown to love so much. It's because of me. I'm the one who broke our marriage.

"I know we grew apart, but we're still together. Even if you want to pretend like we're not for a little while," I tell her. Climbing off the bed, I take a step to go to her, but she shakes her head slightly, crossing her arms and taking a step back.

"It was only one last time, Evan."

My mouth falls open just slightly for me to tell her last night wasn't the last time. I won't let it be. But the words don't come out. There's no conviction in that thought.

My eyes close as the phone in my hand buzzes again and I don't miss how Kat looks at it, a question in her eyes.

"It's James." I answer her unspoken question

She chews the inside of her cheek and doesn't acknowledge me in the least.

"I quit and I've just got to sign some paperwork." The

lie slips out so easily. I'm almost ashamed at how easy it's become to hide the truth from her and disguise it as something normal and relatable.

I don't know if she can tell I'm lying, or if she just doesn't care anymore. She leaves me alone with nothing but a small nod in the bedroom we built together.

My blood turns cold and I stare at the open door. The pictures from the hall taunt me. I still hear the laughter. I remember the softness of her skin when they were taken.

The phone goes off again and it pisses me off.

I grit my teeth as I read the messages.

*Get here in the next hour.*

Out of spite, there's no fucking way I'll be at his office by then. I make sure to hit the message so he knows I read it. He can wait.

# CHAPTER
## twenty-five

### *Kat*

I t's supposed to hurt this much. I remind myself of that over and over again.

That's what a breakup is. It's pain. It's removing someone you once loved from your life. Erasing them as if they don't exist. As if they've died. And that's the most painful thing one can experience.

That's why it hurts so much. Because I'm supposed to be in agony.

"You look tired," I hear Jules say before she rests her hand on my shoulder, bringing me back into the moment. Standing in my small kitchen, with its clutter and a pile of dirty dishes in the sink, she's so out of place here. "Are you all right?" she asks me softly.

Before I can answer, the sounds of Maddie and Sue

laughing over something drift into the room. The wine has been flowing, and half of the only remaining box of pizza is left on the counter. It's what I said I came in here for, another slice, but really I'd just remembered my time with Evan last night and then this morning and I wanted to be alone for a minute.

"You can tell me anything, Kat," Jules says in a voice drenched with empathy. I've always loved the person she is. But never more than now.

"I don't think I'm all right and I don't know if I ever will be," I answer and then arch my neck to stare at the ceiling, keeping my eyes open and trying not to bring this night down any more than I have.

"Is it normal to cry so much?" I ask her. "To be this emotional and this exhausted?"

"When you lose someone you love, yes." She answers easily and calmly, sending a wave of calm through my body, but even that makes me feel that much more exhausted.

"I wish I was past this stage."

"It'll happen before you know it. One day, the reminders won't hurt so badly. The mention of his name won't cut you to shreds. One day it'll feel like it's supposed to be this way."

"But I don't know if it is," I confess to her and then Sue ambles in from the dining room.

Her wineglass clinks on the counter as she sets it down and then she catches a glimpse of me, her expression morphing to one of sympathy. An expression I learned to hate growing up, but right now, while I'm weak and feeling so lost, it's an expression that makes me lean into her when she opens her arms.

"You're all right, babe," she says softly and wraps her arms around me. Sue's arms are filled with warmth and she kisses my cheek too. "It's all right babe, we're here for you."

"Aww," I hear Maddie coo as she makes her way into the room.

"Let it all out," Sue says but I shake my head, my hair ruffling on her shoulder as I sniffle. Sue smells like wine. She sways a little and squeezes me tight. She's definitely more than tipsy.

"I'm sorry, guys. It wasn't supposed to turn into this." I push out the apology, wishing we were having the fun night I promised as I stand up straight and pull my shit together. Sue tries to hold on to me a little longer, but I push her away. I can handle this. At one point in my life I was so good at being alone.

"I'm fine," I tell them, stepping away for a moment and shaking out my hands. "I'm sorry."

It takes a few deep breaths and Sue refilling the empty glasses of wine on the counter for me to get over whatever this breakdown was.

"Don't be sorry. It's a sad time no matter how much you don't want it to be." Maddie's the first to say something and Jules nods.

"It's going to be okay, though," Jules says and then Sue chimes in with, "You've got us, babe. We'll always be here for you, and that's all you need."

"Well, maybe a vibrator too," Sue adds a moment later and a genuine laugh erupts from my lips. It's short and un-expected, and fills the room. But it felt so good to laugh. To smile. To feel anything other than this darkness that's been a constant shadow over me.

"Do you want another?" Sue asks me, nearly spilling the wine from a glass poured too full as she tries to hand it to me. I haven't had a drink all night.

"If I do, I'm going to pass out." Just as I answer, another yawn hits me. "It's been a while since I've been able to sleep through the night."

"I'll take it," Maddie offers and immediately sets it back down on the counter.

"So it's really over?" Sue asks and then takes a sip. For the first time, I see something in her eyes I haven't before. I see sorrow. Genuine pain. As if even Sue was rooting for us. Sue, the valiant heroine against men who cheat and lie.

I nod, ignoring how the emotions swell up again. I haven't told them that he cheated on me back when we first started dating. I can't admit it. I don't want to say the words out loud and make them real. I don't want them to see him as a villain. I love him too much to paint him in that light. Or maybe it's the shame that I still love him even after knowing what he did.

"We're just in two different places and it's better to be apart." I shrug and add, "But we always were, you know? Like this shouldn't be too shocking."

"He doesn't want to change?" Maddie asks. There's always hope in Maddie and I wish I could hold on to that.

"Men don't change," Sue says woefully. "I'm sorry. I'm doing it again," she says, shaking her head. "Sometimes it still hurts, you know? And I don't want you to go through what I did. I promise you, it's the last thing I want for you." Her voice gets a little tight, but she shakes it off quickly.

I love Sue, and I remember how hard her divorce was on her. But I swear this is different. *It has to be.* Her ex was vile and brutal. Evan isn't any of that. He'd never hurt me intentionally. He's just ... he's just Evan.

"He said he wants to fix it," I answer as I watch Maddie sip from the glass without picking it up. Instead she crouches down, bringing her lips to the rim to sip. My lips tug into an asymmetrical smile for just a moment at the sight.

"It's not what he says." The hardness in her voice is absent, but there's still a finality in Sue's statement. "It would be hard for him to change, wouldn't it? He's been this way for years."

It's meant to be a rhetorical question, but the answer rings clear in my head. He did something bad. Something that he needed an alibi for. That's enough of a reason to change everything at once.

I stare at the dark red liquid. Sue's voice turns to white noise as she tells a story about something that makes the other girls laugh and I laugh too, when they do. I don't know if it's the first time he's needed an alibi. Or the second or the third. But it's the first time he changed. I knew something was off before the article. Before he told me anything. Before the lies.

I knew something was different.

And I didn't even bother to ask him what he'd done.

# CHAPTER
## twenty-six

### Evan

THERE'S A SLOW PRICK OF IRRITATION CRAWLING down my spine as I sit in the chair across from James. Every limb feels the need to move, like a spider is climbing its way down my back. My fingers dig into the hard wood of the armrests as I stay perfectly still, staring down my former boss. Former friend. Now enemy.

"You aren't the best at listening," he says from across the room as he closes a drawer. The city lights creep in through the window behind him, casting shadows over the large desk.

"I don't follow orders," I grit out from between clenched teeth. My words come out menacing, but I don't mean for them to. One more meeting, and this is over. I'm done with him. He's yet to get that message or to tell me what the hell is going on.

James leans forward, clasping his hands together and his perfectly tailored suit wrinkles beneath his arms, making the fabric look cheap. He's always looked just a bit cheap. Regardless of the brand or how expensive his tastes are. Some assholes will always look like a knockoff.

He taps his fingers on the desk, but my eyes don't leave his. "The reason I called you in here is simple, Evan. The new client we have likes to live on the reckless side, and I'm concerned about drug abuse."

A gruff exhale leaves me from deep down in my chest. "I quit." I ignore the fact that he's hinting around what happened with Tony. My skin tingles and that feeling of a spider crawling on me comes back. I can't help but think he's recording this conversation. Everything in my gut has been telling me there's a setup and that I'm going to take the fall for what happened.

It was my fault, so I should be taking the blame regardless. On my terms, not this prick's and he's responsible for the way it went down. Some of the blame rests on his shoulders.

"I know what you said, but I assumed you'd come to your senses," he says, waving off my curt response. "Like I said, the new client has been known to behave a bit recklessly and I just want to make sure the policy we had in place remains the same."

*The policy.* I smirk at him, my grip on the arms getting tighter although my fingers are all that move.

The policy where the clients get what they want, but we don't say it out loud to anyone. The one where we're given clean stashes of the best drugs in the rec rooms. That's the policy. Instead of clarifying the policy, I answer, "After what happened with Tony I would think it's more than clear that we should advise our clients against anything too reckless."

James's eyes narrow. He knows I know that he's recording this. I'm not a fool. The only question I have is why. Why record it? More blackmail? Or evidence? What's he after?

I stare him in the eyes as I ask, "What is it you really want? You know you've provided drugs to clients before." I cock my head to the side as I ask, "Are we changing the policy?"

"I've never given anyone anything illegal," he states and I notice how he stiffens slightly but still tries to act casual as he shrugs and adds, "There's no change to the policy."

My wife has this thing she does. It's a smile I hate. A smirk really. I hate it when she gives it to me. It's one that tells me she knows I'm full of shit. While I sit here, staring at this asshole, I can feel the corner of my lips tug up into that sarcastic smirk. It doesn't stay there for long, though.

"Did you know the coke was laced?" James asks me and it takes a moment for the question to register.

The coke I gave Tony.

That doesn't make sense. Our shit is clean and pure and the best there is.

It's also provided to us in the recreation room by the company.

"I wouldn't know a thing about that." It's the only answer I can force out. Keeping a hard stare on my face even as my blood heats hotter and hotter.

Is he serious? It was laced?

I know the laws in and out. I can't admit to any knowledge that could lead back to me. I can accuse him, but not admit to participation or any foresight of drugs being gifted so freely when asked.

I raise my hand as if I'm the one in the wrong. The one who misspoke. "None of it matters anyway. I told you, I quit."

"And I told you, that you—"

"I'm done," I say and my words come out hard as I stand up and tower over the desk. James is quick to get up, tugging at one sleeve and then the other on his suit. "I thought you had something to tell me. Something useful and not some delusion that you could use to blackmail me."

His eyes glint with a darkness at my words. "It's not blackmail. I haven't—"

"Fuck you, James," I say, cutting him off as I turn my back to him to stalk out of the room. It'll be the last time I come here.

"You know what I can do to you," James says the threat to my back.

"I'm calling your bluff," I respond out of anger and instantly regret it, but I don't stop. All the weeks of not knowing if him or Samantha would tell the cops what happened, all the guilt and denial rise up in my chest and cause the next words come out without my consent. "Tell them what happened."

Just the thought of the truth getting out lifts a weight off of me.

"Tell them I gave him the coke. Tell them I set him up to get high and came back to him dead. Tell the press. Tell everyone," I say and my heart beats faster and faster as my hands ball into white-knuckled fists. I realize what I've just done. I realize I've said it out loud. But I don't care. It doesn't change anything. None of it matters anymore.

"It's murder, Evan, and you know it," James says as I face the door to leave. Not bothering to acknowledge him in the least.

Yes, it's murder. And it's not the first time something's happened under my watch. But it's the last. I'm done with this shit and this life.

I didn't lace a damn thing. If that stash was messed with, it wasn't me and I'm not going down for a crime I didn't commit. I'll own up to everything else.

I want to pay for my sins and chase what truly matters to me.

A love I took for granted. A love I don't know if I can salvage.

# CHAPTER
## twenty-seven

### Kat

*Pulled in every direction,*
*Too dizzy to stay still.*
*My feet stumble beneath me,*
*My body frozen from the chill.*
*No more of being numb and weak,*
*No more of waiting, left in vain.*
*I've had enough of lies,*
*I've had enough of pain.*

THE BUZZ FROM THE TOWNHOUSE SPEAKER ROUSES me from my seat in the dining room. Buzz. Buzz. It's an annoying high-pitched sound that I can't stand. My head's already throbbing. It's been like this for hours, ever since I got home and took the test. I can't go back and look at it. It's hard enough to wrap my head around everything that's happening.

And the guilt ...

As I walk to the front of the townhouse, hustling down the stairs so I don't have to hear that damn noise again, I realize it's nearly nine and I'm still in my pajamas. At least I have pants on, but the matching light gray cotton shirt has a large spot of coffee on the front and I'm sure my hair's a mess.

"Who is it?" I ask in a voice that sounds more together than I feel as I push the button down and then release it. The only person I can think of is Henry, Evan's father.

"Sorry to bother you, I was just hoping for a quick meeting," a voice says on the other side and it takes me a moment to recognize it.

"Jacob?" I say into the intercom.

"I hope you don't mind. I was in the area and wanted to stop by," he replies and his voice breaks up over the speaker.

I know it's rude to make him wait, it's unkind not to answer him immediately, but this is so unexpected. I don't know how to react or respond.

"I'm not quite dressed for company," I tell him and then close my eyes from embarrassment. He still hasn't signed with the agency and I haven't spoken to him since running into him on the street.

"That's all right with me," he answers easily and I lean into the button, keeping it held down as my head throbs again and my eyes close with frustration.

"Is it all right if I come up?"

"Of course," I answer out of instinct. "Come on up," I tell him and then hit the buzzer to let him up. My heart races as I consider why he's here. I know why, deep down. It's my fault. I led him on.

A sarcastic laugh leaves me as I throw my head back and wipe my tired eyes with my hands. How self-centered and presumptuous I am to think he's here for anything other than business. I ignore the guilt and the worry that riddle my body and glance in the large oval mirror in the foyer as I wait for Jacob to make his way up the stairs.

There are bags under my eyes and a smattering of eyeliner from yesterday still remaining. I wipe carefully under them and pull my hair back, but I still don't look professional. My simple black leggings and a baggy shirt are made somewhat better by slipping on a crocheted sweater. It's better than nothing, laid back at the very best. I find it hard to care that much about my appearance as I open the front door.

I'm caught off guard as he walks up the stairs and comes into view. Of course I look like hell when he looks charming in a relaxed kind of way. His hair is ruffled, but probably gelled to look like it's slightly messy. It's his stubble, though, that gets me. I have a type, and Jacob fits that type to a T. Maybe that's how I know this is going to be trouble.

He gives me a wide smile and doesn't seem to care about my appearance in the least.

"I was just going to call it an early night," I lie, trying to stand with dignity in front of Jacob.

"Oh shit, I'm sorry, Kat." It's odd hearing him call me Kat. Most of my clients don't use my nickname. It's too casual. A type of casual I usually put an end to immediately, but I can't bring myself to correct him.

"What are you doing here, Jacob?" I ask warily. We don't

have an appointment, and quite frankly I'm not in a state to be professional.

"It's Jake, remember?" he answers playfully and God help me, but I blush. "I was wondering if I could maybe take you out for coffee? I was hoping for dinner. If not tonight, then …"

"I'm sorry, I don't think that's something," I stammer over my words. "Jacob …" I clear my throat and continue, "Jake, I hope I didn't give you the wrong impression." I suck in a breath and push the stray hairs out of my face.

"It's nothing at all that you did, I just," he pauses to take a deep breath and smiles before letting out a small laugh. "It was stupid of me. I'm sorry, Kat. I just thought maybe there was a little attraction on your side?" he asks although it's a statement.

"Jake, I'm …" I want to say married, taken, in love with another man. The last line would be true. I'll always love Evan, and nothing will ever change that.

"I thought maybe you would like some company," he states, tilting his head as he leans against the wall. The muscles on his shoulders ripple as he does it. "I went through something a bit ago and I know I could use a distraction."

*A distraction would be nice.* I can't help that the thought makes me more relaxed each second that passes.

His half smile and gentle sigh are what do me in as he shrugs and slips his hands into his pockets. "I thought maybe you needed someone. Or that you'd like the company." He's even more handsome when he looks at me like that. It's a look that makes me feel warmth running through me. Compassion and understanding.

I've never been so tempted in my life. I so desperately

need someone. I need someone to pick me up and force me to think about something else, because I'm a hopeless wreck.

"It's very sweet of you and I won't lie," I start to say and then hesitate to finish the thought, but settle on the basic truth. "I wouldn't act on anything because I just can't right now. I would never forgive myself and it wouldn't be fair to you." My words are rushed at the end, trying to defend my decision and assuage me of the guilt I'm feeling.

"Hey," Jacob says with an easy tone that breaks through the anxiety washing over me. His reassuring voice forces me to look into his gentle gaze. It's comforting and relaxing and makes me not trust myself. "How about this? How about you call me if you think you want to hang out or talk, or whatever it is that's on your mind?" he asks in a soothing tone that's almost melodic. It calms me, each word a consoling balm to the hurt that rages through my body.

*I want that.* More than anything, I want this pain that I feel to stop. I would give anything to make it go away. Jacob could do that, but it would be short-lived. I blink away the haze of lust, the cloud of want and desire leaving me slowly, very slowly. I clear my throat and look him in the eyes as I tell him, "I can't."

"'Cause we're going to work together?" he asks, although the way he tilts his head and strains his words makes it more than obvious that he knows why I can't. My lips form a thin straight line as I shake my head no.

"You love him?"

"I do, but that's not why. I'm just—I'm not okay and I need to figure things out …" I can't finish the thought, but thankfully I don't have to.

"I understand," Jacob says and runs his hand through his thick hair. My eyes are caught in his as I nod in thanks.

"Let's pretend this didn't happen then?"

"I'd rather you remember," he says with a grin that makes me crave him more. "I'll be here when you're ready," he says and then turns to leave. To walk away from me and leave me alone in my misery, just as I asked.

For a second I want to reach out and stop him from leaving; I don't want to go back to what's waiting for me. I don't want to face what I have to do.

But my fingers grip the edge of the foyer doorway as Jacob turns away and heads to the front door.

"I'll talk to you later then?"

I should say no. I should cut off whatever this is. It's dangerous and I can feel myself heading toward an edge where I won't be able to balance. I can see myself falling. And that's why I give him a small smile and nod my head. "Later," I say, the word slipping from my lips like a sin.

# CHAPTER
## twenty-eight

*Evan*

THE RADIO IN THE CAR IS SILENCED AS I TURN OFF the ignition. It's not often I get a parking spot so close to the townhouse. It was a sacrifice we made when we bought the place a few years ago.

My head falls back against the leather headrest and I stare up at the building, at the top two floors on the right side, knowing that Kat's in there. So close, but so damn far away just the same.

My phone pings just as I open the door to get out and drag my sorry ass up to tell her everything. To lay it all out there, beg for her forgiveness, her understanding. But most importantly for her to stay with me. I'll give her space and time. I'll give her everything she asks. All I need is a deadline or something to work toward. I need her.

If she can still love me, after all I put her through and everything ahead of us, then we can get through anything.

I expect it to be Kat who messaged, but it's not her that texted me. It's Samantha.

*I heard you quit.*

*News travels fast,* I respond quickly and then debate on how to tell her I won't be responding anymore to her. It's not fair to my wife and now that I've left the company, there's no reason to have any type of relationship with her.

*What about what happened?*

I stare at the text on my phone as the lights in my car dim, signaling me to leave. She follows up the question with another that makes my stomach churn. *He knows about what happened and you know he won't let it go. He'll hang this over your head until he gets what he wants.*

My brow knits as I read the message. I don't give a shit what he knows or what he wants. For a moment, I think maybe she's messaging the wrong person. I settle on my response.

*I have nothing to give him.*

*He knows about us, Evan.*

I stare at the text message, letting it sink in.

*You told him?* I ask her, my gaze shifting from the phone to the lit townhouse building off the busy city street. The lights are on in her office and the living room. So close. She's so close.

My phone vibrates in my hand and I look back down to see her response. *He's known for years.*

My hand clenches tight as I realize he's been playing me. He's never let on that he knew I fucked his wife.

My first instinct is to blame Sam. *You didn't tell me you told him*, I text and then hate myself for it. I didn't know she was married; we were both high and I wanted any excuse to end things with Kat.

*I didn't think he cared.*

*It was years ago. So now what?* I swallow the ball of heat rising in my throat. It doesn't change anything. If he wants to be pissed, he can be pissed.

*I don't see him letting this go. Not when he can get back at you. You need to be careful.*

A frustrated groan travels up my throat.

*Fuck him. He can do what he wants, but I'm not his bitch.*

My phone immediately vibrates as I slip it into my pocket, and I cuss as I take it back out. Not to read her response, only to shut it off, silencing it and ignoring all the problems that wait for me. I'm done with both of them. I'm done with it all.

I swallow thickly and step out into the cool night, the city traffic surrounding me as I shut the car door and leave it all behind.

Everything is crumbling around me, but the only thing I care about is losing Kat. I don't see how I can hold on to her when I don't have a plan and I've lost control.

She needs a better man, and I swear I can be one. We'll start over and do it right this time.

I run my hand down my face. Hitting the lock, the car beeps and the bright headlights flash in the dark of the night. The sounds of the city streets are loud as I walk up the sidewalk, past men and women who carry on with their busy lives and don't have a clue how mine is being ripped apart.

I'll confess and then pack a box, and let her know it's only a separation and that even after I'll still love her and want her. That I'll do anything. I'll keep coming back, fighting for her. I'm not saying goodbye, I'm only doing what she asks because I love her and I know she needs time.

The keys jingle in my hand as I make my way home. Every second I'm trying to think of the best way to come clean about everything to Kat. She deserves to know, even if she hates me once she finds out. I have to tell her first.

A heavy breath leaves me as I turn the lock and walk into the building, running a hand over my hair and trying to block the image of her disappointment from my mind.

I can imagine how her deep green eyes will widen, how her lips will part and how she'll think I'm lying at first. I already know how she'll look at me, how she'll question who I am and why or if, she loves me.

My footsteps are heavy as I grip the iron railing and head to the top of the stairwell, to our home we've built together, the one she's kicked me out of. My gut feels heavy, churning with a sickness that rises to my chest as I hear her voice and recall the memory of her telling me to get out. My fingers wrap tighter around the rail, keeping me upright as I force myself to continue. I need to confess and come clean.

I want Kat back and the life we once had. It's all I need to live.

Every thought is lost at the sight in front of me. My blood turns ice cold when I stop at the top of the stairs where Kat's talking to that asshole from the café. Her voice is kind and nurturing and the way she offers him a sad smile … fuck no.

My legs feel like they're trembling; my body's shaking

from the sight of him. Jacob, the supposed client Kat said was no one. *No one.* Yet he stands only feet away from the front door.

Anger rises quickly as I watch them. I knew there was something between them. I could tell. I know my wife and I know men like this prick.

"You motherfucker," I sneer the words without thinking twice. The door to my townhouse is still cracked when this dumb fuck looks up at me.

"What are you doing?" Kat calls out with shock as she stands in the doorway.

# CHAPTER
## twenty-nine

### Kat

I'd recognize Evan's voice anywhere, but the anger is terrifyingly new. The second I grip the cold handle and open the door, my body freezes and the shock makes my mouth hang open and my eyes go wide. My heart beats in what feels like slow motion.

"Stop it!" I scream at him. My words echo in my head as he slams his fist against Jacob's jaw. It's instantly red and swollen and Evan's already got his other fist up.

Holy shit!

"Evan!" I scream as I run out of the foyer and into the hallway. "Stop it!" I yell and grip onto his arm. I slam both of my hands into Evan's chest, managing to separate the two men as Jacob grabs his jaw.

"You fucked my wife," Evan yells over me, screaming at

Jacob and this time I want to smack Evan straight across his face. I don't. I don't give him any reaction except to turn toward Jacob to apologize.

"I'm so sorry," I offer Jacob who keeps a surprised smile on his face, as if it didn't bother him in the least.

"You fucked—"

"Stop it!" I scream again, and this time my voice feels raw and it pains me to scream. My body's hot and shaking, adrenaline coursing through my blood as my heart races.

"Get out of here," I say as I usher Jacob away. His green eyes flash with something, perhaps disbelief.

"You're cheating on me," Evan says it as if it's a question, his nostrils flaring and his hands still clenched into fists.

"You're an idiot," I say, keeping my voice low, apologizing again to Jacob and feeling the heat of embarrassment.

"It was a sucker punch," Jake says loud enough for Evan to hear. "And no, I didn't sleep with Kat." He looks Evan dead in the eye with the last line.

Embarrassment and horror wrap themselves tight around me as Jake leaves.

With my throat tight and arms crossed, I face Evan and say, "I'm not the one keeping secrets, you fucking asshole. He's a client and nothing more." My gaze almost shifts away from him. I know there was something, a chemistry that kindled between Jacob and me. A tension that I wanted to push. But it's only because I was hurting, and I never submitted to the temptation. I couldn't hurt Evan like that. I never would.

"What is wrong with you?" My question is dripping

with nothing but disdain. For a moment I think of all the questions on the tip of my tongue, asking him why he's doing it and when he turned into this man. But this is the man I married. I'm the one who's changed. Not him.

Evan takes a step forward and his hand raises to my shoulder. I smack him away, barely feeling his hot skin against mine. "Don't touch me," I yell at him. My hand stings from the impact and I can't stand it.

I can't stand what we've become.

Evan's shoulders rise and fall steadily.

"Kat," he says and his voice cracks, like my name strangles him as he whispers it again. He takes a hesitant step forward, raising his arms and the blood from his torn knuckles is all I can see.

"What were you thinking?" I can barely ask him. Evan's expression falls and he looks past me. It's only then that I turn and see that Jake is gone. "What's wrong with you?"

"What was he doing here?"

"I've never cheated on you, and I wouldn't. Ever. Evan, I can't deal with this. The partying and what you're doing. Punching people for no damn good reason!"

"I quit, Kat. And you sure as hell know what it looked like. If he didn't fuck you, he wanted to."

"What the hell are you doing here?"

"I came to tell you everything," he says and his admission changes the tension in an instant. The evening is seemingly colder in the blink of an eye.

"I might … I might have some things happen." He closes his eyes and moves his hands to his hair. Hands with split knuckles and traces of blood.

Was he always like this? I want to hold and comfort him. But it's no use.

"I was stupid."

"Evan, you've had years to be stupid. Years of me begging you to grow up." Every word hurts more and more. I know I'm not going to give him what he needs. I can't anymore.

"I wanted you to be my partner." I whisper the words, my voice laced with disappointment.

"I thought that's what we were."

"I need someone who's ready for the next stage of life." I barely get the words out as my throat dries and closes, threatening to suffocate me. But I finish the thought, making my heart split into two as I look deep into Evan's eyes and tell him, "Or no one at all."

"Kat," Evan says, whispering my name as if it's a threat. One against him. Or maybe it's a plea. "I'm sorry, okay?"

My head shakes and the words won't come out.

"I'm sorry I hit him, it looked bad at first. It looked like something else to me, but even then I shouldn't have hit him."

"No, you shouldn't have."

"It was shitty of me. I'm sorry. I'm so sorry," he says and I believe him. But it's not enough. He's still the same Evan.

I wipe the tears from my eyes with the back of my hand as I shake my head. "I can't do this anymore." It's the truth and even though it's the worst pain that I've felt in my entire life, I know it needs to be done. "I will be better on my own."

"Don't say that," Evan pleads, but he stands there not

moving, his hands by his sides and his body stiff with disbelief. Or maybe fear. "I can't lose you," he says. I feel like my heart is breaking, but I shake my head.

"Maybe I should just be alone." My eyes burn with more tears as I shake my head again and say, "No, I need to. I need to be alone. I'm sorry," my voice fails me as I whisper the apology. I hate hurting him; I can't stand the pain in his eyes and expression. He doesn't try to hide it in the least, and it shreds me.

But we're just not meant for each other, not with the lives we're leading.

"I love you."

"Love isn't enough!" I yell and hate myself. I truly do. "It's not enough anymore," I say, steadying my voice although it's still low. I cross my arms and try to keep myself together, I try to hold my body upright although it begs me to collapse.

"Is that what you want?"

"I want a divorce," I say the lie in a single breath. The words all come out at once, bunched together and needing to be said, to be heard. To be felt to the very core of who Evan is.

My fingertips dig into my forearms as I slowly raise my eyes to his and the conviction wavers.

He doesn't speak, although his lips part once and then again. He licks them as his brow furrows and he visibly swallows then looks past me at the empty wall. Again he starts to say something but stops, clasping and unclasping his hands and trying to find some way to tell me what he's thinking.

The worst part is that I want him to say something. I need him to give me something to hold on to him.

I'd go mad waiting to hear him tell me he'll make this right. For him I'd fall again, I know I would. There isn't enough strength in my body to keep me from Evan.

But he doesn't say a word; he never does when I need him to.

It takes a long moment. Each second my heart beats, the steady sound is all I can hear. And then he turns his back to me and walks away without saying another word.

My body is freezing as I slowly turn from the hall and head toward our door. I can't breathe, but somehow I am. I can't manage a thought, but my mind is whirling with the image of what just happened.

The way he spoke my name like he needed me. The way his voice was laced with desperation and his eyes shined with determination, but then failure. The way his expression crumbled when he realized he lost me.

I don't stop walking until I get back to our bedroom, barely glancing at the unmade bed and remembering the last time we shared it and everything about that night. I can still feel his lips on my neck, his hands traveling ever so slowly down my body as he whispered how much he loves me. And I believe the sentiment. No one has ever loved me like Evan, and no one else ever will.

It's just not enough.

For me, I'd go back to him. I'd let him do what he wanted and I'd pay the price. I head into the bathroom.

I pick up the small plastic stick still hanging off the edge of the sink.

My head's been a mess the past month. I didn't realize I'd missed one period, let alone two.

It's the brightest set of pink lines. I may not be the best friend I can be, or the best wife for that matter. But for my child, I'll be the best mother I can be and that starts with saying no to the life I once lived and had with Evan.

My hand splays on my lower belly as I lean my back against the edge of the sink. I have to tell him and I will, but not yet. I need to stop loving him first. I need to move on and focus on what I can change and make better for what's to come.

It's not just me who deserves that anymore.

# CHAPTER
## thirty

*Evan*

*I promise to love you forever. And that's the easy part.*
*To honor and cherish you.*
*To keep your wishes and dreams my own.*
*To comfort you and keep you safe, always.*
*Till death do us part.*

**M**Y WEDDING VOWS HAUNT ME. THE PARTS OF them I can remember, at least. I can't stop seeing the look of complete devotion on Kat's face on our wedding day, as I read my vows from the scrap of paper where I'd written them.

My heart raced as I spoke each word, my gaze straying from the paper to look back at her. She was so beautiful, with a love that I knew I didn't deserve.

I can still remember the feel of her soft skin as I cupped her cheek in my hand. I can still smell the sweet fragrance that drifted toward me as I leaned closer to her, all of our friends and family clapping and cheering as I took my first kiss from my wife.

I can still taste her lips on mine.

When I said those words, I meant them. I thought they'd be so easy to keep, to be honest, and it never occurred to me that I'd forget.

A large metal door opens at the end of the hall and I look up, my view obstructed by steel bars of the jail cell.

It's been a long damn time since I've been locked up. Years. Almost a dozen years, to be exact. I knew I'd be back soon, though.

It was only a matter of time before they brought me in for questioning. Samantha tried to warn me but it was too late. Soon after I left the townhouse the cops picked me up and brought me in. I sit hunched over, resting my forearms on my thighs as I wait for the attending officer to come get me. With the footsteps echoing down the small corridor, my gaze raises in anticipation, only to drop again to the cement floor. He walks right past me without a glance in my direction and I drop my head, focusing on the cracks in the concrete and recalling every detail of the night that put me here.

My hands sweat as I twist my wedding band around my finger. I can't think about Kat right now or what she'd say. I haven't told her a damn thing about this and we're in the same place we were when I last left.

The worst part about all of this is that I don't have a

way out yet. I'm falling into a dark hole, not knowing how I can escape, or if it will ever end. Never in my life has a situation seemed so dire and I'm more than aware that I miss her presence the most. It would make all this hell seem insignificant if only I knew she still loved me.

Someone coughs and I slowly turn my head to the left where it came from a few cells down, but I can't see a damn thing but bars and concrete. I think there's only one other person in holding with me. And he's on the same side so the rest of the cells are empty. I guess Tuesdays are slow days for the station.

My foot tap, tap, taps on the ground as I wait. The cops haven't given me any information to go on yet. Other than the word *murder*. My best guess is that they think I gave Tony the coke and knew it was laced with something deadly.

Even if I didn't know it was tainted, I'd still be held accountable. At least here in the state of New York, I am. If it was deliberately tampered with, though ... then someone *wanted* him dead. Although the only two people who knew it was even there were me and James.

My shoulders rise with a heavy breath as the anger gets the best of me. Rage seeps into my blood just thinking his name. The image of him flickers in front of me the second I close my eyes. He smiled as he patted my back, walking out of the room after making sure it'd be ready for our client, Tony.

He's the one who put it there. The only question I have on my mind is whether he's the one who laced it. I can't imagine he did. He wouldn't be that stupid, but I'm not taking the fall for murder. Not to save his skeevy ass. I'm not a rat, but if James plays his cards against me—the proof that I was with Tony before he died, then I'm taking that fucker down.

"Thompson," the cop's voice bellows and echoes off the walls of the small cell.

"That's me," I answer, looking the detective square in his light blue eyes. I don't recognize him as he puts the key in the lock and opens the door wide for me to get out and walk to the interrogation room. Adrenaline pumps hard in my blood. It seems more intense now than it did years ago.

Maybe it's because I don't know how I'll get out of this. I have an alibi, but if James showed them the pictures proving I was with Tony that night, then I'm fucked.

I have to wonder if he would, though. If that's the case, he was deliberately withholding evidence and they'd have to question his intentions and his involvement, as well as the fact that he lied during the first questioning. He could do it anonymously, though, and knowing his character, he'd sure as hell take that route.

My boots smack against the floor and I walk at an easy pace, making sure I don't do anything to piss off the cop. He's a short guy. Probably in his thirties, I guess. Lots of wrinkles around his eyes, though. Maybe from the stress of the job, maybe from the sun.

"After you," he says with a grim look pulling his lips into a thin line as he opens the door. I give him a nod and walk in; he doesn't follow.

I only hesitate to sit down for a moment. There are two men in the room already. A tall cop with broad shoulders and a thin mustache that I want to shave off and Jay McCann, the lawyer from James's PR firm.

"You're fired," I tell Jay the second I sit down. I don't even look at the slick lawyer. He's represented me and plenty of other clients before, but I know he'd break attorney-client privilege and tell James everything. I don't trust him.

"Are you sure?" the cop questions, not hiding his surprise in the least and glancing between the two of us as McCann stumbles over a response. Jay is obviously shocked and I don't blame him.

"Evan," Jay starts, his voice strong although he instinctively reaches to loosen the knot of the dark navy tie that matches his suit, "I highly suggest we talk about this before you—"

"Yes, I'm sure. Sorry, Jay." I turn to face him and wait for a response, but he stands up and straightens his jacket. His clean-shaven jaw clenches as he grabs his briefcase and I can see he wants to say something, but he holds it in.

Probably a good call on his part.

I watch him walk around the table and exit without another word, leaving me alone with the cop.

"I'm Detective Bradshaw, Mr. Thompson."

"I would say it's nice to meet you, but ..." I reply with a smirk and tilt my hands out with my palms up. Detective Bradshaw doesn't laugh or respond to my little joke and that's fine. They never do in here where it's recorded. I know how this works.

"Have you been informed of your rights?"

"I have," I answer him.

"And do you know what you're being charged with?"

"Charged?" I say and although I keep my voice even, my back stiffens slightly as my muscles tense. "I wasn't informed I was being charged with anything." That statement comes out far too casually for the adrenaline racing through me.

"Well, I imagine there's no refuting the charge on your part. You supplied Tony Lewis with the cocaine he overdosed on."

"You want me to admit to handing over the cocaine to him, so you have someone behind bars to take the fall for a hotshot's death?" I ask him sarcastically, seamlessly hiding how my nerves want to crack and how my blood pounds in my ears. I let out an uneasy huff of a laugh and shake my head. Leaning back in my seat, I look him in the eyes with a smile as I say, "That's not happening, Detective."

"Well, someone is going to go down for murder, yes." He sucks his teeth as he stands up and crosses his arms over his chest. "You'd only be sentenced for your part and we're willing to cut you a deal. Whoever laced it with fentanyl intended for it to kill. There's no doubt in the DA's mind that it's murder, Mr. Thompson. I'd take the deal if I were you."

He waits for a reaction, but I use every ounce of energy in me to not give him anything. I won't say a word. Inside, I'm denying it. No fucking way. There's no way James would give a client something that would kill him. They're wrong. If it wasn't James ... then who?

"We know it's someone within the firm. It's not the first time one of New York Stride Public Relation's clients have turned up dead." He leans back and adds, "As I'm sure you're aware."

As he talks, he half pushes, half tosses the manila folder that was sitting on his end of the table my way. It lands with a heavy thud in front of me and I open it, feigning disinterest.

"Nothing points to that person being you, but this was intentional. Someone wanted whoever was going to be taking this coke to die. It was laced with enough fentanyl to kill instantly."

I don't say anything as he pauses, opening the manila folder when I don't and pulling out a page with charts and shit I don't know anything about. He points his finger to a graph, then taps it far too hard, turning his knuckles white. "Whoever did it wanted even the smallest dose to kill."

Silence. All I do is stare at the man and then force my gaze back down, to the photos of Tony, dead on the floor of that hotel room.

"If you have any information on how we'd go about finding the killer, that'd be useful, and we'd certainly be grateful for that."

I have to calmly exhale a few times, keeping as still as possible and making sure my expression doesn't change in the least before I can respond. "I really liked Tony and it's a shame what happened to him. It's extremely upsetting to think someone murdered him."

"It is, especially since he didn't have any enemies we can find," the cop answers, his voice tighter now and then he leans forward.

"You know, if we can't find who did it, you'll be taking the full brunt of things."

I let a sarcastic laugh rock my shoulders and then look toward the door to my left. The one that leads to my freedom. "I'm sorry, Detective, everyone I know loved Tony and I didn't give him any drugs." I lean forward, mimicking his posture as I add, "It's illegal."

"If that's the way you want to play it." His jaw is tense as he reaches for the folder and I lean back in my seat again and only watch as he collects the papers.

"Am I free to go now? I'd like to leave."

He stands up abruptly, pushing the chair back a few inches, making the steel chair legs scrape noisily across the floor. "I don't think so. Maybe a night in the cells will help you remember something."

Fucking prick. Not that I'm surprised. It's a game of chess and his side has more pieces and a head start. I stay still and wait, keeping my guard up.

"Be back in a bit, Thompson."

I clench my jaw and crack my knuckles as I watch him leave.

It's only when the door shuts and I'm left alone in the room that I realize the extent of what Detective Bradshaw said.

Someone *wanted* to kill Tony, knowing I'd give the coke to him. Maybe even thinking I'd take it too. I'm known for partying. It's why clients choose me to represent them in the firm. My head spins as I try to recall that night. I don't broadcast that I'm not a cokehead and a glass of whiskey is enough for me. Still, everyone in the scene knows I'm down for whatever they're in the mood for. There's no way anyone else could have gotten in there. James had the master key, and he gave me the only other copy.

I was there to party with the clients and make sure they had a good time, but stayed out of trouble. It was easy enough in the rec room.

For the last ten minutes, I've been thinking that someone was trying to kill Tony. It's what the detective was suggesting.

I'd bet anything that James thought I'd take a hit at least.

Maybe it's paranoia, but as I sit alone in the room, all I can think is that the coke was never intended for Tony.

Someone wanted me dead.

This is not the end of Kat and Evan's story. Their duet continues with *You Know I Need You*.

YOU KNOW I

# need you

WILLOW WINTERS

I married the bad boy from Brooklyn.

The one with the tattoos and the look in his eyes that told me he was bad news.

The kind of look that comes with all sorts of warnings.

I knew what I was doing.

I knew by the way he first held me that he would be my downfall; how he owned me with his forceful touch.

I couldn't say no to him, not that I wanted to. That was then, and it seems like forever ago.

Years later, I've grown up and moved on. But he's still the man I married. Dangerous in ways I don't like to think about and tried to ignore for so long.

I did this to myself. I knew better than to fall for him.

I only wish love were enough to fix this ...

*You Know I Need You* is book 2 of the second duet in the You Are Mine series. Book 1, *You Know I Love You*, must be read first for this duet.

Love does not delight in evil but rejoices with the truth. It always protects, always trusts, always hopes, always perseveres.—1 Corinthians 13

# CHAPTER
## one

*Kat*

*You said you'd love me forever,*
*But forever was too long.*
*You said I was your one true love,*
*But the two of us were wrong.*
*It's deceit and lies that broke us,*
*And left me living in pain.*
*Forever was supposed to be ours,*
*But forever was said in vain.*

IT'S NOT EVERY DAY YOU READ IN THE PAPERS ABOUT your husband going to jail. That's one way to find out, I guess.

My heels click steadily on the sidewalk as I make my way to the end of the block; just a little farther until I'm home. The plastic bags from the grocery store on the corner dig into my arm, the grooves getting redder with every few steps.

It hurt after a few blocks, but I didn't care. Now I'm just numb to it. I focus on the front door to my townhouse the second it comes into view. Jail. Evan is in jail and the vise squeezed tight around my heart has been unrelenting since I read the article at the corner store.

It doesn't take long before my gaze is drawn from my building to a figure waiting for me.

Standing in front of the building with her arms crossed over her chest, is a cop. She's dressed in dark navy pants and a matching jacket that's not quite baggy enough to hide her curves. She's short, with her blond hair pulled back into a low bun and covered with a cap. My pace slows as I spot her, and I want to break down all over again.

*If only I'd stayed holed up in the apartment and didn't have to eat.* The thought is bitter as I walk forward. Each step hurts more and more.

I must still love Evan, because knowing he's in trouble twists me up inside.

It was the sign I was looking for, though. The one that drove the nail in the coffin of my marriage. It's really over. He's only in holding, so there's no way for me to get him out of this, but if there was, I'd bail him out and hand over divorce papers the moment we were out of the precinct.

"Mrs. Thompson," the cop says as I traipse up the stone steps.

"Hello," I respond awkwardly, not wanting to look her in the eyes as shame creeps up and makes the cold air feel even colder.

"I'm Detective Nicoli," the woman says and I nod my head, feeling the pinch from the grocery bags digging even deeper into my forearms as I shift on my feet.

"How can I help you, Detective?" I force myself to straighten my shoulders, pretending I have no idea why she's here.

"Could I come in?" she asks me as if I'd let her.

"I'd rather not," I answer, my voice a bit harsh. I struggle with the bags slightly, hearing them crinkle as I let out a low sigh. "It's been a long few days and I don't want company."

"The bags under your eyes could have told me that," she says with no sympathy in her tone.

I huff out a humorless laugh and tell her thanks, the S lingering, intending to walk right by her and into the townhouse, but then she adds, "I'm sorry for what you're going through."

With that, I hesitate.

I stand there, taking the sympathy. More than that, I need it. Tears burn my eyes as I look back at her. "What do you want?"

"It might be better for you if I could come in," she suggests, looking pointedly at the bags on my arms.

I shake my head. That's not happening.

The charge will be murder if the papers are telling the truth.

I'm not interested in hearing from anyone other than my husband. He hasn't been formally charged yet, but for it to be in the papers, there's a fifty-fifty chance they have enough to arrest him as far as I can tell, and I'll be damned if I let her inside, and ... More shame consumes me at the thought of making sure I don't give them any evidence that could help convict him. As if he really did it. There's no way he did. My husband's not a murderer.

"Ask me whatever you'd like, Detective, but make it quick."

"I know you two are getting a divorce," she says and the article from two days ago flashes in my memory. "I'm sure you've heard he's going to be charged with murder, given your position in the social circles around here."

A deep inhale of the frigid fall air chills my lungs to the point that it's painful. The article was all about how Evan lost his job, his wife, and now he's about to be charged with murder. My heart thuds dully just the same it did when I first read it, as if it's lifeless.

"I wanted to know if you had any information that you'd like to give us," Detective Nicoli says and I shake my head, not trusting myself to speak.

"Look, I know this is hard, but anything at all you can give us would be appreciated."

I stare straight into her eyes and I hope she feels all the hatred in my gaze. He's not a murderer. I don't care what they think.

"I don't have anything I'd like to tell you other than that these bags are heavy."

The detective frowns. "If we have to get a warrant and search your place, it's not going to be pleasant for you." She softens her voice and adds, "I'm just trying to spare you that."

I'm not stupid and her good cop routine isn't going to work on me.

I've had to talk to cops before, years ago. I never said a word. I'm sure as hell not going to now.

"Did you know Tony Lewis?" she asks, and I shake my head. Again, not wanting to speak, but she waits for me to confirm it out loud. The pen in her hand is pressed to the pad as she stands there expectantly.

"Never met him."

"Do you know where your husband would go to acquire cocaine?"

My expression turns hard as I tell her, "My husband doesn't do coke." *Any more* almost slips out. He's done it before. He's done a lot of shit that I'm ashamed of, but that was before me. *Before us.* For a moment, I question it. Just one small moment. But then it passes as quickly as it came.

Detective Nicoli smirks and flips the page over in her notepad then says, "We'll have the warrant for a sample from him soon."

Absently my hand drifts to my stomach to where our baby is growing, as if protecting this little one will protect Evan, but I'm quick to pull it back as one of the heavier bags slips forward on my arm.

She doesn't need to know, but I want to tell her. I want to tell the whole world that the Evan I know could never do what they're saying. But I don't tell her a damn thing and I've given her enough of my time.

"Good for you," I tell her and walk past her. I shove the key into the lock and turn it, but before I can open the door, the cop leans against it and waits for me to look at her.

"Please move out of my way," I say as I seethe, my anger coming through. Anger at Evan, anger at her.

"Someone's going down for Tony Lewis's death."

"Someone should, but my husband is not a murderer," I

snap. I grip the door handle tightly, feeling the intricate designs in the hard metal press against my skin. It's freezing and the lack of circulation in my arms hurts. But I can't let go. I don't trust myself.

"I have nothing more to say, so I'm going inside," I tell her, and every word comes out with conviction.

"I'll leave my card," she responds after two long seconds of her hazel eyes drilling into the side of my head. She slips a card into one of the bags dangling from my right arm.

I watch her walk away, biting back the comment on the tip of my tongue for her not to bother.

"What a bitch," I spit out the second I open the door and get inside, then let the bags fall to the floor.

My body feels like ice and my arms and shoulders are killing me. My legs are weak as I lean against the door to shut it and stare absently ahead, my gaze drifting from the empty foyer to the stairs.

I want to cry.

I want to give up.

Mostly I wish I'd been a better wife. I wish I'd kept Evan from whatever the hell he did.

I know him. He didn't do this. I don't know what he did, but he didn't kill anyone.

# CHAPTER
## two

### *Evan*

EVERY SECOND THAT TICKS ON THAT FUCKING clock makes me want to break it.

I haven't felt like this since the first time I was brought into jail. It wasn't here; that place was in a small town, somewhere in the bumfuck boonies outside of Chicago. This restless need to get the fuck out and handle all the hell I created is the exact same feeling I had that first night.

*Tick*, the clock's minute hand moves again and I peer to my right, staring down the woman at the front desk who's processing the paperwork for my release.

My neck cracks as I stretch out my shoulders. I haven't slept a wink and I'm exhausted, but pure adrenaline is pumping through my veins, keeping me awake and fighting.

I need to get the hell out of here.

I knew something was off from the very beginning. James tried to fuck me over. It had to be him.

The only reason I can think of is because of Samantha, though, and that doesn't make sense. It's been years since we had that affair. Years for her husband to get over it. Shit, all he's been talking about for months is how he wants their divorce to be finalized.

I lean back on the metal bench as I force myself not to look at the desk sergeant, and not to look at the clock either. My eyes focus on the abstract patterns of the cheap linoleum tiles and the sounds of the police station fade into the background as my thoughts take the forefront.

The memory of that night comes back to me.

I flinch as I remember the feel of James's hand on my shoulder, showing me where the new rec room in the renovated hotel was and asking me if I needed anything else. My eyes close when I think about him handing me the key card and looking to his left and right before telling me to make sure I showed Tony a good time.

My lungs still and my vision turns red as my teeth grind against one another while my fists clench.

I can't fucking handle this. If that fucker set me up to die, he's a dead man.

Even if it wasn't him, someone laced that coke with enough fentanyl to kill. I'll be damned if I rest until I know who did it. Whether they were after me or Tony, or it was a mistake, it doesn't matter. They're dead.

"Mr. Thompson." A small voice to my right says my name and breaks my concentration. It takes every effort to raise my head and relax my body as if nothing's wrong. As if I'm not envisioning beating in some unknown man's face with my bare knuckles. I'm quick to get to my feet, eager to leave.

Each step smacks off the floor, the sound drowning out the steady ticking of the clock. My heart beats in rhythm to match my pace.

"Your belongings." A weak smile forms on her thin lips as she hands me a ziplock plastic bag and review the contents one by one, going down the list in her hands.

It's all standard procedure, I tell myself.

I shove my hands into my pockets and rock on my heels as I wait. Each second makes me more and more anxious to get out of here.

"And your keys," she says flatly then finally meets my eyes again.

"Thank you," I answer with a tight smile and grab the bag before she can change her mind. As I slip my black leather wallet into my back pocket, I wonder what James will say. Better yet, I wonder how I can get him to confess.

"Make sure you sign here." I smile as I do what I'm supposed to.

*Break his jaw.*

"And here," the woman adds, pointing to another line on the release forms.

*Bash his knees in with a tire iron.*

"You're all set, Mr. Thompson."

*Put a gun to his head.*

My lips tilt up as if I'm happy to be getting out of here. But my muscles are tightly wound and my stomach's churning.

All because of one question: What if it wasn't him?

No one can know about any of this shit. My heart skips a beat and I hesitate to walk out of the station. *Kat.*

My feet nearly stumble over each other at the thought of someone going after her. They wouldn't. Not when she's through with me. They can't. No one better hurt her. No one touches my wife.

I force myself to move forward. I can't go to the cops, not even to protect her. All they'll do is go after me. I don't have a shred of evidence other than a testimony that could lead them to convict me. I have nothing but my word. Inside these four walls, my word doesn't mean shit. I'm well aware of that fact.

The sky's gray as I glare through the glass doors, hating this place and what I've done. I have to tell her the truth and make sure she knows I'll keep her safe and not to trust anyone; I shake my head. I'll have to tell her I'm coming home first and with that thought, I take out my phone. Turning it on, I lean against the door waiting to see what I'm up against.

I bet she's heard I'm locked up, but maybe there's a small chance she hasn't.

As the phone comes to life, a series of pings follows the messages popping up.

A couple from Pops, the first asking where I am and if Kat forgave me. The next asking me to call him when I get out of jail. A numbness creeps over my shoulders at the feeling of disappointment that runs through me. He's too old to be dealing with my shit.

My body sags against the door, the chilly temps from the autumn night seeping through the glass.

I scroll through the messages asking all sorts of questions

from people who don't really give a shit about me, and vice versa. They don't matter.

The one person who does matter, the only one I want to hear from and the only person I want to run to … hasn't sent a single text.

It takes a second for my throat to loosen enough so I can swallow that realization. I check the missed calls to make sure Kat hasn't tried to contact me, hopelessness runs through my veins before I push the glass doors open with a hard slam of my fists.

I hate that she didn't call me. That she didn't care enough to let me know she heard. If Pops has heard, she's heard.

The bitter cold air whips by my face as I move toward the corner.

I check my messages again, searching for her name like I could've missed it. One catches my eye. Samantha. I pause over her name and read her text. *We need to talk.*

My strides quicken at the thought of meeting with her. She might know something. She could be my way to get what I need from James.

I have to go to Kat first and knowing that, I text Sam back, asking when and where.

Glancing up at the next intersection and seeing the Don't Walk icon flashing, I look over my shoulder to hail a cab. I'm going home, whether Kat likes it or not.

I've kept so many secrets from her.

My head hangs low as a cab pulls up and I step out into the busy streets of New York City. The door slams shut with a loud click, dulling the city noises as I tell the driver our address. It's only after a few minutes of quiet, the rumble of the car almost lulling me to sleep, that I rub my tired eyes and think about what Kat would say. What she'd do if she knew the shit I got myself into.

She's already so close to hating me.

She's close to being over me and what we had.

I can't risk losing her, but right now either choice—to come clean, or to hide it from her—feels like I've already lost her. She needs to know, though … I have to make sure she's safe and she's protecting herself.

# CHAPTER
## three

### *Kat*

"I WANT TO THANK YOU FOR MEETING ME," JACOB says in both a charming and professional tone—I'm not sure how that's possible—as my keys clink on the coffee shop table and I take a seat across from him.

It's been three days since Evan came back to the townhouse. And three days since he accused me of cheating on him and punching Jacob. That night I sent Jacob a message apologizing, but then I turned my phone off. Three days of me hiding away in our bedroom and pretending this isn't my life.

At some point, I had to come out. What a fresh hell I walked into.

"I'm so sorry," I tell him again with complete sincerity and my eyes closed tightly as I settle down into the seat. It's a wicker chair with a dark red cushion and the smell of coffee from the café adds to the comfort. This coffee shop has a homey feel to it. Very different from my favorite spot in town, Brew Madison, but I can see why Jacob likes it.

My cheeks are practically frozen from the piercing wind whipping through the West Village, but even still, they burn. "I honestly cannot say—"

"Don't." Jacob stops me from saying more, holding up his hand and waving off my embarrassment.

I can't believe how out of hand things have gotten. As a professional, I'm mortified.

"Please, Jacob." I shake my head slightly then look up at him, staring into his eyes as I refuse to let him downplay everything, especially with a faint bruise hiding behind the five o'clock shadow along his strong jaw. "What happened the other day was ridiculous. Evan had no right to put his hands on you, and I want to thank you for not pressing charges."

"I don't blame him, Kat," Jacob says and waves off my gratitude with an ease that catches me off guard. My heartbeat quickens and it's the only thing I can hear for a brief moment while I take in his words.

"It's fine, really. I mean it, I don't blame him."

I slowly take off my coat as I tell him, "I do. I know it looked a little off." A feeling of confusion clouds my memory of what I'd planned to say.

I was going to thank him for not pressing charges.

Beg him not to hold it against the publishing agency.

And concede that I would not be his point of contact if he did choose to go with us. Obviously, I can't represent him after what happened. I'm prepared for that.

"Evan is in the wrong in every way, and I feel awful."

"It wasn't you who did it." The comfort in his voice makes me slightly uneasy. The next words out of his mouth add to that nervousness. "I'm kinda glad he did."

"Why?" I ask quietly, the nervousness changing to something else. I should stop this. I know that much. It's a slippery slope I'm balancing on.

"You two split, right?"

"Yeah," I answer him, and it makes my throat go dry. My chest feels hollow, with nothing there but the raw emotion I'm trying to ignore. *What am I doing?* I'm feeling something other than the agony that's plagued me for weeks.

"He's not acting like it, judging by the way he talks to you. He's aggressive. He's doing what my ex did to me. And I don't like it."

"I don't know what Evan's thinking right now, but this isn't him. He isn't like this."

"Either way, I don't blame him."

I don't know what to say back. There's a tension between us that's different from what I anticipated.

"I don't like the way I saw him treat you," Jacob states with a softened voice and then raises up his hands as if expecting me to protest. "I know I only saw a small piece." He licks his lower lip and adds, "I just didn't like it. So, if he's going to take it out on me instead, I'll take it."

"It's not like that," I say, attempting to stop what he's insinuating. "Evan doesn't take anything out on me."

"It's just something about what I see between you guys. It gets to me."

"Between us?"

"How you obviously care for him, even though it's killing you," he answers with a sadness in his eyes that could rival mine.

"Either way," he continues, "I'm sorry and you don't have a reason to be, so … let's just agree to let it stay in the past?"

"I didn't anticipate you being the one apologizing today."

Jacob shrugs and it's then I get an even better look at the faint bruise on his jaw. With the rough stubble, it almost blends in, but when I catch sight of it again, I cringe.

Jacob smiles at me and a masculine chuckle makes his T-shirt tighten on his broad shoulders.

"Seriously, Kat," he tells me and moves his hand to the table, turning it so it's palm up. "Don't worry about it. I can see where he's coming from."

Jacob's gaze flickers to his white mug. I glance down at it; it's chai, and a warmth flows through me at the thought of getting myself one.

"So, we're all good?" I ask him.

He shrugs again and takes a sip from his drink. "If you're okay?" he finally answers, and *okay* is not exactly the word I'd use to describe myself right now.

"For you, miss," a woman to my right announces, startling me and catching me by surprise. The barista I barely noticed when I first walked in sets down a mug identical to Jacob's in front of me. The warming aroma of cinnamon mixed with nutmeg hits me immediately and I welcome the scent.

"Thank you," I tell her although my eyes are on Jacob.

"I thought you'd like it," he says, answering the unspoken question with a grin. "I know the shop is new, but I've had their chai almost every day and you have to try it," he tells me like we're good friends. Like we know each other well. After a moment he adds, "Great place to write."

"I can see that." I swallow, feeling a stir of something else in my chest. It pulls at my heart. *Guilt.* I feel like I'm cheating.

Evan and I are separated; I remind myself again. With all the crap Evan's done and put me through, it's over. It has to be.

So this, this little distraction … I refuse to stop it when it makes me feel something other than the turmoil that has been plaguing me.

My hands wrap around the mug and they warm instantly as I take a good long look around the place. The brick walls and picture frames make it cozy and inviting. With the dark wooden tables and wicker furniture, I could see how a writer could make themselves comfy in a corner chair. Using both hands to lift the mug, I take a small sip and then another, much longer one, feeling the warmth flow through my cold chest. And then a third. Even though I feel less consumed with regret about the fight between Jacob and Evan, a different feeling is washing over me.

"So, what do you think?"

I have to blink away my thoughts and try to figure out what he's referring to before a bright blush rushes to my cheeks.

"The chai," he adds comically and nods at my hands.

"It's good," I say with a half-hearted smile and then see the bruise again. "I just …" Why can't I stop apologizing and let it go?

A half-hearted smile graces his lips and it's quiet for a short moment. "Kat, I don't really like your ex."

*Ex.*

My heart hammers and my blood feels as if it's draining from my body, leaving me cold. "I can see why," I respond easily enough, although I can't look him in the eyes.

"Hey, I didn't mean to upset you." His tone changes to sympathetic and I hate this moment. I hate feeling weak and not knowing what to do or say.

"Please don't worry about me, Jacob." My voice is as strong as I can make it.

"First of all," he says with a gorgeous smile, "it's Jake." I can't help the small laugh that slips out at how serious he is. "And second, I'm not worrying, just being there for someone. That's all."

All my misgivings about him leave me as I look into his kind dark green, hazel eyes. He's the rugged kind of handsome I would have been drawn to back when I was single. I'm honest enough to admit I'm drawn to him now.

He's a good guy, and I can feel that in my bones.

"That's very nice of you, but I think …" I start to say and pause as I try to figure out how to word what I'm thinking without sounding pathetic. *I'm still in love with my ex, pregnant with his child, confused and feeling alone. Even if he's in jail and we're separated, I can't stop worrying about him.* Instead, all I can manage is a mix between a groan and a sigh. I conclude with a simply stated, "I'm just a mess over it all."

"Hey, let's just end it there?" he suggests. "I don't have many friends here and I put my nose where it didn't belong. I'm the one who's sorry."

"You're not in the wrong here."

"I'm not in the right either, am I?"

"What do you mean?" I ask him like I'm oblivious. I know exactly what he means.

"I—" he starts to say but then stops himself and lets out a short laugh before rubbing his eyes. "Sorry, I've been up all night working on this manuscript."

I see the opening to steer the conversation back to work and take it. To keep this relationship just business. "I could bury myself in manuscripts right now."

Jacob lets out a charming laugh and I find myself slipping into the one role I know I'm good at. "Have you thought about who you'd like to be your agent and represent you?" I almost roll my eyes at the question.

"You're shameless," he says with a wicked grin.

"I know," I answer him and smile into my cup. The smile is oddly genuine given my state just a moment ago, but Jacob has a way of making me feel calm and relaxed.

"I'm not ready to talk to any publishers. I still don't know what I want to do with this one yet."

"Want to tell me about it?"

"Well, it's about me. Sort of." He leans back and spreads his legs wider, my eyes drawn to his broad chest as he glances out the picture window at the front of the shop. "My ex, really." He runs his hand through his hair.

I nod my head and reply, "So, it's an emotional book for you. Maybe one to feed your soul, more than your family."

"I have no family to feed, so that'd be an easy one," he jokes. "But yeah. It's more just for me, I think."

"What's the plot about, if you don't mind me asking?" I pry gently as I pick up a sugar packet from the table. I have no intention of adding it to my drink, but I think best when I have something to fidget with. Again, I cling to the chance to talk about work. I'm more than grateful for this distraction. I'd rather talk books all day long than anything else.

"We were high school sweethearts who beat the odds, but we just didn't get that happily ever after, you know?"

I feel a sharp pain in my heart, one that knocks the wind out of me. Another romance story gone south. "Why didn't it work out?"

"She'd been cheating on me for a while. I found out when she got pregnant and the dates didn't add up."

"That'll do it," I say as my mind wanders back to Evan. To his infidelity before we were married but still together. And to my little secret.

"Turns out it was my best friend."

"Oh no." A pout pulls down my smile and I feel gutted for him. "Double betrayal."

"That'd make a good title," he replies and then chews on his lower lip.

A feeling of shame settles on my shoulders. Evan and I are over, and I shouldn't feel like this is wrong. But for the first time in years, I feel *something* for someone else.

There's no way I can justify this feeling right now. Not

when I haven't had time to get over Evan. Not when the thought of getting over him cripples me. What's Sue always telling Maddie, though? The best way to get over one man is to get under another. Sitting here right now, I understand the sentiment.

"You think I could sell it?" Jacob asks and holds my gaze as he lifts his cup.

"I'd have to read it first," I answer honestly, even though I know a happily ever after sells better. That doesn't mean there can't be another romance thread added in somewhere. It's not like his story is over. His eyes catch mine and it's as if he knows exactly what I was just thinking ... about another romance thread.

"I'm still in the process of writing it. I think the story is going well, though," he says and every inch of my skin catches on fire. It's the way he looks at me. How his stare holds me captive and the tone of his lowered voice makes my blood race. The air crackles between us and with that, I need to get out of here. Quickly, before this conversation turns into something else.

"Send me the first few chapters?" I ask him and then reach for my purse. "Sorry, but I have to get going. I didn't think our meeting would last this long."

He half smiles at me as he says, "Okay then." He says it like he knows I'm lying, but more than that, like it amuses him.

I take out my wallet, but Jacob stops me. "Don't even think about paying."

"Are you sure?"

"You can get the next one if you really want to, but this one is on me."

I give him a tight smile, although I'm grateful. Truly I am. Even if his intentions are less than pure.

I can only nod then make my way out. It's all too much. Separation, pregnancy. Now Evan's in jail. I can't take how quickly my life is unraveling.

"Hey, Kat," Jake says from behind me as I push the door open and the bells ring. I turn to look back at him.

"It's going to be okay," he reassures me and I say thanks, although it's so softly spoken I don't think he could have possibly heard it.

I have to leave. That's the only thing on my mind because I'm so broken that the words *it's going to be okay* are my undoing.

# CHAPTER
## four

*Evan*

THE WORST SOUND IN THE WORLD TO ME IS THE muffled sobs of my wife crying.

And the worst sight I could ever imagine is her bundled in a ball on the kitchen floor, whimpering against the cabinets. Her shoulders heave as she lets out another wretched sob and it makes me feel that much worse.

I didn't know it could get any lower than this.

"Kat." Her name is a gentle murmur from my lips, nearly a plea for her to stop. She's crying so hard, lost in the sadness, that she didn't hear me come in. My voice startles her and she jumps back slightly, causing the cabinet door to rattle.

Her lips part slightly, but she doesn't say anything. Instead it appears she's holding her breath.

"What's wrong?" I ask and the second the question is

uttered, I hate myself. It's obviously me. I did this. "What can I—"

"Nothing," she answers curtly, cutting me off, more embarrassment and shame present in her tone than the anger I'd anticipated. "I'm fine." She uses the sleeve of her shirt to wipe at her face, leaving her tearstained cheeks bright pink.

"You aren't fine."

"I'll *be* fine," she says, and her tone is harsher this time. "I don't want to cry in front of you," she adds with sincerity. I know the comment isn't intended to hurt me as I walk deeper into the kitchen. Kat's just being honest.

"That's what I'm here for," I tell her and then feel like an asshole. I haven't been here in days. I can see Kat's lips part with some sarcastic response, so I'm quick with my next words. "I know we're going through some shit and I'm not making things any better. But I'm here now."

She doesn't respond as she pushes her hair out of her face and visibly focuses on calming herself down. Glancing up at me only causes her expression to crumple as if she'll start crying again. She rips away her gaze and silence separates us.

I can't help but notice the curve of her shoulders and the way her breasts move as she steadies her breathing. My body is ringing with the need to touch her. The need to make her pain go away. "Whatever it is," I say, "it's going to be okay." I don't know how many nights I've told her that.

And it's always been true. "We'll get through this."

"I'm crying because of you!" she screams at me and angrily brushes away her tears.

"I'm sorry, but I promise, it's not what you think."

She only huffs in disbelief and shakes her head, refusing

to look at me. My blood turns cold and I struggle to breathe, but still I walk toward her. Every step is careful and cautious. I just want to hold her. I want to fix this more than anything.

I can't lose her.

"Kat." I say her name as if it's my only prayer, but she doesn't look at me.

As I crouch down next to her, Kat stands just to get away from me and it kills me. She wipes under her eyes then turns from me, giving me nothing but her back. The cup that was on the counter clinks as she places it in the sink.

Her shoulders shudder.

All I can hear is her heavy breathing as she ignores me. Moments pass, my hands clammy and my body hot. I don't know what to say or do, but I stay. I won't leave. I can do that at the very least. So I stand there, waiting and wanting her to tell me anything. I will wait forever for her if that's what she needs.

"They broke in through the window," she states with a shaky voice, followed by a deep inhale, and my blood freezes.

"Who?"

She shrugs her shoulders, turning to look at me with an expression of disbelief and answering sarcastically, "How the fuck should I know?"

"Where?" I follow behind her as she walks into the guest bathroom in the hallway. The second the door opens, I'm hit by the arctic air coming in through the broken window. It's only a half bath and inside the sink are shards of glass.

"They didn't take anything that I can tell."

"What the fuck," I mutter beneath my breath, my hands

clenching into fists at my sides. "Were you home?" I should have been here. I should have been protecting her.

She shakes her head no, her hair sweeping along her shoulders as she crosses her arms to protect her from the chill. "I called the cops as soon as I got in. I knew something was off. They went through your drawers, by the way. You may want to check and see if you had anything in there."

*Fuck.* My heart hammers as I stand there numb.

I don't know who it was or what they were looking for. But if she'd been here … Fear is crippling. It's the resolute tone of her next statement that forces me to move. "Are you going to fix that or should I call someone?" Her voice is flat and completely lacking in any emotion.

"I'll take care of it, but Kat, please," I beg her, forcing my legs to follow her back to the kitchen.

"I don't want to talk about it," she says without even looking at me.

"Kat, I need to know—"

"If you want to talk, then tell me how jail was. How about that?" she spits back.

"Kat, baby, please—"

"Don't 'please' me, don't touch me, don't anything me," she practically hisses, glaring over her shoulders as she opens a cabinet to get a clean glass then slams the door shut. Her eyes are rimmed in red, and she looks paler than usual.

She fills the glass with water and drinks down half of it with her back to me.

I want to reach out and hold her, but I've never seen her like this. Closed off and nothing but worn out and angry.

"Kat, I can explain."

"Oh, thank goodness. I was worried for a minute." Her voice drips with sarcasm, her back still to me as she turns the tap on and refills the glass.

"Please, if you don't mind, you could start with … I don't know," she says then shrugs and turns to face me, the bitterness in her voice never more apparent than now. "How about why I should give a damn about whatever excuse you have?"

My brow furrows as I take in her stance. She slams the glass down so hard I think it may shatter but it doesn't. With her arms crossed again, she waits. Her hair falls in front of her face, hiding part of her tired eyes and she doesn't bother to sweep it away.

"I don't want you to be mad …"

She reaches behind her to grip the counter, her knuckles turning white, agitation showing in every movement she has. I know right then I can't tell her what I think about James. I can't tell her that I think someone was trying to kill me or that I'm bringing more trouble to her.

I have to be the man she *wants* me to be.

I can do that. Just one last lie, once more. To protect her.

I swear it'll be the last. And only so I can hold on to her and keep her safe.

"Kat, I don't know a thing about the coke overdose or James or whatever the hell anyone's told you."

"You said you needed an alibi," Kat states evenly. She blows a few strands of hair away from her face and then folds her arms over her chest once again.

My stomach sinks as I give her just a little bit of the truth. Just enough that she'll stop questioning me. "This is why. I knew Tony was dead, but I wasn't involved." *Lie.* I can barely stand on my own two feet knowing I just lied to her.

"Why an alibi?"

"To save the company's image. We couldn't be associated with it any more than we already were." It's only a thinly veiled lie. What I've said is mostly true.

Kat nods her head, putting a finger to her lips and letting the words sink in as she stares at the floor.

"So, you gave him the coke?" she asks before lifting her head and her eyes flash to mine.

"No," I tell her and my voice is hard. *Lie. Another lie.* I'm digging my own grave deeper. I add in a truth, hoping it sounds believable enough to cover the lies. "I told you I don't do that shit."

"They're going to test you," Kat says like she doesn't believe me.

"I'll have them show you the results if and when they do," I say, and my words come out bitter.

She turns her back to me again as she fills the glass with more water. I stalk closer to her, careful not to piss her off.

"I mean it. I promise you. It was just a job and I barely drank, Kat. I quit for a reason. It didn't used to be like this and it's gotten to me."

She doesn't look at me as I come closer, close enough to touch her, but I don't.

"I did drink with clients, but that's it. I swear to you. I wouldn't touch that shit or anything like it."

She sets the clear glass down and then looks at me

as she says, "Tony did." She walks past me, brushing her shoulder against mine.

"I quit for a reason," I tell her again and my tone begs her to listen. To forgive me. "I didn't do anything, and if anyone in the world would believe me, it would be you." My voice croaks on the last word and I have to swallow my plea.

"I believe you," Kat replies instantly, hating that she's causing me pain. This is why she's too good for me, but I'll be damned if I'm not going to do everything I can to keep her.

"No secrets?" she asks and there's a change in her expression.

I shake my head no, although I feel like a fucking coward. "No secrets."

"I have one," she whispers softly.

"What's that?" I ask her, sensing the air changing between us, darkening and chilling.

"I have a doctor's appointment tomorrow," she tells me and her eyes flicker to me, right before darting to the floor. She can't look at me and that makes me more nervous than anything else.

"The doctor's? Are you all right?" I ask her, my voice low, the memories of my mother filtering in. I take one step toward her and wait for her to move back, but she doesn't.

She shrugs and stares at the countertop.

"What's going on, Kat?" I ask her, listening to my heart beat hard then harder still as she makes me wait.

Her forehead scrunches the way it does just before she

cries and I chance another step closer to her. I can feel the heat from her body as she sniffles and looks away from me.

"It's okay," I whisper. I reach out to her, praying she lets me hold her, and she does. Her shoulders are stiff at first, but she gives in and I say a silent prayer, thanking God for it. Her soft curves are warm in my embrace and I'm quick to kiss the crown of her head. The smell of her shampoo and every little detail about her is comforting. This is my drug. She's my only addiction.

"Baby, it's okay," I tell her as I pull her small body snugger into my arms. I needed this. I hold her as close as I can, rocking her slightly and loving how she grips me right back.

I hold her like I have for years, and it feels so natural. So right.

"Just tell me what it is, sweetheart," I whisper in her hair as she sobs into my chest. It hurts. Every bit of her sadness shreds me. "I'm sorry," I tell her and pull back to look at her, but she just buries her face back into my chest.

It's a long moment before Kat quietly pulls away.

"I have something you should see," she says and walks off. She wraps her arms around her torso as I follow her toward the stairs.

Anxiousness suffocates me, not knowing what it is she wants to show me.

"Stay here," she tells me, looking over her shoulder as she grips the railing.

I nod and watch her walk upstairs alone. She takes slow steps the entire way. Her bare feet pad softly on the floor as she leaves me.

I wait with bated breath. My body begs me to sit, the

exhaustion making me want to give in and fall onto the couch. But I remain standing.

In the silence all I can think about is the shattered window, the fact that someone broke in. If they didn't take anything, maybe they left something behind instead. Whatever it is, a picture of some shit I did, a text or a letter—I don't care what it is that's making her so damn upset. I'll fix it.

I won't let her go, and I'll destroy anyone and everyone who gets between us.

My head lifts when I hear her coming down the stairs, and my feet move of their own accord.

They don't move for long, though. The second my eyes land on the white plastic stick in her hands, my body freezes.

My mouth hangs open slightly as I glance from the pregnancy test to Kat's face.

She stops in front of me, barely looking at me and holds it out. "I'm sorry," she whispers in a cracked voice. As if this is bad. As if she's done something wrong.

"Baby, why are you sorry?" I look between her and the stick. I can't will myself to take it or to even believe it's real. "You're pregnant?" I ask her. She covers her mouth with her hand and nods.

A baby. A little life just like my Kat. Tears prick at the back of my eyes.

It's the best damn thing I could have ever asked for.

And then it hits me. *Jacob Scott.* I looked into him after that ... 'meeting' we had. My breathing picks up as my blood heats. I don't have the nerve to ask her, but the words are on the tip of my tongue.

I'll kill him.

"I'm pregnant," Kat says and draws in a steadying breath, taking a few steps backward.

I almost ask her, but I can't do it. Even if the baby isn't mine, I don't care. I'll take care of both Kat and her child.

"A baby?" A swarm of emotions courses through me. "This is why you're going to the doctor's?"

"Yeah, a baby," she says and chances a look up at me. Her long, dark lashes glisten with what's left of the tears before she wipes them away.

"That's wonderful," I tell her and close the distance between us, reaching for her hands. She leans into me and I rub the pads of my thumbs against her knuckles. "Kat, why are you sorry about something so amazing? Don't be sorry; I'm so happy."

I can see her expression fall as she tries to stay strong.

"It doesn't change what's going on, but I just found out and I don't know."

"Don't know what?" A numbness creeps up the back of my legs.

"How we're going to handle all of this," she says and starts to pull away from me.

"Kat, you're mine," I tell her.

"You were just in jail hours ago and we're separated. How are you going to take care of your baby?"

"I'll be the best damn father I can be." *Thump, thump.* My heartbeat slows as what she's saying settles in.

"You said that about being a husband too and—"

"And we're going to be fine," I say, cutting her off. "Better than fine. We're having a baby."

I finally look at her stomach. I wrap one of my hands around her hip while the other splays against Kat's belly.

"I love you, and that's what matters."

"It's not the only thing that matters," she tells me back.

Her emerald eyes swirl with so much emotion, I can't stand it. "I'm telling you right now, Kat. Me loving you is the only thing that matters."

# CHAPTER
## five

### Kat

I DON'T KNOW WHAT TO THINK OR DO.

I don't know what's right and wrong.

But I'm so aware of how I feel.

Every inch of my skin burns with need against Evan's touch. He's got a hold over me that's like a spell. It must be some kind of dark magic because he makes me forget reason. He makes me forget how angry I am at him.

I melt into him as if I was meant to be held by him from the very start.

The worst part is that I don't want him to ever let me go. Because the second he does, I'll remember. Reality will intrude, and the moment will be ruined.

One of these times, I'll let him go and never be held again. I can feel it down in my very soul.

YOU KNOW I need you

His hot breath tickles my neck as he whispers, "I love you, Kat."

My soul quiets, the pain soothed. For the moment, I grip him just as tightly as he holds me.

My heart clenches in my chest as I swallow the lump in my throat.

"I'm so happy," he murmurs as he brushes his hand against my belly. "We're going to have a baby," he says reverently.

How can I not fall back into his arms when I know he loves me? How can I not cling to him when he talks to me like this?

I'm exhausted and wretchedly weak. Nothing feels better than this.

Every reason this is a bad idea comes to me one by one, the truth too real to ignore. I don't know if the extreme swings of my emotions are from the pregnancy, or from the craziness of Evan's life.

My nails scrape against his shirt as I push away from him. "We need to talk." I push out the words as he reluctantly watches me move away.

"If we do this, we're moving forward together?"

He nods and says, "I promise."

"I just want to be with you, Evan," I speak from the bottom of my heart and I know it's the bottom because it's all I have left.

"I promise," he says again but his eyes are glossy.

"I'm sorry I wasn't the man I should have been for you." He takes my hand and kisses my knuckles one by one before turning it over to kiss my wrist. "I'm sorry I fucked things up so badly." He doesn't meet my gaze and I can't stand the look in his eyes.

"It's okay," I tell him, desperate to take the hurt away from his expression.

"I love you, and that's what matters," he tells me again. "Don't stop loving me. Please. No matter what happens," he begs me.

"You didn't do anything," I tell him, grateful he's finally told me the truth. I get it now; it all makes sense. "Nothing will happen."

He looks me in the eye and says, "Nothing bad will ever happen to you or this baby. I swear, Kat."

"Our baby," I whisper and put his hand on my belly. He lowers his head and I swear I think he's crying, but when he looks up at me, he says, "Nothing bad will ever happen to you or our baby. I'll never put you in harm's way, Kat." He takes a deep breath.

"Just don't stop loving me," he says, almost like a plea.

"Don't stop loving me," I tell him back and he says beneath his breath, "It's all for you. I won't let anyone hurt you."

"Evan," I start to say as I reach for him, feeling the intensity of his words and the chill that comes with it. But as my lips part, a startled yelp comes out. Evan's strong arms wrap around my waist and pull me to his chest as he carries me up the steps to our bedroom.

He sets me down gently on the bed, which is so at odds with how he kisses me. It's ravenous, reckless even. Desire scorches my skin and makes my core unbearably hot.

He groans into my mouth as his hands slip between my

thighs and under my panties. He runs his fingers up and down my hard clit.

"So fucking wet," he says, his eyes darkening with lust. "I love how you're always wet for me."

"Always," I say, echoing him, but my head feels dizzy and the need for him to be inside me overrides any sort of logic or reason.

I claw at his shirt, desperate to get it off and it makes him chuckle, a deep, low sound.

I want to scold him for taking so long and leaving me wanting, but the words stick in my throat as I watch him pull his shirt over his shoulders, revealing his tanned, tattooed skin and lean physique.

I lick my lips with the need to kiss him and he grants me exactly that. Bracing one forearm by my head, he leans down to kiss me, pressing his lush lips against mine and tasting me with swift strokes of his tongue as my eyes shut. He traps my bottom lip between his teeth and pulls back as he pushes his jeans down.

It's a short, sharp pain that spikes through my body, directly connected to my clit. When I open my eyes, letting the sweet gasp of longing escape, I'm lost in his gaze. Trapped by his gaze and waiting for him. I'd do anything for him. I swear there's no way I could love him more than in this moment.

"Evan, please," I say, ready to plead with him not to leave me again. Not to make me choose between a life without him or a life without shame, but he cuts me off, mistaking my plea for what my body feels and not my heart.

"Spread your legs for me." He gives me the command and my body obeys before I can even fully register his words.

Every thrust is slow and deep. The air between our lips heats until I arch my neck with a moan, feeling his thick cock push fully inside me, wanting more of me than I can give.

"Evan," I moan, saying his name reverently as my hardened nipples brush against his chest and he groans into my neck, holding himself still inside me.

"I love you," he whispers and then pulls out slowly. My body relaxes thinking he's keeping a slow pace, pulling himself nearly all the way out before pushing back in. But instead he slams himself into me all the way to the hilt and I scream out, my blunt nails digging into his muscular shoulders as pleasure races through me.

"I'll never stop loving you," he says as he pounds into me again, his hips crashing against mine.

"Evan." His name slips from between my lips as my head presses against the pillow and thrashes from side to side. It feels too intense. Way too much for so soon. My breathing picks up as my toes curl and my legs wrap around his hips.

He rocks himself against me, his rough pubic hair brushing against my throbbing clit and I writhe under him, feeling my skin prick slowly with the need for just a little more. I can hardly breathe. "Evan," I moan and again it comes out as a strangled plea.

"Kat," Evan says then nips my earlobe, sending a shudder through my body, "never forget that I would do anything for you. Everything is for you."

# CHAPTER
## six

*Evan*

I T FEELS COLDER THAN USUAL AS I MAKE MY WAY
down the sidewalk. It's empty and silent, with not a soul in
sight. Not even down the alleyways or in the dark shadows.
Someone's always there. Always watching and waiting.

But not tonight.

The light snow crunches beneath my booted feet and fog fills
my vision with each step I take to get home.

The streetlight outside the townhouse flickers and catches
my attention.

Darkness sets in just as I walk up the stairs and open the
door.

It's so quiet and my first thought is that I'm grateful she isn't
crying anymore. Ever since I told her the truth, Kat hasn't been
the same.

She looks at me the way I've always looked at myself. She's always sad now, with red-rimmed eyes and an expression of shame blanketing her beautiful face, and it's all because of me. I ruined her like I knew I would.

I call out to her in the townhouse. It's the same as it's always been, but there's an emptiness to it. A hollow feeling that emanates from the white walls and seeps into my bones.

"Kat!" I call out again, and my voice echoes.

My boots crunch although there's no snow.

My breathing picks up and again fog clouds my vision as I walk toward the kitchen. "Kat." I say her name, but I already know she can't hear me.

The white mist fades and suddenly I see her. Just as she was yesterday, she's balled up on the floor, but she's not crying anymore.

Crimson red has stained her clothes.

"Kat?" Her name slips from me in disbelief as tears flow freely and I run to her.

"No!" I scream as her limp body lies on the floor and her eyes stare back at me, lifeless, but still rimmed in red.

Praying for God to take it back, I cradle her, rocking her and screaming for it not to be true. A note falls and flutters to the floor with an elegance I hate in this moment. I can't let go of Kat; I grip her tighter, reading the words as the ink on the paper appears slowly. The script is feminine and delicate.

You should have let me go. You should have protected me.

It's all your fault.

And then I hear a baby scream.

My eyes shoot open with terror, a cold sweat clinging

266

to every inch of me. My body's stiff and hot as my heart races, pounding in my chest like a war drum. My pulse is heavy, hard, and unforgiving. *It's just a nightmare.*

"Kat," I say just beneath my breath, attempting to hide the fear before moving suddenly, shaking the bed as I put my arm around her.

It's the soft moan from her sleep that keeps me from waking her.

My heart still races in my chest as she breathes easily beside me.

As if nothing's wrong. Like nothing's happened.

My body trembles, refusing to let go of the visions. I blink away the sleep and fright as the early morning light streams into the room. The white noise of city traffic drowns out the gentle and steady sounds of Kat's breathing.

My body's heavy as I lie back in the bed, wiping the sweat from my brow and trying to forget the look on her face as I held her in my arms in the nightmare.

It's hard to swallow, the fear nearly crippling.

It's not real, I whisper. But I know with everything in me it's so much more.

Time ticks by slowly and sleep doesn't come again for me.

I didn't lie just once last night. I lied twice.

The need to be with her made me do it. The need to hold on to her love and let her feel how much I love her. I had to take away her pain. It only makes today that much harder.

There are two truths I know for certain.

1.  Someone's trying to kill me and if they can't get me, they'll come for her.
2.  But only if they know we're still together. Right now, no one does.

I love Kat too much.

I almost leave a note after going through my dresser drawer. There was nothing in there to take, but I made sure nothing was left behind or planted. The first thing I need to do is have a security system installed. This shit won't happen again and that's how I was going to start the note.

I wanted to write one for Kat saying goodbye and that I'll be back, then leave before she wakes.

She deserves to know why I'm leaving. Only for a little while. Only until I know she's safe.

⁓

"The doctor's appointment is at one I think," Kat says sleepily and I turn to face her slowly, my body stiff. My eyes burn from lack of sleep, but I don't care.

I welcome the pain.

"You're finally awake," I answer her and prepare myself for what I have to do.

The world thinks we've broken up. And it has to stay that way.

"You've been up long?" she asks and then yawns. There's a slight radiance to her. Her hair forms a messy halo on the pillow and a delicate simper is on her lips.

"Kat." I say her name and swallow my words.

I've been thinking about them all morning, the images of the nightmare feeling more and more real. Every possibility of what could happen has been running on a loop in my mind.

"I have to tell you something." I stare at the dresser across the room. I look in the mirror but I can't see our reflection, only the closed door to the bedroom.

"It's only for a short time, but I have to go do something."

"What do you mean?" she asks, the sweetness she had for me vanishing far too quickly as she sits upright. She reaches out to me, her soft, small hand gripping my shoulder.

"I mean I don't think I can go to the appointment today."

Her expression falls and she visibly retreats, pulling her knees up to her chest and wrapping the comforter tightly around her.

"Why not?" she asks with a little heat in her words. With every second that passes, I can see her getting angrier. "What's more important?"

"I don't think we should be seen in public together," I tell her and swallow the painful lump in my throat. No one knows we're together or that she's pregnant. "This has to stay a secret."

"Are you serious?"

"Kat, I have to take care of some things."

"Bullshit! What about us?" she says and her voice cracks. "What about taking care of us?" She motions between us.

"I am," I tell her and my words come out strangled,

shattering the delicate balance that was here only a moment ago.

"If you walk through that door, you're not coming back." Kat's voice shakes as she speaks. Her eyes are wide and the grief I feel is reflected in them. "You can't keep doing this to me. I can't keep …" she trails off and hiccups, on the verge of tears.

"It's only for a short while," I tell her to reassure her.

"I don't understand." Kat shakes her head as if she thinks I'm crazy. As if what I'm saying is incomprehensible and maybe it is, but it's okay. The less she knows, the safer she is. That's the only thing that matters.

"I have something I need to finish."

"You need to stop this, Evan. Please. I'm ready to move forward. We have a baby coming. Our baby. We can do this, but you can't keep going backward."

God, I wish she knew.

I could try to outrun it, but not with her by my side. I'll fight it and come back to her. I just need her to have faith. I know she will. The last thought is what moves me to put space between us.

"Just believe me when I say I love you, but I can't be with you right now."

A silent sob wracks through her body. "Stop it! Stop it, Evan. Please! I don't care what it is, just leave it behind and stay with me. Please, I'm begging you."

"I'm so sorry," I tell her and hate that I'm causing her pain.

"Why are you doing this?" she whispers. "I can't believe … I can't …"

"I love you, Kat, but I can't do this right now." The words come out as if I'm ending it with her, and that's when I realize it's what I have to do.

To protect her and our baby.

"I swear to God, if you walk out of that door, Evan, it's over. I'm done playing games. You're here or you're not." Her words are restrained as she says them, each one sounding more and more painful.

My chest tightens with an unbearable sorrow as I whisper, "I'm sorry, Kat."

# CHAPTER
## seven

*Kat*

**W**INTER HAPPENED OVERNIGHT. AND IT'S A bitter one at that.

My hands are still freezing as I stare at the fire in Jules's great room. Her home has been painted and decorated since I was here only a week or so ago. Jules didn't waste any time making the space feel cozy and warm. The soft gray walls complement the cream furniture and stone fireplace perfectly. She said it's all in "mineral tones" although many of the accent colors are a dark, luxurious purple.

"I love the color," I tell her in an attempt to cheer myself up and break the awkwardness in the room. Usually when we get together it's nothing but laughter. My face can't hide that I've been a crying mess and so laughs have been hard to come by.

"It's called Mineral Ice," Jules says agreeably from her spot on the chenille rug. Her glass of wine hasn't moved from the coffee table since I walked in. Come to think of it, neither Maddie nor Sue are drinking either.

The only one who seems normal is Maddie, and it's because she's lost her mind. I only just texted them days ago with the news I'm pregnant and she's taken it upon herself to start planning every detail of the next nine months for me. I love her and the distraction, but there's no way I can even think about a baby shower right now. It's all up to her as far as I care.

"I think the grays and yellows will be perfect for a neutral theme," Maddie says. "We could do bees or elephants and it will all match this room perfectly."

Maddie has a few bags next to her on the floor. Each from different party shops with samples of all sorts of baby shower accessories and décor. In the group text earlier she said it was a "few" things to look at. Bless her heart, she's ever the optimist. I only wish I could steal some of her positivity.

It was Maddie's idea to meet up today, and thank God they dragged me here. I'd rather be looking at tiny yellow clothespins and paper samples for invitations than hysterically crying on the floor in my bedroom. So, I suppose this is a win.

"Thank you for offering to host it, Jules," I say, pushing as much gratitude as I can into the words, but it still sounds lacking.

I'm not happy, and I just can't fake it. There's a hole in my chest and it feels like there's no way it could ever heal.

The father of my baby left me. Not just left me, but left me *again*. All I can think is that it's karma. I slept with him and kicked him out … and then he fucked me and left. This is exactly what I deserve.

I thought we were whole again last night; I felt it. Everything in me felt the love between us. And yet this morning he walked away. I must've been a horrible person in a former life.

"Okay, so menu …" Maddie says, leaning over the laptop that's on the glass coffee table and clicking the keys.

"Is it a little early to start planning all this in so much detail?"

Maddie stops fiddling with her laptop and looks up at me. "I thought maybe it would be a way to cheer you up a bit?" she says before sitting down on her butt right next to Jules. They're closer to the fire, sitting on the rug, and I'm wedged into the corner of the sofa. "If nothing else it's like window-shopping," she offers up.

"I don't think there's anything that's going to cheer me up," I answer her woefully. My hand drifts to my midsection, but there's not even a tiny bump. There's no way I'd know I was pregnant if I wasn't peeing on a stick every other day to prove that it's real.

"Do you … want to …" Maddie trails off as she struggles to suggest something else.

"Do you want to talk about what's going on?" Sue pipes up. "We can listen, you can vent. I could get a pillow and you can hit it?"

"I'm so fucked up right now …" I say and almost swallow the confession, but then I blurt it out, "that I'm actually considering starting to write letters again." I remember how I used to write to my mother when she died. It was what my therapist had suggested. "That's how low I feel," I tell them, emphasizing each word.

"You can tell us, you know?" Sue says and Jules nods in agreement. Maddie's soft gaze loses its ever-present happiness and all that's reflected in her expression is a sad smile.

"I'll probably cry too much to get it out," I respond and huff a sarcastic laugh to keep from completely losing it again. "I just wish someone could explain it. I feel crazy."

"Well, you're pregnant so you're allowed to be crazy," Maddie says as if that's a known fact and it actually makes me laugh. It's just a little bubble of one, but it's something at least.

"So let's have the complete update," Jules says and squares her shoulders as she gives me her full attention.

"It's over." The words come out easier than I thought they would. Maybe I'm just numb to them, I don't know.

"For real, for real?" Maddie asks me.

"Yeah, I'm not," I pause and shake my head then close my eyes. "I'm not doing this back and forth. I know where I want my life to go, I know what I need to do, and Evan just isn't there."

"Did you tell him you're pregnant?" Sue asks me cautiously.

"Yes." The single word nearly strangles me and I swallow down the pain that threatens me. "I told him, and he was so happy." I have to put my hand up to my mouth to keep from getting emotional again.

"I think it's okay if you cry," Sue says gently. "You're going through so much and you can always blame it on hormones."

A soft but genuine laugh sneaks in, shutting down the overwhelming heartache.

"I told him, and he still chose to leave."

"Why?"

"He didn't say," I tell them then correct myself. "No, he said," I try to quote him although I'm not sure if it's exact, "'I have to finish something, but it's only for a short while.'"

"What the heck does that mean?" Maddie asks with her face scrunched up.

"I don't know," I say, raising my voice in exasperation and that's exactly how I feel.

"Maybe he's worried about the stress from everything he's going through getting to you?" Sue suggests and I don't mean to, but I'm well aware that I stare daggers at her. "As if leaving me is any better?" I practically snap.

Her hands fly into the air defensively as she says, "I take it back. He's such an asshole."

"Here's your tea, sweetheart." Jules sits next to me on the plush sofa, holding out a cup for me. The steam itself is comforting. The seat sinks in slowly, dipping as she gets comfortable beside me.

"I'm still so happy you're pregnant," Maddie says, offering up a distraction as she leans forward and reaches for my hand, squeezing it gently. "You're going to be the best mom," she says with such certainty even though she looks so sad.

"Do you want one of us to go with you to your next doctor's appointment?" Sue asks, but I shake my head.

"I'll be fine."

"It's not about being fine, love," Sue says. "I could take pictures or something."

"Of her hoo-ha?" Maddie jokes and Sue rolls her eyes.

"Just to have someone there," Sue says.

"I would love to go with you," Jules says.

"I rescheduled the one I missed yesterday but it's not for

a few weeks," I tell them, shrugging it off like it doesn't matter. Like I'm not worried my baby can feel my pain and that every night I cry alone in our bed I'm damaging this tiny life.

Like I'm already a horrible mother and all this shit is going to hurt my baby.

"They couldn't get you in sooner?"

"I told them I wasn't free until the end of the month. I just want to get my life together," I say and take in a calming breath. "I know what I want, and I'm going to go for it whether or not Evan is beside me." Picking at nonexistent fuzz on my sweater I add, "I'm going to need some time before I can … before I can be the kind of happy and grateful I want to be when I first see my baby … even if it is only a little blip on a screen."

"You deserve happiness," Maddie says and the other girls nod.

"Instead of the appointment, I watched a bunch of men I don't know install a security system and fix a window."

"A window?" Maddie asks and Sue tilts her head in confusion that matches Jules's furrowed brow.

Huffing out a breath, I decide not to elaborate on that. "I wish Evan would stop living like he's twenty-one and doing stupid things … like leaving me."

"I can't imagine him walking away when he knows you're pregnant," Sue says although I'm not sure it was intended for me. She stares absently at the roaring fire, the crackling filling the silence that follows her words.

"I think that's what hurts the most. It was so … When I told him, he was just so …" I have to pause and close my eyes. I remember the way he held me and kissed me, and it kills me.

"Hey now," Sue says. "You're going to be fine regardless. He's got a situation he's dealing with."

I roll my eyes at the word "situation."

"The fact that he has any *situation* is the problem." All of my frustration flies out of my mouth. "We should have our lives together. Stability and a family."

It's silent once I've finished. Maddie looks down at the rug and Jules has an expression of sympathy, although neither says anything.

"I agree," Sue responds gently after a moment.

"It's going to be okay," Maddie speaks up although she doesn't look at me, she just picks at the rug. She shrugs and says, "Being pregnant and single is like the new trend anyway."

I let out a little laugh, and it breaks up the tension. Maddie even smiles.

"Well, at least it's fashionable then." My hand moves to my belly subconsciously and a surge of strength eases my pain.

I can do this, and I deserve happiness. I'm worthy of that. If Evan doesn't think so, then he'll have to deal with the consequences.

"Forget him," I tell them. "If he wants to act like he's perpetually twenty-one, then he can do it alone."

I move a throw pillow to my lap and hold on to it.

"You're going to be fine regardless," Sue says, repeating her earlier sentiment.

"And we're going to throw you the best shower ever," Maddie adds, taking over the conversation again. Bringing it to happier topics.

"What theme do you want? The elephants or bees …

or whatever else is in that bag?" Jules asks me as if it's all we should be talking about. I suppose it is. I'm done with Evan and this instability.

"I'll have to think about it," I answer and bury myself into the sofa. "Maybe when we know if it's a boy or a girl, then we can decide?" A light feeling seems to lift my shoulders like a weight is gone. Maybe it's the feeling you get when you're truly done with someone. When there's no way they can make it right again and you've come to accept it.

Maddie steers the conversation toward baby shower talk, and her voice is peppy as she says something about a Pinterest board.

My gaze falls on each of the girls in turn, all of them here for me. Jules catches my eye and rests her hand on my thigh, mouthing the words, "It's going to be okay."

For a short moment, maybe a second or two, I feel like it might.

Evan needs time to realize what it means to be the man I need.

Hopefully the time I need to get over him completely and stop falling for his charm is less than that. Because I can't do this again. I can't, and I won't.

Diary Entry One

Mom,

It's been a while.

I miss you guys, but you already know that. I could really use your advice now.

I know Evan loves me. I can feel it when he looks at me,

279

but when he's not with me, I feel like he doesn't. I know I'm insecure, but he's been so weird lately. He's acting crazy and it scares me a little. You wouldn't like it.

I don't even want to tell you. I'm so ashamed.

It's that bad.

I know you never met him, but I swear he's a good guy. I know he is.

But the thing is, he's not doing good things.

The worst part is that he's not stopping.

He knows we're pregnant, and he's not stopping. It doesn't get much worse than that, does it?

I don't know what to do.

He wants me to wait for him and I love him so much.

But I'm scared, Mom.

I cry all the time. That can't be good for our little one.

I remember you crying when I was little and how you held me and sang lullabies to me. I'm trying that late at night. I hold my belly and try to sing lullabies instead of crying. I'm trying so hard, but I'm afraid I'm already failing.

I don't think I can be with someone who isn't willing to stop doing what he knows is wrong. It's not just me anymore.

But it gets worse.

I can't stop loving him. I don't know what's wrong with me, Mom. I could use your lullabies right now.

# CHAPTER
## eight

*Evan*

*Threats can make you weak,*
*To think of what's to come.*
*To avoid seeing what's here and now,*
*Living life as if you're numb.*
*The lies are spinning webs,*
*To trap and hold you still.*
*The sinners hiding in plain sight,*
*Hold your fate against your will.*

NEW YORK CITY IS A SIGHT THAT NEVER FAILS TO impress. It's a mix of things—the nightlife, the skyscrapers, the people themselves. But winter is when it's the most beautiful, I think.

Only the trees are wrapped with Christmas lights this

early in November, but soon everything will be covered in white and blue lights. The shop windows in Rockefeller Center will be decorated with luxe details and high-end staging, and people will come from around the world to see it.

It's stunning, but what's best about it, is the crowds. During the winter months, this block is constantly packed. That's exactly what I need right now.

I need to remove one of my gloves to turn on my phone and check the messages. My foot taps on the hard cobblestone beneath my feet as I wait on an iron bench.

The phone goes off in my hand and I stare at the message from my father.

*Just a bit overworked because of my dumbass son.*

*Are you sure you're all right?* I ask him and ignore the insult.

*I'm fine.*

*If you went to the hospital,* I text him, *it must've been bad.* On the subway here, I got the message from my father that he was being released. He said he felt light-headed in the grocery store and the manager called an ambulance. He said they were just being dramatic, but I know my father. He's stubborn and hates hospitals.

*I'm fine. Go make it right with your wife,* he tells me, and I have to tear my eyes away from the phone.

*I'm trying.*

I hesitate to tell him, but the heat flowing through my veins begs me to text my father. *She's pregnant.* I can't help it. I'm so fucking proud. Like I did something amazing for the first time in my life.

His response is immediate.

*Thank God. Now she has to forgive you, right?* he texts back, and I let a small chuckle escape.

I wish it were that easy. *That's not how it works, Pops.*

He messages back, *It's Pop-Pop now. I'm so happy for you two. You better make it right with her.*

My phone pings again and this time it's not my father, it's the person I've been waiting for. *I'm here.*

A few children shriek with laughter as they run by me and I lift my eyes, watching them chase each other. That's when I see her. Samantha.

I shove the phone in my pocket, stand up and put my glove back on, then shove my hands into my coat pockets as I walk toward her.

"Thank you for meeting me." Sam greets me with bright red cheeks that match the tip of her nose. Her hair's been blown around her face by the wind, even though she has on a white cable knit beanie and a matching scarf. She slips her phone into her fur-trimmed jacket and declares, "I feel like I'm being paranoid."

I don't want to be here any longer than I have to. The only reason I agreed is because I have questions as to who could have broken in and if she has a lead on anything at all. I've got nothing and no one. There's not a soul in the industry I'd trust with this information, sure as hell not with the cops on my ass for murder. "Tell me what's going on."

"James messaged me and said what happened to Tony could happen to me. He told me to lay off the demands for the divorce." Her bottom lip quivers and again she glances over her shoulder.

"As in … an overdose?"

"I don't know." She takes a deep breath and looks to her left and right as her face crumples. "I think … I think he was threatening to kill me."

Anger threads itself through me as the woman in front of me breaks down. "Are you all right?" She shakes her head.

"No," she says and her voice cracks. "He didn't really kill him, did he?"

"The coke was laced with enough fentanyl to kill an elephant and the cops are convinced it was intentional," I tell her.

"I would say I don't think James is capable of that," Sam murmurs with sad eyes. As she speaks, her breath turns to fog. "But he's done things before …"

"Things like what?"

"He's choked me, thrown me against the wall. He's threatened me in the past. But he's never …" Her eyes become glossy as she says, "I didn't think he would ever do it."

"You think he killed Tony? Do you think the threat was a real one?"

She nods her head once, a frown marring her face as she gets choked up. "He said it was for you," she speaks softly, her eyes flicking from me to the cars passing behind us. The chill of the breeze bites down to my bones as her words sink in.

It was James, and the coke was intended to kill me, not his client.

I don't give her a response in the least, hiding the anger as my heart thuds hard in my chest at the confirmation of what I already suspected.

"What did I do?" I ask her.

"It's because of me," she says and her voice cracks.

"You didn't do this."

"You don't understand," she says, gaining more composure and wiping under her eyes as the wind whips between us and forces her hair behind her. "He wants me to give him everything in the divorce. The properties, our investments, the business, he's not budging on any of it."

"I thought it was finalized?"

She shakes her head and says, "I pushed back." Her words come out hard. "He's pushed me around for so long and he thought he could just get rid of me and throw me away like he did his first wife. But I made the company what it is today."

"So why go after me?"

"To prove a point."

"And what point is that?" I ask her.

"That he could eliminate whomever he wants."

Anger narrows my gaze as I tell her, "He missed his shot."

"He'll do it again," she says, "and I'm scared."

"It'll be all right," I tell her although I'm not sure it will be. I'm already trying to figure out how to end this. All roads lead back to James and the only thing I need to know is the fastest and safest way to put that asshole six feet in the ground.

"Please help me, Evan," she begs, and her voice is rife with agony. "I don't know where to go or what to do."

"The police," I tell her and it's the first time in my life I've ever thought of going to them. "You can tell them everything. Tell them he threatened you with that."

"He has them in his back pocket," she says bitterly then adds, "You know that. Did they tell you anything?"

I shake my head and say, "Only that the coke was laced enough to kill. It was made into a murder weapon."

"Oh, God," Samantha says then lets out a gasp and

hunches forward slightly. I feel the need to put my arm out to steady her and she clings to me.

A moment passes in the wintry cold, where I think back to a few times we've gotten out of tight spaces. I thought a client here and there would go to trial, but they never did. I didn't think it was because of James, though. I thought they didn't have enough evidence.

"He'll go down for what he did," I assure her as one name and one face come to mind. Mason. Jules's husband. He's gotten off for murder, just last month. There's more corruption in this city than there are tourists. Mason knows it as much as I do and I can trust him.

He killed his father, and everyone knows it. Well, the whispers in certain circles are sure of it.

He's from a different world than me, but I know him from back in the day. Back when both of us were a little too eager to cut loose. I helped him out back then and never called in the favor I'm owed. I haven't spoken to him since I split up a fight a few months ago.

He owes me for that too. And Mason's the type of man who pays his dues.

"What are you going to do?" she asks. Samantha scoots closer to me, almost too close, and I take a step back.

"I know a guy," I tell her and she's quick to nod, but then her face falls.

"Shit," she whispers, her eyes focused on something behind me and I whip my head around to see what she's looking at.

"It was him," she says then covers her mouth. "Shit," she repeats with tears in her eyes.

"He can't hurt you." I turn around and keep an arm behind me to protect her. My eyes search the crowd, but I don't see him.

Her hands tug at my arm, pulling me back to her. Her bright red lips glisten as she licks them and tells me, "He went down to the subway, but he saw us. I know he did. At least I think he did," she says then closes her eyes tightly and takes a step back. "It was definitely him."

"Is he following you?" Her eyes are still on the subway entrance and her body's still as she holds her breath.

"I don't know." Her bright blue gaze flickers to mine as she says, "I'm scared, Evan."

"You should go to the cops, Sam—" I start to tell her she needs to protect herself, and if she doesn't trust the cops she can always hire private security, but she cuts me off.

"It's not me. I'm not worried about me. If he thinks you know, you're not safe."

"I don't care what he thinks. Or what he thinks I know." I stare into her eyes as I tell her, "I'll kill him before he touches either one of us again."

# CHAPTER
## nine

### *Kat*

H E KNOWS WHAT HE'S DOING.

Jacob Scott.

*Coffee? I could use some advice.* I reread the message as I sit in a booth at the back of the coffee shop we met at last time.

*His place, not mine.* The thought makes me huff sarcastically.

My blood rings with guilt and regret. Even as I sit here, looking from my cup of chamomile tea to the entrance of the shop as the bell hanging above the front door rings, granting entry to temptation himself.

I should tell Jacob I'm pregnant. That I'm not at all ready to think about moving on, although I wish I were after the weeks of hell and on-again, off-again hardships Evan and I have been through. I should tell Jacob no. I should tell him sorry for not telling him sooner.

But I don't do any of that.

I give him a small wave and force my smile to stay put as he walks over to me. His shoulders shiver and I can feel the faint chill of the November air flow through the shop.

"I'm so glad you could come," Jacob says, greeting me with a smile, shrugging his jacket off his shoulders. I offer a smile in return as I see the waitress approach, carrying the cup of chai I bought for him.

"You have good timing," I tell him, biting the inside of my cheek and knowing I'm playing with fire. "Now I don't owe you."

A genuine chuckle fills the space between us as he's given his drink.

"Touché, Kat," he says, accepting it and thanking the barista.

I mouth thanks to her as she turns. She's sweet and young, but I don't miss how her gaze trails to my ring finger, then to his. She keeps her smile in place, but it doesn't reach her eyes.

My heart stutters and I wish I'd taken my wedding ring off. I wish I could solidify the separation as easily as Evan walked out on me.

"You okay?" Jake asks and grabs my attention again.

"Yeah." I force a smile to my lips. The singular word was spoken tightly, so I pick up the tea to take a sip.

I clear my throat and try to shake off the unwanted feelings. "Do you want a muffin?" I ask him absently. "Or a cookie?"

I read last night about all the foods you should and shouldn't eat when you're pregnant. Oatmeal seems to be a winner, so the thought of having an oatmeal raisin cookie or two sounds like a win to me.

"A cookie?" Jake smirks and I almost tell him why. But I don't. I gesture to the display cases; I can't be the only one who smells all the baked goods.

"You got the drinks, let me get the snacks."

"Oatmeal raisin?" I ask him and he nods with another smirk before tapping on the table and making his way to the counter.

I stare down at my not-so-big-yet belly and feel slightly guilty. An onlooker may think I look bloated. There's zero evidence I'm pregnant at all. Other than the box of pregnancy tests. I've taken four of them now, just to make sure the pink line turns darker each time.

At least I'm not crying and wallowing in despair. I'm simply crazy with worry. My hand gently rubs my belly.

"At least I have you," I whisper in a sweet, sorrowful voice as I rest my hand on my lower belly. I want a doctor to tell me it's real. That I really do get to have a baby. This little one who will love me, and I can love them back and give them every part of me.

As I take another sip of the tea, watching Jake at the counter, I start to think that maybe it was supposed to be this way. Maybe I don't have enough in me to love both a child and my husband. God must've known it and that's why Evan left me.

I nod my head before pulling the mug back to my lips quickly to hide my face from Jake. There's a reason for everything, isn't there?

He sits down slowly, and I know he saw; I can see it in his eyes.

"Sorry," I say and shrug. "I read this manuscript earlier and it shredded me," I lie.

He hands me my cookie and I feel foolish for a moment, but then he says, "Really?"

I nod like a fool.

"You want to talk about it?" he asks, and I get the impression that I could tell him anything. I think I could tell him the truth right now and he'd know it's exactly that. I could spill my guts to him and say it's all something I read in a book. And he'd let me. He'd give me that bit of kindness.

I'm so grateful for it.

But I'm not ready.

I shake my head, my hair spilling over my shoulders as I do. "Maybe another time."

He nods, peeling back his muffin wrapper enough so he can take a bite. "Good thinking," he says after he swallows. "Very good call on the muffin."

My shoulders rock gently with another small laugh as I take a bite of my cookie, once again feeling the ease that Jake gives me.

"It's okay to not be okay, do you know that?" he asks me.

I snicker and pick at the cookie.

"You can roll your eyes and laugh, but it's true," he says as he peels at the wrapper, exposing more of the treat as he talks.

"If I'm not okay, though, that means I need to talk about it." I point my finger at him and pick off another small piece of the cookie. "And I don't want to," I say smartly and pop the bit into my mouth.

"Nah, you can be not okay, but talk about something else instead. That's a thing, you know?"

"How's that?"

"It's okay to let something bother you, that's all I mean."

"You authors speak in code, do *you* know that?" I use his phrase right back at him.

Now he's the one who laughs. "Well, I guess what I'm saying is that I'm not really okay. I'm sort of running from my own problems. But now I'm okay, 'cause I'm here."

"Here in New York?"

"Just here," he says and gives me a small smile, but I read the real answer in his expression. *Here with you.*

"So, what are you running from?"

"Are we sharing stories?" he asks me in return.

"I'm not sure how much sharing I'm willing to do," I tell him honestly.

"You afraid you'll wind up in a book of mine?" he asks with a sly smile then adds, "One second, before you start I just want to grab my pen and paper."

He acts like he's reaching for an imaginary bag on the floor and I let out a loud laugh, then cover my mouth with both my hands as a lady looks up from her phone at me with a pissed-off expression from across the room.

Jake likes the laugh, though. Enough that he smiles widely as he settles back into his seat.

"You don't have to tell me anything. I just want you to know that you can be not okay around me. I get it. Some days I'm not the best, and it's nice to just go out and get a chai ... and a muffin."

"Like today?" I ask him.

"Yeah, like today."

"I have a hard time getting a read on you, Jake," I tell him.

"What do you want to know?" he asks me.

"What do you want from me?" I ask him then immediately regret the blunt question. It's rude and risks losing him and the only distraction I really have.

"Just company, until you want more," he says with his dark green, hazel eyes staring straight into mine as they heat.

"I don't know that I'll want more, though."

"I think you lie, Kat. I think you already know you want more."

"It's only because I'm lonely." The words slip out and I hate that they're true, but a weight is lifted with my confession. I expect Jake to react negatively. Maybe to be angry or offended, but instead, he nods his head.

"Yeah, I know. I am too."

"Sometimes I do stupid, reckless things when I'm lonely."

"Well, if you ever want to be lonely together, I'm free."

I should feel guilty about how Jake makes me feel.

Wanted, appreciated, like he doesn't want to lose me.

It's foolish to entertain what's between us. But I feel so rejected. My husband doesn't want me and yet Jake does. Even if it's only because I'm the only person in the entire state who he knows.

We can be just friends.

At least I can pretend we can, for a little while. Or what did Evan call it? *A short while.*


Diary Entry Two


Hey Mom,

I have a secret to tell you. Do you remember how I told

you about Markie in middle school? He's the one who was in Mrs. Schaffer's math class. He had a crush on me and passed me that note. It wasn't important really and I doubt you remember. But I had this feeling back then and I kind of have it now.

It's weird and it's mixed with all sorts of other things.

Obviously, I shouldn't see him, and I shouldn't even be considering talking to this guy, but I've been crying almost every night for so long. I started playing sad movies on the television at night, so I could blame it on that. I know I'm lying, but I'm so tired of crying.

I'm exhausted, Mom, and this guy gives me something else to think about.

It's wrong, isn't it?

I don't even have to ask you to know that it is.

I'm using this man, and I'm still married to Evan. My heart is still waiting for him, even though he's given me every reason to stay away from him for good.

Maybe I'm a bad person. Maybe I deserve all this.

I don't know. Could you tell me, please? You used to give me little signs. I know they were from you. I could use one now.

I don't know what's going to happen and I'm really tired. I'm ready for change and some sanity. The exhaustion is probably from a mix of what's going on with Evan and the pregnancy.

It's wonderful that we're having a baby, isn't it?

See how I changed subjects there? I hope that made you laugh.

I'm so grateful for this baby and I want to feel happy, Mom.

But my life isn't okay and I kind of hate myself right now.

This guy, Jake, changes that. Does that make it better?

Please tell me it does, because I want it all to be okay for the baby. Not the mess that it is.

I know it can't last, but maybe just for a little while?

# CHAPTER
## ten

*Evan*

"I T'S BEEN A WHILE," MASON SAYS AS I SIT DOWN at the booth in the back of the restaurant.

"I saw you just a few weeks ago," I point out to him.

"Not what I meant," he says, correcting me. "It's been a while since the two of us have been up to no good."

That comment pulls my lips up into an asymmetric smile and he follows suit with a wicked grin. "And how do you know that's what I'm here for?" I used to buy some good shit through Mason and vice versa. I came from the poor part of town, and he was from the rich. The only real difference that makes is which drugs you're doing. Pot or snow.

And if you want a taste of the other, all you need to do is make friends with the right people. Long story short, that's how I met Mason and as I moved into his circle, he made a spot for me when I needed one. When he got into trouble, I got him out. It was years ago, but a pact like that never dies.

Mason shrugs at my question. "I'm going to take a guess and say that whatever you want from me, it's something I could go to jail for."

I huff a sarcastic laugh and toss my phone down on the white tablecloth, then glance around casually to make sure I don't recognize anyone. The place is mostly empty, with only a few guys at the bar and a couple in the corner of the diner.

"Are we good if that's the case?" I ask him.

"We're good," Mason answers. "I have to say, considering what's going on, I'm intrigued."

"Intrigued is a word for it, I guess."

The waitress saunters over with a beer, setting it down with a smile and I thank her, although I didn't order it.

"I got you an IPA, seasonal."

"Thanks, man," I tell him gratefully, but I don't touch the tall glass sitting right in front of me. I take off my coat and hang it over the unused chair to my left as the waitress pulls out her notepad and a pen. She's a skinny little thing, which makes her look even younger than she probably is.

"Welcome to Murray's," she says evenly. Her top's unbuttoned a little too much and the way a blush colors her cheeks as she looks at us makes what she's thinking more than obvious.

"Can I get you guys anything?" She bites down on her lip and Mason raises a brow at me.

"Not me," I tell him and lean back in my seat, not looking back at the broad and risking leading her on.

He waves her off politely. "We'll just grab the drinks from the bar," he tells her and her smile falls. She seems to falter, and she clears her throat.

"Sure, if you need anything …" she says and shrugs, "just let me know."

"So, how you been?" I ask him as the pretty little blonde walks off.

"Better now," he tells me.

"I'm sorry to hear about your father."

He readjusts in his seat, making it groan, and looks away as he takes a long swig of his beer.

"I know it's got to suck either way." I choose my words carefully. Word is Mason killed him. Shot him dead. Still, it's his father and I don't know for a fact that Mason really wanted him gone. There was tension between them and rumors they were at odds, but I don't have a firm grasp on the truth when it comes to that situation.

"Yeah," he says without looking me in the eyes. "Thanks, but let's cut the small talk. It's not often I get a call from you."

I nod and crack my knuckles one by one with my thumb as I look out the window, scanning the streets. "I think I need to hire someone," I tell him.

"You're going to need to be a little more specific than that," he replies.

"There's a guy," I say then pause and lean in closer, resting my elbow on the table and moving my hand so that my fingers cover my mouth as I talk. Just in case someone's watching and trying to lip-read.

"He tried to kill me." I blurt out my theory. "Tony wasn't supposed to die. It was meant for me."

"You're still doing coke?" he asks as he eyes me then takes a drink from his glass.

"Not in years, but he didn't know that. It would hurt my reputation if the clients thought I was clean, you know?"

"That's what I thought. I was just asking 'cause that means whoever went for you doesn't really know you."

"I think it's my boss."

"Wouldn't he know?" he questions and for a moment a tinge of insecurity washes over me.

"He never really asked. He doesn't ask any questions so long as the clients are happy."

"All right." He tilts his head slightly and lowers his voice. "So, why does he want you dead?" Mason asks.

"It was years ago," I start to tell him and feel sick to my stomach. "I fucked his wife. Before I married Kat."

Mason's eyes assess me as if he's trying to figure out if I'm lying.

"I've never cheated on her," I say, talking louder than I should and in response to my raised voice, Mason looks to his right.

I lick my lips and calm my racing heart.

"He wants to scare her, so he went after me to prove what he could do to her. That no one's safe from him."

"But you gave Tony the blow?"

I nod my head once, the memory of his dead eyes looking through me flashing in front of me and sending a chill down my spine. "With the stuff James left in the room for me."

"So, your boss, James? You want him dead? You want to prove he did it, frame him, what do you want?"

299

"You have a fucking menu?" I joke with him to lessen the tension in my body.

An asymmetrical grin forms on his face.

"I don't do anything. I'm not involved in any of the process."

My body feels heavier with his words.

"Doesn't mean I don't still have connections," he adds and I nod. "So, for a friend, what is it that you want?"

"Three things," I tell him. "First, your lawyer."

"That's a given. He's already on retainer in case they take you in again."

"Second, someone to watch Kat. I need her safe."

"Is he after her?"

"He might know that I know, and I can't risk her safety." He merely nods and I add, "I can't lose her. I'll fucking lose it, man."

"The safest place for her is distance. Well, anywhere fucking away from you."

"I know … I know."

"Good thing you're separated, huh?"

"She tell Jules that?" I ask him as dread races through my blood. Before I can tell him we're not, and that there's no way I'm leaving her, he laughs at me.

"Jules tells me everything. I know the papers got it wrong."

"I'm not leaving her; I'm just protecting her. There's a difference."

"If you want the world to think you're broken up," he says, "then you need to treat her like you are."

"I don't know if I can treat her like that. She's pregnant."

"I heard." He lifts his beer in a mock cheers. "Congrats

on that, man ... but doesn't that make it even more important not to risk anything happening to her?"

"Don't make me feel worse than I already do." My words are bitter and my heart sinks. "How long's it going to take?" I ask him to get back to the point.

"To dig up dirt, plant evidence, figure out how to kill the guy ... it could be a while."

"I don't have a while," I bite back. "Every day is a day I have to put her through this."

"There are worse things you could do."

"I can't lose her," I tell him and he nods in understanding.

"I'll watch her myself," he offers and a small sense of peace relaxes me, but only a fraction of the way.

I rub my eyes with the back of my hand and finally pick up the beer on the table.

"If anything happens to her ..."

"Nothing's going to happen to her," he reassures me before asking, "What's the third thing?"

I look him in the eye and tell him, "I want him to go to jail for what he did. Whether you get real evidence or have to create some. And if that's not possible, I want James Lapour dead."

# CHAPTER
## eleven

### Kat

"I THOUGHT YOU WERE TAKING TIME OFF?"

I didn't even hear Sue come in. I glance at the clock in the upper right of my computer screen. It's already five o'clock and time for our dinner date. The girls are taking turns keeping me occupied. It's almost like they're babysitting me and if it was anyone else, I'd hate it.

But I can never turn down a date with Suzette.

"You of all people should know that working is all I'm good for." My voice comes out flat although I meant it to be funny. God, I'm tired. I'm always tired now even though I'm finally starting to sleep like the dead.

I guess the first trimester of pregnancy will do that to you.

"Oh honey, have you not looked at your shoe collection

recently?" she asks, quirking a brow. "You're good for so much more than work."

I stand up slowly, feeling every muscle stretch with a sweet ache as I do and grin at her. "Ha-ha," I say sarcastically, but the smile on my lips is genuine.

"So, what place tonight?" she asks as she turns on a lamp in the corner and settles into the one comfy chair in the room… which isn't even the desk chair.

"Order in takeout, getting pretty and hitting the town?" she suggests then takes her scarf off and looks around the office.

She doesn't even give me a chance to answer her before practically scolding me. "Why the hell haven't you decorated this room?"

I shrug as I follow her gaze. I have a bookshelf in the back, but all the books are still in boxes on the floor.

"Just not a priority," I answer her honestly. "I look at the screen more than anything anyway."

"It's like your décor inspiration was a depressing cubicle."

I snort at her response, but it makes me laugh so hard.

"Maddie should focus on redecorating in here before planning a baby shower."

I don't think the remark was meant to be taken seriously, but I actually love the idea. "I should tell her. I'd like that."

Twisting the scarf around her hand, she crosses her legs. "I'm sure she'd love to."

"Well, actually. I totally forgot to tell you, but I may move in with Jules for a little while so Maddie could really go to town."

Cocking a brow at me, Sue leans forward with her mouth

a bit more open than it should be before she says, "You sure you want to be around to hear them when they … enjoy their newlywed activities? I feel like that's the number one concern here."

I roll my eyes. "It was Mason's suggestion, so I'm sure he …" *Ugh.* The thought of them doing it in the room next to me is a thought I'd rather not picture.

"I get it," Sue says, sensing exactly what was on my mind. "You shouldn't be alone, though. Not when you have so many people who love you."

I shut down my computer and give her a tight smile. "That's basically what Jules said."

She adds, "Good. Because you're not alone, and there's no reason you should feel it right now."

Today's been so much better than the last few and Sue's sweetness threatens to change that. "Damn it, Sue, stop it," I admonish her and shake off the unwanted emotions as they creep up on me. "I'm fine."

"I know you are!" she says, pushing herself up from the seat. "And that's why we're going to go out and go somewhere fabulous."

My phone dings on the desk, indicating a text as I start to tell Sue that I don't really think I want to go out.

Holding back a yawn, I cautiously look at the message. I've had four texts today already. Each from a gossip column editor wanting a statement or my reaction to the recent events. Evan's been spotted with Samantha again and the rumor mill is churning with tales of scandal.

They can go screw themselves. I believe that was my response to each of the columnists. Probably not the best quote I've ever given. He promised he wouldn't see her. I guess I got my sign.

"You okay?" Sue asks, and I nod when I see it's a text from Henry this time.

He messages me almost every other day, which makes the fact that Evan hasn't bothered to call me back that much harder to take.

"Just Evan's dad. Wanting to drop by with some lemons."

"Lemons?" she questions.

"He said they helped Marie when she was pregnant and nauseated."

"But you aren't …" Sue trails off with a hint of confusion.

"I know!" I answer jokingly as I text Henry, *Thank you, but I'm fine. Really it's sweet of you but I'm not nauseated.* I wonder if I should ask him how Evan is. Where he is. Or anything at all.

Before I can, he answers that he wants to meet for lunch soon.

"You know, he's really sweet," I tell Sue, feeling guilty and torn about what to do.

"So, that's where his son got his charm from then?" Sue asks sarcastically then mouths she's sorry when she sees I'm not amused.

"I'll just tell him I will, but I can always bail," I reason out loud as if I need her approval.

"Yeah, that's a good way to handle it." She nods with pursed lips then looks me up and down. "You should probably put real clothes on."

"How fancy?" I ask her, setting the phone down as I realize I'm still in sweats and a baggy T-shirt.

"Let's go fancy, fancy." I hope she can see how the thought of getting prettied up makes me perk up. I could really use a night out, feeling beautiful and carefree. I'll just pretend I don't feel like falling asleep at the table.

"Fancy-pantsing it up tonight?" I ask, already feeling better than I did before she got here.

"You know it."

# CHAPTER
## twelve

*Evan*

ALL I CAN FOCUS ON ARE HIS TELLS.

You learn them fast in the line of business that led me to this moment. The sweat on his brow. The way his right foot won't stay still. His dilated pupils and quick breathing.

He's one of two things: high as a fucking kite, or going through withdrawal.

Judging by the look on this prick's face, James Lapour is fiending for his next hit.

I peek over my shoulder. His office is on the first floor. There are apartments above us and plenty of witnesses in case some shit goes down. More importantly, just outside those doors is Mason, sitting in his car and waiting for me in case I need him.

I've got two goals in coming here like this.

1. Warn him to back the fuck off.
2. Get any evidence I can.

Seeing as how he's in his office, goal number two will have to wait unless I can get a confession. The tape recorder in my pocket is already running.

It takes everything in me to keep my hate down, but the memory of Kat from my night terrors is all I can see. I can't sleep; I can't do anything without thinking about losing her. It's as if my sanity is steadily eroding. Blinking away the image of her, I prepare to do what I have to. For her. For us. All I want is for this to be done and over with, so I can be with her and be the man meant to stand beside her.

I walk into the office, the wooden floor beneath my ox-fords creaking eerily as I do. I've been standing outside the open door watching him for a few minutes. He didn't change the locks and there's no one else here on a late Wednesday night. Just him and me. Well, not quite, there are a few broads in the far back. I can hear them from here. Maybe they're waiting for him with exactly what he needs. I wouldn't be surprised.

"Taking a break from the snow?"

"What the fuck are you doing here?" he sneers at me, ripping his red-rimmed eyes away from the computer screen. With the city lights peeking through the drawn blinds, the room is bathed in a diffuse glow. It's darker than I'd like it to be in here with only the lamp on his desk illuminating the space.

"What I really want to know is, why?" The question leaves me coldly as I stalk closer to him.

"Why what?" he asks me, leaning back in his seat and I can faintly hear him pulling out a drawer, ever so slowly.

Racking the slide on the gun in my hand, I raise it slowly. "Uh, uh, uh," I reprimand him. It's been a long fucking time since I've aimed a gun at someone. I've never wanted to pull the trigger more, though. "I wouldn't do anything stupid if I were you."

He raises his hands slowly, cocking his head and letting out a sick laugh. "So, you here to kill me now? Is that it?"

"I should, shouldn't I?"

"For what, exactly? Spit it out, you coward," he scoffs at me. His eyes appear nearly black with the lack of light.

"I'm the coward?" The ridicule comes complete with an arched brow. I have to be careful with the loaded gun. My anger is putting me on edge, the adrenaline in my veins pumping hard and every second that passes makes my body temperature go up just a little more.

One of the girls from the back room yells out, "You all right in there?" in response to my raised voice.

Before I can respond, James answers her. "Just stay where you are." Good old James, he knows how to talk to the ladies.

"What do you want, Evan?" he questions, slowly placing his hands palm down on the desk.

His arm twitches and I can tell he's fucked up.

"What's going on with you?" I ask in return. "You're not looking so good."

"You look pretty fucked yourself," he spits out without wasting a second and forces a smile to his face.

"We saw you watching," I say, offering him a small piece of the puzzle.

"Watching what?"

"At Rockefeller Center."

"Is that so?" I hate this game. This back-and-forth where no real information is given. "And what exactly was I watching?" he asks with a smirk on his face although I can see in his eyes he's curious.

I shrug and say, "Doesn't matter, does it? What I want to know is what you plan on doing."

He laughs abruptly, deeply and from his gut, but any trace of happiness is immediately replaced with pain. He nearly doubles over and I raise the gun again, my heart beating hard as I prepare for him to come up with a weapon.

He doesn't, though, and when he sees the gun aimed right between his eyes, he forces his hands to the desk again.

"You stop doing coke? I guess Tony told you it was bad for you," I say flatly, swallowing thickly as my hands sweat and the gun feels heavier.

He groans an answer I can't hear then winces again.

"What the fuck is wrong with you? You got the shakes?"

"Fuck you," he manages to get out as his eyes shut.

"You paranoid now? Worried someone's going to do to you what you tried to do to me?"

He opens his eyes slowly, the light shining from the lamp creating shadows on his face. "The fuck are you talking about?"

"The coke you laced. You scared someone's going to do the same to you? Give you what you have coming?"

"It was from my personal stash, you prick."

I almost call him a liar, I almost tell him to shove it and put a bullet in his chest, so I can get back to Kat and end this shit. But the look on his face stops me.

310

He's always been a damn good liar. I know that much about him. But I'm better with tells.

He adds, "If I wanted you dead ... well, I know how to use a gun."

"You want to know what I think?"

"Sure, you can say that I'm intrigued," he retorts.

"I think you're greedy," I tell him as I lower the gun.

"Greedy?" he repeats with a crooked smile.

"I think you wanted to prove a point to your wife." I lay it out there for him. I'm not messing around; I want this prick to know that I'm fully aware of what he's doing.

"That bitch has got nothing to do with this."

There's a skip in my pulse. With a slight cock of my head I ask, "Who does then?"

His mouth parts, but then slams shut a second later. "Fuck you."

"I won't stop until I find out everything. Until every bit of dirt I can get on you is dug up and exposed."

"You know how much shit I've got on you, Thompson?" He seems to find his strength as he leans forward on his desk.

"This is a warning to stay away. From me and Samantha." I almost bring up Kat. I almost say she's pregnant. Every ounce of my being craves to demand that my family's off-limits. But that would only give him that much more of a reason to hurt her. So I keep her name out of the conversation; I keep her safe.

I'll do anything for her. Anything and everything. Fear stirs in my blood at the thought of her being on his radar. It's gone as quickly as it came, eased by his next line of questioning.

"So, it's true then?" he asks with a snort. "You two are together?"

It takes me a moment before I realize he's talking about Samantha and referring to the rumors. "She came to me for help."

"I always knew she'd cross me. I didn't think you'd be the dick she picked to go down with her."

I raise the gun and take a step closer. "Give me one reason I shouldn't kill you right now. You and I both know you deserve it."

He shrugs. "I have the evidence that proves you lied to the cops, for one. I have evidence on both you assholes."

"A dead man can't do shit with evidence."

"The cops will find it, and you know it. You don't want them poking around in here."

"What are you doing back here, baby?" A high-pitched voice rings through the hallway and I look quickly over my shoulder. I hear the door open and James smiles.

"Oh yeah, there are two other reasons. In all the years I've known you, you've never put your hands on a woman. Well, other than Sam, I mean."

"Shut the fuck up," I say, gritting the words through my clenched teeth.

"Come on back, sweet cheeks!" he yells out. He's calling my bluff and I'm quick to lower the gun, hiding it behind my leg.

My heart beats slowly and I can see it all playing out. Killing this fucker and the two girls from the back room screaming, running. I can see the red and blue lights reflecting off the glass.

"Are you ready for us?" A young woman walks in, skinny

as a rail with a sharp blond bob. It looks so perfectly straight, my guess is it's a wig.

The smell of perfume floods the room as she enters, swaying her hips and wearing light blue ripped shorts that ride up her ass.

Hookers.

"Let me just finish this conversation really quick," James tells her as the second girl walks in a bit behind the first. The blonde rounds the desk, peeking at me, but stalks toward James to perch on the corner of his desk.

"Whatever you want. I'm not in a rush."

"Hi there," a little brunette says. Her voice is softer, sweeter even, which matches her look. She's got a look that's more innocent, with clothes that actually cover her ass. She might sound sweet, but there's a devil in those baby blues of hers. Her eyes are bloodshot, and she can barely walk straight. She tries to lean against me but I take a step back, and when I do she sees my gun.

Her eyes widen, and she stumbles backward with a gasp. The two girls exchange a look while holding their breath, both on edge and realizing they shouldn't have walked back here.

"I was just on my way out," I reassure them. I tuck the gun back into the waistband of my jeans.

"I want to ask one question before you leave, Thompson," James says to my back as I turn away. "Wives aren't off-limits anymore, are they?" My blood rushes into my ears and I almost do it. I almost kill that fucker, consequences be damned.

"Ah, I see not all the rumors are true. Are they, Evan?"

"Leave her the fuck alone, James." My blood pumps hot as I stare into his beady eyes, but all he does is smile.

# CHAPTER
## thirteen

*Kat*

I T'S BEEN THREE DAYS NOW.

Evan hasn't come back or even texted. Just the thought makes my throat tight. My eyes are filled with sadness that I can't shake. A piece of me feels like it's mourning, but not ready to let go of hope.

I've texted and called, remembering how he said he loved me and this was only going to last for a short while. It was pathetic of me.

I'm lonely, emotional, pregnant. I was desperate to believe he still loved me.

The text was simple. *It's really hard without you. I'm sorry; I was wrong to give you an ultimatum. Please forgive me. I miss you and I really need you.* That's what being lonely does to me. It makes me weak and wish he'd just come back to me.

Brushing under my puffy eyes, I stare down at my phone. It's my raw heart and the very last pieces of the shattered thing that bring me down this low. I never heard anything back.

I thought it would get easier, but somehow Evan refusing to talk to me is making it harder. He doesn't return my calls, doesn't text back. Nothing. The only contact I have with him is an excerpt from the Page Six column quoting him as saying that we've split.

I remember how he said it was just for a "short while." Maybe that's how he got me. He left me with hope.

That fucking bastard.

It's like my body doesn't want to hate him and instead, the blame is falling on me.

It's my fault I pushed him away.

My fault I gave him an ultimatum.

Why am I the one hoping he'll forgive me?

Why am I the one praying he'll write me back, leaving voicemails saying he's sorry?

At least at night. And only late at night.

The days are so much easier. Although I know I'm to blame too. I know I contributed. If only I could take it back, I would.

After the unanswered texts, I started packing everything of his to place into storage. Starting with his clothes from a basket of clean laundry. Removing those clothes from my sight didn't make any bit of difference with the sadness. The harsh tears and sobs came when I started ripping the photos off the wall and throwing them into a box.

It was my breaking point, the moment I knew I'd lost it and couldn't stay here, surrounded by pieces of him.

So I moved out and into Jules's guest room.

I don't know if I'm insane, hormonal, or how the hell I'm supposed to react to all this. The only thing I really know is that I'm not the first woman to have a man leave her. I won't be the last, either. It is what it is, and every second that goes by with Evan not saying a word is one more layer added to my armor.

"What about her?" Jules questions and I lift my gaze to her, trying not to show how messed up I am. It's not her fault.

She's cuddled up on the couch, a soft cream and brown striped throw over her legs with the computer in her lap. She turns it toward me so I can check out the profile and résumé she's looking at.

*Personal Assistant—Angela Kent*

She has experience and an impressive résumé. My gaze scans down the lines on the screen, but it's hard for me to focus. Interviews are a must at this point; I have to hire someone to help me. Or take on less work from the agency. Both are viable options. I only need to pick one. Hopefully sooner, rather than later. I'm drowning in work, but struggling to do any of it.

"Maybe," I tell her and lean back into the sofa. I let my head fall back and wish I had one thing figured out in my life. Just one.

It seems like nothing can go right anymore.

The doubt only lasts seconds and with a deep breath, I find myself glancing back to the screen to read the applicant's résumé again.

"Hey, come on," Jules says, attempting to console me. She places the laptop on the ottoman so she can scoot forward and lean against the armrest of my chair. "It's going to be okay.

YOU KNOW I need you

No matter how dark the night gets, the sun will come up in the morning." She gives me a soft, encouraging smile to cheer me up. It's one of the lines from her first book she gave me as her agent. The memory takes me back to the high point of my life and then it crushes me.

"I'm sorry … It's just that the nights are hard."

"I get that," she says, her kind tone adding extra comfort to the small words. "Do you want me to make you some tea?"

I shake my head. "I think I just need to sleep," I answer her but I really don't know what I need, and that's the problem. There's no solution to this because it's out of my control.

"If he said he's coming back, I guess the real question is: Do you wait for him?"

"I told him it's over." I sniff and absently pick at a snag on the corner of the throw. "I told him if he walked out, I was done."

"I know what you said. But it's obviously not over, not for you."

I mutter softly, "I would be stupid to take him back."

Jules smirks at me as she says, "We've all done stupid things. Haven't we?"

She continues the conversation as she stands, letting the throw fall to the floor so she can stretch her back and adds, "Besides, forgiveness isn't stupid, and neither is love." She speaks so confidently and in a lighthearted tone as if they're so obviously true.

"Can I beat the crap out of him first?" I peek up at her with a half grin, feeling a bit upbeat just from her being with me. She's a damn good friend and I hope one day I have the chance to be as good of a friend back to her as she is to me.

"I think I'll allow it," she responds as her own smile grows.

Mason's footsteps can be heard approaching from down the hall. He's not quiet in the least and part of me wonders if he wants us to know he's coming. "Sweetheart?" he calls out and we both turn to the open doorway before he enters.

"You wanna come to bed?" he asks Jules, bracing his hands on either side of the door jamb before leaning just his upper half into the room. Like he's checking to see if he's welcome.

"I don't know," Jules answers him, but her last word is distorted by a yawn. She's never been a night owl.

"Go to bed, I'll be fine," I tell her, knowing darn well she's only staying up for my sake. I wave her off. "I'm tired too."

"It might be silly," Jules says as Mason strolls toward her and wraps his arm around her waist, "but I'm really happy you're here."

"Thanks," I reply and mean it. Such a simple admission makes my heart swell. That's how badly I need someone right now. "I'm lucky I have you," I tell her. "And I guess you too," I say to Mason, suddenly feeling awkward that he's in the mix of this chick lovefest.

"You staying up?" he asks me.

"Nah, I'm exhausted. I think I'm just going to watch something and pass out."

"I can stay up with you," Jules offers, and her voice is even peppy. She's eager to help me, but she's not the one I need.

"I'm good. Seriously," I tell her easily and for a moment I think I will be when she yields and they say good night. As their footsteps slowly quiet to nothing, the television proves useless as a distraction, because the memories of what happened only nights ago come flooding back. It all haunts me, refusing to let go.

How I opened my heart to Evan, when it was raw and damaged from his doing.

How accepted I felt when he said he was happy we were having a baby. Not just accepted, but complete and whole and like everything was going to be better than okay.

How loved I felt when he held me and kissed me.

How I didn't want to be anything other than *his* when he laid me down in bed.

I think that's the part that hurts the most. I would give up everything to just be his.

And he can't be bothered to text me back. Not even today, and I really could have used his support today. It was hard enough to keep my composure for the full two hours. I didn't say anything the entire time. But on the way back home, I felt a pair of eyes on me. It was like a prickle at the base of my neck, like a sixth sense that told me someone was following me.

I hailed a cab and texted Evan immediately. It was out of habit more than anything else.

I was probably just crazy with paranoia and all the hormones and raging emotions coming with the pregnancy. At least I'm honest with Evan, open and raw. If nothing else, I'm giving him everything I have to offer. He can't even send me a reassuring text.

Absently my hand falls to my belly. It's been doing that. Reminding me that there's another small life in the mix. I focus on taking deep breaths in and out. More than anything, I need to stay calm.

I pick up my phone, intent on texting everything.

He can ignore me all he wants, but I'm going to tell him everything I feel. I deserve that much. To at least be able to tell him what's on my mind. *I'm not the one who keeps secrets. I'm not perfect*, I text him. *I'm slowing down at work. I have to, I'm so tired. I love being pregnant, though. I love knowing we're going to have a baby.*

*I'm afraid I'm hurting him by being this way. I don't know how to get better, though.*

I delete the last two lines and stare at the ceiling as tears threaten to come.

I used to do this when my parents passed. I used to write to them like I did when I was a kid at camp. After they died, I'd write to them telling them how angry I was. I begged them, pleading with them to come back.

It's not fair that Evan is alive and says he wants me, when a very large piece of my heart feels like I've lost him forever.

*Please, Evan. Please come back to me.*

Just as I delete all the words, not sending him a single message, my phone rings. It's a number I don't recognize, and I let it ring again in my hand before answering it. "Hello?"

"Hello. This is Dr. Pierce. Is this Katerina Thompson?"

"Yes, can I help you?" The nervousness wracks through my voice at the knowledge that there's an unfamiliar doctor on the line.

"I'm so sorry to call you, but Mr. Thompson's phone has you listed as his daughter. Is that right?"

I'm confused at first, imagining that Evan's in the hospital, but then I realize it's his father, Henry, who the doctor is referring to.

"Is he in the hospital?" The question comes out hurriedly

as I sit up straighter, my mind waking up from the fog it was just in. Rather than correcting the doctor and telling him I'm Henry's daughter-in-law and soon-to-be ex-daughter-in-law at that, I rush the next question out without waiting for a response to the first. "Is everything all right?"

The doctor exhales on the other end of the line, but it's not out of exhaustion or boredom. It's the type of sound that accompanies bad news. The kind of sigh that says, *I'm so sorry, I wish I didn't have to tell you.*

No. No, no, no. Denial overwhelms me.

"I would like to first apologize for having to break this news to you over the phone," the doctor says, and I'm taken back to middle school. Sitting down in the principal's office, wondering what I did. I sat there, my legs swinging nervously as he brought in the secretary, then gave me such a sad look before leaving the room. He was so sorry to tell me. They're always so sorry to tell you.

No one wants to be in the room when you learn your parents have died. No one wants to be the person to tell you. I could see it in Mrs. Carsen's eyes.

"Sorry to tell me what?" I ask with caution, but my body is already prepared for it. My heart feels both swollen and hollow, and my head light with denial. I lower myself to the floor, my hand shaking as I hold the phone to my ear.

"Mr. Thompson suffered a blood clot, and unfortunately it traveled to his lungs."

I remember the way the bell rang as I cried and the other students ran through the halls, going about their lives and not knowing my life had changed forever in that moment.

The same agonizing pain rips through me and tears fall freely as I end the call.

He can't be dead. Not Henry. I just talked to him; a voice in my head whispers the reminder.

He was the only dad I had, and I threw him away. He was supposed to be with me tonight. Like he wanted.

If I had met with him, if I hadn't blown him off ... Regret consumes me.

I can hardly breathe as the phone drops next to me and I cover my face. He didn't deserve to die. It's an odd thing to think because it means others do. But Evan's father should still be here. He wasn't supposed to go. Not yet.

My body shudders as I hold back a sob.

I've cried so many tears over the past weeks. So many shed on my pillow, in my hands, soaking into my heated skin.

These tears are different.

It's not from a fear of loss. It's not because I'm disappointed in myself. It's not even because I'm hopeless.

When you shed tears over something that's truly gone, those are the tears that never leave you. They drown your soul and take a piece of your heart. That's what death does.

I have to force myself to text Evan once I've finished speaking with the doctor. *Call me as soon as you can, please. It's urgent, Evan.* I can't help that I add, *I love you.* I'm not conflicted about adding it either, because I do.

I can't tell Evan the news over the phone, though. I want to be there for him. To hold him and ease the pain. Even more, I need him to hold me right now.

I hesitate but then add, *It's about your father.*

The phone shifts out of focus as my eyes blur and my hand shakes, but I hear it ping after only a small moment.

It's not Evan, though, it's Jake. *Hey, you want to grab coffee?*

I have to force myself not to message him. I have to force myself not to tell him that I'm not okay. With how badly I want to be held, I wish I could, but I refuse to use him.

But after an hour going by and a dozen more text messages unanswered by Evan, I cave. I have to tell him, and so I do. I tell him over a text that his father passed away and after crying for hours and seeing that he read it, I still get nothing back.

I text Jake, *I'm not okay.*

# CHAPTER
# fourteen

*Evan*

*She won't wait for you forever,*
*There's no way she ever could.*
*Time changes by the day and life,*
*Brings both the bad and good.*
*It creeps into who you are,*
*Deep down in your soul.*
*The person that you left behind,*
*Will never again be whole.*

I T'S FITTING IT WOULD SNOW TODAY. I SHUDDER AS I watch men dig the hole my father will be laid in tomorrow. The ground's hard and stubborn. Like my father, in a way. The frigid air isn't doing a damn thing to aid me in keeping my composure.

All day, all I could think is that it was James who somehow found a way to kill my pops. Mason's the only reason I didn't go back to his office and kill him. Even if he wasn't there, there's no place he could run.

I'm paranoid. I'm desperate. I'm fucking lonely.

I want my wife. I need her. A weak man would go to her and she'd be made a target. Mason assured me she's safe, and this would only help reinforce to James that Kat and I aren't together anymore and she shouldn't be on his radar in the least.

The snow crunches to my right and I turn toward the small parking lot. Mason's early. I didn't even hear him come up behind me until now.

"Thanks for coming, man," I greet him and take his outstretched hand.

"I'm so sorry," Mason tells me as he looks behind me to the gravesite. He found Kat downstairs and I'm still devastated that I wasn't there for her like he was able to be.

Every piece of me is begging to go to her. She can make me feel better—not right, but better.

"You hear anything from your guy?" I ask Mason as I turn from the two men digging my father's grave. I'm desperate for someone to blame this on. It's hard to grasp it's real, let alone just a random occurrence. I'll fucking lose it if he says yes, but that's what I'm praying for. I'm already on edge. Anger is so much easier to handle than despair. If this was because of me, I'll never forgive myself. My heart clenches as Mason stares back at me.

"It was natural causes," he says lowly with more sorrow

than I anticipated. I have to turn from him and face the nearly empty parking lot as the wind whips at my face.

I bite back the need to cry and simply nod my head.

Just a blood clot. Just bad luck. There's no one to blame or kill.

That's what hurts the most.

"I'm sorry," Mason says, offering his condolences again. He gives me the space I need as I walk off a few feet closer to the empty plot and I'm grateful for it.

"Your girl," Mason starts and then clears his throat. "You've got to do something for her." His voice is weak like he's begging me.

"You're the one who said I can't," I remind him as I turn back to face him. He told me not to. To not even think about texting her back. James is tracking my phone, just like we're tracking his. He'll know the moment I message her.

"When I asked about her being followed, you said it wasn't your guy," I add.

"This is different," Mason says like it wasn't devastating that someone could've been watching her. If they're watching her, they could be setting her up. If she really felt eyes on her, that is. There's not a hint of activity at our place and we haven't seen anything ourselves.

"She's not doing too well." My blood turns to ice as I wait for him to spit it out. *Not her.* I swallow thickly.

"This morning she said, 'everyone in her life dies,'" Mason tells me with a deep crease in his forehead. "She needs someone."

"You're the one who said she has to believe it too. That we're over with."

"I know, I know," Mason says.

"So, which is it?" I practically scream, the words ripping their way up my throat. Light-headed, freezing and desperate for this all to be over, my world spins around me, too fast for me to keep a level head.

"I'm sorry, I just … it's rough seeing her like this." I can't stand it. This is torture. Maybe it's the punishment I deserve but it's as if I'm dying from a thousand tiny cuts, and I can't stop a single one.

With a chill hammering into my bones, I finally face Mason. My voice is ragged when I ask, "Do I go to her, or not?" If it was up to me, I would. I would hold on to her and lie in bed, denying everything and hiding away with the woman I love. All I can imagine, though, is that the door would be kicked in at some point. He'd come for me, and she'd be right there.

Mason's expression falls and he runs a hand down his face before taking a half step closer. "My mistake, man, I'm sorry. Jules is there. She's not going to leave her. Just … just wait a little longer."

"How much longer?"

"We don't have shit. Lapour's record is clean and there's no evidence of anything. We'll have to plant it. Including tampering with his emails and credit card data."

"How long?" I question again, not bothering to hide the irritation in my voice.

"Only days."

Days … I can wait days. Everything will be right again after that, and I'll make it better. I nod, pacing in a short circle. Just days. The seconds tick by so slowly.

"After what happened in his office …" I voice the concern that's repeating in my head on a loop. "The way he brought her up. Like he was …"

"She's safe. I have her locked away with Jules and she doesn't even know it."

"Locked away?" I ask, stopping in my tracks.

"No one's getting into that house. And Jules knows not to take her out. If Kat wants to go somewhere," Mason says and snaps his fingers, "there's a security detail that'll be on her the second the door is opened."

"So, she's safe?" Knowing she's all right makes not being with her a little easier to swallow. She's protected and that's all that matters. I can't lose her too.

"She's safe and this helps take any heat off her," Mason answers me. "We're tracking his emails and calls, and her name hasn't been mentioned. Yours is, though."

I snort at the idea of James planning a hit on me. "And what's he saying?"

"Wants eyes on you. Wants to know what you're doing and who you're seeing."

My heart sinks at the thought. "Who I'm seeing," I echo, feeling crushed. It's like he wants me to have to stay away from her.

"Yeah," Mason says with a defeated tone. "Could mean his ex, could mean lawyers or cops …" He doesn't finish but I hear the unspoken addition, could mean Kat.

My resolve hardens, but it sends a shooting pain down my chest. I twist the wedding ring on my finger and look back at the grave. I'll be buried with this ring. Either now or years from now. Forever hers.

"Call her from a different phone, just one call?" Mason suggests as I watch the men shoveling piles of dirt. "Not with your phone. From someone else's." I barely register Mason's words.

"If I see her or talk to her," I say, my words coming out as numb as my body feels, "I don't know how I'll walk away again."

"It's a tough call," Mason says faintly.

"She's not at risk now?" I ask him again. It's fucked up, but part of me wants her to already be in the line of fire. Just so I can go to her. To hold her, and take back everything. I hate myself for thinking that for even a second. I'm weak. I need to be stronger for her.

Diary Entry One

Dear Pops,

I've seen Kat do this a few times.

Writing a letter to talk to her parents. It's how I knew back then that she wasn't doing too well. I'd give her extra attention and keep a closer eye on her whenever she took out that journal. I'm not doing too well now, and I need you. Thought I'd give this a try; I don't have anything else.

I miss you already.

If you're with Ma, tell her I miss her too. That I love her and wish you two were here.

God, I do. I need you two.

I'm sorry I wasn't there. I'm sorry I wasn't a better son.

I'm so damn sorry that the last conversation we had was

about how disappointed you were in me. I promise I'm trying to do what's right. It's so hard to know, though.

It's too many lies to know what the truth is. Too many secrets to hold on to what's real.

I'm afraid of losing everything. It's like it's all crumbling around me and I can't stop it.

I'm so damn alone, and it's my fault. I'm terrified to be close to anyone right now.

I need you to do me a favor. You gotta look out for Kat.

She misses you and she's not okay.

She used to say that when she'd write, her parents would be there in some way. She said she knew they were watching. She knew they heard. I hope you can hear me now.

Can you go to her? Please?

Give her a sign that you're there and that you love her.

I'm trying, Pops, but it's so hard to know if I'm doing the right thing.

If I lose her too, it's over for me. There's nothing left.

So please, don't watch over me. Stay with her.

I love you forever.

# CHAPTER
## fifteen

### *Kat*

*It's memories that hold me back,*
*The visions of yesterday.*
*Back when we were so happy,*
*And our faith did not yet stray.*

"THANKS FOR MEETING ME HERE."

"No problem," Jake responds with a charming smile as he sits down across from me in the booth.

We're back at Brew Madison and not the café closer to Jake's place. It's "my place," but it feels different. Everything feels a bit different now. Nothing feels like it did once; that feeling of being home isn't the same without Evan.

"Tired of the chai?" he asks, and I have to laugh.

"No, it's just that Jules, my friend who I'm staying with for a bit, wanted to meet across the street after we're done, so I asked her driver to bring me here."

"Ah, gotcha. What are you guys going to do?" His question is casual as he looks up at the menu across the wall. It's a large black chalkboard with all their drinks written in elegant flowing script. I'm pretty sure it's not actually handwritten, but I could be wrong.

"The chai is better at your place," I tell him and snag my caffeine-free pumpkin spice coffee from off the small table. Apparently, Maddie's tastes have rubbed off on me. Either that or the baby has ruined my taste buds and given me a temporary sweet tooth.

He chuckles as I take a large gulp then tell him, "I think we're getting dinner at a little Italian place Jules loves. Or maybe heading to the new bar below the hotel a few blocks over." I shrug and add, "She hasn't decided yet, but it's girls' night, so we're doing something."

He lays his coat over the back of his seat as he stands. "I'm going to go with straight black coffee."

"Oh?" I ask him. "Is it one of those days?"

"You tell me," he responds and instantly my smile falls. It's been a week since Henry died and each day is worse than "one of those days." They blur together and time has flown by, but somehow, it's only been a week.

"Give me a sec?" he asks me before leaving, as if he's checking on my well-being, gripping the back of the chair. I nod, not trusting myself to speak.

My fingers play at the edge of my coffee cup. I wore lipstick today and the outline of my lips mars the white rim.

There's a statistic I read once about how lipstick sales and alcohol sales both go up during depressions, while sales for everything else plummet.

The alcohol ... well, you drink when you're happy and you drink when you're sad.

The lipstick is because in hard times, we just want to feel special, pretty. We want to feel like we're worth it. As in, if we look pretty and put together, then maybe we can be.

I need to buy more lipstick, I think.

It only takes a moment of me checking my phone before he's back with a brighter spirit and the robust smell of fresh black coffee joining him from the cup in his hand. "So, what's going on?"

"Wow, that was fast," I say to stall a moment longer.

"I'd rate them an A-plus for the service. I'll have to admit that," he answers with a pleasant smile.

I give him a soft one in return, but I can feel it breaking down as I try to formulate an answer to his question.

"Evan's father died." The truth rushes out and my expression crumples regardless of how hard I'm trying to keep it in place.

"Shit," Jake murmurs beneath his breath as I desperately work to maintain my composure. "You all right?"

"I'm fine," I answer in a choked voice, refusing to cry again. "I'm dealing with it. It's not the first time I've lost a family member, but it still hurts."

"What happened?"

"It was sudden. He had a blood clot that traveled to his lungs." As I pick up a napkin from the table and blot under my eyes, I remember the doctor's voice and how calmly he spoke. My lashes graze the napkin as I blink and it comes back black.

"I'm sorry; I'm such a mess," I tell him, flipping the napkin to the other side and being careful not to smudge my makeup too much.

"Don't be." It's only then that I realize how close he is. He's so warm. "Evan," I say, blurting out his name as my tired eyes feel heavy and the need to be held makes my body hot. My fingers itch to lay across Jake's lap. "I tried to call him and got his voicemail."

"About his father?" Jake asks, and I find myself leaning closer to him. Jake doesn't let on that there's any more tension between us than usual. The air between us has shifted. It's something closer and vulnerable. Something I should be wary of, but I need it. God, I need it.

I nod once, twisting the little shreds of the napkin I'm destroying in my lap. "The doctor called me. I was my father-in-law's emergency contact." My throat tightens yet again and my words are choked, thinking about how I was listed as his daughter in Henry's phone.

"And Evan?"

"He didn't answer."

Jake leans back, putting a bit of distance between us and seems to question whether or not he wants to respond. He takes a heavy breath as if he's going to, but sips his coffee instead. I study his face as he stares straight ahead.

"I'm sorry, I shouldn't even be talking about this. I just—"

"Stop saying you're sorry, Kat." Jake turns his head and gazes deep into my eyes as he tells me, "You have nothing to be sorry for, and I don't understand why anyone would make you feel like you do."

My breath comes in shorter bursts, my heart beating faster. But all I can think about is how I wish Evan would say those words to me.

My teeth sink into my bottom lip as I reply, "I am sorry, though." I don't know what else to say. It's just how I feel.

"Well, I'm sorry too. I'm sorry about your father-in-law. And I'm sorry your ex isn't there for you. I'm sure he's going through his own things, but it doesn't seem right that he's ignoring you like that. He's got to know it hurts you."

"He doesn't feel like my ex most of the time," I admit to Jake with my eyes focused on my fingers as I continue to shred the napkin.

I'm anxious for Jake's response. It would lift a weight and burden for someone to understand, and I feel like Jake can. Even if he can't, I don't think he'll judge me. I hope he won't.

"You've been married for years, right?" I nod at his question. "And you only just split?" I nod again to confirm.

"You're going through a lot, and he's not even talking to you. I don't get this guy. I wouldn't throw you away like that."

"I don't think he's throwing me away so much as putting me to the side while he tries to …" An uneasy sigh slips into the silence when I can't finish my own thought.

"I read in the papers about what he's got going on," Jake says, and I'm forced to look at him, my heart beating slowly as I wait for his judgment. "I don't get how the two of you fit together, honestly."

"We have more in common than you'd think."

"Still have? Or had?" he asks me. Without waiting for a

reply, he shakes his head. "Tell me to fuck off if you want," he offers then closes his eyes and takes a quick sip of coffee. "I'm only here if you want to talk. And if I cross a line—"

"You're not crossing any line," I reassure him and find myself reaching out, letting my hand fall on top of his. Mostly for fear of him backing away and leaving me with nothing again. "I don't talk to anyone else really." The plea is unsaid, but Jake hears it. I'm already a burden to my friends. I know I am, even if that's what friends are for. The one thing I know, though, is that they'll remember everything Evan's done, and they'll hate him like I do right now for treating me how he has. Even if they don't say it. So all of this animosity and worry over him and his actions? I can't give it to them. I need someone else. Someone like Jake.

His soothing gaze assesses me and stays on mine as he tells me, "I don't want you to get upset with me because of an opinion I have when I only know a small fraction of the truth. I know the past goes deeper than that."

It's small kindnesses that kill the pain. The tiny bits break down walls, making them crumble all because they hit at just the right spot, at just the right time.

"Just don't hate me for still loving him," I whisper.

"I think you still have feelings for him because you haven't let anyone else in," he says and leans just a bit closer to me.

*If Evan would give me just a little, I wouldn't be here.* The thought flies through my mind as Jake leans forward a bit more, his gorgeous dark green, hazel eyes focused on my lips.

*If Evan would only comfort me or let me comfort him, I wouldn't have even called Jake,* I think as I close my eyes and breathe in the masculine scent of Jake's cologne. The deep forest fragrance fills my lungs as he gently presses his lips against mine.

*If Evan really wanted me, if he cared about me ...* the thought is lost when my hands move to Jake's hair, my fingers spearing through it as my lips part and Jake deepens the kiss.

The problem is that when my eyes are closed, I picture Evan. It's his fingers that thread through my hair and cup the back of my head. It's his lips pressed against mine.

The problem is when I open my eyes, it's not Evan. No matter how much I want it to be him.

Diary Entry Three

Dear Mom,

I really could use you today. You had such great advice when I was younger.

Evan's father passed away and I don't know what to do. I want to be there for him because I love him even though he's not here for me. But he didn't want me to be there for him. Not even at the funeral. He hardly looked at me.

Mom, I think he blames me in some way. Or there's something I don't know. I don't understand it. You know how you told me to be honest with my emotions? I feel like I'm dying inside. I can't describe how badly it feels to stand near him and be completely ignored because "hurt" doesn't do it justice. It's an emptiness I don't know how to fill.

I love him so much, but I cried alone in the car at the funeral. He didn't hold me. He didn't talk to me. He only hugged me like he hugged everyone else. Like I was no one special.

I thought for a second he would let me cry in his arms.

Or that he would cry in my arms like he did when his mom died. But he didn't. He just left.

He didn't need me, Mom. He didn't need me at all and it feels like I need him just to breathe.

There's something else too. Something that you might not like. Or I don't know, maybe you'll like it now that you know what Evan did.

I kissed someone else.

I can't help feeling like I'm cheating on Evan.

But if Evan doesn't want me, it's okay, right? It doesn't feel okay. Separated or divorced, I still love Evan.

This guy, his name's Jake, he treats me like he cares about me. Not that we've done anything really. I don't even know him. I think I want to, though, and that scares me.

My heart belongs to Evan, but there's someone else who wants to take it.

Seeing Evan at the funeral is what broke me.

I don't know what to do.

I tell you that a lot, don't I? That I don't know what to do. But for the first time, I want to do something. I'm ready for something to change. I know you'd know what to do.

I wish you were here. I miss you. I love you.

# CHAPTER
## sixteen

*Evan*

T HE PILES OF DIRT ARE GROWING LARGER. THE metal shovels pierce the frozen soil. The sound cuts through my bones, one and then another and another.

It's been constant as I stand here helplessly. I've never been colder, the bitter wind and blustery snow besieging my body, but I still don't move.

I can't take my eyes from the two graves.

The shovels spill the dirt, the piles mounting as my eyes drift to the tombstones.

The first my father, a man who died before his time. A death of tragedy.

And then to my wife's. My love's. No one believes me. He put her there. James killed her.

*My eyes pop open wide when I hear Kat whisper, "It's all your fault."*

I wake up gasping for air, my heart pounding and I swear I can feel Kat's hot breath on my neck even though I'm alone. My eyes dart around the room as I slowly lift my body into a sitting position on the bed.

Just a terror. The same as last night.

I'm quick to grab the video monitor for the security system from the nightstand and flick the button on to bring it to life. Mason set it up for me to keep a close eye on her.

It's only when I see Kat in bed that my heart starts to calm, and my heated skin seems to succumb to the chill of reality.

She's okay.

I close my eyes and when I open them, the monitor displays an image of her rolling over in bed. *To my side.* My fingers brush the glass where she is. I'll be there soon. I'll be with her and it'll all be over.

It's that promise to myself that brings me any sleep at all anymore. *It'll be over soon and then I'll be with her.*

∽

"There's a lot of shit you aren't going to like," Mason states matter-of-factly the second I close the door to his car. He doesn't even wait for my ass to hit the seat. He's situated outside the park and I focus on the people walking by. Moving through their day and carrying on with their lives, while mine's slowly deteriorating into nothing.

I needed this meetup to get the fuck out of this rut and

talk to someone. Even if it means hearing something I'm not going to like.

"Let's start with the easiest."

"You have a tail. Hired by Lapour," he says, and his sentences are short, clipped. I nod my head. I figured as much. I've been scoping James out and James is doing the same in return.

"The cops are coming around your place more often too and they've been poking around your family home, looking through the garbage. A few tags on the station's search engine too."

"They're not going to give up, are they?" It's not really a question. The leather of the seat groans as I lay my head back.

"They just need one thing to pin it on you."

"James has the evidence they'd need to do it." The photos come to mind and anxiousness makes my chest tighten. I'm waking up to heart palpitations and I'm constantly exhausted, but not able to sleep. My right leg rocks from side to side as Mason speaks.

"We can wipe them from his computer, but the hard copies will have to wait until tomorrow. My associate will ensure the place is clean, but then he'll know."

"That works. Whatever it costs."

"It takes time to get a batch of drugs that matches," Mason says and I know it's not about the money. It's about the time and executing it correctly.

"It would have been easier if we'd found it on him," I say, stating the obvious.

"Yeah, it would have," he agrees and then it's quiet.

"I'm failing. All this money paying other people to do shit and we're coming up empty."

"You're doing everything you can."

I can't stand the waiting anymore. "I want this over with," I confide in him. A couple of days turned into a week. And now the weeks are bleeding into one another.

"I'm walking around this city," I tell him, "stalking a man who should be dead. I *need* to do something." It's killing me to wait, driving me fucking crazy. I can practically feel my sanity slipping away.

"You have to be careful when you … take care of someone," he says as if I'm being impatient. "If you're reckless, you get caught.

"Besides, I don't have anything on James. Not a shred of evidence that shows he purchased the fentanyl."

"We need evidence or to set him up if there isn't any. Or we can just murder him and end it all." The thought has been festering in the back of my skull. Picking away at me. I just want to kill the fucker and be done with this.

"You kill him before it's ready, and the cops will be looking for his murderer. Is that what you want?"

I know he's right, and I can't answer. I respond with the only thing that matters. "I need my wife back."

"That's the other thing," he tells me while looking out his window.

"What thing?" I question, a deep groove settling down the center of my brow as I stare at the back of his head, willing him to look at me. "About my wife?"

"She's seeing someone," he answers and it's like white noise.

"You're wrong." Time slows. She isn't. There's no way she's seeing someone.

"She went out yesterday and we kept an eye on her like I promised you we would. My guys saw some things."

That's when a man's face comes back to me. My hands clench into tight fists at my side as I shake my head. Jacob whatever the fuck his last name is. My breathing comes in ragged pants as he says, "Jacob Scott is his name. A potential client of hers."

"Not my wife," I say, biting out the words although I already know it's true. "She's not going to move on so fast."

The worst part is that I don't even blame her. I'm dying inside. Every night I think about how my father should still be here and my wife should be in bed with me. Instead I'm alone, clutching a fucking T-shirt Pops always wore. He gave it to me when he gained a little weight and it didn't fit him any longer. It's just a shirt from a shop he used to work at. The shop's not around anymore.

I didn't give a shit about it back then, it was just a shirt, but all I can see when I hold it now is him. It's funny how the little things that don't matter are the most sentimental when you lose the ones you love.

That's my life. Hiding away and mourning my father alone. Hating myself and not being able to fix it all. I can't fix a damn thing.

"I told you she wasn't doing well," Mason says like I should have known better.

My teeth grind against each other as I seethe. "I can't do both at the same time, lead her on that we're broken up, but also be there for her." Pounding my fist against the window once like a madman, I hold on to the anger. I'll prolong every other emotion I can until I'm forced to deal with it at night when sleep refuses to comfort me. I know I must look like I'm fucking unhinged, but I am. So, I suppose it's fitting. "I can't protect her and have her in my life at the same time. There's no way for me to do it!" Exasperation gets the better of me.

"Well, if you're not there for her, someone else will be."

My heart's in my throat. That's the only explanation for what I feel. It's not in my chest where it's supposed to be. Only pain lingers there.

"I want to kill him. That Jacob fuck."

"Now I know that one isn't serious."

"He's seeing my wife!" I bite down on the inside of my cheek to keep from screaming, but Mason doesn't react.

He's silent as my rage slowly subsides.

"What would you do?" I ask him out of desperation as I imagine her calling him. Alone and desperate for someone to take away her pain.

Mason answers with a shrug, "Kill the asshole."

"You're a real wiseass, you know that?"

"It could be worse," he says.

"How's that?"

"She cried for a while when she got back from dinner with Jules."

I wait for him to continue, not understanding. "Why was she crying?"

"After seeing the guy, she cried all night. She's not moving on. She's not okay, Evan."

"What am I supposed to do? She's everything to me. And all I can see, all I dream about at night is her dying because of me." Mason doesn't answer me.

YOU KNOW I need you

No one has an answer for me. "If I lose her, I have nothing. There's no reason to live if I don't have her."

"You could always go with the locking her in a room option. She likes her office, right?" Mason jokes and I don't know whether to thank him for lightening the mood, or punch his fucking face in.

"Do you think James would go after her if I took her back?" I ask him. "Tell me honestly."

"If someone wanted to hurt you, the first thing they'd do is go after her." Mason says exactly what I already knew, and I rest my head against the window.

"He still might, but the chance of that seems low. Right now, James is only interested in three people: you, Samantha, and a man named Andrew Jones. Obviously, a cover."

Before I can ask, Mason adds, "We're paying him a visit soon. As soon as we track down his location."

I nod, agreeing with the plan, but all I can think about is that prick with his hands on my wife.

"What if we paid Jacob a visit?"

"You really think that's the way to go? Like Kat won't find out?" he asks me, and I grit my teeth.

"What if she goes home? What if you go home? Just be quiet about it. Rent a hotel room and make sure you're seen there for your tail. But go to her at night and make sure she keeps quiet."

"Kat can't keep a secret for shit."

"She's talking about going back home anyway. You're going to need to be there."

"You think she'd be okay with me just slipping in at night?

Maybe if I told her what's going on. But in and out, coming and going as I please? She'd kill me."

"Don't tell her shit. Are you fucking crazy?"

"Lie to her? Kat's always been able to see right through me. Lying is what made all this worse."

"I'm not saying lie to her. I'm just saying this is how it has to be. Right now, she needs comfort … She'll take what you can give her. James thinks you're with Samantha, so be seen with her, then head over to your place."

The very idea of being seen with Samantha makes my stomach coil. "You want my wife to hate me?"

"It's the only real option you have right now," he says and looks me in the eyes to add, "She'll never know."

He's a fool to think that. She'll find out. There's no fucking way I'm going to do that to her. She deserves better than that.

# CHAPTER
## seventeen

### *Kat*

I HAVE TO TELL EVAN ABOUT JAKE, BUT HE DOESN'T want to talk to me.

He's ignoring me. Intentionally hurting me.

Yet there's still a sense of obligation. As if I owe it to him to let him know that I'm moving on now. I've finally got a grip on my self-respect, but I need him to know it. I roll my eyes at the thought and heave out an aggravated sigh.

I don't care if it's weak or pathetic. He was everything to me.

I nearly trip as I realize what I thought. *Was.*

Is it really over? I struggle to breathe in the cold air as I think maybe a small part of me wants to move on. No, that's not it. It's simply accepting that it's time to move on.

*Say something, I'm giving up on you ...* song lyrics play

through my head as my throat dries and I force myself to keep walking up the sidewalk to 82 Brookside. Evan's family home.

The sad lyrics of the soft song are what keep me from knocking on his door at first. I attempt to compose myself because if Evan doesn't open this door, or worse, he does but doesn't hear me out? Then I have no hope left.

I know deep down in my gut, this is my last and final effort.

*Say something, I'm giving up on you* ... and then the melody stops, a feminine voice cutting through. The voice of a woman I recognize. Sadness freezes over, replaced quickly by something ... more gruesome.

Samantha.

I hear her laugh and then a muted voice. His voice. She's in there with him. Shock keeps me paralyzed. I listen a moment longer, denying it at first.

The only movement I can make is to hide my hands in my coat pockets as the winter wind brutalizes me. I thought my heart was already broken. Apparently, it was only torn because at this moment, there's no denying my heart's been ripped ruthlessly in half.

I'm numb as I stand in the harsh cold, trying to listen to the faint sounds as I lean my body toward the window to my right. I can barely see her, and I can't see him at all.

There's no way I can make out what they're saying, but I watch her put on her coat.

It's funny how anger can so easily replace sadness. Almost like rock paper scissors. Anger beats sadness, sadness beats ... I don't know what, and in this moment, I don't care in the least.

My heartbeat rages; my breathing shallows as I watch

that woman I once trusted standing in Evan's parents' home. He can't really be with her.

Time passes, maybe a minute more before I come to terms with it.

What a fucking fool I was.

This is why he left me. Of course. My breathing falters as I take a few steps back from the door, my warm breath turning to fog in front of me. Shoving my hair out of my face, I collect myself before I can fully fall apart.

With my arms wrapped tight around my shoulders, I hug myself as I walk aimlessly down the street. My shoes crunch the thin layer of fallen snow beneath my feet as I get farther and farther away. I let my mind whirl and my emotions stir into a concoction of self-doubt and recklessness.

"He thought I would wait for him while he had one last fling?" I whisper under my breath but then shake my head. "Maybe he's trying to pick which one of us he wants …"

Like a madwoman I talk to myself, ignoring the horns honking and cars speeding along the street next to me. I let out a sarcastic laugh and think, *his choice is made.*

He already left me, and I already told him it was over.

How dumb can I really be?

My hands fumble inside of my jacket as I turn the street corner. I bite down on the fabric of my glove and pull it off so I can unlock my phone.

*Evan's cheating on me.* I tell Jules first. I've talked to her more than anyone else since she's welcomed me into her house.

*No, he can't be!* She's quick to respond and I find myself standing still in the middle of the busy sidewalk, texting her back. Everyone walks around me, ignoring me and my mental breakdown.

*I'm pregnant with his child and he's cheating on me.*

*Why would you think that?* she texts back as I type my response.

*I just saw her.*

*Saw who?* she asks.

*Samantha.*

*And they were kissing??? That bastard!!*

I bite the inside of my cheek and hate that I can't say yes. They weren't kissing. I told him to stay away from her and she's inside his house, though. Isn't that enough?

*I didn't see them kiss. She's in his house.*

*What were they doing?* she asks, and I find my anger turning on her.

*I don't know!*

*What were you doing, spying??*

*OMG Jules! YES, of course, I was!* I stand there numb, reading the text messages and feeling like I truly am crazy.

*What did he say?*

*About them? I didn't go in,* I text her. I'm left with silence for a moment with no response back. The wind seems to pick up and my ears burn from the cold. Or maybe from people talking about me.

*I'm going to get proof.* I text Jules and spin around on my heels, shoving the phone into my coat pocket and ignoring the dings of her return messages.

I'll confront that bastard and make him pay for the hell he's put me through. All the while I work myself up. Each step back to his house is taken with stronger and stronger resolution.

Until I get there and his car is gone, and just like my gut told me the second I saw the empty spot in front of his house, the door is locked.

"Motherfucker," I scream out as I bang my fists against the door. The chill in the air makes each impact hurt more and more.

I start to text him even though my hands are aching from the freezing cold. One line saying, *I know.* And then I backspace until it's erased. That's not good enough, it's too mysterious. I text him a paragraph about what I saw, but I delete that too, knowing he'll just deny it.

Outside of his parents' house, outside of the house where I fell in love with him, the light dims from the sinking sun and the sudden sheets of gray signal more snow is coming.

Defeated, I slip my phone in my pocket, realizing only now that I've been trembling.

I'm not going to text him or confront him. Nothing. I'll figure out the truth and make sure I have evidence, but I'm giving Evan exactly what he gave me … nothing.

Diary Entry Four

Mom,

I'm worried about the things that I think sometimes.

I'm worried about how angry I get. Did you get like that ever?

I don't know if you would have. I did it to myself by marrying Evan.

I'm filled with anger more than anything anymore. I don't want to be like this, but it's what he's done to me. Maybe that's an excuse. That's probably what you'd tell me, isn't it? I'm responsible for my own actions and no one else's.

I've never been this angry, and I'm afraid of what I'm going to do.

# CHAPTER
## eighteen

*Evan*

I HAVEN'T BEEN THIS NERVOUS SINCE KAT AND I WENT out on our first date.

It was an easy date, a place I knew well. *My* club. I didn't own it; I never got into commercial real estate, although I have thought about it. It was still my club, though. At least that's how I felt. I should've felt in control and powerful to meet her in front of the doors, the music drifting out into the street, but one look at her stepping out of her car had my heart pumping faster and the back of my neck sweating.

Kat's always been able to stun me like that.

As if I don't already know she's beautiful.

It's something else, though, that's got me this nervous.

It's the sense that I can't hold on to her no matter what I do. That's the feeling I had flowing through my veins that night, and that's the feeling flowing through me now as I get ready to step up to the doors of Mason's house in the Berkshires.

I check my phone again to see if I have any more texts from him, but I don't. The last one said she was packing her stuff and planning on moving back to the townhouse.

I rap my knuckles on the hard oak doors, the cold air making it hurt just a bit. My body urges me to do it harder, to embrace the pain and focus on that and not the anxiety of rejection.

I would deserve it, after all.

The door opens in one tug, and the glow from the foyer chandelier carries to the porch. There she is. Holding the door open with her lips parted in shock.

"Evan." She says my name as she stands perfectly still.

A faint dusting of snow settles around me as I take her in. From the white socks on her feet, to the silk pajamas that must be a gift from Jules, because I've never seen them before in my life.

"Hey," I greet her and then swallow the lump in my throat. "I heard you were here."

Her expression hardens instantly as she seems to get over my surprise arrival.

"What do you want?" she asks me, although it sounds like an interrogation. Before I can answer, she takes a half step forward to come outside rather than letting me in, like a fucking lunatic.

"What are you doing?" I ask her with complete disbelief as she tries to shut the door.

"I'm not having this conversation in Jules's house," Kat

says as if it's an admonishment, like I'm the one who's lost their mind.

"Baby, get inside, it's freezing out!"

"Don't tell me what to do!" she yells back at me, and her words strike me across the face. I take it, though. I take one step back and watch as she crosses her arms over her chest and her cheeks quickly turn pink from the wind that won't let up, followed by the tip of her nose. "What do you want?"

"Are you sure you don't want to go inside?" I question her as calmly as I can, attempting to be reasonable.

"I went to your house today," she states. The blood drains from my face.

"Is that right?" I somehow manage to reply, knowing what's coming, my body tensing up. All I can hear is my heart pounding as I feel her slipping away from me.

"I don't want anything to do with you, Evan." The cutting words are spoken with a cracked voice. At least there's emotion left. If there's that, then I still have a chance.

"I don't know what you think you saw, but …" I start to tell her and then flinch from her shriek.

"Think?" she yells. "I saw her!" She moves in closer, getting in my face to scream at me. "Samantha. You left me to be with her," she says and seethes, the accusation coming out hard.

"Did you see me touch her?" I ask her, taking a step closer to her. "I know you didn't, because I never would. I'm not seeing her. I didn't even want her there."

"She was with you," she says the words then breathes out with nothing but pain and agony.

"Yeah, she was. A few times in the last week," I confess.

I don't want her to find out any other way. "I'm trying to fix things and she's—"

"I want you to go," she says, cutting me off.

"I won't until you tell me you believe me." I look her in the eyes, silently begging her, and wait for it.

"I told you not to. Just go!"

"Never. I would never stray from you." As I say the words, it's crippling. Because I know she did what she's accusing me of. She's the one who's seeing someone else, but I gave her the space to do it. I left her side.

It's all fucked.

She doesn't answer me, merely shivers in the cold as her bottom lip starts to turn a purplish blue.

"Let's go inside," I urge her, but she doesn't respond. "I want to talk."

"I thought the funeral might be a good time to talk," she finally says with tears in her eyes. "Guess you didn't?

Her words slice through me, down to my core. "It meant a lot to me that you were there," I manage to say, but I can't look her in the eyes. The tips of my fingers turn numb and the feeling flows through every inch of my body.

"Didn't seem like it," she replies, although she's lost a bit of strength in her voice.

"I'm having a difficult time handling it," I tell her, scrambling for an excuse, but there's so much truth in those words.

James was there at the funeral. He even shook my hand, the fucking bastard. The reason is right there on the tip of my tongue. I wanted to go to her, to hold her. To go home with her and get lost in her love. More than anything.

"You think it was easy for me?" she asks me after a moment of silence.

"You think it was easy for me?" I shoot right back and the memories of the grave, the service hit me. I have to pinch the bridge of my nose and close my eyes as I see the visions of the nightmares mixing with the memories. *I shouldn't even be here.* Regret flows through my veins. What am I doing?

"I'm sorry," she whispers, and her breath turns to fog. The wind blows, and her hair falls in front of her face as I tell her, "I'm sorry too." I get a little choked up, but I manage to tell her, "He loved you so much."

He really did. His voice telling me to make it right keeps playing in my head and it kills my strength.

"I told you I just needed time." I try to make the words come out strong, but instead, it's a plea. I don't know what to do anymore.

All I want to do is protect her. *Maybe that means losing her forever.*

She shakes her head. "What part of us moving on with our lives didn't you understand? I don't have time for games or whatever trouble you've gotten into."

"I'm fixing the trouble." I refuse to give up. "I just need more time."

"And how much longer is that going to be? How much longer do I have to sit on the back burner and wait for you to love me again?"

"I still love you," I say.

"You don't act like it."

"There's a reason for everything, I promise." I have to blink away the scenes of the funeral, of the night terrors.

"I don't want to hear your excuses anymore," she says and wipes under her eyes. Her voice is drenched with defeat. "You're supposed to be here for me."

I question everything in that moment. I'm so afraid of losing her, but the image of her dead on the ground makes me harden my resolve. I hesitate and immediately regret it.

"I need you to go, Evan. For good."

"It's because of Jacob, isn't it?" I can't help but blurt it out. I want someone else to blame. Someone else to hate other than me. "You're moving on with him?"

I can't help but point out that she's the one who wants someone else. I only want her. I won't lose her. I'll fuck her so good when all this is over, she'll forget any other man exists.

"You think I need a man? You think I need someone?" Her voice is coated with an anger I haven't seen from her before. "I never needed anyone! You're the only one I ever let in. You were the only one I let get close and I'll be fine, living the rest of my life alone."

"You want him more than me?" My jealousy gets the best of me.

"Get away from me!" she spits out as she opens the door to head into the house.

"I'm coming back for you," I tell her, and I mean it.

"Well I won't be here, and I'm changing the locks on the townhouse. So good fucking luck with that."

# CHAPTER
## nineteen

### *Kat*

I T'S A HEAVY, SINKING FEELING IN THE PIT OF YOUR stomach. It rocks back and forth, making you queasy and your body can't sit still. That's what it feels like when you know you're about to hurt someone.

At least that's how it feels right now.

I don't need anyone at all and I don't want anyone either. Maybe I'm proving it to myself, or maybe to Evan. I don't care which.

My pulse quickens, and I try to swallow the spiked ball in my throat when I hear the bell at the front of the café.

Jacob smiles sweetly with genuine happiness as he strolls over to the table, letting his jacket slip off his shoulders. I'm going to miss that charming grin he has. I'll miss the comfort his presence brings more.

"One more nice day before winter comes in," he says easily. It's felt like winter for weeks now to me, but he's from farther up north, so I suppose it hasn't been as brutal to him as it's seemed to me.

"One more nice day," I repeat, nodding my head at the ceramic mug on the table. I have to force the smile to stay on my face, but it doesn't fool Jacob.

"What's wrong?" he asks me, not touching the mug of chai already waiting for him.

I hate that I get choked up. It's stupid really. Childish and I'm far too grown for little kid games.

It was just friends, then just a kiss.

But it never should have been anything.

"Nothing," I answer and shake my head slightly then pick up the mug. Jake's face falls, but he still tries to cheer me up.

"So, I never got your answer about the movies tomorrow night." He's quick to change the topic, gracing me with that ever-present kind smile. "I heard it's going to be good."

My mug clinks on the small saucer as he adds, "I love coffee shops and all, but it'd be nice to do something more."

*More.*

It would be. I can see it. I can feel it. If my heart didn't belong to someone else, I could see Jacob being so much more. Well, not only that. I'm going to be a mother. My priorities have nothing to do with dating or starting anything new that doesn't involve the little life I'm carrying.

"I have to tell you something." I get the words out before I change my mind and swallow them. Before I give in to getting over Evan by getting under another man.

Jacob visibly winces then scratches the side of his neck as he looks to the right. "That doesn't sound so good."

"I kind of lied to you," I confess, feeling a viselike grip on my heart.

"You're not separated?" he says.

"No, we are. But I don't want to be."

"You still love him. I know you do."

"There's more," I continue, not daring to look him in the eyes, and hesitate.

"Just tell me," he urges me as if this is going to be easy, moving his hand to mine, and I stare down at where his skin touches mine. It's gentle, kind. It's the comfort I desperately need. But I can't be expected to always have someone to lean on. More than that, I want to stand on my own.

"I'm pregnant," I tell him and the only reaction I get is that his brow raises just slightly. It's comical really, and the small movement forces the corners of my lips up. I'd laugh if my heart didn't hurt as much as it does.

"*That*, I didn't see coming," he responds, keeping a small bit of humor in his voice. Slowly, he pulls his hand away but keeps it on the tabletop. I notice the absence of his touch instantly, though.

"Not far along?" I shake my head no at his question, feeling the end of my ponytail swish around my shoulders. "How long have you known?"

"A while," I answer honestly.

"So that's the lie?"

"Yeah … I'm sorry. I never should have kept that from you."

"Don't be," he tells me and waves it off, as if it's no big deal.

"I knew better. It was just …" I trail off and swallow my words, staring at a stain on the table. One that will never go away.

"It was nice being *okay* with someone. Right?"

I chance a peek up into his eyes. There's nothing but understanding there. "Yeah," I answer him and chew on my bottom lip. "I wanted to pretend to be okay for a little bit."

"Well it's not pretend," he continues and adjusts in his seat. "You can be okay if you want to." It's hard to hold his gaze as he brings his hand back to mine.

"Does he know?" I answer his question with a nod, my throat too tight to speak.

"And he …?" he starts to ask, but doesn't finish the obvious question.

"Says he's happy but he's still not with me. He's not committing and carrying on like he was. I want him, but I need him with me and he's not …" I'm ashamed of the answer.

It's quiet for a short moment. The ceramic mug in my hand slides against the wooden table and it's the only noise to be heard. The itch in my throat matches the prick behind my eyes. I've cried enough over all this. It's been weeks and this is simply how it is. With a sip of my peppermint tea, I accept it.

"So, do you want to go to the movies?" Jacob asks then picks up his mug. "I'd still like to go if you would."

My heart does this little flutter, a quick flicker of warmth that lets me know it's still there. It's gratitude and I think that's all I could give anyone else. It's all I'm willing to do.

I shake my head, once again, and give him a sad smile.

"I had to ask. I think it would've been good," he tells me,

forcing a smile then covering his disappointment by taking a large sip of the chai.

"You going to be okay?"

I shrug, honestly unsure of whether I'll ever be okay. "Some people are meant to be alone." *Or waiting for a love that may never come back.*

"You sound like me," he comments with a huff of humor that doesn't reach his eyes and then he takes a deep, heavy breath. "Gets tiresome, though."

"A story for another time perhaps?"

"I think it's the same story mostly, with only one big difference."

"What's that?"

"I think Evan may love you back, just like you love him. Whether or not he deserves it … well, that's a matter of opinion, I guess." I can't respond and instead, I let my gaze wander back to the stain on the table. "It wasn't the same for me. It was very much one sided."

"I'm so sorry, Jake." It's all I can respond and I genuinely am.

"Don't be," he says easily. "Fate puts people in our life for a reason." He takes a steadying breath before saying, "And now I know it's possible."

"What's possible?" For a moment I worry that he thinks the two of us being together is still an option when it's not at all for me.

"Not this like you and me," he says, rushing out the words as if hearing my unspoken thought. "Trust me, I wish it were. But I meant … just that there could be someone else for me."

"You could always write the story. Although I doubt you'd want me to be your agent, huh?"

"No … I don't think that would work really," he says with the same sad smile on his face that I've been giving him.

"Maybe we could still be friends?"

"I don't think that's for the best, Kat. I can't just be friends with you."

My hair tickles my shoulders as I nod and reach for my coat to leave. My movements are sluggish; I don't want this to be the last goodbye. But it is. I know it. I barely touched my drink and didn't have anything to eat, but that's okay. I knew I wouldn't anyway. Morning sickness has been rough this week so it's not like I'd be able to keep it down anyway.

"How about this," Jacob offers as I pull my wool coat tight around my shoulders. "You call me if you're ever not okay and want more. But I won't call you or text you again. It's in your hands."

"I'm sorry, Jake." I say the words, but they don't even make a dent in expressing what I feel.

"Stop being sorry. Do that one thing for me, will you?" he questions, his dark green, hazel eyes shining back just like they did the first moment I met him, and I merely nod and say my goodbye.

Every step back to my townhouse, I want to go back.

Every breath, I wish I could tell him that what he did for me, I can never repay, and I'll be forever thankful for that.

But neither of those things happen. I walk back to my townhouse alone and the first thing I do when I get home is delete his emails and his number.

I don't want to have the option to run back to him.

Jacob is a good man, but he's not for me. I don't need someone else to love me. I need to learn to love being alone again. So I can be whole for my child. So I can be a good mother.

Diary Entry Five

Dear Mom,

It's not so bad being alone. I'm not really alone, alone. Not with this baby growing, but I can't feel him or her yet. I still talk to him, though. I think it's a boy, but I won't know for weeks.

Like I said, though, I think it's going to be all right being alone for now. I remember having that same thought for a while after you guys left me. I know it's not your fault.

I just can't stand to think of needing someone. Not when it hurts so freaking bad when they leave you. Did you see what Evan did? I gave him that power and that's my fault. I won't do it again.

I should have known better.

If you could just remind me, maybe? The next time he comes around and says he wants me and that he loves me, can you give me a sign? Something that will remind me that he's just going to leave me again and how much that will hurt?

People don't change, and some people are meant to be alone.

I promise I'll be okay from now on, Mom.

I just forgot that I'm one of those people. But I remember now. I won't forget again.

# CHAPTER
## twenty

*Evan*

I'M USED TO SNEAKING AROUND. I'VE DONE IT ALL MY life. I'm a professional at it, after all.

The door to the townhouse opens and I turn to look over my shoulder at the cold, barren street. No one knows I'm here and I need to keep it that way.

The pictures of my wife and me stare back at me as I slowly close the door. Feeling the warmth and familiarity of the home I built with Kat makes the ache deep in my chest twist and turn to a sickening degree. She took down several of our photographs, leaving dark rectangles on the wall where they used to hang and the sunlight failed to lighten and fade the paint behind them.

The large clock on the back wall ticks loudly as I move through the place we made together. It's nearly 3:00 a.m., but still, I make sure I wasn't followed. With bated breath, I check the surveillance system … again.

The life I led destroyed the only thing I ever had that I wanted to keep. My marriage.

The knowledge pushes me forward, each step bringing me closer to her. Closer to the bed we once shared, and closer to her warmth under the covers. As I push the door open, my heart beats slowly. With every second that passes my skin burns hotter and the worry threatens to consume me.

But the sight of her steady breathing and the faint movements of her body as Kat stirs in her sleep put all my worries behind me. She's safe, and that's what matters.

Her eyes flutter open and I stand as still as possible, terrified she'll see me, but she merely rolls over in bed, moaning slightly, pulling the thin white sheet with her.

The moonlight filters in through the curtains and leaves a trail of shadows that accentuate her curves as they fall across the bed. She's still as gorgeous as ever. Even in her sleep with no makeup on and her bare skin kissed by the faint light of the early morning, she holds a beauty that, for me, surpasses all others.

How many nights have passed with me failing to see that? How much time have I wasted?

I can't let a soul know I still love her. They'll use her to get back at me.

My eyes widen and my grip tightens on the door as I hear my name slip through her lips. "Evan." It sounded like a prayer, or maybe a plea. A soft moan escapes her as I take a hesitant step forward, wondering if she saw me or if I'm only with her in her dreams.

I start to question if she even said it, but then she says it again. The sweet sound of her soft cadence whispering my name is everything I need to keep going.

I swallow thickly, hating myself for what I've done and what I've put her through.

I dare to whisper the only thing that helps lure me to sleep at night, hoping it'll soothe her too, "I'll make it right, Kat. I promise, I'll make it right."

# CHAPTER
## twenty-one

### *Kat*

**M**Y EYES POP OPEN AT THE FAMILIAR CREAK FROM the stairs. My heart races faster and faster as I lie as still as I can, not daring to move a muscle. My body's hot and the covers are making me even hotter, but I don't move. I try not to even breathe as I wait for another sound. But nothing comes.

It's just my nerves. Maybe a nightmare.

Slowly, my breath comes back, but I'm still too scared to move. Nearly paralyzed still, I blink away the sleep and tilt my head just enough to look at the clock on my nightstand. 04:14 AM stares back at me in bright red digital numbers.

The sounds of the city streets filter in and my quickened heartbeat fades. It was nothing, I whisper and reach for my glass of water, downing it then wishing there was more.

*Get up.*

I will my body to move. I wince and crack my back, letting my bare feet hit the cold hardwood floor. Sleeping alone has never been a favorite of mine. Until Evan, I spent years with poor sleep patterns, both in falling and staying asleep. Even more than that, I don't like how Evan's side of the bed doesn't have the faint smell of him anymore. I can feel the solemn expression on my face as I glance at where he used to sleep, but it only pushes me to stand up straighter and wipe the sleep from my eyes.

The floor protests as I walk, and I let the feeling that someone was in here leave me. I have the security system … but I think I'd like a dog. *A big dog.*

The corners of my lips tip up into a smile as I walk down the stairs.

Pushing back the hair from my face, I slink down to the kitchen and turn on the light. It's early, but I'm starving. To sleep, or not to sleep becomes the question.

It only takes a glass of water, two Twinkies and a couple handfuls of grapes before I don't feel so hungry anymore and sleep is calling me upstairs again.

Passing through the dining room, I check over my shoulder just to make sure there's no one here. That eerie feeling still clings to me.

I think I'll name the dog Brutus. My lips purse as I wonder how dogs do with infants … I make a mental note to look that up first thing tomorrow.

I think I'm starting to really *feel* pregnant. It's beyond being exhausted. It's something else, something that makes me rub my belly and talk to him or her as if they're already here. Some type of knowing and it makes me smile.

Before I can head back upstairs, my eyes catch sight of the flowers on the table. The flowers Jacob sent me when Henry died are already wilted. Bright yellow sunflowers. They're large and the stems are thick. They'll eventually die and by the look of them, that time is coming soon. What a shame ... that's what flowers do, though. They die.

Next to the vase is my laptop and I absently pull it toward the edge of the table then take a seat. My body aches, my hips especially, and sitting up feels better than lying down. I might as well get a little work in before I try to sleep again.

A yawn leaves me as the dim light of the computer brightens.

Studying the flowers again, I think about how twisted it is that I turned down a man who could have been perfect for me. A shrink might have something to say about that decision. My fingertips brush gently along the petals. I'll never know if we could have been more, but right now I'm content with that decision.

It's time I took control of my life.

My to-do list is already set. First step: I need a new place. Somewhere near the Manhattan Bridge, I think. It's far more family friendly. Dog friendly too.

I check my messages and emails, simply out of habit. A few of the candidates I picked to interview to be my personal assistant emailed me back. There are two of them I really like. I might actually hire both of them. Maybe that's really the first step. And then finding the perfect place will be step two. A smile plays across my lips and I nod to myself in approval of my "early morning can't sleep, aha" moment.

Those two tasks are momentous and huge leaps for me. Delegating work and settling down somewhere my child can have deep roots. Resting my hand on my belly, I promise I'll make it happen. I may have failed to be there for Evan, but for this baby, I'll do anything. I'll have it all fixed and ready before this one gets here. He or she will never know this place or all the hell that went on here.

My gaze drifts across the room and the night that started it all plays out in front of my eyes. Suddenly, it hurts. That numbing prick comes back. It's been happening like that. I'm so sure, so ready to move on ... and then I remember. The visions of myself sitting there in the dining room chair like a ghost, drinking wine and wanting to deny it, and at the same time hating Evan because I knew he was lying.

A dreadful breath leaves me, and a sadness weighs down on my chest, but there's conviction there too.

A new place, a new way of life. My fingers drift to my belly button and then lower. A new life entirely.

Diary Entry Six

Hey Mom, can I take back what I said? I don't think I want to be alone.

I don't think alone is the right word. Alone hurts my heart a lot. It hurts more than I want to admit. Mom, it feels like the worst thing in the world sometimes. Now that I know what it's like to not be alone, I'm not sure that's really what I want.

I think that's why I clung to Jake. I just didn't want to be alone. You probably knew that, didn't you?

More than that, I want to be loved by someone who can love me the way I need and I can admit that.

How did you know Dad loved you the way you needed? I just laughed a little writing this. I'm sure he made it obvious. He didn't hurt you like Evan does to me.

I hope what Evan did doesn't make you mad. I don't think he means it. I think he doesn't know any better and I knew that when I married him.

Everything has settled now, and I know I want more, Mom. I really want someone to love me.

I want them to love me like Evan used to love me.

I don't know if it's possible.

I'm going to find someone one day. There's a lot to do between now and then, but I promise I won't settle for being alone.

Maybe not now. I don't know when. I'm not going to use them or compare them to Evan. It'll take time, but I think eventually I'll be able to do this.

This baby makes me feel loved and I know I love him or her.

I promise I'll give him every bit of love I have. A little extra too, lots of kisses from you. I know you'd love to hold him. I'll hold him extra tight for you. And for Henry. Henry would have loved this baby too.

# CHAPTER
## twenty-two

*Evan*

SHE TOOK OFF HER WEDDING RING TODAY.

I watched on a tiny-ass security monitor as she slipped it off and held it between her fingers. Miles away with the sins of the city between us, all I could do was watch her stare at it, as if wishing it would answer some unspoken question for her.

I hold my breath as I quietly open the door.

Kat didn't change the locks like she threatened to do, but that wouldn't have stopped me anyway.

This is the point that I've truly gone crazy and I know it. She's set boundaries and I don't give a shit about them. It's the first time in my life that's happened, but losing the woman you love will do that to a man. Watching her walk away when you know she loves you and you love her; it's a torture that's immeasurable and the destruction it leaves is irrefutable.

One slow step in, and not the faintest of sounds. The front door to the townhouse closes behind me softly. She'll forgive me one day. I'll hate myself forever if I stayed away.

Maybe I should have called, maybe I should have announced myself, but it's my home. She's my wife and this is where I belong.

I can accept that now. If I can keep secrets, so can Kat. I swallow thickly, closing my eyes and hating myself as I lock the front door. *She better be able to.*

I'm a desperate man. If anything happens to her, I'll end it. I already know that. But I'm so fucking weak that I'm risking it. If only she can keep a secret, we'll be all right.

My head whips around to the sound of the microwave beeping in the kitchen.

*Beep, beep, beep* followed by the click of the microwave being opened and a soft hum of satisfaction.

*Kat.* My love.

She's only a room away, and knowing what I'm about to do makes my heart race as I find it hard to swallow.

My body doesn't wait for me. My feet move on their own, pushing me closer to her. I need to see her, even if she doesn't see me. I can't explain why it needs to be in person.

The only light in the townhouse that's on is the kitchen light. It's early morning and I wasn't planning on her being awake.

Maybe the fact she's awake is a sign. A sign that I can't be a coward any longer.

That's what a man who waits in the shadows is. That's what a man who hurts his wife is. A fucking coward.

Stalking into the kitchen, I expect her to see me, but her back is turned as she stirs something in a bowl then slips it into the microwave, still humming something. It takes me a moment to realize it's a lullaby.

In nothing but a thin cotton sleep shirt, she tempts me.

Fuck, I've missed this view. When she raises her arms, the T-shirt she has on slips up past her thighs and gives me the smallest peek of her cheeks.

I almost groan from primal deprivation. It feels like forever since I've held her, laid her in bed and enjoyed her in every way possible.

"Kat." I say her name softly as the microwave starts and she whips around, backing into the cabinets with her hand on her chest.

"Sorry," I say and there's not a single second of hesitation when I apologize. "I know you said not to come … I just …"

I can see the outline of her breasts through the shirt and with her dark brunette hair a mess from sleep, she's never looked more beautiful. More fuckable. More *mine*.

"You scared the shit out of me," Kat whispers after a second, breathless.

"I'm sorry," I repeat. "I didn't mean to." I take a chance to move closer but stop at the kitchen counter. Boundaries. I've already broken so many of them. It's hard to keep my distance, but I'll wait.

"What are you doing here?" The microwave beeps and she rips the door open without taking the bowl out then slams it shut. Merely silencing it before crossing her arms over her chest.

I cock a brow at her anger, but she doesn't react.

"I brought these." Slipping my hand into my jacket pocket, I pull out the pair of baby shoes I got from home. They're the same pair I wore when I was little. Smooth leather and simple, but before me, they were my father's. I found them in a box in Pops's basement. Ma put them there. It's her handwriting.

Kat pinches the bridge of her nose and turns her shoulder to me, hiding her expression, but I saw it. The sweep of sadness cuts me to my core.

"Baby?" I whisper softly, cautiously even. "I—"

"What are you doing?" she says, cutting me off as she stares daggers in my direction.

"I know you're angry." My tone is placating, but it does nothing to soothe her.

"Angry doesn't even begin to cover it."

A second passes, followed by another as I struggle to form the right words. "I have faith you'll forgive me," I tell her with feigned confidence.

"Fuck off," she spits out.

"Because you love me. And you know I love you."

"You love me?" she questions with a deep scowl. Storming toward me, she sticks her finger in my chest as she yells. "This is what love is?" She shoves me back and I take it, loving the fight in her. But it doesn't last long.

"Your father died, and I had to be alone." She murmurs the truth I already know and takes a step back. "You chose to be alone," she whispers. She tries turning from me again, but I grip her waist.

"I didn't want it to be like that. I swear to you." Bringing up my pops hits me hard. I keep forgetting and that's how I want it to be. I keep thinking he'll call or text. I keep thinking when all this is over, we'll have dinner together on Sundays again. I hate it when I remember he's not here anymore. I can't handle losing them both at once.

"I'm not all right." I whisper the truth to her as something pricks at the back of my eyes. "I'm sorry." Sincerity is there, but I don't know that she can hear it anymore. The feeling of worthlessness washes over me.

"Sorry doesn't cut it." She takes in a deep breath meant to steady her, but it seems to do the opposite.

"You know what loving you means?" I ask her, raising my voice. "It means protecting you."

"You can take all those words and—"

"They're in my vows," I say, heaving out the words as I interrupt her, my emotions rising and the thought of losing Kat forever becoming more and more real. "Protecting you is in my vows."

"Don't talk to me about vows." I've never seen her so angry. The look in her eyes is pure hate mixed with mourning.

"Come here," I tell her and her eyes narrow.

She tilts her head to the side and looks at me as if I've lost my mind. My heart feels like it does a somersault, a painful flip in my chest as she says, "Don't tell me what to do."

"The only reason I've been gone is that being seen with you would put you in danger." I hate myself the moment the confession slips out. Weak. I'm so fucking weak. I need to be a better man for her, but I've never been good enough and we both know that.

Kat's silent, but her expression is unchanged.

With a hesitant step forward and my hands held out to her, I add, "I had to do it."

"You don't have to do a damn thing but breathe," she finally responds, her voice hollow, the devastation I've caused ringing out clearly.

"I was only trying to keep you safe." I say the words quietly as the sight of Kat in front of me becomes more of a reality than my fear ever was.

She hates me. I've made my wife hate me. Pain ricochets through every piece of me.

"Well, thank you for that," she answers sarcastically with tears in her eyes as she shakes her head.

"I swear." I feel tears prick my eyes as I fall to my knees in front of her. I'm not in control anymore. I'm not in control of a damn thing and purely at her mercy. "I'm here right now because I can't stay away any longer." My heart crumples at the words that I choke on.

Kat takes a small step back, brushing against the counter as she does, and I wish I still had a grip on her.

I murmur my apology. "I didn't know it would take this long. I'm sorry. I fucked up. Repeatedly and I'm trying, but I'm failing."

"Didn't know what would take this long?" she asks, crossing her arms and refusing to look into my eyes, but she's full of emotion and on edge waiting for me to open up to her. I know her, and I know that's exactly what this is. That's what made her fall in love with me. I swallow the thick lump in my throat and pray I'm not making a mistake.

"I'm …" I can hardly breathe as the words *threatening, investigating, framing* get caught in my throat.

"Tell me, Evan." Kat licks her lower lip and stares down at me with tired eyes. "I've had enough and I'm over the secrets and the lies. I'm over this," she says and gestures between us although as she does, her expression morphs into pain. "What was so important that it had to be done to protect me?"

"It's going to sound crazy," I warn her, staring up at her from where I am as the dawn slips in through the windows, playing with the shadows on her gorgeous face.

"It already does."

"James is the one who's responsible for Tony's death." I confess still on my knees, although I let go of her. I hate myself for telling her and bringing her into this, and I almost don't say another word.

"He was trying to kill me, not Tony." My throat is dry and scratchy as the words slowly leave me and I rise to stand, feeling the weight of it all rain down on me. "And he knows I know."

Denial forces Kat to shake her head, a crease settling between her brow. It's a small motion of disbelief, but she doesn't speak as she drops her arms, listening.

"It's because of his divorce. He wants Samantha scared and he wanted to prove he'd do anything. So he tried to kill me, thinking I'd do a line of it. It backfired."

Her mouth opens and closes, but she still says nothing. A lightness carries me forward, knowing she's listening. At the very least, she's listening.

*Please believe me.* "I've been tracking his schedule and

routines, breaking into his house and office looking for evidence or something that can prove it."

A huff of disbelief so faint I almost think I imagine it leaves Kat's lips as she turns from me, facing the sink and putting her fingers to her lips.

"Talk to me, please," I beg her and a trace of anger flashes in her eyes.

"You could have gone to the cops," she finally says. "Like a normal human being."

"I couldn't go to the cops with nothing on him. James has proof I was with Tony. It's his word against mine, and he has photos. I listened to him that night. I went along with the alibi and lied to the cops. I fucked up and he tried to blackmail me, but I called his bluff."

"Jesus Christ," Kat says then exhales.

"You see why I didn't tell you? It's too much and you're pregnant. If he's after me and he knows I love you, he'd go after you too." My biggest fear slips from me and I can't control how my eyes glaze over as the terrors I've dealt with every night for weeks linger between us. I've pictured her here on the floor, just by my feet, dead almost every night.

Yet I'm here. I've told her. And there's a chance I just brought that reality to life.

"You could have messaged me; you didn't have to hurt me."

Swallowing thickly, I gather my composure, refusing to let the fear win although everything else has failed. "He's tracking my texts, babe, he's following my every step. Just to get here, I had to make sure to lose the guy he paid to follow me around."

"This is insane, Evan. You know that, don't you?"

"I know, and I'm sorry. I have someone working on it and we're trying."

"Who?" she asks and when I don't answer she adds, "No more secrets, and no more lies. I want all of it."

"Mason," I confide in her, and it takes a moment to register.

"Does Jules know?" she asks, worry riddled in her down-turned expression.

"I doubt it."

"So, because you think I could have been in potential danger, you left me alone, treated me like I was … like I was nothing?"

"He would have killed you," I tell her, stressing the truth of the situation.

"You don't know that."

"I met him, and he brought you up." My throat goes dry at the memory. "He would have gone for you, Kat."

She shakes her head in disbelief.

"If I lose you, I have nothing!" The words are ripped from my throat, desperate for her to see what I've been seeing. To feel what I've been feeling, complete and utter loss. I calm my voice and take a step closer to her then say, "If he killed you, I would have nothing to live for."

She stares into my eyes with a look I can't quite read and whispers, "I'd rather die beside you than live without you."

"I would kill myself if anyone hurt you because of me. I don't know how you can't see that." She appraises me for a moment, her shoulders rising and falling with soft breaths. "I promise it's almost over. I promise you Kat, I wouldn't do this if I didn't have to."

"You should have known better than to keep it from me. What if you had died?" she asks me, and I can't answer right away. I'd never considered it. "What if he killed you? I would have never known."

"My only thought was to keep you safe; I wasn't concerned with anything else.

"If you do what I say, we can still be together," I tell her and the reaction I get is nothing like what I'd planned. She's not at all moved by my confession. She can't tell a soul or let on that we're together. "If we're together," I say then stop mid-sentence, afraid that we're not. Afraid that it's too late.

"You don't control me anymore." Although her words are spoken easily, and she seems to understand everything, her walls are still high, guarding her from me.

"Kat, I love you, but I will lock you in a fucking room to keep you safe. If you don't listen to me, then you leave me with no choice. I swear to God I will."

*Smack!*

My face burns with a stinging sensation as the sound rings in the air. My lungs halt as my eyes widen, taking in the vision of a pissed-off Kat in front of me with her hand still raised. My hand slowly rises to my jaw.

I've never seen Kat strike a person in my life. She's not a violent person by nature.

But I guess I had it coming to me.

"Don't you dare tell me that you love me."

I don't fucking hesitate to respond, "I love you more than anything, and I'll never deny it. I'll tell you every single day for the rest of my life." Even with my jaw stinging from the impact.

"I can keep a secret too. You could have told me. You

didn't have to put me through this with everything else I'm dealing with."

"One slip is all it will take. If anyone even thinks we're back together … that's all it would take."

"Well, you told me now," she states with finality and I take her hand in mine, forcing it up so she can see.

"Because you took off your ring," I tell her, not holding back the pain it caused. "Because you kissed someone else." Her fight vanishes, not all at once, but slowly as both of us breathe heavily, the air between us growing hotter. "Because I thought I was losing you forever."

"You left me with no choice," she says although a look of regret flashes in her eyes.

"I didn't have one either. You have to believe me."

"You really love me?"

"I do. You must know it's true. I know you do."

"You want to be with me? You want to keep me yours?" she asks, completely serious as if there's any other option for me.

"Yes, it's all I want. And to keep you safe."

"Evan." She utters my name softly but as it rings through the air, I hear the threat that comes with it. Her eyes pierce through me as she stares back at me.

"You'll come back to me, every night. Every fucking night. You'll message me back every time I text you."

"I can't text you back from my phone." Her eyes narrow and I'm quick to come up with a solution as I offer, "But I can get another."

"Damn right you will," she answers me and I find the

corners of my lips kick up in amusement. I love my wife and she loves me. *Thank fuck.*

Just as that truth begins to comfort me, she adds, "I don't like you doing this."

"I promise it's almost over."

"Evan, you better never do this to me again."

"I promise, baby. I promise never again. Everything's going to change from here on out. I promise."

"We can get through anything, but never this again," she whispers, and I know I have her. I have her back and I'll be damned if I ever let her feel lonely again.

# CHAPTER
## twenty-three

### Kat

"Talk to me," Evan says again, and I want to. God, I do, but there's so much to say.

"You want to hear what I've been wanting to tell you for weeks?" I ask and even to my own ears, I sound like I've lost it.

"Kat, you—"

I don't care what he has to say, I'm going to lay it all out there for him and he can decide what he wants to do with it. I have a plan, I have needs. Either he's in, or he's out. I'll accept either; I'm willing to give it a chance. There's only so much that's left of me, though, and he needs to be very aware of that.

"I'm exasperated. Just because you said sorry doesn't take away everything. It doesn't make it all just fine and back to normal. I'm still ... *feeling*." The spiraling that's come over me day in and day out threatens to take me over now, and I let it happen. "I feel like someone's run over my body with a truck and then backed up. My hips and back hurt. I can't sleep. And that's just the pregnancy." With a deep inhale, I continue before he can interrupt me.

"You know, the baby you put in me? That's still happening and by the way, pregnancy doesn't just pause because things have been insane. So, I'm dealing with hormones, and I cry way too much for no reason. I feel sick and I can't sleep. I'm paranoid and I'm so damn alone that I've truly been scared. I feel crazy and I don't even know what part of this is normal and what part isn't." The words leave me in a fluid mix of emotions. Like a purge of everything I've been feeling, piling up until it drowned me. With a shuddering breath, I attempt to calm myself, not knowing how he'll take any of it and very much aware I'm an absolute mess.

After a moment, he speaks. "I want to hold you," is all he says. I'm caught, shaken and uncertain as I stand in front of him in nothing but a T-shirt in our kitchen. My God do I want him, but murder? People trying to kill him? I can barely handle normal life. "I want to make all the pain go away; I'll take it from you. I promise," he says in a deep cadence that washes a sense of calm over it all. Evan slips closer to me, wrapping a hand around my waist and I can feel myself falling back into the same trap. Because he does that to me. He makes the pain go away and he makes it so easy to give in.

"Stop," I say, pleading with him. "It's like history repeating itself." My body and my thoughts are at war with each other. I'm brought back to every kiss we've had, every time he's held my hand, every heated moment that's left me consumed.

The world is nothing without him in it and I know it, mind, body and soul.

"It's not," Evan says matter-of-factly to me, his voice begging me and my body persuading me to once again fall into his arms. Which is right where I want to be. The very thought tugs at every string wrapped around my battered heart.

"We have a baby coming and I can't put this baby through what we've been going through, Evan," I say, admitting my fears to him. If only he knew how much it hurt. "I'm afraid every time I cry the baby can feel it. I terrified I'm hurting him already." As I say the words, tears prick my eyes.

"Him?" Evan asks. "You think we're having a boy?" The shine in his eyes is of pure devotion. That's how he breaks me down. By truly loving me.

"Don't change the subject," I warn him although it warms my heart and I can't help but feel it resonate. "I want you, Evan. But I want you here with me, and committed to me and this baby."

"I know," he says. "I love you, Kat. I love you with everything in me and I won't stop proving that to you every day for the rest of our lives."

Even though he's saying all the right things and I love it, I have to be honest. "I swear I can't take it anymore."

"Never again. I can't stand not being with you," he tells me, and my body succumbs to a warmth that's been there all along, waiting just beneath the surface.

He pulls me into his arms and I let him. Even more, I grip onto his shirt as he wraps his muscular arms around me and I breathe in his scent of fresh forest after rain. This is home. This is what feeling complete feels like. I'm so very aware of everything he said only moments ago. The threats and danger are legitimate, but it all comes with him. I can keep a secret. I'll do whatever I have to if it means I get to have Evan completely.

My eyes shut tight, willing the unwanted thoughts away as Evan whispers just beneath the shell of my ear, "I want to make it all better." He's so close that my hair tickles my neck as it moves gently with his breath.

He says the right words. He's always been good at that.

He lowers his lips to the sensitive part of my neck. "I only want to love you, and have you love me back."

My poor heart has barely survived all this time without him, but it rages now, pounding against my rib cage. I suppose it's only beating still because it hasn't belonged to me in years. *It's always been his.*

I nod my head and look down at his chest, inhaling his scent I've missed for so long, feeling his touch I've been craving.

"You're still wearing your jacket," I comment softly as I run the tips of my fingers down the zipper. I lift my gaze to his dark eyes, swirling with desire. "Take it off."

I bite my lower lip then take half a step back as he keeps his eyes on mine and slips his jacket down his arms.

"Your shirt," I say in a breathy voice and in an instant, he tugs it over his head then carelessly drops it to the floor. The fabric puddles at his feet. He closes the space between us as desire spikes in my blood. Like the first night I saw him, knowing he was trouble, yet I can't resist.

"What now?" Evan asks, moving his pointer finger to the bottom of the cotton T-shirt and slipping it upward, tugging ever so gently until he reaches the peaks of my breasts. He closes his fingers around my nipples with a slight pinch and then tugs. Gasping, I let my head fall back. The sensation is directly linked to my clit and it forces me to part my lips with a soft moan. "What now, baby?"

"Mmm," I manage, and that's all I can offer as lust clouds my judgment. I missed this. I missed him. Such a small touch and yet it feels all-consuming.

"How about this?" Evan suggests and then he unbuckles his belt. The sound of his pants being unzipped fills the small kitchen and my body aches to reach out to him.

His pants fall to the floor and he pushes his boxers down with them, stepping out of them and exposing his already hard cock. Every nerve ending in my body lights just seeing him bared to me. Knowing how much pleasure he can and will give to me.

A rough chuckle distracts me from focusing on his erection and I look into his eyes.

"You still want me?" he asks and it's only then that my cheeks warm with a blush. My body sways slightly. I murmur my answer. "Always."

Evan runs the same pointer finger along my upper thigh past my panties and traces the center seam of the cotton, brushing my throbbing clit and sending sparks of heated pleasure through my body. My body leans forward, my hands gripping onto his corded forearms.

"I will never risk making you unhappy again. I promise," he says. My head is so dizzy with desire, I can only moan in response.

"Tell me," he says as he slides his fingers under the thin

fabric and runs them along my hot core. He pushes against my clit with just the right amount of pressure then nearly slips into me as he runs his fingers back down. My hands fly up to his chest, gripping onto him for balance as my toes curl and my body begs me to ride his fingers.

"Tell me," he repeats then stops. My heavy-lidded eyes open, and I pull back to object. "Tell me you still want me."

"I still want you," I whisper without hesitation; the words rush out of my lips with need and desperation. Before the last word is even spoken, Evan splays his hand on my lower back and pulls me closer to him, forcing my chest against his.

"Fuck, you're so wet," he groans in the crook of my neck as he forces two fingers deep inside of me. I cry out in pleasure, clinging to him as the sensation nearly topples me.

"Evan." I moan out his name, but he doesn't answer as the pleasure builds. It's been so long but I don't remember it ever being like this.

It's so intense, so overwhelming that I know I can't remain standing for this.

"Evan," I plead for him to understand, but my head flies back and strangled moans fill the air, both from him and from me as I find my release on his fingers.

My body buckles and shakes as the orgasm rocks through me. I'm paralyzed as Evan moves me to the counter. It's cold and hard, and I lean against it for balance as slow waves mercilessly continue to flow through my body.

"And your shirt?" Evan asks me as if I didn't just experience the strongest orgasm of my life.

I grip the counter tightly while I catch my breath, staring at him.

"I want it off," he commands and with my back to his chest, he tugs the shirt off me. My body sways easily, caving to his every whim. "And these," he tells me, pushing his hand back down my panties. I'm trapped with my back to his front and his strong arm pinning me to him, his other hand on my hip, keeping me still.

My fingers clutch at his wrist and my blunt nails dig into his flesh as he strums my sensitive clit.

"Evan." His name is a plea as my body falls forward, and I struggle to take more.

He's not gentle with his strokes in the least. And I love it. My nipples pebble and my body goes weak with a numbing, blinding intensity.

The pleasure stirs deep in my belly, but like a flame it grows hotter and hotter, warming me and threatening just the same.

It's only when I come again that Evan slowly pulls my panties from me, leaving them by my feet. I'm not blind to the fact that they're damp with my desire.

Evan moves his hard erection between my thighs and I widen my stance slightly. He kisses my ear as he runs the head of his dick up and down my folds. A shiver runs through my body. Every inch is covered with a heated pleasure so sensitive to touch, that I shudder from just his hot breath on my neck.

"I love you, Kat," Evan whispers as he pushes himself deep inside of me. Slowly, stretching my walls. My head falls back onto his shoulder as he wraps his arm in front of me, holding me to him. He reaches up and grabs my throat.

Buried deep inside of me, he whispers, "Tell me you love me."

"Always," I say and the word slips out easily, my eyes still closed. I slowly open them to see Evan's expression. I'm struck by the intensity of his gaze. The need, the desire, the possession. "Say the words," he commands.

"I'll always love you," I tell him softly, the words barely audible.

He crushes his lips against mine as he bucks his hips. The sudden spike of near pain makes me push my head back and scratch along his forearm. He doesn't stop pounding into me, letting the pleasure build.

He pistons his hips relentlessly, each thrust forcing a pleasured groan from me. I try not to make too much noise, I try to be quiet, but I can't.

I come again and again, each climax feeling more intense than the last. Evan's ravenous as he kisses me. He doesn't stop his hands roaming over my body. He doesn't stop until I have nothing left, and only then does he bury himself in me to the hilt and find his own release.

Diary Entry Seven

Mom,

I think I've lost my mind.

Evan's like a tornado in my life.

That's not news to you, but I think that's how I want it. Crazy and reckless, but deeply rooted and unstoppable.

I'm ready to fight for him, Mom. For us. I'm eager to, even.

I love him. I love what he does to me when he's with me.

Mom, I'm afraid you'd be ashamed of me if you were still here. That's the only part that hurts.

But believe me when I tell you that I love him and in all his fucked-upness, he loves me.

That hole I was telling you about before? It's the one that came when you left, but it's not there when Evan's with me.

I think he has a hole in his heart too, Mom.

And I think I'm the only one that can fill it.

I told you I've gone crazy, didn't I?

Maybe it's not the worst thing in the world, though. I don't know. I don't think I care about it much anymore. So long as I keep Evan close to me.

I hope I make you proud. And if not, I'm sorry, Mom. I didn't choose this, but I choose him. I want to see it through.

# CHAPTER
## twenty-four

*Evan*

THE PAPER RUSTLES IN MY HAND. IT'S A LIST Pops left on the counter. He didn't tell me about it, but I'm sure it was for us.

Bottles.

Pacifiers.

Bibs.

Onesies.

It goes on for a bit, but it's everything I need to buy. I'm not sure if he was going to give it to me, or if he was going to get this all himself. A pain radiates in my chest, right where that beating organ is. I miss him. I've never needed to talk to him as much as I do now.

*You have to do it.* I read the text that buzzes through and then put both my phone and the list in my pocket. I already know what Mason is getting at.

He's convinced I need to be seen in public. To make sure the tail James has on me sees me keeping my distance, moving on. He wants them to back off and that means I need to look like I'm backing off too. No more of this tit for tat. The plan is to let them think I've moved on from looking into James. That I've given up or simply decided it wasn't worth it. It doesn't matter which.

I stare down the aisle as a kid runs past, holding up a plane in the air and making swooshing noises. It's crazy that one day, I'm going to have one of them. A kid. A baby first. And before that, a pregnant wife.

It's fucking terrifying.

This particular setting isn't what he had in mind and I made sure no one followed me here. Family first, though, and then I'll take care of the mess. Bars and old hangouts. Then back to the apartment every night before I sneak out to go home. She's a saint for putting up with me and all of this.

"Hey," I call out as a young guy in a blue Kiddie Korner T-shirt walks by with a clipboard in his hand. He has to push his glasses up the bridge of his nose when he looks at me. "Can I help you, sir?"

"Yeah, I was looking for simple baby things. Like bottles and tiny clothes. Things like that," I tell him. "I can't find them anywhere in here."

"We don't have infant merchandise. You'll have to go to Little Treasures," he responds and starts walking to the center of the store to point. "Two blocks down and make a right. It's a bit of a walk, but it's right there on your left."

"Thanks."

I rub my tired eyes and walk out of the shop, hearing

the ding of bells above my head and I'm instantly accosted by the bitter cold.

Just as I'm shoving my hands into my pockets, I catch sight of Detective Bradshaw.

"It's one of those days," I mutter under my breath as he kicks off the wall. Guess the prick was waiting for me.

"Mr. Thompson," he says, greeting me without a hint of emotion as he closes the distance between us.

I take a few steps forward as a couple of kids run behind me and into the store. Meeting him halfway, I answer him, "Detective Bradshaw, nice to see you again." *Not fucking really.*

He huffs a laugh like he heard my thought and says, "I'm glad I found you here."

"A bit odd that we just happened to run into each other." Holding his gaze, I let him know that I know he must've been following me. "Not my usual hangout."

"Yeah, I noticed. Your schedule's a bit different now?"

"A bit."

"For the best, I hope?" he asks and a prickle runs down my neck. I don't like it.

"Yeah," I answer, and my word comes out hard. My back's stiff and my muscles are wound tight. "You taking me in?"

I wait as he assesses me, enjoying the suspense.

"Should I?"

"I can't think of any reason off the top of my head." He doesn't think my answer's funny in the least. My lips quirk up into a smirk at his hard-assed expression. "I'm good to go then?"

"You got any new information for me?" he asks, getting to the point of this meeting.

"I got nothing to say."

"Why are you doing this to yourself? Protecting someone who wants to issue harassment charges?" he asks me, and I can't help that my forehead creases with both confusion and anger.

"Oh," Detective Bradshaw says, finally showing a little joy. "You didn't hear?" He rocks on his feet like he's happy to deliver the news. "James Lapour wants us to keep you away from him. He filed for a restraining order and all."

"That's why you're here?" I ask, not sure what to make of James's move. He went to the cops and maybe I grew up different, but that's something you just don't do when you're neck-deep in criminal shit.

"He said you were snooping around, making him uncomfortable and issuing threats."

"Threats?" I echo, getting more pissed off by the second.

"Nothing solid we could work with, so I thought I'd give you a shadow."

"Ah, and thus this wonderful meeting." I don't talk to cops. Never have, never will. Half the city's cops are in someone's back pocket. *Someone's* like Mason and James; the rich *someone's*. Not *someone's* like me and the kids I grew up with.

"I'm sorry to say I couldn't really give two shits about James Lapour so if you want me to stay away, I'm happy to keep my distance."

Detective Bradshaw's less than pleased with my statement. "Just thought you'd like to know."

"Thanks, Detective, am I good to go now?"

"Have a good day," he mutters as he walks past me, brushing my shoulder as he goes.

I finally bring my hands out of my pocket and open my

clenched fist only to see the scrap of paper balled up. My breathing comes in shorter and my blood heats.

This shit has to stop. Right fucking now.

Diary Entry Two

Dear Pops,

I'm ashamed. I feel like I've lost complete control and I know it's hurt Kat.

Help me to be a better husband and take the nightmares away. Please. Just get them out of my head.

It's just getting worse every night, and it's scaring my wife.

What kind of a man am I? Dreams are tearing my life apart.

I can't sleep without seeing you. Don't get me wrong, I love and miss you so damn much, but you always die in my dreams. You're gone. All of the memories of our life together are changing. I don't want them to, but I don't know how to stop it.

I have them with Kat too, and it's killing me.

I yelled in my sleep last night, and it woke me up. Kat was crying next to me, Pops. She said she'd been trying to wake me up and that's when I started screaming.

She's worried, and I feel like less of a man and husband because I can't stop it.

Please, Pops, if you're there and you're able to, please help me.

I miss you. I can't stand this.

Please just take it all back.

# CHAPTER
## twenty-five

### Kat

**A**T WHAT POINT DID THIS BECOME MY LIFE? I've been asking myself that question all morning. I've showered, I've eaten and cleaned most of the townhouse. But my mind is fuzzy with disbelief.

A sigh leaves me at the thought as I hail a taxi just outside our townhouse. The winter weather has lightened up some, and I almost feel like I could wear a light jacket and not this heavy wool coat. Maybe I've just gotten used to the cold.

It doesn't take long for a yellow and black cab to pull to a stop in front of me. Ushering myself in, my mind still fails to grasp all the details of everything that's happened in only months.

If an author submitted my story to me as a manuscript, I'd tell them it's too unbelievable. What's that quote from Mark

Twain? Something about how truth is stranger than fiction because fiction needs to make sense.

"Where to, miss?" the cabby asks me as I get in the back seat and close the door.

"Saks on Fifth, please," I answer confidently, although my nerves creep up. Evan would kill me if he knew what I was doing, but it's not going to stop me. I need this.

There are only two things I'm certain of.

1.  I can't afford to let Evan leave me again or else I'll truly lose my mind.

2.  I'm not going to stay out of this like Evan wants.

The car moves forward, taking me away from the empty townhouse. He's gone off to meet with Mason and tell him what we agreed on. He's staying with me, committing to me and our baby. And he promised to move past this. I'll listen to what he tells me to do, but every night he comes back to me and sleeps with me in our bed. No more secrets and hiding. I have to help him, not let the fear of what might happen ruin what we have in the present.

I'm still pissed that Mason knew when I didn't. It's the second knife in my back, but I let it slide simply because it's not his ring on my finger.

Instead, I focus on the real target here. Samantha Lapour. I'm not over her being with him when we were separated. The hate and jealousy are still there.

She loves Fifth Avenue. What rich New York socialite doesn't?

I remember her bragging about her apartment above Saks when I first met her. She was so happy to keep it even though she and her husband were happily married. It wasn't so much a humblebrag as it was just bragging.

That should've been my first clue we were never destined to become friends, but her smile was charming and her stories were alluring. I'll admit, I was dazzled.

The cabby stops before I'm ready, my nerves getting the best of me, and it's only then that the weight of what I'm doing makes my stomach churn.

I pay the cabby, slipping out and onto the curb to avoid the traffic.

My pulse races faster and faster, adrenaline surging as I make my way through the throngs of people and into the apartment foyer, disappearing from the crowd and readying myself to knock on her door on the fourteenth floor.

I don't know the exact address, though. There are only so many up here, so if at first I don't succeed, I'll simply try again.

My legs are shaky as I climb the stairs; I should have taken the elevator. Some small part of me is quite aware that the decision was made to eat up time.

"Good evening," a feminine voice says, and I have to raise my gaze to watch an older woman with a stylish white bob and a small Pomeranian in her arms close the door to 1401. There are only two other apartments on this floor, the one I'm sure Samantha told me about.

*But that was years ago …*

"How are you?" I greet the woman as if I'm supposed to be here, as if I'm visiting a friend and not a woman I have every intention of warning to stay the hell away from me and my family. In an effort to be convincing, I open my clutch, keeping my eyes on her with a simper plastered on my face. I'm sure it looks like I'm getting out a key or maybe my phone to call a friend.

The woman simply smiles tightly and nods then carries on her way, not answering the question. I hesitate, glancing between the remaining two doors and wondering which one I should knock on first.

*This is crazy.*

My heart races and a mix of adrenaline and anxiousness make me question why I'm even here.

The real answer, the absolute truth, hisses in the back of my head.

*She was with him. In his family house.*

Two confident strides and I knock, one, two, three times on 1402. I don't breathe until I take a small step back and wait.

Silence. No response. The confidence threatens to leave with every second that passes, but the moment I take a step to the right, to knock on the only other option, the door opens.

In red silk pajamas and her hair in curlers, Samantha looks so different from any other time I've seen her. She wasn't expecting company, that's for sure.

Her expression is nothing but irritation at first, and then she recognizes me.

"Oh, hello," she says, greeting me somewhat easily but with her lips pressed in a thin straight line as she stands up straighter. "Kat."

I have to clear my throat before I can answer her. "Samantha," I respond in the same stiff way. "I apologize for dropping by with no notice. I was hoping I could talk to you." Clutching my purse with both hands in front of me, I add, "It's about Evan."

She crosses her arms, instantly on the defensive and I'm quick to add, putting on a bit of a show, "I'm worried about him. About the loss of his father and how he's handling it." The words are the truth and the emotion that comes with them is genuine. But I just want an in so I can get a better grip on exactly who this woman is … and maybe details on her estranged husband.

"I'm so sorry for your loss," she responds tightly, still looking me up and down as she considers what to do with me.

"I know you've spent a little time with him and I was just hoping you could tell me how he is."

She nearly flinches then has to take a moment before she can answer. As if she has no idea how he's doing. Or maybe she's shocked that I know she's seen him, but it's all over the papers, so why wouldn't I?

Evan's told me one side of this story, but there are always three sides … sometimes even more. In this case I'll stay away from James, for Evan's sanity, but I'm sure Samantha will have a thing or two to gossip about.

"Did you guys talk at all?" I ask her. My throat tightens as I add, "He doesn't talk to me at all anymore."

"Oh, God," Samantha says, sounding exasperated and then tells me, "We didn't talk about his father. I'm sorry." She struggles to gather a response. "I'm sure it's difficult and I understand you two are going through something, but I assure you that I'd like to stay out of it."

With the creak of the heavy door, she attempts to close it, but I'm quicker.

My palm smacks against the door and I plead with her,

"I just need someone to talk to. Please! If you could just let me in."

My blood rushes in my ears as I wait, the door remaining right where it is, only slightly cracked. She opens it again cautiously, pursing her lips and appearing more irked than anything else. As she lets go of the door, it opens with my weight and she nods her head, letting me in.

"What is it that you want?" she questions as she walks with her back to me inside of the apartment. I close the front door myself and take the place in.

It's a barren disaster.

I nearly ask her if she was robbed, but looking to my left at a cluttered kitchen I can easily spot a potential cause of the state of her place. Three small bags of white powder and a line wait for her. Right next to them is a colorful bag of pills. A mix of what could be Adderall and pain meds.

She turns with a smirk on her lips. "Like the place?" she asks sarcastically. "My prick of an ex made sure to sell all my belongings when I went out of town."

"Oh my God," I say, the words coming out in a whisper of disbelief and pity, neither of which truly resonate with me. There's only a sofa in the living room, a sleek gray contemporary sectional. I imagine it would look beautiful if the living room itself wasn't devoid of any other piece of furniture. She settles down onto one end and I take the other.

Glancing up at the chandelier I tell her, "I'm so sorry. I'm sure it was beautiful …" my voice trails off and she doesn't say anything.

"You could go to the cops," I offer her, and she laughs with ridicule. If she weren't so arrogant, I'd feel sorry for her.

With her cheeks sunken in and the silk pajamas baggy on her slim frame, she appears far less beautiful and enviable than I remember her.

"He's got them all on payroll, sweetheart. I'm barely surviving."

"I am so sorry," I say, at a loss for words and feeling so much more uncomfortable than I anticipated. I even feel bad for her to some degree.

"Divorce isn't always a bad thing, love," she says and then takes in my expression. "I'm sorry for you two, though, I really am."

It's hard to judge her tone, so I'm not sure how to take it.

"I actually had something to ask you about your husband." I shift on the sofa, preparing to question her. Samantha reaches for a pack of cigarettes and slips one out.

She lights it then asks, "What's that?"

There's a glint in her eyes and her back stiffens slightly.

"Evan doesn't like him much anymore," I offer her, gauging her reaction and she lets out a small laugh that's accompanied by smoke.

"I don't much like the asshole either."

"Can't blame you," I say, keeping my tone agreeable as I set my purse down beside me and feign a casualness I don't feel.

"He told me weeks ago he thinks James is trying to hurt him." I hold her gaze as I say, "I think he's paranoid, but he's worried about his reputation since leaving the company."

Samantha takes a long drag of her cigarette, ignoring the question until I tell her.

"I was hoping that if I talked to you, you could tell me the truth. Evan's just being crazy, isn't he?"

Every nerve is on edge in my body. There's something about how she looks at me. It's as if she's wondering what to do with me.

I don't trust the look, and I don't trust her.

"Evan told you what, exactly?"

"Evan told me that James tried to kill him, thinking he'd do coke left out for him."

"Did he?" she asks condescendingly. "I'm surprised because from what he told me, he didn't want you to know."

I hate her in this moment. I hate the expression of disinterest.

I hate that Evan was with her when he should have been with me.

I hate that she knew he was keeping secrets.

More than that, I despise that she has any hold over my emotions at all. How could this woman affect me so much? My inner voice hisses, *because you let her.*

"It was a mistake on his part," I lie to her, my fingers tensing as I grip my purse harder. "He got drunk one night a few weeks ago and lashed out at me. It's the last time we spoke." Her expression changes slightly, but only slightly, with a raised brow and the hint of a smirk. Amusement. I fucking hate her.

"Maybe it was a mistake to come here. I thought you'd know or maybe get a sense of how Evan's doing since you were with him."

"I have no idea what you're talking about." Leaning forward, she puts out the cigarette in a mug that's sitting on her furnace. It's then that I know she's not going to tell me a damn thing. She's far too stiff and closed off.

"My apologies for coming then," I say, shrugging it off.

There's some piece of me that wants to confront her about the affair years ago. A part of me that wants to tell her I know.

She's a liar, though. It's so very clear. There isn't anything I need from this woman.

"It was a mistake on my part," I say then offer her a sad smile, taking in the room once again. "I hope you get everything you want from the divorce." I leave her with that false sincerity. The only thing I hope is that I don't have a reason to ever think of her again. She's nothing more than a waste of time and breath. Every second I've wasted on her is one I'll never get back and this woman isn't worth my time.

# CHAPTER
## twenty-six

*Evan*

"WHAT'D YOU DO TODAY?" KAT asks as I turn on the stove, listening to the clicks before the gas lights.

"Not much," I answer her as I look over my shoulder. *Just hunting down the identity of a drug dealer.*

"What do you think you want to do?" Kat asks me as I pour olive oil into a pan. Chicken marsala for dinner. My throat goes dry as I remember how Pops taught me how to cook it; it was one of his favorites.

"Like do for work?" I ask to clarify and put the chicken in the pan. The sizzle is perfect.

She shrugs and hops up on the counter, setting her ass down and letting her feet dangle. "I know you have some investments."

"'Some' is putting it lightly. If you're worried about money, don't be. We'll be fine." I haven't checked in a week or two on some of the stocks, but the savings account is more than enough. We've been here so long, both of us working and not doing much of anything else, the money piled up. "I promise we'll be fine, baby. You don't have to worry about that."

"I'm not really worried about money, it's more about what you're going to do with yourself." She's kept her distance in an odd way I haven't experienced before. She's careful with me. Every question seems planned, every touch cautious. It's obvious that she's still scared.

I flip the breasts over and pick up the pan, making sure to spread the oil before setting it back down. Just like how Pops used to do.

"We have a baby coming and you want to move," I answer her and stride over, my bare feet padding on the floor as I go. Standing between her legs with my hands resting lightly on her hips, I tell her, "That's all I've been thinking about for now."

There's a small hesitation before she speaks and a tension that flashes between us. *That and James.* His name is always on the tip of my tongue for any conversation we have. The threat of him lingers, even though we pretend it doesn't.

"The baby won't be here for a while," she finally says and threads her fingers through my hair. I love it when she does this. When she loves on me. I missed this. "I'm worried about you," she adds and I back away slightly, but she keeps me there, tightening her legs around me.

"Don't be upset," she says and her tone begs me to listen.

"I'm fine," I respond stiffly and even I know it's a lie.

"You just lost your father, and …"

"Stop worrying about me."

"You scared me last night with the night terror. And the ones you've had before," she adds.

"It'll be over soon," I reassure her and get back to cooking. "I have sleeping pills and that's going to help." It's quiet for a moment, but that doesn't last long. Kat's not the best at giving up on what she wants.

"What about seeing someone?" she asks.

"What, like a shrink?"

"They aren't called shrinks," she says, reprimanding me. Some days I think she thinks it's all in my head. Like maybe I'm crazy.

"I'll see one. I promise." It's on my to-do list. It's just at the very bottom of it for now.

The tension clears as I reach for the Italian mix of spices. With just a pinch of cayenne.

"Thank you," she whispers and before I can respond, she asks again, "So what do you *want* to do?" At least she moved on from talking about Pops, the nightmares, and seeing a professional about all the shit going on in my head.

Peering back at her and wiping my hands with a kitchen towel, I note the devotion in her gaze. It'd bother me, if I didn't know how damn much she loves and needs me.

"I'm not worried about keeping myself busy."

She purses her lips and nods, but she doesn't seem convinced.

"I'm going to be fine," I say and stir the sauce before layering it onto the cooked chicken.

411

She murmurs in that sweet voice of hers, "You better be."

"You know what I'm going to do?" I ask her as I continue cooking and ignore the sick feeling in the pit of my stomach about everything *currently* going on. "I'm going to move us out of here and into our forever home. I promise," I say, and she rolls her eyes.

"For the love of God, hire a moving company this time," she states with exasperation and I give her the laugh she's after. The move here was … something for the books.

"I'm going to find a house you love and help you make it ours." I tap the tongs on the side of the pan as I pull it off the burner and then walk back to her. "I'm going to set up our baby's room and make it perfect with all the little details."

She likes that. Kat sways on the counter like she's giddy at the thought and a genuine smile lifts up her lips. Making them that much more kissable.

"I'm going to make sure the two of you have nothing to worry about and that the three of us are happy and healthy, and all that good stuff they write about in fairytales."

She lets out a small laugh and wraps her arms around my shoulders. That's what I'm after. That's all I'm after.

"I love you, babe," I tell her, and she leans in for a small kiss.

"I love you too … I just hate seeing you anything other than happy."

"I'll be better when this is over with," I say, bringing up the one thing I don't want to speak about. She kisses me soft and sweet, and it feels right. She's a balm to my soul, but it doesn't take the pain away.

She doesn't release me like I think she will. Instead she holds on tighter.

"I'm worried about you," she whispers against my lips.

I brush my nose against hers. "It's not supposed to work that way."

Her green eyes peek up at me through her thick lashes and she says, "Yeah it is. It works both ways. Don't you know that by now?"

# CHAPTER
## twenty-seven

### *Kat*

"I THOUGHT WE WERE JUST GOING TO ORDER OUT," Evan says from across the table. The silverware clinks in his hand as he picks up the white cloth napkin and lays it on his lap.

The Savinga Grill has always been one of my favorite restaurants since I first discovered it years ago. With exposed dark red brick, raw wood beams, and high ceilings, it's rustic, it's cozy, and it's only a cab ride away.

That's what I told Evan to get him here when he asked where I wanted to go. *Just a cab ride away.*

I shrug and say, "I wanted to go out."

"It makes me nervous," he tells me. I know it does. I realize this is a risk and one he didn't want to take, but time is not on our side and I've waited long enough.

I lay my hand on the table, palm up, and wait for him to take it. "Mason said you need to be seen."

"Me, not *us*." He emphasizes the word "us."

"It's part of us moving forward together." The smile on my lips is small but it's still there. "I won't let someone keep me from you or us from our lives."

His lips twitch with a response, but he doesn't say anything. Two weeks have passed since I told him we were pregnant. Two weeks came and went, and I'm officially in our second trimester now.

"We tried this your way, now we try it mine," I tell him, and my words come out hard.

"And your way is to go out and risk being seen?"

"I want us to go out, yes … like we used to." My answer is blunt as I pull my napkin across my lap. "I'm not going to hide away in some dark room and let my fear cripple me." My voice is stern but also sympathetic. "If someone wants to know if we're together, let them know." He woke up last night with sweat pouring down his face. He was screaming in his sleep. I refuse to play this psychological game. I'm going to be there for my husband. I'm going to do everything I can to make him better. And that means not hiding and not being scared.

I'll be strong for him. I'll be strong for us both. At this point I don't know what to think of his ex-boss or how Tony died. I know my husband is letting his fear kill him, though. It's shoved itself between us and I can't let that happen anymore. He refuses to go to the cops. He's not ready to see a psychologist. I'm okay with that, but I'm not okay with nothing changing for the better.

"I won't let a single person keep us from moving on with

our lives. That means being together and going to my favorite restaurant to celebrate."

I flash him a smile as the waiter walks over to us. Like this conversation doesn't put me on edge.

It's quiet while the water is being poured, and stays that way except for the waiter informing us of the specials and handing us a pair of menus.

It's only when he leaves us that I continue what I was saying.

"Yes, I want us to be seen. I also want to celebrate being pregnant. I want to buy a new house, a bigger one closer to the park." My fingertips play along the stem of the water goblet and I rest my elbow on the table as I talk while reading the menu, even though I already know what I want. "I want to slow down with work and I want the world to know it all. I want to move forward, Evan. I want everything that happened to stay in the past."

He only responds with a tight smile.

"I'm not going to let this change us and who we are."

"I don't want you to be in danger," he answers me, leaning back in his seat and casually glancing to his left and right. I recognize a man sitting alone a few tables away. Occasionally he glances up at us. It was Evan's concession and I allow it.

"Too late, baby," I say and my smile falters.

"I feel uncomfortable being here," he says and guilt digs its claws into me at his admission. I'm trying to do what's right. That's all I want to do.

"I feel like"—taking a deep inhale, I steady myself to continue, meeting his concerned gaze—"like you're perpetuating your fears by hiding away and only focusing on them. Not just focusing, but allowing them to dictate everything." My voice cracks with the confession. I have to take another sip of water to calm myself down. "I hate that you're constantly on edge when we leave the house."

"You don't understand," he tells me with a frustrated sigh that pisses me off.

"It felt like you'd died when you left me," I say. "So, I think I do understand." I take another drink of water and ask, "What if the cops stop looking into what happened? They have no leads." I stress the basic truth. "What if James gets away with it all? What then? Will you carry on like this?"

He doesn't answer, although I can see his will to fight me has left.

"I just want us back," I say. "That's really what it comes down to."

This time it's Evan who puts his hand on the table and I'm more than happy to reach for him. He kisses my knuckles then my wrist. "I'm sorry," he whispers against my racing pulse.

"I know you are, but what am I?" I give him a joking response to lighten the mood and it works somewhat.

As Evan's lips pull into a smile and he relaxes his posture, he takes my hand in his.

"You know I miss this side of you?" he tells me.

"What side?"

"The playful side," he answers and squeezes my hand … kind of like how my heart squeezes. This is the version of my husband I want all the time. The man I know and love.

"Can I tell you a secret?" I whisper just before the waiter walks up to us. "I miss it too."

"Are you two ready to order?" the waiter asks, looking between us and clasping his hands in front of him.

"You first," Evan says and gestures at me.

"The lasagna please, with a house salad." I almost order a glass of cabernet but then I stop myself. Every time I remember we're having a baby, it's a gift in itself.

"I'll have the same," Evan says, and it surprises me.

When the waiter leaves, I comment with a questioning smirk, "You never have lasagna."

He shrugs and says, "I guess I want to try it your way."

"We have the next doctor's appointment coming up and since you're no longer working, I assume you're coming with me?"

"Of course," Evan says then nods and leans forward, lowering his voice and adding a huskiness to it that makes every inch of my body tingle. "You know you look beautiful, right?"

I can't help the smile and blush that spread across my face at his compliment. "Stop," I say, brushing him off.

"Never," he answers playfully, his handsome asymmetric smile toying with my emotions.

That warm cheery feeling in my chest slowly drifts away as I remember my own little secret. Not so little, really.

"I have something to tell you," I say, uttering the words even at the risk of upsetting Evan. I guess I waited intentionally for us to be out in public before I could tell him. "I did something that I don't think you're going to like."

"What's that?" he asks easily, although I notice his shoulders stiffen.

"I was curious about something and I think it's something only I would know how to ask appropriately …"

I don't know how to word this, and I find myself staring at the ice in the glass of water.

"You can tell me. Whatever it is."

"I went to see Samantha a couple days ago. At her place on Fifth Avenue," I tell him, confessing before I can stop myself. The air instantly changes as Evan doesn't respond. He seems uncomfortable if anything.

"I had to know for myself."

"What did you have to know?" He shifts in his seat

"I had to know if she was your type. What she was like. So I know how to react when her name comes up."

Evan runs his hand down the back of his head as he looks away from me. "Her name isn't going to come up ..."

"You don't understand—" I start to explain but he cuts me off.

"There's no one else for me, Kat," he tells me bluntly, his hands hitting the table and rattling the small plates. The couple a table down from us glances in our direction and Evan grimaces. Sometimes he doesn't realize his own strength.

"I knew you would be upset—" I begin my apology and again he cuts me off.

"But you did it anyway." His cocked brow adds some humor although I still feel guilty over it all.

I nod my head once. "I did. And it's over."

The tension between us lifts a bit as I look him in the eyes and say, "It's over. There's nothing there and I'm fine now, but I had to tell you."

"You're fine?"

"Yes," I answer and I am. "There's no way she's your type."

My response gets a short laugh from Evan. A genuine smile even. "You know you're crazy?" he asks me.

"I do. And you made me this way."

"Fair enough," he says but then his expression gets serious.

"I know, don't do it again," I say before he can tell me.

"I'm serious," he says, and I nod.

I glance to Evan's right, toward the front of the restaurant as another couple walks in. "I was surprised that Samantha does pills," I say absently. More to gossip than anything else. Well, maybe to throw her under the bus a little. I can admit that I'm not a big enough woman not to.

"What?" Evan asks.

"There was coke on her kitchen table, lying out in the open." He looks back at me with an expression that's not quite disbelief, but something else.

"Coke?" he echoes. "Sam doesn't do drugs."

I ignore the fact that he called her Sam and nod my head once while I add, "And a bag of pills. She had a variety pack, Adderall and a mix of things. It was like a grab bag. I would never have guessed she does drugs." I wait for him to say something.

"Speed?" he asks me again although it's not quite spoken like a question.

"I didn't say speed," I reply.

"Adderall is speed," he tells me with a concerned expression.

"Oh, I didn't know. I don't know what they were. I just know what I saw and I was shocked. I'm just guessing it's Adderall." I swallow thickly, wishing I'd just kept my mouth shut and saved the gossip for the girls.

I watch as Evan's forehead pinches, but there's something else in his expression that catches me off guard. It's hard and unforgiving. Something that sends a chill down my spine. Even his hands clench into fists on top of the table. I glance at them and then his eyes, but movement behind him at the front of the restaurant catches my attention.

"Is that Suzette?" Even with the shock of seeing her stride in just now, I don't think I've ever been happier for a change of subject. I wish I could snatch the last two minutes of our conversation from the air and shove them back into my petty mouth.

"It's definitely Sue," I say, holding up Evan's end of this conversation since he's still silent. I'd know that blunt bob anywhere. She walks slowly as she digs in her purse, looking for something at the front of the restaurant.

I'm pushing my chair out from the table when my mouth drops open at the sight of a man coming up from behind her.

He's much taller than she is even in her heels. I don't recognize him; he's facing away from me. In a black suit, he stalks up behind her, moving his hand to her waist and pulling her close to him.

"Who is that?" I say beneath my breath, but when I look to Evan and try to get his attention, he's busy on his phone.

"Babe," I say, not so quietly trying to get his attention. It's not every day you see one of your good friends being felt up by someone you don't know. I much prefer this conversation. It's easy and Evan always has something to say about whoever Sue is "dating."

I have to turn my head when I look back up to keep my

eyes on them and try to follow them down the hall. But they're gone before I even get the chance to stand.

I swear it was her and I go to reach for my phone to send her a message, but glancing at Evan, he stops me in mid reach.

"What's wrong?" I ask him as he stares at his phone.

"We have to go." His response is hard and nonnegotiable.

"We just got here," I object, but that doesn't stop him from standing up abruptly as the waiter returns to our table.

"I'm so sorry, we have to go," Evan tells the waiter. "Please cancel the order."

"Are you serious?" I hiss as the couple from before looks at us again.

"I'm sorry, but something just came up," he tells me and there's a look in his eyes that's begging me not to push him.

"Please, Kat," he says, ushering me away. "We need to leave. Now."

# CHAPTER
## twenty-eight

*Evan*

"THIS ALLEY SMELLS LIKE PISS," MASON SAYS as we stop between a Chinese restaurant and a shoe store. I met up with him on Prince Street and we walked our way here. Just me and him … and business to take care of.

I take a whiff and immediately regret it. "This is where he's going, though, right?"

"Should already be there," he answers.

"That's what it said on his profile. 'Getting ready for the party,'" he elaborates beneath his breath and shoves his hands in his pockets.

It's bitterly cold and the city streets are packed with people shopping and moving about like normal.

"I don't believe in coincidences," I tell Mason and bring it up again.

His eyes flicker to me and then back across the street.

"There's no way she happens to do speed," I tell him. I've known Samantha for a long damn time. "Her husband dabbles in all sorts of drugs recreationally. But she doesn't touch it. She never has."

"It's possible she does it on the down low," he suggests. "You'd be surprised how many people do coke nowadays."

I shake my head. "There has to be a connection between her and the dealer."

"We're gonna find out, aren't we?" he asks me, although it's a rhetorical question.

"What's the plan?"

"All we need is an address."

"Just follow him, then?" I ask with disbelief.

"Only for a bit, then we switch off so we aren't seen."

"Switch off to who?"

"I got some guys," Mason says, and frustration gets the best of me.

"I want to be the one—" I start, but he's quick to cut me off.

"You want to keep her safe? Getting into this shit isn't what you need. That's not what the man who deserves to be at Kat's side would do."

That shuts me up, but I fucking hate it. He's been edging me out of this. Giving me less and less.

"So, we just wait?" I ask him again.

"Yeah," he answers, and his breath turns to fog, "just wait."

Almost an hour passes before I think about going back to Kat. She has no idea what this could mean. I'm sure she'll be pissed I took off in addition to cutting our date short. Sirens wail in the distance and the busy city night reminds me of how things used to be.

"Fuck me," I say out loud and run my hands down my face.

"Sorry, you're not my type," Mason says so matter-of-factly from his spot next to me, I grunt a short laugh despite myself. "I feel so fucking trapped."

"I know the feeling," Mason tells me, and I give him a sidelong glance. His stare only hardens. "I know what it's like to be in a lose-lose situation where the stakes are high." He looks forward, staring at the opposite brick wall in the thin alley. "Too high," he mutters under his breath.

"So, what do you do?" I say and get his attention again. "How do you win?" I ask him with complete sincerity as if he has an answer that will put an end to this hell.

He shakes his head as he looks down at the ground and replies, "Sometimes there's not a way to win, only a way to survive."

I have to tear my eyes away from him, knowing he's right and when I do, I spot something. My arm reaches out and I smack him in the chest.

"Visual." The single word is barely spoken from me, and Mason doesn't hesitate to take out his phone and call the tail. "He's here," he speaks into the phone as both of us watch the perp, chatting with some guy in an open doorway on Twentieth and Broadway. Even from his profile, I know it's him.

Every muscle in my body coils, ready to fight. It's been weeks of holding back and not being able to do anything.

And just across the street is the last piece to this puzzle of fucking misery.

Dark black hair slicked back and tanned skin with a tattoo scrolling up his neck. It's definitely him. We got this prick.

The second he's walking down the stone steps, we're moving out of the alley and following from across the street. I keep my eyes on him, walking through the thick crowd with my jaw clenched.

"Johnny, we got him." Mason talks into his cell phone as we walk. I try not to make it obvious that we're following the fucker. At the same time, I'm holding back every desire to chase the dealer down and beat the shit out of him to get every bit of information from him.

Mason says we should bribe him. It's not exactly my style, though.

"Heading down Twenty-second," I hear Mason say and instinctively I glance up to look at the street sign before turning left to follow him.

My blood's pumping hard and with every step it gets harder and harder not to pick up speed.

Right as we get to the end of the block and the cross-walk sign turns to a red hand, the fucker walks out, ignoring the oncoming cars and nearly getting hit, but he keeps going, yelling out, "Hey, watch it!" at the drivers as if it's their fault. I move to do the same. We can't risk losing him, but Mason puts his arm out in front of my chest to stop me.

"He's got him," he tells me, his eyes glued to the dealer's back as he vanishes into the thick crowd. "Johnny's on him."

My shoulders rise and fall with my heavy breaths. I'm calm on the outside, but inside I'm pacing. The nerves eat away at me. "I need to do something," I tell him, ignoring how the woman to my right turns back to look at me as if I've lost it. Maybe I have.

"Then go home," Mason says and turns halfway around to walk right back up the way we came.

His leather jacket bunches in my fist as I pull him back to me. "I can't sit around and do nothing," I say, pleading with him to understand.

"The best thing for you to do is go home to your pregnant wife and stay right the fuck there," Mason tells me. That's it? That's all I can do when this is the prick that laced that coke? When he's the one who sold the tainted version and he's the only one who can tell us who he sold it to.

I swallow thickly, feeling guilt settle in my stomach. "She needs you to be there," Mason asserts, with caution thick in every word. I wonder if he's just saying that to make me listen to his order, or if he really means it.

"You told her you were done with this shit. Be done with it. You saw him, you know we got the guy. It's just a matter of time now."

# CHAPTER
## twenty-nine

*Kat*

EVAN IS ... NOT HIMSELF IN THE LEAST. His shoulders are hunched, and he keeps checking his phone like he's waiting for something.

Ever since we left dinner last night, he's been closed off. I wish I'd never brought up Samantha. It was a mistake.

Evan checks his phone again as an explosion on the television booms through the living room. He doesn't flinch or react. He's numb.

I scroll through the list I've added to the baby registry. Maddie sent me a check-off chart and it's so, so long. All the clothes in miniature and every odd and end, from pacifier holders to little mittens, should be enjoyable to add, but there's a nagging feeling that claws at my chest.

I peek up at him again, scooting closer into the cushion

and pulling the throw tighter around me. "Why do you keep checking your phone?"

"It's nothing," he answers.

I'm slow and deliberate as I arrange myself into a cross-legged position across from my husband on the sofa.

The expression on his face is one I've seen before, the "what is she doing?" look.

He sets his phone down beside him, and I don't take my eyes off his, but I notice how he tries to hide it.

"No secrets," I remind him. "You promised."

Another loud boom from the television distracts me and I reach for the remote without hesitation, bending over Evan to grab it from where it sits right next to his phone. As soon as the television screen goes black, I toss the remote behind me.

Giving him my full attention I tell him, "I feel like maybe you have something to tell me." I hold his gaze and his expression gives me nothing.

I'm so close to snatching his phone out of his hands just to prove him wrong, but before I pull the trigger on that idea he says, "I don't want to bother you with these things."

"You're my husband. You're supposed to bother me." I say it with a little humor, but again, he doesn't react.

"Tell me, Evan. I *want* to know." I scoot closer to him, just a bit so my leg touches his and I rest a hand on his thigh.

"It's something you said. About Samantha having drugs." Dread washes over me. I never should have gone to see her, confront her or spoken her name. I regret it all. He glances away from me at the far wall in the room. "It's something bad," he adds.

"Her having drugs is … what? I don't understand." I hate

that an inkling of jealousy creeps up on me, but it's quickly followed by a darker realization. The coldness that came with the dread sinks down deeper, coating every inch of my skin.

"The coke that killed Tony was laced with another drug. High amounts, enough to kill." He looks me in the eye and slowly the pieces come together, one by one.

A chill sinks into the marrow of my bones. Samantha. Not James. "Did you tell Mason?"

He nods and then adds, "He thinks he has something concrete."

"What?" I ask him, eager for more. I can't lie. There's a part of me that's afraid, but a bigger part that needs to know. Ever since Evan told me his theory, I've questioned it. I've questioned his sanity even. I started to think it was all in his head.

"He can't tell me over the phone," Evan says as if that's the end of the discussion.

"Is it good or bad?" I ask him, guilt and stupidity both weighing down my words.

"Good, I think." He hesitates, but then adds, "He said it's done and to come see him. I'm just waiting for the time and place."

"It's done?" I question, feeling my eyes widen with hope. My lungs stay perfectly still until Evan nods his head once.

"Just waiting for the time and place." He turns his attention back to the television and then glances at the remote.

There's an eerie feeling that settles between us, a darkness I can't seem to grasp.

"You know I love you, right?" he asks as he brushes the hair out of my face.

My eyes flicker from his chest to his eyes as I say, "I do."

His lips twitch into a smile and he leans forward to kiss me. It's chaste and quick, but he rests his forehead against mine, his hand still on my jaw.

"I don't like this," he whispers.

I can't respond. The words are caught in my throat and I have nothing to say other than, "I love you too. I'll wait with you."

# CHAPTER
## thirty

*Evan*

I STARE DOWN AT THE PAPER AND THEN LOOK BACK TO Mason. I've known since Kat told me. Samantha's the reason that coke was laced, and it wasn't meant for me at all. It was James she wanted dead. I'm a fucking fool.

Anger rolls through me like a low tide. Slowly rising and each wave threatening to take more and more of me away.

"She was fucking him," Mason says.

"Fucking who?" Kat asks, still clinging to my side. With my arm around her, I pull her in closer. She insisted on coming and at first, I didn't want her here. I didn't want to involve her in this more than I already had.

Now though, knowing she went to Samantha, that she spoke to her, and was inside her apartment, so close to a woman capable of murder, I need her here with me.

She's not allowed to leave my side until this is finished.

I rub soothing circles along her hip as I look past Mason and out through the picture window in his sitting room. I need to feel her. I need to know she's still here, alive and by my side. Away from any danger.

"Samantha was fucking Andrew, the dealer. They planned to kill James and it went sideways. He was supposed to do the coke, not give it to Evan to share with Tony."

"Do you have evidence?" Kat asks, and I look down at her. She's standing there as if she just asked for a receipt for an item she wants to return to Nordstrom, not at all affected in the least.

"Enough of it," Mason answers and I look back at him when I can feel his eyes on me. "Shots of her with Andrew taken from his own surveillance feed. You can't tell it's him, since it's his back and he's wearing a hoodie. More importantly, my guy was able to grab a sample."

We can plant the tainted coke. That's easy enough. Send the picture anonymously to Detective Bradshaw, plant the coke and boom, there's the evidence they've been after. There's the matter of what she'll say when they come for her, though. Who she'll blame and throw under the bus.

The details still need to be decided, but the truth is there. Now we know what happened.

"She wanted James dead because the divorce wasn't going to leave her with anything?" Kat asks Mason and he's quick to respond.

"She's the one who cheated and according to their pre-nup, if we go by the gossip columns, a divorce would leave her without a penny to her name."

"Better to kill him than to finalize the divorce," Kat comments under her breath and steps away from me, walking to the far side of the room to pick up the cup of hot tea she left on the side table.

"What about James?" I ask him. "He really had nothing to do with this?"

Mason shrugs. "Still a prick, and now he's onto his wife because of the nudge we gave him, but I don't have shit on him."

I break eye contact and wipe a hand down my face. I feel like a fool. Guilt and regret swirl together, and the mix of emotions makes me numb. I have to remind myself that all I need right now is Kat, just my wife.

"You were wrong," Kat says from across the room.

"I wanted to kill him … I would have," I admit to them, and it hurts to do it. The past few nights I've lain awake, thinking about all the ways I considered murdering him. As I stood outside of his house, I knew it'd be easy. I craved to see his body lifeless on the floor.

"It's because of her," Kat speaks lowly, but her breathing picks up as anger gets the best of her.

"It's not hard to focus on revenge," Mason says as if reading my mind. "It's not your fault for wanting this over so you could protect your wife."

The clink of ceramic on glass gets my attention as Kat sets down her mug and makes her way back to me.

"So, what do we do now?" Kat asks then leans her back against my front.

Mason smirks at her and looks between the two of us. "See, this I love," he says, tapping the folder in his hands.

"We came up with a plan. The cops have to find out. James and Samantha need to be focused on each other and forget about me."

"So … what's the plan? Leak it to them somehow?" Kat questions.

Mason steps in and says, "James is going to post about how Samantha's fucking a drug dealer. He's going to write all about how he found coke and a grab bag of pills in her office and that's why they've split."

"How do you know that?"

"Because my guy has access to his email account. And he drugged him about two hours ago. James is going to wake up with a hangover and unleash hell when he realizes he emailed his contact at the *News Journal*, who's eager to post anything at all about this case.

"The cops are itching for something and they know they have nothing. This city talks, and Derek at the *News Journal* will foam at the mouth to have the inside scoop before anyone else," Mason answers Kat.

I hope it's enough to satisfy her. She can't know the last piece. Just one more secret. One final release.

"James will be relieved more than anything else," I add, trying to ease her worry. "He's a time bomb of paranoia waiting to go off." Mason backs up, leaning against the back of a sitting chair as he adds, "And Samantha will be behind bars by morning."

"She can't deny the pictures of the evidence," Kat murmurs, grasping the plan, but quickly licks her lower lip and shakes her head, seemingly finding a gap in the details. "She'll make bail."

"With the cops James has in his back pocket?" Mason looks at her with disbelief. "No way. She's done." He's good at convincing her this will work, even though I'm still not convinced. If anything, I know nothing is bulletproof.

A moment passes and I let my hand slip to the small of her back. It takes everything in me to assure her, "It's done. This will work and it's done." There's a nagging feeling in the pit of my stomach, knowing either one of them could mention my name. I could go down too. But it's a risk I have to take for all this to be over. I can't outrun it and I'm willing to take a deal, I'm willing to do anything to put an end to it all.

"Good," Kat says with finality.

"Do you need me to do anything?" I ask Mason as Kat cradles her body against mine.

"I can take it from here, but I'd stay inside and keep a low profile until there's word about the arrest."

I give him a tight smile then lean down to kiss Kat's hair, savoring every moment. I'm doing it for her. With my throat tight and everything inside me ringing, I whisper, "Let's go home, baby."

*One week later*

"Is he in there?" I ask Mason as we sit in the car.

Andrew Jones, also known as Mathew Staller, is about to meet his maker. The man who sold Samantha the drugs, helped her plan a murder, and got off with nothing has to pay for what he's done.

He didn't get a single charge that stuck to him. Not a damn thing. Samantha protected him and pled guilty when it came down on her. So did James, accepting the weaker charges that were merely slaps on the wrists. I slipped under the radar, although I'm certain Mason had something to do with that.

Andrew got off completely. Until now.

"Yeah, this is his address," Mason answers as he unbuckles his seatbelt. The click is loud in the still night air.

I watch the light at the end of the street turn green, but there's not a single car down the road where Andrew's house is. Not a person in sight, in fact.

It's only him and us.

I guess he liked being out here for his privacy, away from the city in a Podunk area … maybe it's where he cooks up the drugs. Or maybe he's lying low since it all went down only days ago.

I don't know, and I don't give a fuck. All I want is for every person responsible to pay the price.

As I step out of the car, the chill of the evening creeping into my bones, I tell Mason, "You better never tell Kat."

He grins at me and says, "It's our secret."

The doors to the car close softly, although they cause a gentle thud to resonate in the bitter cold. I keep my gaze on the warm yellow light coming from the upstairs of the two-story house.

"Sticking to the plan?"

I nod at Mason's question, not stopping my pace, and not taking my eyes off the light upstairs. Duct tape and rope are in the trunk.

I crack my knuckles one by one, all the pent-up anger and fear from the past couple of weeks raging through my blood, begging for revenge.

I came so close to losing everything because of this fucker. My wife would have been a pregnant widow. And it's because of this asshole.

"Yeah, stick to the plan," I answer Mason.

He grins at me. "I'll get the front, you get the back."

Just as we break, the man of the hour walks right out the front door, hoodie on and straight out onto the sidewalk, only feet from the car.

"I don't do meets here, get the fuck out," he informs us with a threatening tone that only heats the rage coursing in my blood.

"Not here?" Mason questions as if we're here to buy or sell or whatever the hell Andrew thinks we're here for.

"Yeah, like I said, I don't do meets here," Andrew repeats and then opens his coat, flashing a gun tucked in his waistband. "So get the fuck out."

Dumb prick should have had the gun in his hand.

The rage turns my vision red.

Before I know what I'm doing, I go for the first punch, slamming my fist right in his jaw. It's reckless, but it's a damn good release of all the tension I've been carrying. My blood rushes in my ear as he and Mason both fumble for the gun. Mason grabs it from him as a bullet goes off, flying through the air and ricocheting off the car. Crouching down, I get in another punch, stunning the dealer. It's cold and the freezing air bites into my white-knuckled fist. Over and over I feel my muscles tighten, gripping onto his collar, then letting the rage pour out of me, blow by blow. My teeth grind against one another as I don't hold back a damn thing.

*Crack!* The prick's jaw snaps and I feel the bones crunch under the weight of my fist. I see the images that haunted me for weeks.

Andrew pulls back his arm and lands a single solid punch to my cheek. It'll bruise, but it barely affects me. Nothing can pull me from this haze of vengeance. My head snaps to the side as another punch lands on my chin. I throw all my weight forward, pushing him to the ground and feeling my body fall on top of his, slamming hard onto the concrete sidewalk.

"Fuck!" he screams out just as I pin him under me and throw punch after punch. His nose cracks under one of them; I don't know how many I get in. I can't stop.

"Evan!" Mason cries out, his fingers prying into my shoulders then my chest, desperately pulling me backward, but I get one more hit in that snaps Andrew's head to the side and for a moment, I think he's dead. He lies there nearly life-less. Blood's covering his face and soaking into my knuckles. Red lays in streaks everywhere.

Andrew spits blood onto the street next to him and coughs it up as I attempt to rein in my heaving breaths.

"Snap out of it. It's not the plan." Mason repeats, "It's not the plan. This isn't the plan." There's a ringing in my ears that won't quit. One that balances out my tunnel vision and the stinging pain that shoots from the split knuckles on my hand.

When I finally catch my breath, Mason is on top of him on the ground, pinning him down. Andrew knees Mason in the stomach, desperately trying to win a losing fight. But I'm too quick, grabbing his own gun and shooting him once in his thigh.

I don't want to kill him. That's not my job to do.

He's not for me. But I'll be damned if I didn't love beating the piss out of him.

Andrew screams out in agony and Mason, still wincing and holding his gut, socks him right in the mouth.

Mason catches his breath as he slowly stands up and Andrew stares up at us, begging for mercy.

"Are you Andrew Jones?" I ask him and he hesitates to answer, so I fire a shot off right next to him.

"Yes!" he screams. "Fuck! Yes!"

I crouch down in front of him, gun still in my hand. "The same Andrew Jones that left those messages for Samantha? The ones convincing her to murder her husband?" The blood drains from his face as I talk. I'm not some dealer looking to get more turf. I'm not a cop. True fear permeates the air as the fool shakes his head. "The same Andrew Jones that gave her tainted coke so she could end his life and pay you half of what the insurance company was going to give her?"

"I don't know any Samantha ..." he tries to lie, and I shoot off the gun again, feeling the shockwaves run up my arm. It's closer to him this time and Andrew screams out.

"He pissed himself," Mason comments and when I look,

sure enough, his sweats have a dark wet ring around him. He's pathetic.

"That Andrew Jones?" I ask him.

"She wanted him dead!" he yells. "She was going to do it whether I helped her or not."

"You can tell her husband that; I'm sure he'll understand," Mason says and then tosses handcuffs at his feet. "Put those on. First your feet, then your hands."

"Please," he begs. But there's no mercy for what he's done.

It takes a good fifteen minutes to tie him up. The gagging was the hardest part.

The trunk slams shut, and the dark night seems so empty. Empty is what I needed, though. It's done and over.

Mason turns the car on, the keys jingling in the ignition before it roars to life and we leave in silence, listening to the fucker in the back. It's already starting to snow. They're calling for ten inches and that will wash away any evidence of us being here. Not that anyone will come looking for a while. Like he told us, he doesn't do meets here.

My heartbeat slows, and the end feels so fucking close. Every loose end is finally being resolved.

"Thanks for doing this," I tell Mason, ignoring Andrew's muted thumps in the trunk as we go over a speed bump and then another.

"No problem." His nonchalant response is as if I've only thanked him for picking up milk on the way home.

"I just needed to do something about it all." I feel the need to explain. We could have let Mason's guy take care of him. I needed some kind of part in seeing this through, even if I promised Kat I'd stay out of it. It's the last secret and I'm done. One last deal to see through.

"It's not like he doesn't have it coming to him."

I nod at Mason's comment and listen to Andrew's muffled screams.

"You sure he's going to be here?" Mason asks me as we pull up to a vacant lot.

Even as the car slows, I can see James inside, moving aside a curtain in the bedroom.

"Yeah, I'm sure," I tell him.

I know James is here. He's waiting for sentencing and not going anywhere near the city. *He's hiding.*

I know what that's like.

"You ready?" Mason asks me, and I nod once again. "Let's do this."

We'll leave Andrew bound and gagged on James's porch. And the hard copy photos James kept of me are already in my possession.

It's a truce of sorts. I give him his final piece, he gives me mine.

More than likely he won't see a day in jail and half his charges were already dismissed. His wife is sentenced to prison for life, his worries behind him. All but the drug dealer. He was foaming at the mouth to get him.

It was an easy call to make.

Andrew's slamming every which way, but it's 4:00 a.m. in the suburbs. There isn't another house for nearly half a mile. Even if I took the gag out of his lying mouth, there's no one here but us and James.

James is right there in the doorway, rifle ready.

"Just leave him here," I tell Mason and we let Andrew drop to the ground with a muffled scream piercing the air. "James will take him from here."

With the cold air blowing in my face and the city skyline lighting up the dark night, I finally relax into the leather seat. The bite of pain that hovers over every cracked knuckle is all that's left of what happened. It'll heal and my life will go on.

I'm done now. It's all done.

It's just me and Kat now. Just the two of us.

No. The three of us.

# CHAPTER
## thirty-one

### *Kat*

"DO YOU THINK HE TOLD THE COPS ANYTHING to try to get a lighter sentence?" I ask Evan as the newspaper in my hand rustles.

Samantha pled guilty to multiple attempted murder charges and got life in prison.

James pleaded guilty to his charges as well, but his sentence is nothing compared to hers even though they found him complicit in his client's death. It's rumored that he gave up information to cut a deal. He'll be out of jail in a year or less according to what the rumor mills are saying. The dealer got off scot-free and now people are saying he skipped town in case more evidence comes in.

"Told them what exactly?" He doesn't look back at me. Instead he lifts a picture frame off the wall of his parents' dining room. He considers it for a moment before wrapping a handful of bubble wrap around it like he has the others.

The moving company is going to be here tomorrow, but Evan wanted to box up the pictures and a few other things himself. The *valuable things* is what he told me when we left this morning. All he's packed up so far are pictures and I wish I could steal the pain away that reflects back in the glass as I catch his gaze.

"That you were there," I say, whispering the words quietly as if it's a dark secret no one can ever know. "With Tony," I add. A part of me thinks it's just too easy. I can't shake it just yet. I can't quite grasp that I get to have my happily ever after with Evan.

He shrugs a heavy shoulder and then looks me in the eyes, gauging my reaction as he lowers the wrapped picture into the box. "He doesn't have a reason to say anything. He wanted Samantha to go down, and we made that happen." His lips are pressed into a thin line as he makes his way around the table to pull out the chair next to mine.

"You really want to talk about this?" he asks me.

I glance at the article and him, swallowing my words and not knowing how to feel. The entire situation makes me uncomfortable. Worse than that … dreadful. "I want to know it's going to be okay." I offer him the truth. "I want to make sure *you're* going to be okay."

Evan smirks at me then leans forward, kissing the tip of my nose, which makes me close my eyes. "You're cute, you know that?"

I love how at ease he is. It feels like I have my husband back. Truly. Yet I'm still waiting for the other shoe to drop.

Reaching up, I quickly grab his hand and keep him close to me. "I'm serious," I say as I look him in the eyes. "I want to know you're okay."

"Baby, I told you there's nothing to worry about." He brushes his hand against my cheek, forcing me to let go. Evan pinches my chin between his thumb and forefinger, and stares into my eyes. There's a look there that makes me all warm and fuzzy. He's always been able to do that, and I love him for it.

"You promise?" I ask him softly and he pecks my lips once, then goes in for a deeper one before answering me.

"Well, we do have a baby coming," he says, still staring at my lips. "So, I'm sure we've got some things to be worried about, but that mess is over."

The stir of desire drifts away, dissolving instantly when I peek back down at the article. The picture they chose is one of Samantha giving James a death stare as she was arrested. The papers paint her as the villain she is.

"And you got that package too," Evan comments, bringing my attention back to him. My heart flickers once, then twice as I bite my lip and shrug.

"It was really nice of him," Evan says, and I feel the need to smack his arm playfully as he stands up to keep packing.

I place a hand on my belly and tell him, "It was a good-bye and good luck gift from a friend."

"A friend you kissed," Evan reminds me.

"A friend who was there for me when you weren't," I point out.

His shoulders stiffen a little as he stops midway from taking another photo off the wall. "I know," he says beneath his breath.

"It was a nice gift, though, wasn't it?" I ask him. Evan looks at me with an eyebrow raised and I have to laugh. "He doesn't have our new address anyway and he didn't put his on the package either."

"Yeah, yeah, yeah," Evan says.

"I really like it." I shrug my shoulders and remember the gift box Jake sent. Inside was a baby book called *I'll Love You Forever*. I can't read it without crying. All the note said was that he gave a copy to all his friends who were expecting and he didn't feel right not giving me one. One last kindness.

"It was nice of him, but it better be the last of him," Evan warns me jokingly. I love the trace of a smile on his lips. He knows I'm all his.

I lean back in the chair, and a yawn escapes before I can stop it. I'm halfway to telling him off in some way or another, but the words are stopped.

"You ready to go home?" he asks me and I nod my head, but add, "Only if you're all done."

He takes a look around the half-packed house and shakes his head. I have to admit watching him cleaning up his father's place makes my heart ache for him. I know I can't take the pain away. It'll always be there.

"You know our baby is going to be tough, right?" he comments just as the emotions start to get the best of me.

I rub my swollen bump in smooth circles as I pray our baby is okay in there and doesn't know how sad I am in this moment. I only want love for him or her.

"I hope so," I whisper as Evan comes back over to me. He wraps his arms around my shoulders and pulls me into his chest. I'm more than grateful as I wrap my arms around him and my cheek presses against his shirt.

"It's true. When a mom goes through hell during pregnancy and handles it as well as you have, the baby can handle anything, you know?"

I let out a sad but genuine laugh into his shirt and try to calm myself down as he rubs my back.

I peek up at him and smile as his lips touch mine.

"Everything's behind us," he adds.

I feel the need to remind him, "There's good behind us too, isn't there?"

"So much good," he says and then kisses me again before splaying his hand on my belly. "And so much more to come."

# epilogue

## Kat

*Little blips, they come and go,*
*In rhythm and in time.*
*Black lines that paint a picture,*
*And soft lullabies in rhyme.*
*You're everything, and the reason I need,*
*To love and to forgive.*
*My only wish is to keep you safe,*
*For as long as I shall live.*

SEEING THAT LITTLE BLIP MAKES IT REAL. "I CAN see his heartbeat."

"You're still convinced it's a boy?" Evan says although he doesn't take his eyes off the monitor. A trace of a smile is on his lips and it only grows when the little one moves.

"We'll find out soon," I tell him with a little more glee in my voice.

"Soon as in right now," the doctor comments, breaking up our little moment. With Evan to my right, I hold his hand as I lie back on the white paper, hearing it rustle under me. Dr. Harmony holds the wand right above my belly button. My belly is covered in clear gel and there's more than a little bump now that I'm twenty weeks along.

I'm quiet as the sound of a steady heartbeat comes through the speaker. *Lub-dub, lub-dub, lub-dub.* The only thing that distracts me for a moment is Evan placing his second hand over our joined one.

"Our little baby," he whispers in awe.

"Your little *boy*," the doctor corrects him, pointing to the screen. She keeps the wand there for a moment, tapping on the keyboard to take photos before removing the wand and the soft, rhythmic heartbeats are gone. But I heard them, I heard that steady heartbeat and that sound will stay with me forever.

"He's healthy?" Evan questions and my heart swells.

"Perfectly healthy," Dr. Harmony says as she wipes down the equipment and tosses the paper towels into the trash.

"I'll be back in just a bit with some pictures for you two." The young blond doctor has a pretty smile; it's one that reaches her eyes.

"Thank you," Evan and I say in unison.

"A boy," I murmur to him before he cuts me off with a kiss.

"We're going to have a son," Evan says, running a hand down his face. "It's real."

"Does it feel real to you now?"

Evan takes my hand again and kisses my knuckles before nodding his head.

My gaze moves from Evan to the screen. The little heart is beating in a perfect rhythm.

"I have a feeling it's going to be really, really good," I tell him and get a little choked up.

"It is," Evan says and kisses my hand once more. "I know it is."

# Evan

*The morning brings a bright light,*
*Hope and laughter too.*
*And with time comes a new love,*
*Faded dreams become anew.*
*Just remember to hold tight,*
*And fight for what you love.*
*For our lost ones will watch over,*
*And keep us safe from up above.*

"We should name him Henry," Kat suggests as we walk into the house. The homes near the Manhattan Bridge are an expensive area to live, but the park is close, and this school district is where Kat wants to live for our little one, so how could I say no?

She tosses the keys onto the side table, walking past a row of cardboard boxes and a stack of dishes I brought back from the old place last night. "I've thought a lot about it. And I think we should."

"Henry." I say my father's name and a swell of unexpected emotion catches me off guard. I slip the jacket off my shoulders and move to busy myself, opening the window in the dining room and ignoring the look Kat gives me.

"I know it hasn't been a long time since he passed," Kat says. "It feels like it was yesterday."

She holds her swollen abdomen and drags out the head chair in the dining room. At least this room is mostly put together. Kat's nesting has her up all hours and doing shit she shouldn't do. Like carrying heavy boxes and climbing on the furniture to hang curtains. She's ever the stubborn one.

"I wish he were here with us," she murmurs and gets teary eyed; she's been crying a lot more recently, probably due to the third trimester pregnancy hormones. "But we can give him this, you know?"

Her voice is tight with emotion and I nod my head, understanding what she's saying but not wanting to voice it.

The wind blows through the house. It's warm for late March. The breeze gently moves the napkins on the table so I'm quick to tuck them into the holder and attempt to form a response. I miss my father. More than I ever could have imagined.

"He'd have loved to help us move down here." I say the thought out loud to offer her something.

"At least this time you hired movers," Kat says with a bit of humor, but her voice is solemn.

She winces with pain and grabs ahold of her belly, her eyes closed tight and my heart races.

"Babe?" She ignores me, just like she's been doing. For some unknown reason, I continue to think she'll respond during these Braxton-Hicks contractions.

Hovering over her, I eye her carefully then walk slowly to her and wait, afraid to do anything wrong.

I may have made mistakes while learning to be a good husband, but Pops showed me how to be a good father and I won't let him down.

"Oh my gosh, that was a long one." Kat finally breathes out as her body visibly relaxes.

"Do you want to go in?" My nerves are all on edge. I'm terrified, but I won't tell Kat. I've never even held a child, let alone having one depend on me to live.

Kat rolls her eyes at me. "For one contraction? I think not."

She reaches into the bag at her feet and pulls out a water bottle. "Besides, I read a baby comes when you're ready and relaxed, and we have four more rooms to set up and get settled in before I'll be anywhere near relaxed. And another two weeks until our due date."

A huff of humor leaves me and I move the top box off the nearest stack, ripping the tape back to expose what's inside.

"So, what do you think?" she asks me.

"About what?"

"About naming him Henry?" She tilts her head to the side and her long hair falls over her shoulder.

"I think Pops would have loved that," I say, getting out the answer before my throat goes tight and take in a deep breath. "I think he'd be proud."

Lowering myself to the floor in front of her, I let my hands rest on her thighs and bring my forehead down to rest on her belly. "What do you think?" I ask our son and Kat's belly shakes as she laughs.

"You think it's funny, but he's going to know my voice."

Kat doesn't hesitate to lean down and kiss me. The first one is a peck on my cheek, but then she moves her hand to my jaw and keeps me still for a longer one, a deeper one.

It's slow and sensual and makes my blood heat.

"I know he will, and I love you for it."

I take her small hand in mine and look deep into her eyes. She's seen so much of me. All of my bad along with the little bit of good I have in me, and she still loves me. There's no way I could doubt that. "I know this past year has been rough, but I'm going to do everything I can to make our lives easy for … forever."

A small smile seems to tickle Kat's lips, still a darker hue from our kiss, and she moves her fingers to them.

"I mean it, Kat. I love you and this baby more than anything." Tears come to my eyes and I only pray she knows that I love her just as much as she loves me.

After a moment, she nods. "I know you do, and I know you will."

Moving my hand to her belly, I feel our little one kick just beneath the small bit of pressure. It still gets me every time.

"He knows too," Kat says with a smile that lights her eyes.

"So, Henry?" I question, feeling a swell of pride in my chest.

She nods her head, her eyes getting glossy as she puts a hand on her belly.

"Henry."

Diary Entry Three

Hey Pops,

I wanted you to know, every day I think about what I should do to make you proud. Even the days I mess up. I guess those days especially. Your voice is always there, telling me to make it right.

Lately, I've been doing good. I think you'd agree. Sometimes I make mistakes. Like when little Henry peed through his diaper last week at four in the morning. I changed his diaper but didn't change the onesie. Kat let me have it for that one.

Common sense and all that goes out the window when it comes to him. She didn't tell me to change the onesie too. I should have known, but I'm just so careful around him. She's teaching me, though, and we're learning together. You'd love it. We miss you so much.

He's so small, Pops, I can hold him in one hand. I'm scared I'm gonna break him some days. Kat tells me I'm fine, and that I look good holding him. But I'm terrified I'm going to mess up.

I guess I'm just nervous to ruin it, so I keep waiting for her to tell me what to do.

She's taking good care of me. Especially in that department.

She's not going to mess up and that's the only thing that makes me think it's all going to be all right.

Kat's not gonna let me get away with anything anymore.

The best part about that is that I love it.

I wish I'd listened to you sooner, Pops. I want you to know, I'm trying to make sure my marriage is like yours and Ma's.

I've got to go. I just really wanted to talk to you tonight. Some nights are harder than others and I'm not sure it'll ever get too easy. Even if it does, I'll be thinking of you and wanting your advice.

I love you. We all do.

# ABOUT THE
# author

Thank you so much for reading my romances. I'm just a stay at home mom and avid reader turned author and I couldn't be happier.

I hope you love my books as much as I do!

More by Willow Winters
www.WillowWintersWrites.com/books

9 798885 921244